Beneath *the Scars*

New York Times Bestselling Author
Melanie Moreland

Dear Reader,

Thank you for selecting Beneath The Scars. The majority of my stories are set in Canada. This story is set in the cliffs of Maine's seashore. The rugged, isolated coast fit my hero.

Be sure to sign up for my newsletter for up to date information on new releases, exclusive content and sales.

Always fun - never spam!

xoxo,
Melanie

ALSO BY MELANIE MORELAND

Vested Interest Series

BAM - The Beginning (Prequel)

Bentley (Vested Interest #1)

Aiden (Vested Interest #2)

Maddox (Vested Interest #3)

Reid (Vested Interest #4)

Van (Vested Interest #5)

Halton (Vested Interest #6)

Sandy (Vested Interest #7)

Insta-Spark Collection

It Started with a Kiss

Christmas Sugar

An Instant Connection

An Unexpected Gift

The Contract Series

The Contract (The Contract #1)

The Baby Clause (The Contract #2)

The Amendment (The Contract #3)

Mission Cove

The Summer of Us

Standalones

Into the Storm

Beneath the Scars

Over the Fence

My Image of You (Random House/Loveswept)

Copyright © 2014 Melanie Moreland

Published by Melanie Moreland
All Rights Reserved
ISBN # 978-1-9936198-3-0
ISBN Print #978-0993-6198-2-3
Copyright registration #1115209

All rights reserved. No part of this book may be reproduced in any form or by any
electronic or mechanical means including information storage and retrieval systems-
except in the case of brief excerpts or quotations embodied in review or critical writings
without the expressed permission of the author.
The characters and events in this book are fictitious or are used fictitiously. Any
similarity to real persons, living or dead, is purely coincidental and not intended by the
author.
Cover Design by Moreland Books, Inc.
Formatting by Moreland Books, Inc
Edited by D. Beck

DEDICATION

To Matthew,
who sees beneath the scars I carry
and loves me so fiercely, it takes my breath away.
You are my world.

In honor of my darling mom, who would have loved
every single moment of this ride. I miss you every day.

1

MEGAN

The more the miles flew by, the more I relaxed; my shoulders loosening as I left the city behind me for wide-open spaces. I didn't speed, but took my time driving, enjoying the scenery. Classical music drifted through the speakers; the gentle swell of violins and cellos soothing my fractured nerves. Normally, I'd have contemporary music playing, but at the moment, I needed the calming sounds of Bach to surround me. I rolled down the window, releasing my hair from the tie holding it in place. I hated wearing my hair up, although often did for work or in the heat of the summer. For now, though, I could enjoy feeling the breeze flow through it, cooling my head and neck.

I smiled as flashes of water became more frequent; the vista around me changing from congested traffic to empty roads. The hilly landscape was dotted with trees, still barren from the passing winter, waiting for the warmth of spring to return them back to life.

The metaphor wasn't lost on me.

It was late afternoon when I pulled up to the small general store in the town of Cliff's Edge. The coastal community was quiet. That time of the day most of the shops were closed; the sleepy town almost empty except for year-round residents. It was the exact sort of place I wanted to be.

The urge to leave Boston had hit all of a sudden. My friend, Karen, had offered the use of her beach house a few days ago and I took her up on it today, not even stopping to pick up the keys. Instead, I followed her instructions to get the spare set of keys from the owner at Cooper's General Store.

Karen hadn't been happy about me leaving so late in the day, urging me to wait until tomorrow, but I needed to be gone—to escape. The email I received mid-afternoon was the final straw.

I refused to think about that, though. Instead, I focused on where I was heading: the beach house. Karen's words of "private" and "isolated" echoed in my head—both of them sounding perfect.

With a deep breath, I stepped out of my car, stretched my cramped back muscles, then headed into the brightly lit store to collect the keys and get directions.

The house was farther out of town than I'd thought. The directions were confusing, so Mrs. Cooper graciously offered to show me the way. I followed her car along the steep, unfamiliar roads, sighing in appreciation when at last we stopped. As the Ford's taillights faded, I shut off the engine, letting my head drop to my chest, and enjoyed the new sounds surrounding me. It felt good to be here; somewhere different, alone.

Getting out and slipping my jacket back on, my first plan was to let Dixie out of her car carrier and take her inside right away. I knew she had to be tired of being cooped up in that tiny space, but it was safer for her when driving. As I opened the back door, my little dog shot out of her carrier, having somehow released the small latch and immediately headed for the thick woods at the edge of the property, barking and wagging her tail furiously. I lunged after her, and we played a game of tag for a few minutes before I managed, with Mrs.

Cooper's help, to corner her, and snap on her lead. Panting, I leaned against the car while Mrs. Cooper laughed at our antics. "She must keep you on your toes," she chuckled.

I nodded. "She loves to explore." I drew in another deep breath. "Thanks, Mrs. Cooper, for escorting me out here. You were right—I'd never have found the place."

Her smile was kind as she bent down to stroke Dixie's soft ears. "I still can't believe you arrived so late in the day, Megan. I'm glad you let me bring you here. I was surprised when Karen called and said you were coming up today instead of tomorrow. She was a little worried about your arrival time."

I shrugged as I tugged on my ear. "I just wanted to get away." I turned toward the sound of the water in the distance, already smelling the bracing sea air. "I wanted to wake up here; if that makes any sense."

She clucked softly in sympathy as she tucked the keys into my hand. "You have everything you need?"

"I brought a few things. I'll come to town tomorrow and buy some more." I had made sure to pick up my two favorite things while at the small but surprisingly well-stocked store. I planned on a great dinner of over-buttered popcorn followed by rich ice cream. I forgot the syrup but would get some next trip into town.

"Okay, dear. It's all ready for you. Mr. Cooper came out right away after Karen called and made sure everything was in order. I sent a few items with him as well so you should be fine for the night." She paused. "Did you want me to come in with you?"

I smiled at her thoughtfulness. "Thank you, but I'm fine. I'm going to take my stuff in, then Dixie and I will go for a quick walk and have a quiet night."

"Don't go far. As you can see, the woods are pretty thick and it's easy to get lost."

"No, we'll just have a short jaunt on the beach." I stepped back from her car. "Good night, Mrs. Cooper."

"Okay. Take the flashlight on the counter with you on your walk.

I made sure Mr. C put fresh batteries in it. You have my number. Call me if you need something, dear."

With a smile and a wave, she was gone, and I was alone.

A sharp bark made me smile and I scooped up Dixie, laughing as her rough tongue met my cheek. I stroked her head in return and carried her up to the porch, grateful all the keys were labeled on the ring. Opening the back door, I took her inside; wanting to make sure she was settled prior to unloading the car for the night. I walked through into the front of the house, scanned the comfortable looking room, and stopped dead at the sight that met my eyes, my breath catching in my throat.

Setting Dixie down, I stepped forward, never taking my eyes off the large front windows. The sun had almost set, the last of the evening light casting rays over the water. I was transfixed by the beautiful scene laid out in front of me. The house was set back, somewhat elevated from the beach below; close enough I could see the waves breaking on the rocky shore. I could also hear the sounds of the surf even through the window. Beside me, Dixie was up on her hind legs, looking through the glass, tail wagging with excitement. I smiled down at her, scratching her ears gently. "The car can wait, Dixie. Let's go for a walk!"

Ensuring her lead was secure, I picked up the flashlight, and we made our way to the beach. The air was fresh and sharp, the salty tang filling my lungs. The wind was cold on my face, and as we got closer to the water, I could feel the icy spray as the sea crashed against the rocks. The vast expanse of water and sky caused my throat to tighten. The sheer beauty—the only sounds around me, of wind and water—brought unexpected tears to my eyes. I wrapped my arms around my torso, as a long, shaky breath left my chest. I was glad I came today. Dixie ran around as far as her lead would allow, sniffing and barking happily. After another deep breath, I wiped the damp from my cheeks, and we walked the shore, both of us enjoying the openness around us. I clutched my jacket tighter around me and stood with my back to the water, looking at the house where I would be staying.

The front was all glass, allowing the beautiful view that had drawn me out to the beach to be seen with ease. Edged with rugged stonework, the house had a large deck, but it wasn't as large a place as I'd have thought, knowing Karen's taste. I had to smile—that was obviously her husband, Chris's, influence. The lines were simple and clean, almost sparse. He came to Cliff's Edge a lot, Karen only staying for short time periods. The town was too small for her liking—no nightclubs, huge shops or spas to keep her entertained. Whereas Chris, like me, would be perfectly content with a book, a cup of coffee, and the panoramic view; for Karen, it would wear thin pretty fast.

My gaze drifted to the only other two houses on the very private stretch of water. There was one, just up off the beach, somewhat larger than Karen and Chris's, then at the end, high up on the bluff, was the one house Karen told me was occupied year-round. I could see muted lights in the windows. I felt a small sense of comfort knowing there was another person around the deserted beach—even if, as Karen told me, he was intensely private and not very approachable. All three houses backed onto the dense forest but faced the ocean in front. As I found out, the road leading up to the houses was difficult to find and not something you would stumble upon without great effort, thereby ensuring privacy for homeowners. Even though I hadn't listened to her, I understood now why Karen told me to drive here in the daylight. I was grateful Mrs. Cooper had been in her store when I stopped to pick up the keys and had insisted on driving ahead of me, so I didn't get lost.

A bright light caught my eye. I glanced back at the house on the bluff, thinking how spectacular the views must be from those windows, given how lovely the scene was before me. The largest house of them all, it was three stories high and light was spilling out from the top floor. It was the most secluded, set back from the water and nestled close to the forest behind it.

Dixie pulled at her lead, and I shook myself out of my thoughts. "Come on, girl. Let's go inside. We can unpack and make some popcorn and cocoa! That huge sofa I saw is calling our names, and I have a book I can't wait to start reading." I sighed, feeling content— my idea of a perfect evening would now be enhanced with the muted sound of the ocean crashing on the sand and rocks. As we made our way toward the house, I heard a distant, eerie howl, deep within the forest. A shiver, icier than the sea, ran through me as I bent down and scooped up Dixie, remembering Karen's warnings of wild animals in the forest.

"You, my girl, are staying on your lead while we're here." I nuzzled the top of her head, grinning as she turned and licked my face affectionately. "You'd make a tasty snack for one of those coyotes or wolves—whatever they are." Another long, mournful howl had me shuddering as I hurried inside, putting Dixie in the guest room and shutting the door, so she was safe. Then, even though the howls were far in the distance, just to be safe, I turned on every outside light while I unpacked the car, grateful when it was done, and I could shut the back door firmly behind me.

2

MEGAN

The next morning, smiling and feeling less stressed, I swung my arms widely as I walked on the beach, marveling at the beauty stretched before me. It was still cold enough the sand was packed hard beneath my feet. Ahead of me, Dixie was running, stopping often to sniff and bark at whatever inanimate object drew her displeasure, making me laugh with the simple joy of watching her. It was early, the sun having come up a short time ago, the light casting multicolored hues across the water and highlighting the sand. The sheer relief of last night had settled, leaving only elation behind. Lifting my arms, I twirled around, spinning until I was dizzy, and had to drop to the damp sand, amused at my own antics. Dixie jumped on top of me, licking my face, and I sat up, hugging her close. The wind lifted my hair away from my face and I tilted my head back, enjoying the sensation.

I closed my eyes and inhaled deep lungfuls of fresh air, listening to the sound of waves beating on the shoreline, the crying of gulls flying overhead and feeling the spray kicked up by the wind on my face.

Here, I hoped, I could find my calm. Surely, I could find it in me to write again, to put aside the past few weeks of terrible hurt and embarrassment—to find my feet and to continue forward. I opened my eyes and looked out over the vast expanse of water. There were no distractions here. No cameras or intruding phone calls prying into my once-private life, no threats from my ex-boyfriend, and no one telling me how disappointed they were with my betrayal. Standing up, I brushed off my pants and turned around. I looked back at the house, its clean lines even more evident in the light. Here I could work. Recover. Find my balance.

A distant bark had me turning my head. From the other end of the beach I spotted a dog, charging toward us. I picked up Dixie, unsure of the large creature lurching our way. As he got closer, I could see it was a golden retriever, his face friendly, tail wagging in excitement. I extended my hand, which was sniffed then licked before he turned a couple times, barking and whining in the back of his throat. I kneeled down while he and Dixie sniffed each other cautiously. Once I was sure he meant her no harm, I sat her back on the sand, where the two of them explored each other. I had to smile at them; one so large and excited, the other small and wary. He was very gentle with her, nudging her playfully with his great nose, licking her head. She looked at me as if to say "What?" then sat down between his great paws, letting him shower her with attention. I chuckled watching them—two instant friends.

I was startled as a whistle cut through the air from the end of the beach. A man was standing partway down on the stairs, which led to the beach from the house on the bluff, a dark overcoat billowing out behind him in the stiff breeze. The dog stood up right away and started running toward his master, who made no move in our direction. I raised my hand in a wave, thinking it would be a good time to go and introduce myself. There was no return salutation; he remained motionless on the stairs. I stepped forward a couple of feet, wondering if he hadn't seen me, and waved again.

Finally, his hand lifted in a brief wave. I looked down at Dixie, smiling, taking it as an invitation. "Let's go meet our neighbor, girl."

Looking up, my steps faltered. He had retreated and was already at the top of the stairs, his large dog right behind him. It was obvious; he had no desire to meet me.

"Unfriendly," Karen had said. "Closed off."

"Private," Chris had insisted. "Reserved."

I watched him disappear and assumed he went inside. His house was even larger and more imposing in the daylight; built in stone and cedar, high above the water, set amongst the trees, a fortress unto itself. Private and closed off—much like the man himself.

I sighed—unfriendly, indeed. Rude was more like it. I had wanted to introduce myself—nothing more. Our dogs had already met and become friends. I shook my head, deciding it didn't matter. I wasn't here to meet new people or make friends. I was here to find some peace and solace, then get back on track with my life.

Rude neighbor or not!

———

"You find everything all right, dear?"

I smiled at Mrs. Cooper. "Everything was great. Thank you for the extra things you left. I never even thought of some bread for toast. The butter I bought was for my popcorn."

"Not a problem. Are you heading right back to the house?"

"I thought I'd look around a little, actually."

"Excellent. The gallery down the street is lovely. I'll have Mr. Cooper load up your car, while you wander around. Not everything is open this time of year. But if you're hungry the café makes a great lunch."

"Thanks. I'll check it out."

"Where's that little dog of yours?" Mrs. Cooper grinned as she looked behind me.

I chuckled. "I left her at home, sleeping. She had a big walk on the beach this morning." I paused. "We met another dog while we were walking—a golden retriever. Very friendly."

"That would be Elliott. Zachary's dog."

Ah, the neighbor had a name. It was only then I realized Karen had never mentioned it and I had never thought to ask. "I didn't meet him. He never came down to the beach."

For the first time since I met her, Mrs. Cooper looked sad. "Zachary is very, ah, private. He pretty much keeps to himself." I was sure I heard her utter "poor man," but it was so quiet I could have been mistaken.

"I waved at him."

She smiled, although it didn't quite reach her eyes. "Did he wave back?"

I shrugged. "After a fashion. I got the feeling he wasn't interested in meeting me."

"Don't take it personally, dear. A wave is more than most people in town have had the entire time he's been living here. As I said, he keeps to himself."

Her tone told me she had nothing more to say about my private neighbor. So, I smiled, thanked her again and told her I would see her in a few days.

Once outside, I looked up and down the rather deserted streets. I could imagine, during the warm, summer season, the sidewalks would be full of people—tourists checking out the local wares and eating in the restaurants—but right now it was like a ghost town except for locals. A grim smile curved my lips; it was exactly what I needed.

As I waited to cross the street, an SUV with dark-tinted windows drove past me and turned the corner. It was very new and shiny, which seemed out of place amidst the various older-style cars parked around town. I frowned, watching it drive away, having no idea why I even noticed it, other than the fact it was going so slow. I continued my exploration of the shops, stopping in at a couple of places. I picked up some more bread and cookies at the local bakery, a few bottles of wine, then went into the café and had a quick lunch. Mrs. Cooper was right—the food was very good, so I got some soup to go for the next day.

After leaving my purchases in the car, I decided to visit the gallery Mrs. Cooper mentioned. The sign in the window told me they featured local artists; again, I was sure in the summer they did a brisk business. A bell over the door chimed as I stepped inside. It was empty, but I could hear voices coming from the back of the shop. A man appeared a moment later, smiling, assuring me he would be right with me. I smiled too and told him I was browsing, so not to hurry.

The glass cases held an impressive collection, and not what I expected. There were none of the cheesy, touristy things I expected to find. Instead, there was beautiful stained glass, delicately carved woods, handmade silk scarves and jewelry laid out in a tasteful manner. I suppressed a grin. Karen must love this place.

At the back of the gallery was a beautiful collection of paintings. There were numerous different artists featured, but one person's work caught my interest. Several pieces hung in their own small room; the artistry evident even to my untrained eye. Ocean views, deep forests, scenic beaches; all so vivid, with attention to detail so great, it was as if you were looking at a photograph. The use of light and color was flawless and stunning. There was no signature in the corner—only the initials **Z D A** in bold script adorned the pieces. One painting in particular captured my attention, and I was spellbound by the beauty. It was the image of a storm moving toward the shore, coming closer, as though it was aiming for me. Its ferocity and power had been captured to perfection. The steel gray and white of the angry clouds, as they whipped up the violent waves on the water, crashing on the rocks, were so striking I could almost feel the cold coming off the canvas. The swirling mass of colors the wind kicked up in the water was mesmerizing; their chaos so equally matched it was almost impossible to tell where the water started, and the clouds ended. It was as if the artist had caught my own churning emotions and had thrown them on this canvas for everyone to see. For several moments I stood, staring at the picture until a noise startled me. I felt someone brush past behind me, and I gasped softly as I inhaled. The scent of the ocean, with all its heady, earthy fragrances hit me. It was as though the sun, sand, and water itself were slipping by me.

Turning, I caught the briefest glimpse of a tall man moving away from me in hurried strides. The collar of his coat was up, shielding most of his face; a knit beanie pulled low on his head. His broad shoulders tensed as he opened the door leading out the back of the gallery. Before he disappeared from view, I caught a quick glimpse of his profile—a straight nose and stubbled jawline. His long fingers rested for a brief instance on the doorframe as he yanked the door open. There was something on the back of his hand—a birthmark or scar perhaps? He hurried so fast I couldn't be certain.

I had the strangest feeling; I wanted to call out to him and halt his departure, to come back, but I stopped myself. I realized my hand was extended toward the picture, hanging midair as I stood in front of the art. Self-conscious now, I lowered it, unsure what had caused that reaction in me. The squeal of tires out back let me know whoever had left, was in a great rush to do so. I groaned in frustration. I seemed to be causing all men to run away from me today.

The mystery man was forgotten, however, as I brought my eyes back to the painting, once again swept away by its power. Captivated by the beauty, I was determined. I had to buy this one. I *needed* to own the painting.

"Brilliant, isn't it?" Another man appeared beside me. He was tall; his gray hair caught back in a long ponytail. His smile was open and warm, and I found myself returning it.

"It's mesmerizing," I replied, my smile now fading. "The pain in it...it's so blatant, I can feel it."

"One of our most popular local artists." He held out his hand. "I'm Jonathon. My wife and I run this gallery."

I shook his hand. "Your gallery is beautiful. I'm Megan."

"Thank you. My wife, Ashley, makes all the jewelry and scarves. Are you passing through, Megan?"

I shook my head. "I'm staying up at the bluffs."

His eyebrows lifted. "Friend of the Harpers'?"

I laughed. "How did you know?"

"There are three houses on the bluffs. The Smiths never have visitors, you aren't a friend of Zachary's, but you're the perfect age for Karen." He grinned. "Karen is a frequent visitor, when she's here. She and my wife get along very well."

I wasn't a friend of Zachary's.

The rude neighbor.

Interesting—maybe I wasn't the only one to whom he was rude.

"You're very astute."

He started to laugh. "I may also have heard from Mrs. Cooper that a friend of Karen's was coming to town."

I joined in his laughter. "I guess I'm big news." I'd been greeted and made welcome everywhere I went that morning. I turned back to the painting. "I see why this artist is so popular. All his work is astounding. I'd like to buy this one, though."

With a slight shake of his head, he indicated a small sign in the corner. "This one is not for sale. The artist was kind enough to loan it to us for a short time."

"I see. I noticed there's no signature."

"No. He's very private."

I frowned, feeling sad. "Would he listen to an offer?"

Jonathon shrugged. "I could ask him next time he's in. He seldom changes his mind, but perhaps if the offer was right, he may reconsider. Leave me your number and I'll ask him. How long are you here for?"

"A couple of weeks—maybe three."

"He'll be in again next week. He left only a short time ago, actually."

I paused, looking at the initials on the painting. **Z D A**. The tall man—the stranger who had rushed by me and smelled like the ocean—was he the unfriendly, mysterious Zachary? How many people lived in the area whose first names started with 'Z'?

"Just now?" I asked. "In a dark overcoat?"

He hesitated before answering. "Yes."

My neighbor had been wearing a long overcoat when I caught a glimpse of him this morning. It had to be the same person.

He must have recognized me from the beach and, it would seem, had no desire to meet me at any point. I looked over at the painting. I still wanted it. What the man lacked in social graces, he made up for with his paintbrush. Something about this painting called to me.

"Our dogs met on the beach this morning," I offered. "Zachary was also wearing his overcoat then."

Jonathon only offered a slight nod of his head but didn't confirm or deny my statement.

I wrote down my number for Jonathon and said I would check in the next time I came to town. I also told him I would be happy to speak to "the artist" myself, if he so wished, seeing as he was my neighbor. Jonathon smiled sadly, the same strange look I had seen passing over Mrs. Cooper's face showing on his. "No, as I said, he's very private. If there're any negotiations to be done, he prefers me to do it on his behalf. I suggest you don't bother him, since it, ah, might end any chance you have of purchasing the painting. Which, my dear, I must caution you is slight. As I said, he seldom changes his mind."

I nodded, confused. It was clear Zachary took his privacy to the extreme, but if it meant I could have that painting, I would do whatever it took to get it.

My eyes drifted back to the imposing canvas and its brilliant imagery.

I had to have it.

3

ZACHARY

"No." I shook my head in frustration. I couldn't believe we were having this conversation again.

Jonathon's voice was patient. "Think of all the opportunities this would open up. Your name's becoming huge, Zachary."

"My initials, you mean. That's all they get. We've discussed it before, Jonathon. I don't *need* any opportunities. I'm very happy with the current arrangement and the way my life is now. I don't need my name out there."

"Zachary..."

"I said no."

Jonathon leaned back in his chair, regarding me in silence. "People want to know the man behind the brush."

"Well, they can't have it or me. Either you sell my paintings as we agreed, or I'll pull them." I wasn't backing down—it was the only way.

He held up his hand. "No need to be so defensive with me." He hesitated. "We could do voice interviews and only use your first name."

"No promotions. I let you show my paintings on your website and sell them here. That's it. No interviews, no meet the artist, no first name, nothing."

"There may come a time you can't say no."

I shrugged, well aware of that fact. "Then I'll stop painting."

"Don't say that—wasting your talent would be criminal. Fine, I'll drop it. You can remain just a set of initials on a canvas."

"It's what I want."

He sighed. "I don't understand why, but it's your choice."

He didn't understand?

My eyes narrowed as I looked at him, struggling to remain calm. Of course, he didn't understand. There was a time I wouldn't have understood, either, but my name out there meant a door to the past could be opened up. Questions, *pictures*, people looking at me, talking about the past; the gossip and memories that could resurface. I couldn't allow that to happen. I was happy with the way things were. People liked my paintings. I enjoyed making them. It was a simple, easy process; one I wasn't willing to change, no matter how much Jonathon wanted me to. Internally, I shook my head, knowing it wouldn't be the last time he brought up the subject.

"It's my choice, Jonathon. The subject is closed."

"Fine. I'll shut up. I don't want to lose your paintings. Business would slide, and besides that, my wife would kill me."

I allowed a small smile. Ashley was a huge supporter of my work. It was because of her friendship I even allowed my canvases to be available for sale. She and I shared a bond Jonathon didn't—*couldn't*—understand; as much as he loved his wife. Her connection was a small light in my dark world, but one I would give up if I felt I had no choice.

His phone rang. "I'd better get that, then go out and see if I still have a customer."

I stood up, anxious to leave, my emotions raw from the day. "I'll be in touch."

I opened his office door and slipped out, going my usual route of exiting the back of the building. Rounding the corner, I came to a complete standstill at the sight in front of me; my heart began to pound hard in my chest, as waves of small electric shocks ran through my body.

It was the woman I had seen on the beach last night and again this morning. Elliott's low bark had alerted me to the fact something was outside, and when I checked I saw her on the beach. She had stood, drawn in on herself and motionless, staring at the water. I wondered what she was looking at—what was holding her attention. This morning, she was running and playing with her small dog, her long hair blowing in the wind as she laughed, the lilting notes drifting up to where I stood in silence. The sound had fascinated me and drawn me off my porch to get closer to the source of the sweet noise. As I watched her, the way she had twirled around on the sand and thrown her arms open made me smile. There had been something so simple and joyful in her actions; I even chuckled as she fell to the sand, the dog jumping on her and licking her face.

Then she had waved when she saw me on the stairs, trying to get Elliott back to my side before she came over. I had barely acknowledged her friendly wave and slipped into the house. I didn't want her to get some silly idea in her head of following me; that thought alone almost caused a panic attack as I rushed up the stairs to safety. Nonetheless, I had stood at the window and watched her disappear into her own house a short time later. I had seen her again, as I drove down the street on my way to the gallery to pick up some supplies Ashley had ordered for me. She was standing on the sidewalk, waiting to cross the street, not doing anything to draw attention to herself, yet I found her quite captivating. I had slowed down to watch her again, unsure of my reaction to this stranger.

Now, she was standing, frozen, her hand outstretched in front of my *Tempest* painting. Her fingers were reaching, caught midair, not touching the canvas but simply hovering, trembling. She was mesmerized; her face a study of shock. It was as if her entire being was caught in the swirls of paint. I could feel her emotion from where

I stood, gazing at her in wonder. Never before had I seen such a visceral reaction to that piece, prior to today. Her body was expressing the emotions I felt when I painted it. Pain, longing, and unending chaos were etched into that canvas, and she was feeling every stroke, living them herself. Her display of emotion caught me unprepared, and I steadied myself against the wall before I did something I would regret; like move forward and touch her. I wanted to feel the satin of her skin under my fingers.

The angle I had offered me a perfect view while I stared; her entire being lost in my work. When I first saw a woman on the beach last night, I assumed it was my neighbor, Karen. I knew this morning, though, I'd been wrong. This was definitely not her. Small and petite like Karen, but her features were soft, almost delicate in a way. Karen carried an intense, confident beauty I remembered from our brief first encounter, when we bumped into each other in the shadows of the woods and a couple other awkward meetings. This woman's stance was timid, her bottom lip caught up in her teeth as she worried the plump flesh. For some reason I yearned to step forward and pull her teeth away, wanting to see if her lip was as soft as it looked. I wanted to taste it. Sweep my tongue over it before I kissed her.

I shook my head at the strange thought. I couldn't remember the last time I wanted to kiss a woman or be close enough to another person the way I wanted to be close to her.

The gallery was filled with natural light and it caught the color of her hair: deep, rich coppery auburn, which contrasted dramatically with her pale skin. There was a smattering of freckles on her cheeks, standing out in contrast to her pallor. Her hand was small, the fingers tiny, as she reached toward the canvas. I noticed how tired she looked. Her dark, wide eyes were weary as she lost herself in the image in front of her, and her entire face awash in emotions. A sudden, intense longing tore through me—a feeling that seldom, if ever, happened in my life—I wanted to help her. The need to offer her comfort, to ease whatever pain made her look so vulnerable, had me reaching out, wanting to grasp her hand in my larger one and soothe her. However, I realized what I was doing when I caught sight of the back of my hand, bringing reality crashing around me. She would never want or accept soothing from me. No woman ever would.

Putting my head down, I rushed to the back door, passing behind her. I could feel her as I went by in long strides, moving as fast as my feet would go. Her scent hung in the air around her, as soft and delicate as her sweet face. I felt her gaze shift from the painting to me and I walked faster, hoping Jonathon didn't come from his office and call my name for any reason. I wouldn't stop, even if he did; my panic was too great.

I groaned as I grasped the door and wrenched it open, almost running to the SUV, in my haste to get away from there. My hands shook as I struggled with the seat belt, finally hearing the click as the buckle connected. My tires tore on the pavement as I backed out of the lot and headed toward the house.

I struggled to control my breathing as I drove away; my mind was a chaotic symphony of thoughts. One was more prevalent than the others.

I wanted her. I wanted her in ways I hadn't wanted a woman in years.

A complete stranger.

My mind saw us together; limbs entwined as I buried my face in her thick hair and felt her soft curves under me. Her subtle perfume lingered, and I yearned to be close enough again to breathe it in, to hold her scent deep in my lungs. My fingers ached to caress her pale skin, trace that trembling full lip with mine and taste it. I needed to know if it was as sweet as I thought it would be—or even sweeter.

I wanted to see her reaction to other pieces of my work. Watch the wonder on her beautiful face as she studied the canvases.

I could see her in my studio, her brilliant hair lit by the sun. I wanted to capture her image on canvas.

I wanted so much more than that with her.

Slamming my hand on the steering wheel in anger, I cursed. I could never have her.

I could never have any woman.

She would never want me.

I needed to stay away from her and keep her away from me.

If she got close to me, I wasn't sure I could resist her.

4

MEGAN

From: Jared Cameron
To: Megan Greene
Subject: Running from the truth Megan?
Did you think hiding was the answer here? Stop
ignoring me. Why don't you do the right thing—
everyone makes mistakes. Recant your state-
ment and let it go, and I will drop it. Don't you
think it's enough I have to suffer not only finding
out my assistant/girlfriend used me, but also
tried to claim my work as hers? I've been hurt
enough, Megan, and still, I forgive you. I have to
in order to move on. I loved you once and your
betrayal has cut me to the bone. Stop the pain for
both of us.
Jared

Damn it, he was good. Another pleading email, which would, no doubt, *somehow* be leaked to the press. It showed not only

21

his pleading with me to stop hurting him, but his forgiving nature. All designed to make me look like the bad person; just the way he intended. There were also texts and a voice mail from him, all spewing the same lies, keeping up the front that *he* was the injured party. I was so tired of this mess. The fact of the matter was that I was almost ready to walk away, no matter how much Karen told me to keep fighting. He had done a good job. He managed to destroy my credibility, ruined my career, killed my hopes of becoming a published writer, and made me feel worthless all at the same time. How could I overcome all of that?

I sat back with a groan, rubbing my forehead. This was not helping the building headache.

Outside, the skies were low and overcast; a storm was slowly approaching. Staring out the window, my eyes drifted to the end of the beach and the house on the bluff. I hadn't heard from Jonathon since I'd been at the gallery two days prior. The urge to walk across the sand and knock on Zachary's door, begging him to allow me to buy his painting, had been one I'd been resisting since I came home. Instead, I had gone for many walks on the beach, spent hours sitting in front of the computer screen. I tried and failed to find inspiration to write again, always ending up on the same site run by the gallery, looking at Zachary's paintings.

I had no idea what his full name was—they were all listed as painted by **Z D A**—but even his initials fascinated me. I stared at the images of the paintings for hours. Even the simplest, softest ones of the beach and sand held so much emotion; I could feel it even through the screen. It was as though he captured emotions on all his canvases. On some, like *Tempest*, he brought out hidden ones, the kind a person kept to themselves.

I glanced back at the computer, then the thick pad of paper beside it. My fingers itched to pick up the pen, sit on the sofa, and allow myself to write the way I liked to. Except after what happened, I wasn't sure I could ever do that again. Unless I copied every page immediately, locked all of it up into a vault, and never spoke of it to another person. A small huff of frustration left my lips. I didn't know if anyone would ever read anything I wrote, even if I was able to do so again, not after this fiasco, anyway.

The headache started to build, and my fingers rubbed at my temples, trying to effect some relief. Caffeine hadn't helped and neither had my spur of the moment idea. Drawing in a deep breath, I grimaced at the lingering odor of nail polish hanging in the air. When I had seen the electric blue bottle of polish in the drawer, I hadn't been able to resist painting my toenails with it. I was, after all, at the beach. It seemed almost wrong not to. Now, though, I needed to go for a walk and get some fresh air. My toes were still drying, but Karen had flip flops I could borrow to protect them.

Looking over at the chair, I smiled. Dixie was sitting on the cushion, looking at me, her little body almost trembling in excitement. She loved it here with all the open spaces to run and investigate. The beach below us held endless exploration for her, and I didn't even need to keep her on her lead in the daytime. She stayed close as we walked, running up and down the packed sand together, often playing fetch. If we went for a walk later in the evening, I snapped on her lead, just in case something spooked her. The large retriever hadn't come for another visit, but I could only assume Zachary was keeping his dog away from the beach, in order to not interact with me. I imagined him to be the quintessential artist: aloof and brooding, eating only when necessary, holed up in his studio, creating and gnashing his teeth as he swirled paint on his canvas, shunning the world around him.

I chuckled at my imagination. Then a quiet sigh broke through my lips. I could understand shunning the world. That was the same as what I was doing. Maybe he could give me some pointers.

As I descended the few stairs to the beach, I was surprised to see the large golden retriever as well as the mysterious Zachary. I stood for a minute, observing him in private. He was standing, barefoot in the surf, staring out over the water as his dog frolicked close by. Zachary was a tall, dark silhouette against the sand and stormy, strange-colored sky of the late afternoon. Wearing dark jeans and the same overcoat that showed off his broad shoulders, a beanie once again pulled low on his head, he stood with his hands in his pockets, motionless, as the water swept across his bare feet. The rolled-up edges of his pants were dark with the ocean spray clinging to the material. I shivered just watching him. The water had to be freezing.

Seeing her new friend, Dixie let out a happy, little yelp, which had the retriever bounding over to her, once again licking her head and huffing as he greeted her. The two of them took off, heading right toward Zachary. He leaned down, greeting Dixie, allowing her a sniff, then patted her head and straightened up. He didn't turn around or acknowledge my presence. With a roll of my eyes, I walked forward, stopping when I was close enough to be heard, but not have my feet in the frigid water. I waited, but he said nothing, ignoring me completely.

Unfriendly indeed.

"That's Dixie—my dog."

His chin dipped with a brief nod. "Elliott."

I couldn't keep the sarcasm out of my voice. "You or the dog?"

His lips quirked at the edges. "My dog."

"I'm staying at the Harpers' house."

He nodded.

"I'm not Karen—I'm a friend of hers."

His sarcasm was thick. "I realize. I *have* met her—more than once. There is a slight resemblance, perhaps, but I can see you aren't her. Your hair rather gives that away."

"I'm sure it was a thrill for her," I murmured, surprised to hear the trace of a British accent in his voice. I chose to ignore the remark about my hair.

Nothing.

"They're letting me stay here for a while."

"How kind."

I shook my head. *Was he for real?*

"I'm Megan. Megan Greene."

Silence.

I searched my brain for something to say. "Looks like a storm's coming in."

"Observant."

I frowned at him—definitely rude. His voice, however, despite its unwelcoming tone, was low and rich sounding, his subtle accent curling around the words when he spoke. I wanted to hear more than a few monosyllables from him, and to hear him say my name.

"Aren't your feet cold, *Zachary*?"

He glanced down and shrugged, still facing the water, not even acknowledging the fact I knew his name. "Not really. I'm used to the cold."

I decided to try a different subject—maybe one that would open him up a little. "I saw your work at the gallery in town; you're very gifted."

Again, he nodded.

"Your *Tempest* painting is"—I searched for the right word— "exceptional."

"It's not for sale."

Disappointed at his words, I studied his partially hidden profile. Again, his jaw was covered in stubble, and all I could really see was his nose and the downturned set of his full mouth. Some wayward hair sticking out from his beanie was blowing in the wind, its color not easy to make out. I was sure it was dark, but I couldn't see enough to determine if I was correct. I wanted to step forward, force him to look at me, but there was something about his tense stance that screamed "back off." He was obviously uncomfortable with me being this close, so I remained where I was, even though I felt some bizarre sort of need to get closer. I had to struggle not to move beside him, slip my hand into his, and offer him some sort of comfort, to loosen the tense set of those broad shoulders. I shook my head at the strange urge.

"Would you perhaps reconsider?"

"No. Jonathon already inquired on your behalf. I have it on loan to the gallery as a personal favor. It's not for sale—at any price."

I smiled, attempting to tease him. "Everything has its price, Zachary."

I wasn't prepared for the venom in his voice when he spoke.

"I'm fucking aware that's the way most of the world works. I don't conduct my life that way."

Then he turned and walked away, his long strides eating up the distance, his unbuttoned coat billowing out behind him. He whistled for Elliott, who dropped the stick from his mouth and chased after his master.

Both Dixie and I stood staring at the retreating figures. Not once did Zachary pause or look back, while Elliott raced ahead of him. I waited until he had climbed the stairs and disappeared from sight, never taking my eyes off him.

I blinked and looked over the water.

Now I could say I had met my neighbor.

That went well.

The fresh air helped, but the ache lingered in the back of my head, making me feel sluggish. Dixie and I spent the rest of the afternoon quietly napping on the sofa, watching a movie, and in an effort to be somewhat productive, I made some banana bread—the only thing I could bake with any success. As it cooled on the counter, I looked out the window; the sun was beginning its slow descent for the night, breaking through the low hanging clouds. Crystalized colors reflected off the water, light dappling on the long swells. I walked onto the deck, breathing in the crisp air and letting the sounds drift over me. Movement caught my eye and I was surprised to see Zachary on top of the rock formation, a camera held to his face. One leg was bent behind him as he crouched, his upper body twisting and moving as he sought the perfect angle. His overcoat had been replaced with a long, gray hoodie and jeans hugged his stretched legs. I felt bad for upsetting him earlier and as the scent of fresh coffee hit me, I came up with an idea on how to apologize. Hurrying inside, I filled a small basket and with a deep breath for courage, walked toward the rocks.

ZACHARY

I felt her before I saw her. There was a subtle shift to the air around me, a break in my concentration and I knew she was coming toward me. My instant reflex was to make sure my loose hood was up, and I was angled away from her. The temptation to turn and walk away quickly was strong, but I stopped myself; I refused to run away again.

"Hello," her gentle, quiet voice spoke. She was close—far too close for my liking and instinctively I shifted away but nodded in silent greeting. Her next words surprised me.

"I'm sorry about earlier. I didn't mean to insult you."

I lowered the camera and glanced her way, my throat tightening. The sun was catching her hair, turning it into rich, rivers of color— the strange light surrounding us cast hundreds of highlights through her gorgeous tresses—more than I could possibly ever reproduce on canvas. My fingers itched to try, though. Her expression was sad— remorseful, and I felt ashamed of my harsh words earlier. I had been the rude one, not her.

But I didn't want, *couldn't*, encourage her. I shrugged and lifted the lens back up. "It's fine."

A small basket was pushed in front of me. "I, ah, brought you some coffee and banana bread. I made it myself."

I looked down at the offering, a strange sensation welling up in my chest.

"I didn't know how you took it, so I only added cream. I have some sugar packages," she added. I could hear the hope in her voice. She wanted me to accept her peace offering.

"I like it black."

"Oh."

How she managed to saturate so much disappointment into one syllable, I had no idea. Or why the fact she was disappointed bothered me so much. I reached forward, pulling the basket closer and lifted out a piece of the banana bread. I felt her eyes on me the whole time as I bit and chewed the dense slice.

"It's good," I offered gruffly.

She picked up a piece and nibbled on it, not saying anything. I turned away and lifted the camera, capturing the breathtaking colors and shapes of the unusual, darker clouds as the dying sun spread its magic one last time for the day.

"Do you take a lot of pictures?"

"Some."

"Do you also sell those?"

"No."

She made a small frustrated sigh in the back of her throat. "Where's Elliott?"

"In the house. I came alone so I could concentrate. I didn't want the distraction."

"Am I distracting you?"

"Yes."

"I only wanted to come and say I was sorry."

"You did that."

"Is that a dismissal?"

I huffed out an impatient exhale of air. "I came out to capture the unique light. Not chat."

"You prefer peace and quiet?"

My voice became sharp. "I like quiet—I have no idea what peace feels like."

I started at the feeling of her small hand resting on my arm. The warmth of her tender touch was shocking; my entire body humming with electricity. "I understand."

I stood up with a jerk, keeping my back to her. My heart raced at her close proximity and the strange need to feel more of her touches. "I doubt that very much."

She stood, as well. "That's rather presumptuous of you. You don't know anything about me or my life."

"And I don't want to."

She gasped. "My God, you're rude. I was only—"

I cut her off. "I don't care what you were trying to do. Leave me alone, Megan. I don't need a friend or someone to sympathize with." I pushed the basket with my foot. "I'm not looking for company or little baskets of treats. Just stay away from me."

Only silence greeted me. I knew if I turned and dared to look at her, there would be tears in her dark eyes. Hurt would once again color her expression, but I needed her to stay away.

I lifted the camera back up, even though the light was fading, the colors lessening and losing their vibrancy. I felt her move away—her footsteps withdrawing. I turned and watched her, and unable to help myself, captured her retreating figure on film. Her head was bowed, shoulders hunched in sadness as she hurried from me. Even her hair, still gleaming in the dull light, fell flat over her shoulders, no longer lifting and moving in the breeze. The light of the sun wasn't the only thing that faded in front of my eyes—I had crushed her brightness. I also effectively and completely convinced her of what I wanted: to be left alone.

She disappeared into her house, never once turning back.

My legs felt heavy as I made my way up the steps to my own house.

Alone had never felt as lonely as it did that very moment.

MEGAN

I tossed and turned all night after my run-in with Zachary. He made it very apparent he wanted nothing to do with me or my friendly gestures. His rejection caused an ache in my chest I couldn't explain and everything in me told me his actions caused him the same pain. I didn't believe him when he said he wanted to be alone—I was certain it was the only way he knew how to be.

By the afternoon, the pressure behind my eyes was almost unbearable. The gathering storm from yesterday still hung low and thick, moving in slow. The closer it came, the more my headache intensified. I had every symptom of a migraine: the tunnel vision, sensitivity to light, throbbing pain, and increasing nausea. The only thing I didn't have: my medication. It had been a while since my last headache, so I hadn't even thought to bring it. Some Tylenol in the bathroom cabinet was the best I could do. I knew I needed to lie down and rest, so I left the sliding door open for some fresh air, then curled up on the sofa. Dixie came up beside me, burrowing her little body next to mine. I closed my eyes, praying the storm would break soon and help ease my headache.

A noise woke me, and I sat up, blinking and disoriented. The drapery panel beside the sliding door was blowing, knocking into the wall. Outside, it was darker than before, early evening beginning to settle over the sky, but it seemed the storm was easing off. Although it appeared like we would still get rain, it would not be the huge storm that had been predicted. Grateful the pain in my head had abated somewhat, I stretched and got up from the sofa. Frowning, I realized the invisible screen had drawn in on itself, leaving the door wide open. As I reached to snap it back in place, I looked behind me. Dixie wasn't on the sofa or the chair. I smiled, knowing she had probably gone to snuggle on the bed—she loved to burrow under blankets. Maybe the screen sliding open had startled her; I wasn't sure how long it had been ajar. Walking into the bedroom, I was surprised not to see a little lump under the covers. I checked beneath the bed and in the closet, then tried looking in the other bedroom.

No Dixie.

A chill raced down my spine as I called out to her, searching the whole house. She wasn't there. Panicking, I shoved my feet into some sneakers and ran down to the beach. Becoming frantic, I searched as my heart pounded and tears spilled down my cheeks. I called her name over the sound of the crashing waves, scanning the water in fear of seeing her lifeless, little form.

Darkness was falling, and I didn't know what to do next. She never went out without me. She had never been alone. More tears gathered in my eyes as I stood, wringing my hands, lost and scared on the sand.

I couldn't lose her. Where could she be? I looked up at the house on the bluff, hesitating. Maybe she had gone to find Elliott. After our last conversation I knew Zachary wouldn't be very welcoming, but this was about Dixie—not him. I turned and started to run toward the stairs. Twice I slipped going up, landing painfully hard on my hands and knees, the tears making it difficult to see where I was going. When I reached the top, I looked around and called, but no little ball of fluff appeared. I rushed to the house, climbing the steps and banged on the door. Maybe Zachary had found her and taken her inside, knowing I would come and get her. There was no answer, so I banged again, swiping under my eyes as the tears flowed, my chest threatening to burst with the ache inside.

She couldn't be lost. She couldn't.

Just as I raised my hand up again, the door was flung open and Zachary filled the frame, somewhat hidden behind the door. The encroaching darkness surrounding me, and his dim hallway made it difficult to see, but his harsh voice made it clear he wasn't happy to see me.

"What?"

"Dixie... Have you seen her?" I gasped.

"No. Why would I?"

"She isn't here?"

His voice became impatient, his accent even stronger than earlier. I could see one of his hands curled into a fist at his side; I knew he wasn't pleased to be having this conversation with me. "Why would she be here?"

"I fell asleep...the screen opened up...I think she went outside...I can't find her..." I babbled, my voice quivering.

"She isn't here."

I braced myself on the doorframe, my legs shaking. "I don't know what to do."

He shrugged. "Not much you can do. It's almost dark."

"I have to find her! I can't leave her out all night!"

"How long has she been gone?"

"I don't know. I was asleep."

He stepped back, his hand on the door, beginning to push it shut. "I can't help you."

"Please, Zachary; she's so little. She must be lost...and so scared!"

His voice was angry when he spoke. "You should have taken better care of her, if you loved her so much."

I gasped at his hurtful words.

"I had a migraine and she was beside me when I lay down—" I protested. I looked around wildly. "Oh God, what if she wandered off into the woods?"

His voice was cold. "There's nothing much you can do at this point. You'll have to look in the morning. The only thing you can do is pray a coyote doesn't get her first."

Then the door slammed shut.

5

MEGAN

I stumbled back from the door, my hand covering my mouth.

That man wasn't only rude or unfriendly. He was cruel.

I made it to the top step before my legs gave out on me and I fell down, wrapping my arms around my legs as I sobbed.

My little Dixie.

I had gotten her from a shelter when she was about nine months old. She'd been found in an alley—dirty, scared, and so thin. We'd made an instant connection when Dixie's paw had reached through her kennel, stopping me as I walked down the aisle. I bent down to say hello, and I was in love. The staff at the shelter had named her Dixie since she loved to run around with one of the small cups clasped in her mouth, using it like a toy. It suited her, so I kept the name and she'd been with me ever since—the one real constant in my life.

I felt a few raindrops start and my tears became harder, my sobs wrenching out of my chest in loud gasps. From behind me, I could hear a low whimper, which caused me to lift my head.

Elliott. He heard me crying and was answering me in his own way.

Showing that, unlike his cold-hearted master, he did care.

I had to find Dixie.

With a new determination, I jumped up, wiped the tears away from my face, and ran down the steps. I raced as fast as I could across the sand, stumbling over my own feet in my haste, the space between the two houses seemingly vast all of a sudden. Once my steps faltered as his words "you'd better pray a coyote doesn't find her first" flashed through my head. I lurched forward as nausea washed over me, and I dry heaved onto the sand at the thought of Dixie being hurt because of my carelessness. When I reached the empty house, my hope of finding Dixie waiting for me on the deck, was crushed, so I grabbed two things: my jacket and the flashlight. I had no choice; I had to try and find her. I had seen a path the other day in the woods behind the house—I would follow it as far as I could. I prayed I would find Dixie before I had to turn around.

I tore out the back door and stopped at the edge of the forest. Taking a deep breath, I plunged into the woods. Gloom instantly surrounded me as I hurried forward, calling out Dixie's name. Branches grabbed at my clothes, tearing at my hair as the woods closed in—the denseness around me muffling the sound of the ocean. The way ahead was unclear, and I stopped, panicking. How was I ever going to find Dixie in all of this unfamiliar darkness? I turned, realizing I no longer even knew where the house was located. I had no choice but to continue the way I came. Pushing forward, I began to pray.

I was unaware of how much time had passed when I fell over an exposed tree root, twisting my ankle, crying out in the dark. I had been searching and calling, stopping to listen, praying I would hear Dixie's bark. All I heard, though, were the sounds of the forest around me, the rain as it hit the trees, and my own sobbing breaths. I had been heading uphill for a while and the sound of the ocean was still to my left side, but otherwise, I knew I was hopelessly lost. I should never have come into the woods. The trail had petered out rather fast, but I had continued pushing ahead, my need to find Dixie overriding all my common sense.

Now, I lay sobbing in the wet mud and dead leaves left by the cold winter. Why didn't I bring my cellphone? Why hadn't I waited until daylight? As much as I hated to admit it, Zachary had been right to say I needed to wait until the morning, but it had been his harsh remark about the coyotes that had sent me running in here, in a tail-spin of fear.

Gingerly, I climbed to my knees, wincing as I pushed off the wet ground in an attempt to get to my feet. My jeans were torn, and my hands and knees were both covered in scratches and cuts. I stood, my legs unsteady, but collapsed back down when my ankle gave out as soon as I put weight on it. Crying, I crawled my way over to the closest tree, leaning up into it, hugging my good leg to my chest while my injured one stayed outstretched. The flashlight was lying beside me, its beam focused on the torn leg of my jeans, so I left it on as a form of comfort. Even though I knew the batteries would run out, I wasn't ready to be in total darkness yet. I took in several breaths, trying to calm myself. I needed a plan.

No one knew where I was, so I had to get myself out of the forest. I closed my eyes and listened. The ocean was in front of me, which meant so was the beach. If I went straight ahead, I could get there and then get back to the house. If I'd been going uphill, as I thought, that meant I must be headed toward the bluff. I needed a stick to lean on, a good firm branch that would hold my weight while I inched forward. I only had to rest for a few minutes before I attempted to get to my feet again. I felt fresh tears gather when I realized I couldn't look for Dixie anymore. I would have to call Mrs. Cooper in the morning and ask for help.

Hoping, as Zachary so *kindly* suggested, we found her before another animal did.

Shivering, I closed my eyes and hugged myself.

I'd rest for a few minutes, gather some strength and then I'd get up.

I had to get up. I had to find Dixie.

A sound woke me. Something was moving quickly across the ground, shuffling dead twigs and leaves that covered the forest floor. I pushed back into the tree, gripping the flashlight, ready to use it as a weapon. I shouldn't have fallen asleep—I'd only meant to rest for a moment and gather my strength.

I swallowed, fear racing down my spine as the noises came closer, and I shut my eyes when the sound stopped, too terrified to look at what was now right beside me. Shaking from cold and panic, I bit down on my lip to stop the terrified scream that was building. The brush of fur on my hands startled me, but it was the long wet lick of a rough tongue that caused me to gasp, my eyes flying open as I stared into Elliott's face. My fear was instantly replaced with relief and I flung my arms around his great neck, sobbing. It was when I heard Zachary's impatient voice, and realized he was right behind Elliott, that I raised my head.

He stood, looking down at me, bathed in semi-darkness. With a muttered curse, he kneeled beside me. "Are you hurt?"

I could only nod; too shocked at his sudden appearance to speak.

"Aside from the obvious, where?"

The obvious?

I pointed a shaking finger to my ankle.

He leaned down, his fingers prodding and checking. I winced when he tried to bend it and he placed my foot back down. "I don't think it's broken, but I'm not sure you can walk."

"I know."

He sat back on his heels. "What the fuck were you thinking?"

"Dixie—" My voice trailed off as his anger exploded.

"...was lost." He finished my sentence. "So, you decide to compound the problem by charging into the woods and getting yourself lost, as well? Do you have any common sense at all? What good would it do her if you were hurt? Jesus, if I hadn't found you—" He paused, only to start berating me again. "Do you have any brains in that head of yours, Megan?"

I took in a shuddering breath, startled by his fury.

"You are an awful man."

He laughed—the sound dry and bitter. "Hardly a news flash, my dear." He stood up and reached for my hand. "We need to get you out of the woods and somewhere warm."

"Dixie—"

"She's safe and sitting by the fire, in my living room. I found her not long after you left."

My gasp of relief was almost painful, and the tears started running down my face again. I buried my face in my hands, huge sobs ripping from my chest. Zachary's voice was softer when he spoke again. "Megan, we need to get you out of these woods. I've been looking for you for over an hour; we need to get out of the cold. Give me your hand, please."

He'd been looking for me?

I wiped my eyes and held out my hand, allowing him to pull me up. When I was standing, my legs wobbling, he hesitated. "If you help me, support my weight a little, I think I can walk," I insisted.

He moved closer, wrapping his arm around my waist, allowing my weight to settle into him. Despite the reason he was holding me, my body reacted. Warmth surged through me at his close proximity and I trembled from his touch.

"Try a step."

I stepped forward, the pain tearing through me, making me gasp and stumble.

With a muffled curse, he swept me into his arms and my head fell into his chest as darkness closed in around me.

6

ZACHARY

"Fuck!"

My arms shot out, grabbing Megan before she hit the ground. I pulled her unconscious form closer to my chest, cradling her tight. She was out cold, her body limp and dangling in my arms. Calling Elliott to heel, I hurried back to the house. I was grateful we weren't too far away, and I knew the way well. How she had left the path in the woods and ended up here, was a mystery to me. She must have been wandering in circles, getting more lost each time. Another ten feet and she would have walked right off the bluff and fell the long distance to the hard, unforgiving sand below. The thought of that happening had me tightening my grip on her.

It had taken mere seconds for the guilt to hit me after I slammed the door on Megan, her face gaping at me in shock over my callous behavior. My earlier encounters with her had left me reeling and finding her on my doorstep was unexpected. Her very proximity caused feelings and desires I could never act upon, and it left a bitter taste in my mouth. The longing to reach out and pull her into my arms, to soothe her, was so strong I had to curl my hands into tight fists at my side to stop myself from doing exactly that. I wanted to draw her into my house, sit her in front of the warm fire, and assure her I would find her little dog she was so terrified she'd lost—but I didn't; I couldn't. Instead, her tear-filled eyes and desperate pleas for help had only panicked me further, causing me to treat her cruelly. I shook my head in disgust as I recalled my comment about the coyotes; it was definitely a low point—even for me.

I had stood on the stairs, uncertain, when I heard Elliott's low whines, turning to see him sitting by the door, his tail thumping on the floor in a slow, rhythmic cycle. His look of disdain said everything; I walked back to the door, peered through the glass, my heart clenching at the sight of Megan sitting on my steps, obviously sobbing, her shoulders shaking. Before I could react, she had stood up, her posture determined, then she began hurrying back toward the house where she was staying. She'd run across the beach, tripping and stumbling; at one point she stopped, bent over, then continued on, and disappeared from view.

Groaning, I knew without a doubt, she would go looking for her dog in the woods. I also knew she would get lost. I had sighed, a heavy exhale of air, my head falling onto the thick wood of my door, as I realized there was no choice; I had to go after her. I knew the woods well, since Elliott and I tramped through the dense forest daily. I was certain if Dixie had wandered into the woods, she was probably following Elliott's scent, and there was every chance she would end up on my doorstep—as long as she was safe. It was getting dark, though, the storm was closing in, and I hadn't lied: there were coyotes in the woods. I had to try and find her. I had to try and find both of them.

I had grabbed my coat and called Elliott, guilt eating at me for my appalling behavior. I didn't need to put a lead on him, so side by side we headed into the darkening forest, following the worn trail we had made from so many similar walks. It was only about fifteen minutes later that Elliott's bark alerted me. I found Dixie, trembling and wet, her collar caught on a low lying tree branch, but otherwise unharmed. I exhaled a sigh of relief, tucking her shaking body into my coat as I took her back to the house. Her grateful licks to my face made me feel even worse about the way I had spoken to Megan. With rapid movements, I toweled her off then sat her in front of the fire to warm up, and much to Elliott's displeasure, called him to come with me, hurrying back in search of Megan.

I looked back down at the woman in my arms; she was so pale, with streaks of dirt on her cheeks, concealing most of her freckles. Her coat and jeans were mud-covered and wet; her hair soaked to her head, almost black in its appearance. She was disheveled and dirty, yet I could still discern her delicate beauty, feel the same overwhelming pull to her I had felt when I first saw her in the gallery and earlier on the beach. Tilting my head, I could see her ankle was swelling over the edge of her shoe. I felt the stirrings of anger again at myself that my behavior and words had driven her into the woods, causing her injury.

I broke through the tree line, ignoring the branches that tugged on my clothes and hat. I hurried to the door, wanting to get her out of the rain as soon as possible. Struggling to hold her and open the door, I cursed as I fumbled with the handle, not wanting to jar her in any way. Once in the house, I hesitated, unsure what to do. I felt a tremor go through her unconscious body, and I knew I needed to warm her up. Quickly, I went into the living room, placing her on the sofa. Her coat was heavy with moisture—awkward to remove—and more than once, she groaned before I was able to free her of it. I dragged off her sneakers and dropped them to the floor, to make her comfortable. I hesitated over her jeans, but decided to leave them on, and instead draped the blanket off the back of the sofa on top of her, tucking it in around her tightly. Dixie was whining softly on the floor and I lifted her onto the sofa beside Megan, where she curled into her side.

I shed my own coat, adding more logs to the fire. Then, I went to the bathroom and grabbed a few things, kneeling on the floor beside Megan's still unconscious form. Gently, I lifted her ankle, peeling off her wet sock. I did another quick check, rotating and examining the ankle for broken bones. When I was certain it was a bad sprain, and not broken, I secured it in a bandage, propping it up on a cushion. Frowning, I sat back, and peeled off her other wet sock, tucking both feet under the blanket. Would that make her warm enough? Just in case, I grabbed another folded blanket from the pile beside the sofa and tucked it around her.

I stood up, looking down on her and Dixie, who was staring up at me with wide eyes. I stroked her face as I shook my head. "You caused all this, you furry little fucker," I growled quietly, yet somehow it was without any real anger behind it. Staring down at Megan, I couldn't understand this intense longing I felt; why I wanted so desperately to touch her, to hear her talk, and be able to listen to her laughter. I wanted to watch the emotions flit across her face the same way they did when she had been entranced with my painting. Reaching down, I tucked a strand of wet hair behind her ear, then, unable to resist, allowed my fingers to graze lightly over her cheek, frowning at the scratches I could see under the dirt. Lifting her hand, I grimaced at the cuts on her palms, and I was certain her legs were also bruised and scraped. I hesitated, wondering if I should get a cloth to clean the dirt off her and check her other injuries, but then reality once again hit me.

She might wake up while I was doing that. She would clearly see me. Standing over her, touching her, she would see *me*, and it would scare her.

I would scare her. I needed to move away.

Pulling back, I walked to the corner and turned on a small lamp. With the storm getting closer, the room was getting darker; I didn't want Megan frightened when she woke up to a dark room. She'd be confused enough, I was sure.

I flung myself down in the chair opposite the sofa, just watching Megan. I angled myself so I was almost hidden in the shadows and sat patiently.

Waiting for her to wake up.

Unsure what I would do or say when she did.

MEGAN

Consciousness crept back in slow seconds. My eyes opened and blinked; my head fuzzy and confused. I was warm and comfortable, lying on something soft. I could feel various aches and pains on my body, and my cheeks were stinging. My hand drifted up to my face, and I frowned at the strange texture under my fingers on my cheek. It was dry and rough, and I pulled my hand away looking at the dark smears on my fingers.

Mud?

Images flashed through my mind, and I remembered the events of earlier: Dixie disappearing, Zachary's hateful words, the woods, falling, Elliott finding me, and Zachary appearing.

Zachary.

I lifted my head, trying to work out where I was. My eyes were frantic as I took in the large, unfamiliar room. In the dim light, my heart beat loud in my chest as I looked around, deciding I had to be in Zachary's house. I could hear the heavy pounding of rain on the roof over head, and the low rumble of thunder in the distance. I shifted, stifling a groan as my throbbing ankle protested. Carefully, I lifted back the blankets in which I was wrapped and saw my ankle was bandaged, resting on a pillow. I frowned in confusion. Zachary must have done that. He must have carried me here and looked after me.

He seemed so hateful toward me—why would he do that?

There was a large fireplace, the flames glowing and dancing brightly in the hearth, casting light into the room. Elliott was lying in front of it; curled into him was Dixie. Tears of relief filled my eyes at the sight of her tiny form asleep beside her large guardian. Zachary hadn't been telling me she was safe only to calm me down—he *had* found her. Lowering my hand, I called her softly. She came over, nudging me with her wet nose, licking my face as I picked her up and held her close, stroking her soft fur. She was safe. Despite the nasty words that came out of Zachary's mouth, he had helped to make her safe, and I was grateful. With one final lick to my face, Dixie squirmed away, trotting back over to Elliott. He greeted her with a long swipe of his tongue on her head. She settled back into his side and they both put their heads down with soft huffs.

My gaze moved and took in the chair beside the fireplace and the figure in it. Zachary was asleep in the chair, his face half-turned into the corner of the large wingback as he slumbered. His long legs were stretched out in front of him, crossed at the ankles, arms resting on the chair, hands hanging off the ends. For some reason, his hands fascinated me. Large and wide; his fingers were extraordinarily long and tapered. I could imagine them, gripping a brush as he swirled paint around on one of his canvases. Another unbidden image came to my mind: one where his long fingers ghosted over my skin as his touch danced across my cheek with great tenderness. I frowned in confusion. Where had that thought come from? That wasn't going to happen. In fact, I was pretty sure as soon as he found me awake, I would be asked to leave.

Still, my eyes remained locked on his graceful hands, and like at the gallery, I noticed markings on the back of one of them. I sat up, easing my way to a sitting position, curious as to what I could see. Gingerly, I lifted my foot off the cushion, and pushed myself up onto my feet. Both dogs glanced my way, curling back up, ignoring my slow movements. I tested my foot and was pleased to discover Zachary's bandage afforded me the support I needed to walk, albeit rather awkwardly. I was stiff and sore, but I could move. I inched closer to the chair and stood, remaining quiet as I observed him. His left hand was smooth. The right one, however, was...not. The skin was marred and puckered, blemished. My eyes widened as I realized I was looking at deep scars over the back and extending down his fingers, causing them to bend at an odd angle. My heart went out to him as I thought of the pain he must feel on a daily basis. I wondered how he still painted such stunning images, when his injured hand must cause him discomfort. I looked up at his partially hidden face. It was the first time I had seen him without a beanie on. His hair was thick and riotous, so dark it was almost black, hanging low on his collar and over his brow. Long lashes rested on his cheek, and I remembered the flash of blue that came from under them as he had glanced sideways at me. His lips were full and slightly pouty; my body hummed at the thought of them covering mine. His jaw was covered in thick stubble, and for some reason, my fingers itched to reach out and touch it. He was devastatingly handsome.

He shifted, his head tilting to the other side as he settled, still sleeping, back into the chair. I stepped back in shock.

His face.

The skin on the right side of his face was twisted and marred, stretched tight and rough over his cheekbones. I was certain he had been burned. Small patches of hair were missing from his scalp and jaw, the rough skin showing through in the dim light. One corner of his mouth was twisted, causing an uneven, permanent grimace on the one side of his full lips. There were more scars running down his neck, disappearing under the collar of his crewneck sweater.

A small gasp escaped my mouth as comprehension hit me. That was why he hid from the world.

Zachary's eyes flew open, his startled gaze meeting my overwhelmed one. He blinked, a look of horror spread over his features, and he stood up. His sudden movement scared me, and I stepped back, losing my footing, falling backwards. He lurched forward, grabbing, his arms encircling and dragging me close to him.

For a moment there was no sound in the room other than our heavy breathing. I could feel his rapid heartbeat as he pressed me close, and I had no doubt he was feeling mine. My hands were clutching his thick sweater, my face buried into his chest while his arms held me, his stance rigid and unyielding, yet somehow protective and comforting. I inhaled deeply, his ocean-drenched scent calming and soothing as it enveloped me. Then, as quick as he had come close, he pushed me, stepping back and turning around. With his back now to me, he stood by the fireplace, head hung low, as the flames flickered over his shielded profile.

The tension in the air was palpable. In desperation, I searched my head for the appropriate thing to say. All other words failed me, and I offered the only ones I could find.

"I'm sorry."

He barked out a laugh. "I bet you are."

"No. That isn't what I meant. I meant I'm sorry for disturbing your rest. It was rude of me to stare."

His voice was dripping with sarcasm. "Yes, I'm sure you didn't mean you're sorry you got a full look at me and it scared the hell out of you."

"I'm not scared of you."

He turned; fury evident on his face. "You don't lie well, Megan."

"I'm not lying. I was startled, but I'm not scared."

"You should be."

"Why? Because you have some scars? That makes you scary?"

His eyes narrowed. "Ugliness outside often indicates there's ugliness underneath."

I scoffed at him. "More like you're using the supposed ugliness to make people think that."

He remained silent, his eyes piercing.

I stepped forward, trying to keep my voice soft, the need to reassure him, somehow vital. My heart hammered in my chest as I moved toward him. "Some of the most beautiful people in the world use their beauty to hide their ugliness, Zachary. I've seen that and experienced it myself. I don't think you have any ugliness in you. No matter how hard you pretend or act, otherwise."

"And you know this because?"

"Your paintings."

"*My paintings?*"

"They show your emotions. They show you."

"And what do you *think* you see?"

I hesitated to answer him.

"What do you think you see, Megan?" he demanded again, with a harsh voice.

"Besides the beauty you hide? Pain...confusion...need...loneliness. I see you turning your back on the world you think has turned its back on you."

His indrawn breath was deep, his voice low and furious.

"Get out."

7

ZACHARY

Megan stood gazing at me, her head shaking slowly back and forth, but she didn't move. "You don't mean that."

Why wasn't she listening to me? Why wasn't she leaving?

"Get out of my house. Leave." I pointed to the door, making sure she understood. "Now."

"You wouldn't send me out into a storm, Zachary. Your words are just empty threats to try and get me to hate you." She came closer, her voice soothing and calm.

I barked out a harsh laugh as I stepped back. "You should hate me."

"I don't." She edged forward again.

I frowned at her. Why was she coming closer? She should be backing away; even if she knew I wouldn't throw her out of the house, she should want to move as far away from me—from my hideous face —as possible.

"What are you doing?"

"I'm not afraid of you." She moved forward, closing any remaining distance between us to mere inches. I tried to step back, but I had nowhere to go, my back hitting the stone of the fireplace. I dragged in a shaking breath, only to have my already overloaded senses fill with her warm scent, shutting my eyes as it settled around me like a soothing blanket. When I opened them a moment later, it was to her wide, dark gaze. There was no revulsion or pity in their depths; only a simple calm, beseeching stare. She looked vulnerable as we gazed at each other, the room around us ceasing to exist.

Why was she looking at me like that? What did she want?

"Zachary," she whispered.

It was too much. She was too close and too—

I lifted my hands to push her away, except when they wrapped around the top of her arms, it was as if they had a mind of their own. Time seemed to stop as my fingers caressed the smooth, silky skin not covered by her T-shirt, the warmth of her burning through my fingers to my very core. My arms flexed as they dragged her closer until our faces were almost touching. Her hands held tightly to my loose sweater, bunching the fabric in her small fists so hard, I knew the cuts on her palms would reopen. I knew her blood would seep into the material, forever staining it with her essence. It didn't matter; I couldn't let go of her. I held her so close it was as if I was trying to mold her into my skin and make her part of my body. Her hot breath washed over my face, and I could hear my own ragged, harsh breaths filling the room.

Still, neither of us said a word as we stared, clutching and holding each other, the heat between us burning brighter every second that passed. A small whimper escaped her lips, a pleading, needy sound and I was lost. My mouth covered hers roughly and I jerked her flush to me, not allowing a sliver of space between us. I groaned into her wet, warm mouth as I felt her hands slip into my hair, holding me close to her face. Her tongue was like silk on mine as we caressed and tasted, our tongues stroking and entwining. The taste of her was as sweet as I knew it would be, her lips as soft and her effect on me crippling. I plunged my hands into her hair, tilting her head to deepen the kiss, directing her where I needed her to go with my touch. Megan gripped me tighter as I claimed her, needing and wanting more. Her heart hammered powerfully in her chest, so I knew she could feel mine as well. Small sounds from deep in her throat filled my ears as I ravished her mouth, lost in the heat and wonder that was Megan.

Her hands moved restlessly, stroking and tugging on my hair, and I growled in approval as she pressed closer. I slipped my hand under her shirt, settling wide across the warm skin of her back, caressing and teasing as she whimpered again. I hardened with want, pressing into her heat as she gasped and arched to me. I smiled into her mouth, breaking away only to fill my lungs, before capturing her swollen lips with mine again, unable to stay away. It was as though I was under her spell; she wove her magic around me, drawing me into a world of heat and passion.

It was then I felt it, though. Her hand slipped from my hair. She tenderly cupped my face; her fingers ghosting, light as air, over my marred, twisted skin. The feeling of her gentle touch was so intense— aside from my own hand, my face hadn't been touched by another person since before I'd been scarred, and I jerked away in shock.

Megan stilled, looking up at me from hooded eyes, her hand frozen midair, much like the day I had seen her at the gallery. Her chest was heaving, her hair still clutched in my fist as she stared up at me, confused. Her mouth was glistening and swollen from mine, her cheeks flushed a delicious pink—she looked beautiful.

Too beautiful for me.

That reality crashed around me, and with a roar I pushed her away. She stumbled back, hitting the chair, her hand covering her mouth as she looked on in fear.

Now she was afraid.

I said nothing. I could offer nothing. Rushing past her, I headed for the staircase and I tore up the stairs as if the hounds of hell were pursuing me, not stopping until I reached the sanctuary of my studio. I slammed the door behind me so hard, the paintings resting on the wall moved with the force of the action. I stood, leaning back into the door, my breath coming out in loud, ragged gasps. My hand pressed hard over my scarred cheek—the same one she had so gently caressed moments ago.

I wondered how repulsed she'd been when she had felt the twisted, hard scar tissue covering my face. The long, jagged scars and roughened skin, which served as a reminder to me daily of what I had lost. The words that had been screamed at me as my flesh burned and seared.

Now people can see you're as ugly on the outside as you are on the inside!

Panic filled my chest and I bent over, clutching my knees, as it bloomed and tightened. I dragged in shallow gasps of air, trying to calm and center myself, as I fought against the memories threatening to swamp me. I attempted to find another, better memory as I buried my face into my hands, struggling to breathe. Megan's scent hit me; its floral fragrance on my skin lingering from where I had my fingers wrapped in her thick hair. Greedily I inhaled, the scent calming me enough I could relax and lift my head. I straightened up and pushed off the door, flicking on the lights.

There was only one thing I could do to stop those memories.

I had to lose myself.

I walked forward and stopped in front of a blank canvas I had stretched earlier.

Picking up my favorite brush, I shut my eyes, allowing the images to take over. When I opened them again, all I saw was my canvas.

Everything else had disappeared.

I had no idea how much time passed when I finally set down the brush and stared at the painting. I stepped back, as I looked it over with a critical eye, and grunted a humorless chuckle.

Swirling, angry, black stormy skies circled and threatened over a calm, reflective ocean, its colors serene and in perfect contrast to the image above. The two images were so vastly contradictory; they didn't even belong on the same canvas. Yet, they were, in fact, so starkly beautiful in their differences, that they complemented each other; dark versus light, anger versus calm; intense, hot black amid soft, cool blues and greens. It was good.

I also knew what it represented.

My shoulders slumped in exhaustion. I made my way to the door, opening it with care. Outside, Elliott was asleep, his huge head resting on his paws. He lifted his face to me, his tail thumping slowly on the floor as I leaned down to stroke his thick fur. I listened for a minute, but could hear nothing in the house, other than the wind outside. The storm had passed and judging from the dim light coming in the windows, it was almost dawn. I crossed over and looked outside. Far down the beach I could see the house where Megan was staying. There was a light in the window; therefore, I assumed she was now home safe and sound. I sighed in quiet relief, since I had no idea what I'd say to her if she was still in my house. I couldn't explain any of my actions toward her: my harsh words, my unexpected passion, the horror I had felt when I realized she was touching my scars or the way I had flung her away.

I cringed, thinking about the distraught look on her face as she stared at me before I had stormed off. I'd needed to escape from her; from the intense, overwhelming feelings she elicited in me. Another sigh escaped my lips as I realized, after how I'd acted, she'd probably never come near me again.

I wouldn't have to explain anything.

That was for the best—for both of us.

I gave a weary glance toward Elliott as he stood up, a low whine in the back of his throat. I heard his nails tapping as he ran to the door and a deep thump while he sat in front of it. I listened, tensing when I heard the sound of footsteps, followed by a quiet knock. I remained frozen, sitting at the table, my eyes glued to the mug of coffee I was holding. A few minutes passed, and the knock sounded again. My hands tightened on the mug in reaction, because I knew who it was standing on my doorstep. Somehow, after hours of tossing and turning, before giving up and accepting I would find no rest today, I had been expecting it.

Still, I didn't move.

The sound of her quiet footsteps and fading voice calling Dixie's name, finally allowed me to ease out of my chair. Filled with apprehension, I looked out the window, watching Megan's retreating figure as she walked across the beach. I frowned when I saw how badly she was limping.

Was she looking after her foot? Why did she walk all this way when she was obviously still in pain? I clenched my hands in annoyance. Why had she come back here?

Beside me Elliott butted my leg, pawing at the door. Looking out, like the coward I was, I made sure Megan was far enough away she wouldn't hear. I then eased open the door, surprised to see a large bag sitting on the doorstep. I picked it up and carried it to the kitchen, Elliott following at my heels. Inside were the blankets and pillow I had used in which to wrap Megan, all freshly laundered. I shook my head when I realized I hadn't even noticed they were gone. Looking at the sofa, I noticed it was spotless; the leather gleaming dully in the light—it was obvious she had cleaned it, too. I wondered how long she had stayed after I stormed away. Had she been waiting for me to return?

I placed the blankets and pillow back on the sofa, then picked up the bag. Two more items fell out and Elliott was quick to grab at one of them. A large rawhide bone with a ribbon wrapped around it, made me smile; he loved those. The small tag read: **For Elliott, our hero. Love, M&D**. I grinned as I undid the ribbon and let Elliott run away with his treasure. He plunked himself down in his basket and immediately began gnawing away at the treat.

Curious, I picked up the other item. It was a black beanie, thick and soft. I recognized it as one Ashley sold in the gallery shop. They were made of cashmere and were warm to wear, not to mention indulgent. I turned it over and lifted the small card attached to it.

> *Zachary—I found yours on the beach. I know you were wearing it when you found me. Unlike some things, it was damaged beyond repair, even though I tried to mend it for you. Please accept this new one with my gratitude. I won't give up mending the other. ~M*

I stared at the message. How had she noticed I was wearing my hat? I hadn't even thought about the fact I wasn't wearing it when we arrived home. I was too concerned with her well-being and making sure she was okay. My hat, or lack thereof, never once entered my mind.

I shook my head, confused. I knew exactly what she was saying, yet I didn't understand why. Why did she want to try and get to know me? Or try and mend me?

I was damaged goods. I had nothing to offer the sweet woman who somehow stirred emotions in me, which I didn't understand.

My hand fisted the rich cashmere of the beanie as I thought of our passionate kiss and the feel of her mouth beneath mine. I shut my eyes remembering how perfect it felt to hold her in my arms. How I lost myself with her for a brief, wonderful moment.

Then how utterly horrified I was when reality had hit me, yet again.

I looked down at her small gift, feeling torn.

I had to stay away from Megan.

Except, the thought of doing so made me...miserable.

For a week it continued. Megan would walk over and leave something on the doorstep. I never knew what time of day she would come or even if she'd indeed appear that day, but I found myself sitting, watching for her arrival. The days she didn't come felt endless, and I was filled with a sense of longing I couldn't explain. It felt as if I missed her. Although, when I would see her small figure come into view, I would assess how she was walking, then I would step into the kitchen, hiding from her once again.

She always knocked twice.

I always ignored her.

Still, she always returned.

Elliott would sit in front of the door, his tail thumping out a quiet rhythm as he whined low in his throat. If I was feeling somewhat brave, I would allow him access to the back of the house, where his dog door was; he would push his way through to greet Megan and Dixie on the deck. Megan would sit on the top step and watch them run around the beach or stroke their heads as they sat beside her. She looked so small with her back to the door. I wondered if she knew I watched her; absorbing the enticing sight of her there, her brilliant hair swirling in the wind that kicked up from the ocean. I knew how soft that hair was, and I longed to bury my fingers into her thick tresses again. My body ached to draw her close and feel her flush against me. I wanted to inhale her lovely scent deep into my lungs and taste her mouth with mine. I craved her, yet even as I yearned, as soon as she shifted, I disappeared from sight, for fear she might see me. She always commanded Elliott *home* and waited until he was back inside, before she and Dixie slowly made their way back across the beach, out of my vision. They were the best and worst moments of my day—I longed for them.

Once she was gone, I would open the door and see what little treasure she had left behind.

A small plate of cookies for me and dog biscuits for Elliott.

A pair of warm socks for after my next "wade" into the water.

A slice of pie to share with Elliott.

Even a bag of my favorite peppermints, although how she knew they were my favorite, I wasn't sure.

They were small, thoughtful gestures, accompanied by a tiny card with sweet words of friendship and thanks or a short humorous message; always signed *M*.

As if some other passing angel was leaving gifts and she wanted to be sure I knew which ones were hers.

Today, I opened the door and looked down, fighting a smile. I picked up the small canvas, studying it. It was a very badly done watercolor of the beach with Dixie and Elliott on it—or more like stick figures of them. She even painted the bluff and what I guessed was my house at the top. Turning it over, I let out a chuckle.

Maybe you'd consider a trade? I'd be willing to give this up for Tempest...
One time offer. ~M

I smiled even as I shook my head sadly.
All of this had to stop.

The next day I was waiting. When Elliott's ears perked up, I opened the back door and let him out, following him, remaining silent. I listened as Megan greeted him, then the gentle raps sounding on my door. I stepped out and watched her as she stood waiting, ever hopeful I would open the door. Only this time she didn't repeat her knocks and there was nothing in her hands. Instead, I watched her head bow. I could feel the resigned sadness rolling off her, as she turned and sat down at the top of the steps, her shoulders slumped. Taking in a deep breath, I quietly walked over, and lowered myself down beside her, grateful my scarred half was facing away from her side view. Her startled gasp was filled with surprise at my appearance, but she didn't say anything. I inhaled deep lungfuls of her soft scent, letting it wash over me, enjoying how it soothed and calmed me.

I waited for a minute before I spoke. "You're still limping."

"It's getting better."

"Not much," I huffed. "You're overdoing it, walking here all the time."

She turned, and I felt the heat of her gaze. "Come to me, then."

"You have to stop this, Megan."

"Stop what? Being a friendly neighbor? Thanking you for finding me, bringing me out of the storm, and looking after me?"

I sighed and looked at her. Her brown eyes were too expressive. Normally, dark eyes were flat, but hers were bursting with life and fire, and her fire was directed at me. "My cruelty sent you into that storm."

She shrugged. "Your words were heartless, but I would've gone looking for her regardless." She paused. "You said them to drive me away, Zachary. I know that."

She turned away and looked back toward the ocean. "And I'm not stopping. You might as well give in."

"Why, Megan?"

For a minute she said nothing. I startled when I felt her hand slip into mine, which was resting on my leg. Her fingers curled between mine; our palms meshed together. I looked down at them, noticing the differences: her hand so small and smooth, her fingers tiny as they entwined my longer, calloused ones. The urge to lift our hands to my lips, to caress those tiny fingers, was overwhelming and my eyes flew to hers.

"Why?" I repeated. "I'm not a nice man. I have nothing to give you."

"I disagree. I think you have a lot to give. You're just too scared to give it."

"You're wrong."

"No," she insisted. "I'm not."

"What makes you so sure?"

She squeezed my hand. "This does."

"My hand?" I shook my head at her. "You're not making any sense."

"Not your hand, Zachary," her patient voice whispered. "It's how I feel when I hold your hand, when I touch you." She drew in a deep breath. "How it felt when you kissed me."

"That was a mistake."

"Why?"

I yanked my hand away and stood up. "You don't want to kiss me. You don't want to know me, and you certainly don't want to pursue a relationship with me. I'm toxic. I'm scarred outside and in. Stay away from me." I turned and began to walk away, but I heard her follow me. Pivoting quickly, I found her right behind me, my abrupt stop causing her to begin to stumble. On their own accord, my arms reached out to stop her from falling. As soon as my hands touched her, everything changed. Once again, I felt the heat between us—the unexplained feeling of comfort and desire combining and swirling around us. My fingers tightened on her shoulders, but I fought the urge to drag her closer.

"You need to go," I insisted, but my voice held no conviction.

"Please," she whispered.

Without another thought, my mouth was on hers, our lips parting, as we melted together. I yanked her tight to me, desperate to have her closer. I buried my hands into her thick hair, wrapping the long waves around my fingers, tugging on them gently as I worked her mouth. Hot, burning passion lit up within me, overriding all my other senses. Growling, I pushed her up against the stone of the house. Her hands were wrapped around my neck, holding me close, her body arched into mine. She was so fucking sweet under my tongue, her response so warm and giving. Small whimpers at the back of her throat were answered with my own needy groans. I pulled away, panting, drawing much needed oxygen into my lungs, but right away, my mouth sought out the smooth feel of her neck and shoulder, my tongue tasting her sweet, sun-soaked skin.

"I'm no good for you, Megan," I murmured into her warmth, groaning as my tongue circled her small earlobe and nipped at the skin behind her ear.

"Zachary," she breathed, tilting her head, the other side of her neck presenting itself to my mouth. I trailed open-mouthed, wet kisses up to her ear. A shudder went through my spine when I felt her lips and tongue ghosting over my neck, nibbling and swirling, leaving a long trail of moisture behind.

Until she reached my ear and her lips moved toward my cheek. I stiffened, my body locking down, and Megan's movements ceased as she felt my reaction.

"Don't," she pleaded. "Don't make me stop."

I drew back slowly, placing her back on her feet, then I began to back away.

"Zachary—" Her voice was filled with hurt, which I ignored. "Please—"

I turned away. "I can't. I just can't." Leaning down, I grabbed Elliott's collar. "Don't waste your time, Megan. I'm not some pitiful creature you can save." I laughed, but there was no humor in the sound. "I can't be saved...at all."

Then, once again, I walked away from Megan Greene.

8

MEGAN

The sharp, bitter bite of rejection washed through me, filling every crevice of my body as I watched Zachary turn and walk away. I could still taste him in my mouth; my fingers itched to feel his hair under them again. My entire frame wanted to feel him melded into me.

Never before had I felt such passion for a man. Especially one I hardly knew. Every time he came near me, the air pulsated with electricity and I wanted to touch him.

Never had the sting of not being wanted, of being rejected, hurt so much.

I couldn't explain this need to be close to him; I was sure he felt it as well but refused to allow us to explore it.

A harsh sob escaped my lips, as he disappeared around the corner. I turned and made my way blindly down his steps, knowing I would never again climb them.

He made his feelings crystal clear.

I almost made it to the bottom, when my feet slipped and I fell down the last few steps to the damp sand below, landing on my already sore hands and knees. For a few moments I lay prone, the tears running down my cheeks at my foolish behavior. Bitterness washed over me as I berated myself for thinking Zachary felt the same intense need I felt for him. I pushed myself up, forcing my feet to start their journey back across the sand to the isolation of the house.

There, I told myself, I would cry and rage until I didn't want to cry anymore.

There I would find my strength and do what I came here to do.

Find a way to move on with my life.

Not chase after someone who made it plain they weren't interested in anything I had to offer.

Another sob caught in my throat as my sore ankle protested. Still, I limped forward, ignoring the pain and taking slow, measured steps away from Zachary, each one feeling more agonizing.

I gasped as a pair of strong arms abruptly encircled me and I was lifted like a child into the safety of Zachary's arms. Shocked, my head fell back to his shoulder and I stared up at him. Stormy, pain-filled eyes met my confused ones. "Do you always fall this much?" He growled at me.

"Yes."

"I'll keep that in mind."

He lifted me higher, my head settling in the nape of his neck, as if it was meant to rest there. He turned, called for the dogs, waiting as they ran toward us. I felt the gentle pressure of his lips on my temple, and I tried to ask him why he had come for me. I didn't understand why he even cared if I fell on the sand after he walked away, but all that came out was a small sob.

"Hush," he whispered, his arms tightening. "I've got you."

"Don't let go this time," I pleaded.

His lips caressed again, never leaving my skin as he carried me up the stairs and into his house.

ZACHARY

I carried Megan through the house, right into the bathroom, setting her gently on the counter. It took me a few minutes to gather the medical supplies I needed, then I cleaned her hands, grateful to see, although they were reddened from her fall, only a couple of the cuts had reopened. Before she could protest, I undid the loose tensor bandage and checked her ankle, frowning at how it was still swollen. I tossed the dirty one aside and swiftly rebandaged it, so it would have the proper support it needed to heal. I was glad I could still remember the technique from my first aid courses years ago. Once it was done, and I was satisfied, I glanced up at her, my movements stilling as our eyes met. So much hurt and confusion swam in those expressive eyes. Pain I knew I had caused. Without thinking, I cupped her soft cheek, my rough thumb caressing the skin as our gazes remained locked. The way she leaned into my touch made my heart tighten in my chest, and I fought against the desire to pull her close to me and hold her.

Her voice broke the silence. "Why did you come after me?"

"I don't know." I shrugged, unable to explain how I felt when I turned around and saw her fall off the last few steps. "You were hurt...and I couldn't stand the thought."

"Why?"

"I don't know," I repeated in a whisper. "I feel—" I didn't know how I felt. "Confused."

Her hand covered mine, her tiny fingers warm on my skin as she caressed my knuckles. "I feel the same way."

The air around us pulsated as our gazes held. Slowly, her hand lifted, her eyes begging me not to pull back. She laid her palm on my cheek; her hand a gentle caress on my face. My heart pounded—the rhythm frantic at the feeling of her touch—and I stiffened. I searched her face and eyes for what should be revulsion but found none. All I could see was a silent plea for me to allow her touch. I shut my eyes, swallowing hard, and let myself ease into her caress. Small sparks of anxiety ran down my spine, but I forced myself to stay standing in front of her as she lightly touched me. I jerked in shock when I felt her lips replace her fingers, their softness warm across the twisted skin. It was only one, small kiss; a gentle brush of her lips on me, but the sensation was intense—all at once frightening and beautiful. She didn't linger or push too hard, keeping her touch quick and easy, as if she knew there was a limit to what I could handle at one time. She drew back, giving me a tender smile, a look of contentment on her face. "Thank you," she breathed.

A smile tugged on my lips. She had that wrong. I should be thanking her. In one, simple, giving gesture she had made me feel...normal.

I brushed my lips against hers. "Anytime," I whispered, feeling playful and lighter than I had in years, and wanting to see that warm smile again.

"Now is good for me."

With a groan, I gave in. I brought her to me, my mouth covering hers. Her arms wrapped around my neck, holding me close. Her soft lips moved with mine, as the passion between us started to build. I held her tight to my chest, my arms constricting, needing to feel her as close as possible.

As soon as I allowed her to touch me, I knew...

There was no going back. Nothing would be the same again.

I wanted her, and no matter the consequences, I would have her...but not yet.

It took everything I had in me to break away from Megan. To lean away from the warmth of her mouth, the comfort of her embrace.

We needed to talk.

A s I drew back, I dropped a few gentle kisses on her lips, so she would know it wasn't rejection; I was done rejecting her.

"Why did you stop?" she whispered, as I touched my forehead to hers, inhaling deeply, letting her closeness calm me.

"You need to ice that ankle, and we need to talk."

"Right now?"

I lifted her into my arms, striding down the hall. "Right now."

"Bossy much?" she quipped.

I placed her on the sofa, propping up her ankle. I leaned against the back of the sofa; my upper body pressed into hers. "You have no idea. Get used to it, Megan. It's how I roll."

She let out a low laugh. The sound of it made my lips twitch, wanting to smile with her. "It's how you roll? Really, is that the best you have, Zachary?"

"I said I was bossy, not entertaining. Stay here. I'll be back."

Her smart retort, "Like I have anywhere I can go, since you took my shoes," followed me out of the room. That time, I did smile.

A few minutes later, I handed her a cup of coffee and sat down beside her, lifting the cushion then her ankle up onto my lap, fitting an ice pack over it. The fire was burning, the logs popping and hissing as the flames danced, both the dogs asleep in front of it.

I traced the line of her cheek gently with the end of my finger, liking how she gravitated into my touch.

"How old are you, Megan?"

"Twenty-five."

"I'm thirty-seven."

"That doesn't matter to me."

That piece of information was not really a surprise.

"Why are you here? What brought you to this part of the country so early in the spring? I doubt it was for the admirable weather."

A small frown appeared on her face. "I needed a place to think. Karen and Chris were kind enough to offer me their place."

"Think about...?" I let my question hang in the air, watching her telling eyes change from calm to wary and pain filled. Without thinking, I took her hand in mine. "Can you tell me?"

Her eyes drifted past, to the window behind me, their focus dimming for a minute. I let her gather her thoughts and sipped my coffee.

She sighed, her hand flexing in mine. "I was—am—a writer. I've self-published a few books."

"Anything I would have read?"

"I doubt it"—she shook her head— "unless you read romances."

"Ah, no. Kinda more a thriller, mystery guy."

"Didn't think so." She smirked and I chuckled.

"I was doing okay—not on any of the big best seller lists yet, but I was getting my name out there." She paused to take a sip of her coffee. "I had been working on a story, a much bigger one, for a while. Two years, in fact."

"What happened?"

"I was looking for a job—one that had fairly flexible hours, so I could still write. A friend, who worked at a publishing house, told me about a listing for a personal assistant to a well-known author. I thought it would be perfect. I went for the interview and got the job."

"Not such a good job?"

"No, it seemed fine. Jared was working on a new book. He had finished a series of three books that were huge. All of them best sellers. Expectations were high for his next book. He needed help, not only with keeping up his schedule but proofing his work, etcetera. It was like my dream job."

She shifted restlessly. "Jared and I became close. In fact, we began dating a few weeks after I started working for him. He was almost relentless in his pursuit." She laughed, yet the sound was anything but humorous. "I thought he was crazy about me."

I squeezed her hand that was beginning to tremble a little, knowing we were coming to the crux of her story. "But?" I prompted, keeping my tone gentle.

"The first week I was there, he saw me writing in my book on my lunch break."

"Writing in your book?"

She smiled sadly. "Unlike most people who use a computer, I liked to write longhand. Old-fashioned, I know, but I could always feel the story more. I had to use a computer all day at the office and I hated it. It took longer, but the words made more sense to me when I did that way. I kept everything to do with the book in an old leather satchel, which belonged to my grandfather. I loved it—he was a teacher and it reminded me of him."

I nodded in understanding. I also didn't miss the past tense of "liked."

"He saw me and asked what I was doing. I was rather shy but told him. A couple days later, he asked if he could see it. Needless to say, I was quite excited that a successful author like Jared would ask to see my work, so I let him."

"Did he give you an opinion?"

"He said it was somewhat trivial, not a bad idea, but it required a great deal of work. He said to let him know when it was done and he would reread it, make some suggestions, and possibly show it to his publishing company if he thought it had some merit. I was ecstatic."

"Sounds a little condescending to me," I muttered, suspicious of where this was going.

Megan tilted her head. "Jared was a true artist: mercurial, arrogant, rude at times, and charming at others. He had fits of anger and could be cutting, then turn around and do something kind." Her lips turned up in a small grin. "Remind you of anyone?"

I had to chuckle at her wit.

Her face became serious. "But something he was, that you're not, is deceitful and corrupt."

I slid closer, my hand closing around the back of her neck, soothing the tense muscles. "Tell me."

"Jared's editor was very unhappy with him, which made him unhappy with me—and everything else. His new book wasn't going well. Compared to the series he had written previously, this one seemed 'almost juvenile—full of inaccuracies' according to his editor. I had to agree when I read it—the story line was so disjointed, compared to the outline. Jared blamed everyone around him and became very sullen. He would hole up in his office typing, and cursing away, leaving me sitting for hours with nothing to do, and with so much time on my hands, I finished my own book."

"You told him?"

"Yes."

"And?"

"He said he would read it soon and asked me to leave it with him. The next day, he was back to being Jared. He would take me out to dinner, make me laugh with his stories, and seemed to be better, happier, with his writing. He told his editor it was flowing fast. I assumed he got over his slump; although he wasn't allowing anyone to see what he was working on. He said he didn't want to 'jinx' it yet." She shrugged. "Who was I to argue? As I said, I wrote all of my stories longhand and told no one what they were about until they were done. Everyone works in a different way."

She hesitated, then she spoke again. "A few weeks later, he insisted on going to dinner. He wanted to go to his favorite restaurant, even inviting some of his friends to join us. He was in high spirits, telling them all he was on the verge of another bestseller and how he was writing like a mad man. He was very animated." She looked at me with the saddest eyes and took a deep breath. "When we got back to his place, we found the door kicked in. The house was ransacked. He had been robbed."

"Your book was still there?" I asked. "In his house?"

She nodded. "He had it for a couple weeks. We were going to discuss it when he was finished reading it, but he said he hadn't had the chance to do so yet, because he was busy writing."

"You didn't have a copy of it?"

"No. I never made copies." She sighed. "The only one who I'd ever discussed it with was him. Karen knew I was writing a new, longer story, but I never shared details with her either. I didn't like to talk to anyone about my work—I never did."

"And then?"

"He became sullen again. Nasty. Withdrawn. I thought it was over the break-in. I was so upset myself; I wasn't thinking very well. I didn't know how to start rewriting my story, or if I even could. A couple of weeks later, he broke up with me, and let me go, stating my job position was no longer needed."

"Let me guess," I interjected sarcastically. "Not long after that, he submitted a brand-new-never-seen-before manuscript?"

She nodded. "About three months after we broke up, I heard about it. My friend who worked at the publishing house, and had originally told me about the job, had seen it. I was curious when she said it wasn't at all like what his editor thought he was working on. She gave me the basic outline."

"It was your story."

"Yes."

"He stole your manuscript. He set it all up."

She nodded, her lip trembling a little.

I could feel anger stirring in my gut. "Did you go after him?"

"I tried. I went to him first and he denied it—refuted every accusation I made. Denied he had ever seen me write anything. Demanded proof the manuscript he'd been working on was actually mine."

"Of which you had none," I stated the obvious, arching my eyebrow at her.

"Don't look at me like that," she pleaded.

"Like what?"

Her voice rose in distress, her words rapid. "I know I was an idiot! I kept my book all together, in an old torn satchel because it meant something to me! I should have made copies, kept notes separately. If I'd been smart, I would've told all my friends about it, and typed the damn thing on a computer. I never thought something like this would happen. Once it was finished, I planned on making a copy and then having it transcribed onto a computer, but—"

"But you never had a chance," I finished for her, my tone a little more gentle.

"No. I went to my friend who was a lawyer, and he went to the publishing house on my behalf. They, of course, backed up Jared. It escalated and became the word of a successful, published author and his solid reputation against the word of an ex-assistant, slash, girl-friend, who had only ever published a couple light romances on her own." She shook her head, looking frustrated. "Both he and his team came after me with a vengeance. I tried to use him to further my career. I was trying to destroy his reputation. I abused his trust. I was slammed in the papers and the publishing world. He even went so far as to allow his home to be searched for the "so-called" book folder, which, of course, they never found."

I was sure he'd used the time he had to transcribe it, and then burned the original. It only made sense.

"So, what about proof of when it was written?"

"According to his computer files, it was started months before I came to work for him."

I nodded. No doubt he rewrote an older file.

"Did you try to rewrite it?"

"I have been, but some of it is over two years old. And it's his word against mine. He said he had shown me some of what he had written so it looks like I'm copying him."

"There is no one you told? At all?"

She shook her head.

"But you know the ending."

"No, that part he changed. Just enough so it's different than what I described. He changed a few other things, too."

"Of course," I mused. This guy was either very clever or he did this before and knew all the loopholes. "He's covered all his bases, hasn't he?"

"Do you—do you believe me?"

I looked at her as her words ran through my head. Even given my trust issues, her story rang true. "Absolutely."

"Why?" she whispered. "Hardly anyone else does."

I wasn't sure how to explain something I felt with so much conviction. Maybe it was the pain in her eyes as she spoke or the sincerity of her words, but I did believe her. "I don't know," I answered honestly. "But I do."

"He wants me to publicly recant my statement. His lawyer even drew up papers stating if I did, he'd pay me twenty thousand to drop my ridiculous plagiarism claim and stop seeking attention."

A cheap pay-off compared to what he stood to lose. "All with a non-disclosure of the payout, I assume?"

"Yes."

"This isn't about money."

Her lip began to tremble. "No. It was, *is*, my work. Two years of my life. He *stole* it."

"Then fight it."

"I'm pretty much out of money to keep fighting it. I won't give him what he wants, though."

"So, you came here to try and think?"

"I came here to escape him—it—the whole situation. I was so tired of his emails, the constant barrage of press articles. People following me, calling me names. I couldn't take it anymore. I needed to escape."

I could understand that. I could also see she was growing tired of talking about this painful subject. Her eyes had begun to fill with tears, the tremble in her lip more pronounced, and her shoulders were tense.

I took the cold cup of coffee from her hand and wrapped her in my arms. For a moment, she held herself stiff in my embrace, then melted into me, her head falling to my shoulder as quiet sobs escaped her mouth.

The desire to comfort this small woman was intense. Never had I experienced such a need to care for someone. Realistically, there was little I could do but hold her and allow her to expel her emotions. I had the feeling, that like me, she was very private and rarely allowed those around her to see her pain. Cradling her close, I stroked her back in long, soothing passes, my voice hushing and whispering comforting words I wasn't sure she could hear.

She had been led on, lied to and a part of her had been taken away; all things I knew far too much about. She was right: she was fighting an uphill battle. The asshole had everything to fight for, and with: money, power, and success. She had nothing. It was like David and Goliath.

Only, I wasn't sure this time David would win.

9

ZACHARY

I hated tears. Growing up, my mother had used them like a weapon against my father; bursting into noisy sobs as she slumped onto the kitchen counter or flung herself on the sofa in some dramatic fashion. He always gave in to whatever she was demanding at the time, then the tears would dry up, until the next time—it was a never-ending cycle with them. The day I walked away from them was the first time her tears were real, but they meant nothing to me. Later in life, during my career, I watched women turn their tears on and off with no true emotion behind them, making me that much more indifferent to the sight of them. In my personal life, a woman crying meant nothing to me; even though my own behavior often was the cause. I had the ability to ignore the outburst with no effect. I was never swayed by the sound.

Holding Megan, though, and listening to her cry, was an entirely different story. Her sobs were subdued, almost silent, as her small body shook in my arms. My chest ached with some unknown emotion, the same, almost helpless feeling I experienced when I saw her fall. It was a reaction I wasn't used to nor liked very much. It made me feel out of control, and the one thing I had mastered over the years was being in control. As she cried, I wanted to comfort and fix whatever was causing her so much pain.

It was a peculiar sensation.

Slowly, she grew still, and the muffled, pain-filled sobs ceased. Without a word, I handed her some tissues, allowing her a moment to gather herself as she wiped away the wetness from her face.

"I got your shirt wet," she whispered, her voice gruff with emotion. "I'm sorry."

"I have other ones. It isn't a problem."

Her eyes met mine, the dark gaze wide and confused. We were so close; I could see the flecks of gold that surrounded her pupils like small sunbursts. Her auburn hair, glowing almost copper, glinted in the late afternoon sun that filled the room. Without thinking, I lifted a hand, trailing my fingers through the thickness of her tresses, admiring the colors spilling over my hand. "I'd like to capture you, exactly like this," I murmured. "You're so lovely in this light, with the sun surrounding you, highlighting your hair."

"Do you do that? Paint, ah, portraits?"

I shook my head in wonder. Once again, she was making me feel and say things that were out of character. "I've done a few. I use photography with those. It helps sometimes when the moment is right, and I need to capture something to use later." Teasing, I tapped the end of her nose, wanting her to smile. "Like now. Would you let me take your picture, Megan, if I asked? Paint your portrait?"

"Yes," she breathed, her cheeks flooding with color.

Her sudden shyness and simple answer warmed my chest. I wanted that camera in my hands immediately.

"Maybe later this week we will. I want this light behind you when I do. It's fading now, so when I see it again, we'll act on it."

"All right."

Neither of us acknowledged the fact we both assumed she would be here.

Somehow, though, we both knew it.

Elliott stood up, stretching, shaking his head. "I need to take him for a walk." Easing Megan off my lap, I got off the sofa. "I'll take Dixie, too."

"Are you going in the woods?"

"No. I'll take them on the beach."

"I'll come with you."

"You shouldn't be on your foot." I frowned.

"You wrapped it so well, it feels fine. It'll be good to stretch my legs."

The thought of walking on the beach with her appealed to me, so I didn't argue. It was better than me worrying about her sitting here alone, perhaps crying again. I paused, wondering when the last time I had worried about another person had been, or why worrying about Megan seemed so natural. Offering her my hand, I helped her off the sofa, watching her as she walked in front of me. Her limp was still there, but it seemed manageable. Still, it was probably a good idea to walk in front of her down the steps. They seemed to be her weakness.

Despite the sun, it was still cold outside. Megan grimaced as she observed my usual habit of walking barefoot on the sand. "Do your feet not get cold?"

"Not anymore. I've been walking this beach for so long it feels strange to have shoes on. I do when it snows, but even then, not all the time. I like the cold."

She shivered, and I chuckled at her dramatics. I wrapped my arm around her waist, drawing her close as we walked the hard sand. She fit so well under my arm; her head tucked against my shoulder as we strolled. I kept back from the water, knowing she had no desire to feel its icy fingers wrapping around her ankles, soaking into her skin.

"Have you lived here long?"

"Almost ten years. I've owned the house longer than that but only used it for vacations before—"

"Before?" she prompted.

"Before I came to live here permanently," I finished. I wasn't ready to tell her my story yet; I hoped she wouldn't push me on it today.

She nodded, bending down to pick up a small piece of driftwood, tossing it for the dogs. We spent the next while smiling and laughing as we threw the stick. They bounded up and down the beach chasing it, bringing it back, wanting it thrown again. It felt very strange to be sharing the beach with her, and to be laughing and almost carefree. Done with throwing the stick, the dogs ran around, chasing each other. Leaning against an outcrop of boulders, I looked down at our clasped hands—my scarred flesh wrapped around her perfect, smooth skin—wondering why she allowed me to touch her with such ease. Glancing up, I met her gaze, finding only warmth looking at me. She smiled, understanding in her expression. "Your scars don't bother me, Zachary."

"They should," I answered tersely, feeling the same anxious undercurrent I had whenever anyone brought up my scars or got too close.

"Why?" she asked, her brow furrowed. "Because someone told you they should?"

"Because they're hideous."

She shook her head as she planted herself in front of me. "They're marks. They tell me you survived something terrible. They don't define you."

"They're a pretty good fucking indicator," I sneered. "You don't know me, Megan. Stop trying to romanticize me in your head. I'm not some sort of hero."

She didn't respond to my anger. It didn't have the usual effect of pushing someone away. Instead, she inched closer. Her voice was gentle when she spoke, its soothing cadence comforting to my jumbled nerves. "We all have scars. The only difference is some of them are easier to see. Yours are visible and appear painful, I know. They hurt you physically and emotionally. They hurt me to look at because I know they cause you pain, but they don't make you less in my eyes." She drew in a deep breath as she lifted her hand to my face, cupping my scarred cheek, ignoring my stiffening posture. "I don't see you as a hero, Zachary. I see you as a human being. A man in pain and alone." She stepped closer, her chest leaning into mine. "I don't want you to be alone. Let me in." A soft, shuddering sigh escaped her lips. "Please."

Once again, I was lost to her.

To her deep, caring eyes.

Her sweet words.

The soothing balm her touch provided to my ravaged skin.

Her.

Megan.

Cupping her face, I covered her mouth with mine. When her warm breath met my cold skin, I groaned, surrendering to everything that was her.

I kissed her deeply; our lips moving and shaping, our tongues touching in slow, sensual passes. I moaned at her taste, wanting, needing more. Burying my fingers into her thick hair, I held her face close to mine as our passion began to build. The sounds of the pounding waves and wind ceased. The only thing I could hear or feel was the escalating rhythmic beat of my heart, the roar of my blood as it pulsed through my veins; want, desire for this woman overriding all else. I took everything she offered me: her warm mouth, tight embrace, and the erotic sounds she was making. My hands drifted down her back, cupping her rounded ass, and pulling her up tight to me, letting her feel my desire. Her head fell back with a small gasp, my lips finding purchase on the damp, cool skin of her neck and cheeks, the saltiness of the ocean spray pungent on my tongue as it swirled and laved on the exposed flesh. Lifting her slight body and spinning, I pressed her against the rocks, not wanting any space between us as my mouth sought hers again, desperate for her taste. Megan wrapped her legs around me like a vice, squeezing as my hips thrust forward, both of us moaning at the contact. We were quickly spinning out of control and I pulled back, panting, trying to clear my head. Megan's eyes opened: dark, hooded, wanting. "Zachary, please," she murmured, her hands trying to tug me back to her.

"I don't have..." I paused, panting, knowing we needed to have this conversation. "I don't have what you need to feel safe. I wasn't planning—"

"I'm covered," she interrupted me.

"You trust me?"

"I trust you. Can you trust me?"

Her gaze was fathomless. She was asking that on so many levels, but there was only one answer possible for now. Leaning close, I trailed my tongue softly along her bottom lip. "I want you, Megan. But not here—not a fast fuck against some cold rocks." I ghosted my lips over her skin, grazing her ear. "In my house. In my bed. Let me take you there."

"Yes," she whimpered.

"Hold tight." My body hummed in anticipation as I wrapped my arms around her, lifting her away from the cold stone. Calling the dogs, I strode across the hard-packed sand with purpose, knowing nothing would ever be the same again once we were together. Once I made her mine.

I wasn't sure I wanted it to be, anyway.

She was so right in my bed. Perfect in my arms. The rapidly fading light hid the horrible imperfections of my skin, but her lips found every one. Her tender touch smoothed the rigid, twisted flesh, leaving behind deep, unfamiliar warmth. I watched in wonder as her sweet mouth swept over my chest, her fingertips touching me with the lightest of caresses, healing and soothing. Her bottomless, tender gaze filled me with emotion, seeping through my body, sinking into my soul and making me feel whole. I clutched at her thick hair, hissing at the erotic sensation of soft curls trailing along my flesh as her mouth moved, caressing and teasing me. Her floral scent clung to my skin as she branded me with her essence.

Hovering over her, I halted my movements. "It's been so long, Megan. I've been alone...for so long," I rasped, unsure what I was even trying express.

"I'm here," she insisted. "Right here with you. Be with me." Her teeth tugged on my earlobe, her voice a gentle hum. "Lose yourself with me, Zachary."

With a deep groan, I gave in, letting my body give her what we both wanted.

We were wrapped around each other, skin to skin. Her warmth surrounded me; I couldn't taste or caress enough of her skin to be satisfied. Slipping inside her heat, I stilled, our eyes locking. The intense emotion in her eyes was shocking and unfamiliar. My heart thundered, its rapid pulse matching her pounding rhythm as our chests melded together. "Megan," I whispered as I began moving, the tempo increasing as my need grew. "Sweetheart," I moaned. The sounds she made as I slammed into her over and again, pinning her down on the mattress with my body, drove me crazy. Small gasps escaped Megan's lips, keening whimpers answering my own hungry groans. Her hands clutched at my shoulders, ran down my back, grasping my hips as her legs locked around my ass, holding me close as she met me thrust for thrust. We were wild in our passion, the pillows shifting, knocking the lamp on the bedside table, the bulb shattering as it hit the floor. The sheet twisted under my fingers, tearing sharply as my orgasm tore through me like a live current. I roared her name, pushing into her as deep as I could get, begging her to come with me as I came hard, needing to feel her clutch and pull me in with her.

After the rush of heat and the deep orgasmic release, came the quiet, mindless bliss of resting in her arms, my head buried in her fragrant hair. Our bodies were still intertwined, joined together in the most intimate way, as we slowly recovered.

I breathed in her scent, the soft floral aroma filling my head. For the first time in so long, my body relaxed, my mind calm and at peace because of the woman I was holding. The light outside had faded, the room now dark as she curled into me, her head tucked under my chin, her fingers tracing lazy circles on my chest. There was no need to talk or move. I only wanted to stay right beside her, sharing this warmth. It felt more intimate in many ways than the act itself. I could feel her smooth cheek touching my damaged skin, her gentle fingertips tracing small pitted marks. Surprised at the lack of panic I felt, I let her touch me without restriction.

Her quiet voice broke the stillness. "Will you tell me?"

A heavy breath left my lungs. "Yes."

"But not now?"

"No, not now. I need to think things through. This"—I squeezed her into my side— "is very new to me. I haven't ever had a woman in this house," I confessed. "It's been a very long time since I was with anyone." I didn't tell her that in the past, it was unusual for me to stay with someone after sex. Except what we'd done didn't feel like sex. It felt like something deeper, something more.

"How long?"

"Since the accident. I'm used to being alone."

"Do you want me to leave?"

My arms tensed. "No. Stay with me."

The room was pitch-black when I awoke. My arms were empty, and the other side of the bed felt cold. I sat up, alert and anxious. She'd said she would stay. I wanted her with me when I woke up.

Where had she gone?

I grabbed my pants, ignoring the fact they were still damp from the ocean spray, and raced down the stairs and across the hall, stopping when I saw Megan sitting at the table, idly flipping the pages of a magazine. She looked up at my sudden entrance, confusion written on her expression.

Relief flooded my body, finding her still in my home. The panic that gripped my heart, eased as she grinned. I returned her smile, even as I wondered where all these unknown feelings were coming from or how the sight of her sweet smile could erase my distress.

Crossing the room, I dragged her up into my arms, kissing her fiercely. "You were gone."

"It was late, and your stomach was grumbling in your sleep," she chuckled. "I got up to make us something to eat."

"Oh."

She poked me in the chest. "You need to go grocery shopping, mister. I scraped together what I could for omelets. I was waiting for the toast to be ready, then I was going to come get you."

I noticed then the table was set and the aroma of food in the air. "Okay. I'll go put on a shirt."

"You don't have to; I don't mind."

I hesitated. "I'd be more comfortable with one," I admitted. The kitchen was well lit, and I knew she would see my scars without the softening effects of shadows. I didn't like to look at them and I wasn't sure she really wanted to while we were eating either.

"All right," she agreed easily. "Whatever makes you happy. It'll be ready when you get back."

I walked down the hall, her words echoing in my head. *Whatever makes you happy.*

I wasn't sure there had ever been a time in my life I was happy.

I honestly didn't know if I knew how to feel that way.

Until she entered my life.

"This is good," I complimented Megan. "Especially considering how limited my supplies are at present."

"Do you want to go into town tomorrow and get some things?"

I swallowed the mouthful of omelet as I nodded. "I'll call Mrs. Cooper and arrange what I need. I have to get some things at the gallery."

"Why do you have to call ahead?"

My hand tightened on my fork. "Not everyone is as accepting or polite about how I look as you are, Megan. It's pretty quiet this time of year, but I always call ahead and tell her what I need. She has it all ready and I pick it up from the back. I also use the rear entrance of the gallery."

"You seem comfortable with her and Jonathon. He mentioned you're a friend of his wife," she stated gently. "Ashley, I think he said her name was?"

"I knew the Coopers...before." I cleared my throat and shifted in my chair, already feeling uncomfortable. "Ashley and Jonathon have always been kind." My eyes met hers directly. "Others have not."

"I'm sorry to hear that."

"Don't feel sorry for me," I snapped. I hated pity.

"I'm not feeling sorry for you. I said I was sorry people chose to be unkind because of your scars. There's a difference," she snapped right back. A dull flush tinged her cheeks, her eyes glinting and fiery with annoyance as she frowned at me. Despite her anger, I found her incredibly attractive and my lips quirked.

"What?" she spat at me.

I shook my head as I chuckled and grabbed the bottle of wine to top up our glasses. I might be low on food, but I never ran out of wine. "I was thinking how I wanted to capture you on film again, looking exactly like that."

"Like what?"

"Like a kitten trying to act like a tiger. All growls and swipes of your little paws as you hiss at me, putting me in my place." I reclined back, taking a deep swallow of my wine as I gazed at her over the rim of the glass. "You're very sexy when you're angry. Did you know that?"

"Stop it."

"It's true. Your eyes flash, and the color on your cheeks is sublime. Your glare, which I'm certain you mean to be angry, is more of a turn on than anything."

"I am angry at you. You twist everything I say."

I tilted my head in acknowledgment. "I know. It's a bad habit I picked up after years of being lied to." Lifting her hand, I kissed the knuckles. "I apologize. I'll try harder." I placed another kiss on her skin. "But I still want to capture you when you're angry."

Rolling her eyes, she stood up, taking our empty plates. "Somehow, Zachary, I have a feeling you'll get what you wish for without much effort." She sighed as she walked to the sink. "You seem to be able to make me angry faster than anyone I've ever met."

I closed the distance between us in two large steps. Cupping the back of her neck, I brought her mouth to mine. "Anger is simply another form of passion," I murmured against her lips.

"A tiring one," she returned in a whisper. "And I won't ever lie to you."

"Everyone lies."

"No, they don't. Whatever world you were in where they did, I'm glad you're out of it." She paused, frowning. "I'm glad you're here —with me."

I didn't want to talk anymore. I didn't want to think about the past, or groceries, or even what was going to happen tomorrow. All I wanted was to lose myself with her again. To block out everything else.

I picked her up, striding down the hall with her cradled in my arms, my mouth covering hers.

She wanted me to be happy. Having her wrapped around me, buried inside her, made me happy.

For however long I had her, that was what I wanted.

10

MEGAN

The sun slowly rose, the soft light filling the room as I lay in silence, staring at Zachary. Sound asleep, his face was peaceful, the stress lines, which seemed etched in his skin while awake, now relaxed and smooth on his forehead. Lying on his side, his scars hidden from view, he was, indeed, a handsome man. Long lashes, a woman would envy, rested on his upper cheek, dark and thick like fringes on a cushion. His nose was slightly fuller than conventional, and his face long, with prominent, strong cheekbones. Unshaven, his chin was thick with coarse hair, at least on one half of his face. His hair was so dark you expected his eyes to match, so when you were met with hazel-colored irises, it was unusual.

I wondered if he knew how his eyes changed color to match his mood or how mesmerizing it was when it happened. I'd seen them a bright blue, a reflective shade of green, and when angry, an icy gray. They reminded me of the ocean waves he liked to paint—never ending with the varying shades of color, rich and vibrant with life. They darkened when he was passionate—either with desire or anger. I was already familiar with those emotions. One look from Zachary could cause my heart to flutter in my chest. Never had I felt myself so attuned to another person's emotions; it was as if my soul felt the shift of his mood and transformed itself to match. He could make me feel lust, anger, or happiness so fast; I barely knew it was happening.

I also wondered if anyone ever looked close enough to notice when he seemed angry or dismissive, the expression in his eyes actually belied his actions. They spoke of hurt and pain, of pushing you away before you could push him away. Somehow, I doubted it, since as soon as he began pushing, they began walking. That was exactly what he banked on. *He* chose when you left, not the other way around.

I sighed as he slept on. His heavy arm draped over my waist, where it had been most of the night, not allowing me to move very much. I hadn't been sure if he'd want me to stay or not after we'd eaten, but when he stood up, lifting and carrying me back to his room, my uncertainty vanished. I wanted to stay here with him. I couldn't understand the draw I had or why it was so important for me to be with him, but it was. Never before had I acted like this with another man—or even another person. It was as though I couldn't stay away from him. From the moment I saw his painting: *Tempest*—the angry swirls of paint spoke to me. When I met the irate, scarred man behind the brush, I was drawn to him, as well.

His scars didn't bother me the way he felt they should. They bothered me because of the obvious pain—both physical and mental —they caused him. My heart ached when I saw a grimace of pain pass over his face at times. I wanted nothing more than to ease it in some way. There were so many questions I wanted to ask him, but I was also smart enough to know he wasn't ready to tell me yet. I had to be patient and let him tell me when he was ready. The way he acted, I knew he was as confused by his feelings as I was about mine.

He groaned and rolled on his back, his arm lazily lowering over his face, never waking up. Slowly, so I didn't disturb him, I leaned up on my elbow to study him. I had seen some of his scars, felt them, even kissed them, but this was the first time I was able to really look at them. All on the right side of his body, they varied in degree. His arm and face were the most deeply scarred—the skin marred and puckered in angry looking ridges. His chest had some scars, as well as some pitting scattered on the left side. More ravaged skin ran up his neck and the side of his face, the worst scar reaching to his mouth, twisting the skin up tight. Remembering his words, and the way he made sure to hide that side of his face away, I knew he must have experienced many painful reactions to his appearance. People could often be cruel in their prejudices and the words they used to express them. I had the feeling Zachary had been at the receiving end of many unwelcome stares and words, which explained his regimented way of dealing with the world around him. I understood only being able to handle so many painful words or so much unwanted attention. He acted the way he did to keep people away, to keep hurt away.

I didn't want him to keep me away, though.

He woke slowly, blinking in the morning light. For a moment he was motionless, then turned his head toward me. "Hi," I whispered, unsure of his reaction.

His voice was scratchy and thick with sleep. "What time is it?"

I glanced at the clock. "A little after eight."

"Did I disturb you last night?"

"Um, no...well, other than when you woke me up to, ah—" My voice trailed off, shyness overtaking me. What should I call it? Sex? Making love? I had no idea how he saw what was happening between us. I didn't even understand it.

A small grin lit his face, and I found myself trapped under a warm, heavy chest, pressed into the mattress. Zachary's face was close to mine, his breath drifting over my skin like a summer breeze, hot and damp. "I slept so well," he murmured.

I ran my fingers through his dark hair, the strands feeling like silk. "Is that a rare occurrence?"

His face became serious; his voice so quiet I had to strain to hear it. "I haven't slept that well in years."

"Nightmares?" I whispered, worried if I spoke too loud or too fast, he would pull away.

Lost in whatever memories he had trapped in his head, he nodded.

"That's good then."

Blinking, he looked at me, as if seeing me for the first time today. "It was you."

"Me?"

"You were next to me all night. You let me hold you."

I kissed the messiness of his thick scruff. "I liked you holding me."

"I didn't think there was anyone as sweet as you left in this world."

"You weren't looking in the right places."

"I wasn't looking at all," he replied. "Yet, somehow you found me."

I smiled up at him, loving his gentler, quiet side.

"All night," he repeated in wonder, his grin becoming wider. "Well, other than the 'waking up' as you call it."

I felt my face flood with color. "I, ah, liked that, too."

He pushed closer, lifting my arms over my head and smoothing his hands over the skin. "You approved of the sleep interruptions, did you?"

"Um, yes."

Brushing his mouth over mine, he chuckled—a dark, low sound. "I like it when you're flustered."

"Stop it."

His hands tightened on my arms, his eyes darkening. "What are you going to do about it?"

"Zachary." His name sounded more like a plea than a reprimand.

"Megan," he whispered huskily, his lips tracing over my collarbones.

God, how was it possible I wanted this man again?

"Please."

His mouth covered mine, and once more, I was lost.

"Are you sure you want to go into town with me?" Looking up from my purse, I frowned at his tense expression. "Would you rather I went in by myself, Zachary?"

"I didn't say that."

Trying not to feel hurt over his apparent aversion to my company in public, I strove to keep my voice neutral. "You didn't have to. Obviously, the idea of me coming with you is bothering you, since it's the third time you've asked me. I'll go later and take my own car." Grabbing my purse, I called for Dixie. "We'll see you later"—I paused— "if that's what you want."

His arm shot out, stopping me from walking past him. "Stop it," he growled.

"I'm not doing anything. Dixie and I are going home so you can go and take care of your errands. Alone."

"I don't want to go alone."

My eyes found his, searching for answers. "Then why?"

"It's Friday," he said quietly, as if that would explain everything.

"And?"

"It will be busier in town, even in the off-season." He hesitated. "I don't usually go in this close to the weekend. I, ah, don't like crowds."

My disappointment vanished when I realized what he was saying; I shook my head at my own blindness. It wasn't me going in with him. It was him going into town at all. More people meant more eyes from which he had to hide, and as I was thinking earlier, that made him nervous. I stifled a sigh, tugging on my ear, wishing I could understand his fear. He clearly thought himself hideous, which wasn't true whatsoever, but I had no idea how to make him see that fact. Something, *someone*, from his past had that thought so firmly ingrained in his head it was like cement. I covered his hand that was gripping my arm, with my own in quiet support.

"I could help you, Zachary. Pick up your groceries while I get mine and you can go to the gallery. If we work together, we can be done and home in no time."

His shoulders lost some of their tension as he thought about it. "You could drop me at the gallery, I suppose."

I nodded. "I'll get your order and pick up what I need and meet you back at gallery. You said you had to speak to Jonathon when you dropped off your canvases. That will give you the time you need, right?"

He hesitated, then a small smile played on his lips, a mischievous expression lighting up his face. It happened so quickly I blinked at him, returning his smile. "What?"

"That means you'll have to drive my SUV, Megan. Are you even tall enough to see over the dashboard?"

I huffed at him. "I've driven large vehicles before. I think you can trust me with your truck."

"SUV."

"Whatever. It's a truck to me."

"An SUV means it's fully enclosed," he explained, his voice patient as he educated me in the correct vehicle lingo.

I rolled my eyes. "Truck, SUV...I can drive it."

He chuckled. "Maybe before I agree to this, we need to make sure I can move the seat up that far. You have short legs—shorter than a normal person, I believe."

Then he winked at me, all saucy and teasing. I had to laugh with him, relieved he was feeling less stressed.

He drew in a deep breath. "Please come with me."

Keeping my eyes locked with his so he knew what I was about to do, I stood up on my tiptoes, thrilled when he ducked his head down to meet me, and I ghosted my lips lightly to his rough cheek. "Thank you for asking."

His mouth touched a warm kiss to my cheek. His quiet sigh said all he couldn't with words.

M rs. Cooper regarded me with a confused look on her face. "Sorry dear, I thought you said you were picking up Zachary's order for him."

"I am," I assured her with a smile. "He's at the gallery meeting with Jonathon, so I'm getting it for him. Could Mr. Cooper put it in his truck...I mean, SUV? I have it parked out back by the door."

"You're driving his truck?"

I wanted to laugh at the incredulous expression on her face and evident in her voice. Instead, I chuckled and nodded. "It wasn't without reservations, I assure you. I think he almost had a heart attack a couple times on the way into town. He thinks it's too big for me to handle. And, apparently, I drive too fast."

She stared at me in silence for a moment. "I would have thought he'd be too big for you to handle—too big for anyone to handle." Then she smiled—a warm, open grin. "The fact I'm wrong pleases me a great deal. I'll have his order put in the back while you finish your shopping."

"Thanks."

I walked up and down the aisles, picking up the few things I needed. It wasn't much—some fruit, cream for my coffee, and some snacks. I still had food left, since I hadn't been eating much. Part of me was hoping I wouldn't be eating alone for the next few days either. Zachary's list had been long and detailed, so I knew his house would be well stocked. After I paid for my groceries, and Mrs. Cooper said she would add them to the boxes on the back seat of Zachary's SUV, I went to the café to order some of their soup. It had been delicious when I had it the other day, and I thought maybe Zachary would enjoy some for lunch later. I also planned on running into the bakery for some fresh bread and cookies. Aside from banana bread, I wasn't much of a baker, but I did have a sweet tooth I liked to indulge. The cookies and pie I had left for Zachary had been eaten, so I assumed he would indulge with me. I also picked up another bag of peppermints he seemed to constantly consume. He had a bowl of them in almost every room, it seemed, a few in his pockets, and even in his SUV.

Zachary had been right. The streets and shops were far busier than when I'd been to town last time. The café was full and sidewalks more crowded, bustling with people talking and laughing. I felt a small uneasy feeling stirring as I wondered if the gallery was this busy and if Zachary was all right. I finished my purchases as fast as I could and hurried back to the truck, glad to see all the groceries in the back.

I drove to the rear of the gallery and waited for a minute. When Zachary didn't appear in the doorway right away, I shut off the engine and went in to find him. Several people were milling inside, but I didn't see Zachary anywhere. The door to Jonathon's office was shut, so I assumed Zachary was still inside talking to him.

A pretty color caught my eye, and I went over to a display of beautiful silk scarves. I picked up a brilliant red one, the design shot with gold and orange, thinking how much Karen would like it when a gentle voice spoke up. "Ah, one of my favorites. I only brought it in today."

I met the eyes of a lovely woman, who came up beside me in a wheelchair. Her soft brown hair was a mass of curls, tied back with a scarf and hanging down her back. Dressed in a long flowing outfit, she reminded me of a bygone era with her bohemian look. Kind, smiling, blue eyes met mine as her hand smoothed over the silk of the scarf. "It reminds me of the exquisite sunsets we have here."

"It's beautiful. I was thinking how nice it would look on my friend. She would love it."

"Karen?"

"Yes," I answered, surprised. "How did you know?"

She extended her hand. "I'm Ashley. Jonathon's wife and co-owner of this gallery." I shook her hand as she continued. "You must be Megan."

"I met your husband the other day."

She laughed, a light trilling sound in the air. "It wasn't my husband's portrayal that made me recognize you." She winked at me. "Zachary was far more...descriptive."

I felt the blush creeping over my face. "Oh."

"The artist in him, you know. Somehow the words, 'the beauty with the melting copper-colored hair' would never cross Jonathon's lips. He is far too pragmatic. Zachary mentioned you would be here shortly."

The room got a little warmer. That was how Zachary described me? Beautiful?

Unable to resist the chance, I edged a little closer. She seemed so familiar with him, at ease with mentioning his name. "You know him well—Zachary, I mean?"

She regarded me, a shrewd gleam in her eyes. "As well as he allows anyone to know him."

"He speaks highly of you. He told me you were the reason he allows his paintings to sell here."

A look of sadness crossed her face. "I understand Zachary." Her hand reached up to brush a wayward curl away from her face, the loose sleeve of her dress falling away from her arm. My eyes widened as I took in the puckered, scarred flesh on her skin. She met my eyes calmly, nodding. "I *know* his pain." Her arm lowered and she moved her wheelchair closer to the counter, untying the scarf I was looking at moments prior. "Those of us, who have known physical pain, tend to band together, so to speak. Besides"—she shrugged— "he's too talented not to show his work. It took me a while to convince him to allow us to display it, but I refused to take no for an answer."

My eyes drifted to the back where I could see *Tempest* hanging. "He's amazing," I murmured.

She gazed over at the painting. "I remember the day I met him. He was sitting on a bench in the park, the entire place deserted. It was overcast and gray, far too miserable for anyone to be out, yet there we were, him sketching and me out driving myself around in my electric wheelchair, like I do when I'm restless." She smiled up at me. "As you can imagine, he wasn't very happy to see me, nor was he very friendly."

I nodded, not speaking. I didn't want to interrupt her and have her stop talking. I wanted to know as much about Zachary as I could.

"At first, aside from an abrupt hello, he refused to talk to me, or even let me see what he was doing." She laughed softly as she shared her memory. "But then I leaned over and grabbed his sketchbook out of his hand." Her voice became quiet. "He saw my scars...and for the first time, met my eyes."

"And?" I breathed.

"What do you see when you look in his eyes?"

"Pain, anger," I whispered. "Fear."

"That is what I saw as well, but I didn't give up. I kept talking to him until he started talking back." She smiled as she recalled pushing him. "I think he was torn. He was so used to being angry and alone—"

"But so lonely," I added. I felt his loneliness. I felt the fear he hid beneath his anger.

"Yes. Our, ah, scars were something we had in common. He felt safe with me, knowing I wasn't judging him and was able to open up a little. We became friends, or at least what I would call friends—I'm not sure Zachary thinks himself worthy of being called a friend to anyone. Eventually he showed me his paintings and I convinced him to let us sell them."

"Keeping his identity private."

"Always." Her eyes narrowed; her voice firm. "He surprised me today when he told me you were with him."

"I'm still rather surprised, too. We didn't exactly start off on the best foot."

Her laughter rang out again. "One seldom does with Zachary." She paused, a knowing look on her face. "Today there was something different when he mentioned your name, though, something new in his eyes, something besides pain. His smile actually reached his eyes."

I beamed at her words. I wanted to replace some of his pain. I wanted to be the reason he smiled. Somehow, he also helped to ease mine.

The door opened and Jonathon walked out, Zachary following him. He glanced around, swallowing hard as he lifted up the collar of his coat in an unconscious effort of hiding himself. His eyes found mine and he frowned a little, seeing Ashley and I together. I smiled reassuringly at him, and he seemed to relax. He shook Jonathon's hand and came over to where I was standing. "Scaring her away?" he murmured to Ashley, being sure to keep his back to the few people still milling around the gallery.

She laughed up at him. "If you haven't done that by now, I doubt anything I say can, my dear."

Our eyes met, his filled with trepidation. Without thinking, I reached for his hand. His grip was tight as he clasped mine. I shook my head a little at his words. "No," I offered quietly. "Not happening."

He squeezed my hand, his expression now one of warmth.

"*Tempest* is leaving us, Zachary?" Ashley asked with a frown.

Surprised, I watched Jonathon removing my beloved painting from the wall. I glanced at Zachary, but he only shrugged and nodded.

"Yes. I want it at home now. I left some new ones to sell and another display one for you."

"Have I seen it?"

"No."

"Is it good?"

He snickered dryly. "I'll let you decide that, Ashley."

I smiled, watching him interact with her. She didn't try to be anything but herself with him, and that was exactly what he needed. He glanced at me, lifting my hand and kissing it. "Ready to go?"

Ashley smirked at his gesture and wheeled away, chuckling.

I nodded, wondering how he would feel if I told him I was ready to go anywhere with him.

All he had to do was ask.

11

MEGAN

Zachary surprised me with his humor as he readjusted the driver's seat and mirrors, muttering about short legs and midgets driving his "SUV." His sidelong glance and ill-suppressed smile made me giggle at his unexpected actions. When he voluntarily covered my hand with his, on the drive back, my heart fluttered in my chest and I resisted the urge to cover his scarred flesh with my other hand. The unconscious gesture on his part meant too much for me to push things.

We were quiet on the drive, the silence not uncomfortable, as I watched the scenery speed by the window. The flashes of ocean and open spaces were mesmerizing, and I lost myself to the images. As we approached the long private road that led to the houses, though, Zachary lifted his hand, wrapping it around the steering wheel. Tension emitted from his body, and a quick glance showed me the frown that was now marring his face. Unsure why he seemed upset, I remained silent.

I became even more confused when he pulled up behind my car and cut the engine, his posture stiff.

What now? Was he dropping me off and leaving? Should I ask him?

I swallowed, my throat feeling tight. I didn't understand this need to stay with him, but I knew I didn't want to walk away from him. The idea alone was painful.

Zachary cleared his throat, his voice low. "I can wait," he mumbled.

"What?"

"While you get some things... If you want to come back with me," he stated gruffly. "Or I'll bring Dixie back to you later when I take Elliott for his walk." He paused, his hands twisting and gripping the steering wheel. "Whatever you are, um, comfortable with. Whatever you want." His eyes remained locked straight ahead, and I realized he was waiting for me to make the decision.

He thought I would walk away.

I unclipped the seat belt and edged closer to him, slowly settling my hand over top of his on the steering wheel, making sure my touch was gentle. "I want to stay with you," I whispered.

Some of the tension left his shoulders as he glanced at me, relief and surprise in his eyes. I smiled at him, wishing I could make him understand how much I wanted to be with him. "I want to come back to your home with you."

"Okay then." He nodded, a deep breath leaving his chest. "I'll wait here."

"I can get a few things and walk over."

"With your track record of the stairs leading up to my house, I think I'll wait," he deadpanned, then turned his head and winked at me.

Winked.

Zachary winked at me again, while teasing me. That was twice today.

I liked that side of Zachary—very much.

Pushing up on the console separating us, I grazed my lips across his cheek. I was thrilled when he didn't pull away or tense up but, instead, leaned into my caress.

"Thank you," I breathed into his skin.

He turned his head, slipping his hand around the nape of my neck, holding me close as he kissed me. His lips were gentle and warm on mine, and he tasted of the peppermints he loved. He slowly deepened the kiss, cradling my head, his fingers caressing my skin as he held me close. I felt his smile against my mouth as I shivered from his warm touch. His eyes were dark when he pulled back, breathing heavy.

I liked this side of Zachary, too.

"Thank *you*." He smirked, tapping the end of my nose. "Now go get your stuff."

We were greeted with great enthusiasm when we returned, happy barks and excited chuffs coming from both pets. I picked up Dixie, nuzzling her little head as I stroked Elliott's much larger one. Zachary carried in some bags, and once I put Dixie down, I helped him unload the groceries including what I bought. Zachary's good mood seemed to have returned. He teased me about the cream for my coffee; said I was spoiling the flavor by adding anything to the brew that he drank black. He grimaced in mock disgust when I confessed to also adding sugar. He joked about the food I had purchased, since most of it consisted of snacks like popcorn and ice cream. He shook his head at the large bottle of corn syrup but didn't ask as he shoved it into the cupboard. When he went out to get the supplies he picked up at the gallery and bring in the painting, I heated up some soup and then we ate in relative silence, both dogs watching our every move.

"I'll take them for a walk," I offered. "I'm sure you have things you need to do."

"Yeah, I do. I want to set up some canvases and shift a few things around up there. Let them run on the beach. I'll join you soon."

"All right."

He disappeared upstairs, as I grabbed my jacket off the sofa, pausing when my eyes landed on the *Tempest* painting he'd brought home with us. Even leaning on the wall, it was powerful—the imagery, once again, capturing my attention. I traced the initials in the corner—the **Z D A** so strongly etched into the canvas. Adams, he had told me when I asked. Zachary Dennis Adams. I thought the strong name suited him, and he had grinned shyly when I told him so. Smiling, I shrugged on my coat. There were so many sides of Zachary I hadn't seen yet, but I found the more I discovered, the more I liked him.

It was bright out on the sand as I strolled along, the dogs running and chasing each other around. My ankle felt much better today, thanks to Zachary's ministrations. The sound of waves crashing on the rocks was peaceful; the sky was clear above me, the scent of ocean rich and pungent in my nose. With a grin, I toed off my sneakers, yanked off my socks, and rolled up my pant legs. Hesitantly, I walked into the surf, allowing only the smallest ripples of water to cover my feet, gasping at the icy cold. How on earth Zachary strode through the water daily without it affecting him, I had no idea. I backed up away from the surf and kept walking, trying to get used to the temperature of the icy sand. My blue-painted toenails looked pretty beside the wet granules though; they matched the ocean. I breathed in deep, feeling relaxed and content. I didn't know what was happening later today, or tomorrow even, in regard to Zachary, but at the moment, I was happy, and I was strangely okay with that.

All my life I had done what I *should* do, what I was expected to do—always what was right. I went to school, got a job, paid my bills, acted like a responsible adult. My writing was always a dream and I never let it interfere with what I was *supposed* to do. I put everything else first, and what did it get me? No job, no book, just a lot of grief. I trusted someone I thought cared about me and he let me down, hurting me on every imaginable level.

Zachary was a complete anomaly for me. I felt more for him in the short time I'd known him than I ever felt for another man. He was standoffish and cruel when he chose to be, then at other times, his vulnerability showed through. I knew how much of an act he put forth to cover up his own pain and push people away. He was lost and alone. Maybe that was partially what drew us to each other.

Something had seriously hurt him in the past, and he'd stopped living. I wasn't sure I had ever truly started to live. We made quite the pair.

Arms wrapping around my waist startled me from my thoughts. A teasing voice was close to my ear. "Testing the water, are we sweetheart?"

My heart jumped at his endearment and the gentle way it was uttered.

"It's too cold."

He chuckled, the sound low and deep. "Must be—your toes have turned blue!" Zachary teased as he spun me around, lifting higher, walking toward the water. "You only have to get used to it," he promised, wading deeper—the water rising up to his calves, my toes curling in protest as the frigid water grazed them.

Squealing, I pulled my legs up, wrapping them around his thighs in protest. "No!" I giggled.

His arms tightened around me, chest heaving as he laughed. "Careful," he warned, his lips next to my ear. "Squirm too much...and I might drop you." He snickered, loosening his hold a little; laughing even harder as I gasped, laughing with him, clinging tight. I lifted my legs higher, using his hips as an anchor and holding myself as close to his body as I could. "Don't!" I pleaded.

His embrace became a vice. His voice became gruffer and deeper as his lips brushed down my throat. "You want me to keep you out of the water?"

"Yes," I panted into his neck.

"You trust me? You think I'll keep you safe?"

I tilted my head back, meeting his eyes, which were now filled with passion, swirling blue and green amidst the gray. "I know you'll keep me safe," I whispered. "You make me feel safer than I ever have."

With a groan, he covered my mouth in a rough kiss. Zachary's arms crushed me to his chest as he devoured me with his mouth. The passion was all-consuming; the gentleness from earlier gone. He came at me over and again, claiming and possessing me. His large hands became restless and seeking; one slipped under my coat, the cold of it seeping into my skin, while the other wound into my hair, cupping and caressing my head. Time stood still as we kissed, and only the impatient barking from the shore broke us apart.

Zachary looked toward the beach, muttering a mild curse at the interruption. His hand now cradled my head to his chest as he strode out of the water and stood me back on the hard, cold sand. He opened his coat, enveloping me in it; surrounding me in his scent and warmth. "You give me too much credit," he murmured into my ear.

"You don't give yourself enough," I countered, leaning back so I could meet his eyes.

"When you look at me like that, I feel...like I can do anything."

"You can."

"You make me want...things, Megan. Things I'm not sure I can have."

My heartbeat was so loud in my chest, I was sure he had to feel it against his own. "Things like what?"

His gaze flittered around the vastness of the water. "Normal things. I want to take you to dinner, or maybe out to a movie. Go for a walk and not worry someone will start pointing or make some remark." He exhaled a long rush of air. "I want to be able to let you touch me without worrying about the fact I want to pull away and hide."

"Do you get tired of hiding, Zachary?"

"Yes."

The pain evident in that one word made my eyes sting, and I had to blink and clear my throat before I could speak again.

"We could try," I encouraged him. "Work on it together. One step at a time."

"Why, Megan? Why are you bothering? Why are you so sure I'm worth all this effort?"

Staring into his confused, pain-filled eyes I didn't know how to answer him. How could I explain this pull I felt toward him? That I had felt it so strong the very moment he passed behind me in the gallery. This need I had to be with him was undeniable and frightening in its intensity. The feeling I was the one to help him heal from his past was firm and unyielding. The *want* to be part of his future was overwhelming.

"Because you are."

His finger trailed down my cheek. "You amaze me."

I cupped his unscarred cheek, loving how he accepted my touch. I brought up my other hand and placed it on his rough, thickened skin, giving him the chance to tell me no. His eyes shut, a long gust of air escaping his lungs, and he relaxed into me. Keeping my touch light, I stroked his face, tracing over the scars and healthy skin at the same time, the contrasts between them so vast. They were much like his personality: the rough, angry side plainly visible to people; the softer side very few ever would experience. Both were a part of him— both equally beautiful and ugly.

His eyes fluttered open, the confusion and pain replaced by something else—something quieter and gentle. His arms tightened around me as he smiled. A genuine smile that made my chest ache with its beauty. His voice was rough when he spoke.

"I want to take you home now. I need to be with you." He placed a long, warm kiss to my mouth. "Can I Megan? Will you let me have you, right now?"

"Yes," I breathed. "Please."

He swept me into his arms, calling for the dogs and striding toward the house. He didn't look back to see if they were following. He knew they would.

We would all follow him if he asked.

My head rested on his chest, listening to his strong heartbeat as he carried me to where he wanted to take me.

Sadly, I wondered if we would ever get to the point where he *would* ask.

12

MEGAN

Laughing, I covered my face and turned away from Zachary. "Stop it!"

His answering chuckle warmed my heart. "No, the light is perfect. Look at me, Megan. I just want a couple more pictures."

Pivoting on the sand, I glared at him. "You've taken about a thousand of them. How many more could you possibly need?"

The constant click of the shutter made me roll my eyes and huff in exasperation. Zachary's grin told me he wouldn't be stopping soon.

He'd been at it all day. I woke up to him taking my picture. He snapped more while I was sipping my coffee, trying to wake up. While I read a book from his vast collection, the clicking happened. I was sure he'd stop while we were outside with the dogs, but I was wrong. Slamming my hands on my hips, I narrowed my eyes at him. "Enough!"

Four more snaps of the shutter and he lowered the camera. "You looked positively pissed off in the last one, sweetheart. Perfect."

My heart thumped at his use of that endearment. I loved it when he called me sweetheart. I loved it when he said my name. I loved hearing him talk with his soft British lilt. His laugh made my chest expand with happiness knowing I had made him feel that way. A giggle broke through my lips as I realized how much I sounded like a love-struck teenager, and I covered my mouth to stifle the sound.

The shutter snapping again made me glower back at Zachary. He shrugged. "Sorry. You were too adorable right then not to capture it." He stepped closer, letting the camera hang around his neck, as he tugged my hand away from my mouth. He kissed the palm, his mouth gentle on my skin. "Don't cover up your laughter, Megan. It's become one of my favorite sounds."

"Oh?"

His broad hand cupped my cheek. "I love hearing it fill the house. I never realized how empty it was before you were there."

My breath caught in my throat. The past two days we had spent in peaceful seclusion at his house. We'd been together almost every moment, other than his walks with Elliott or when he was hidden behind one of his canvases. I learned Zachary was a quiet man, surrounding himself with music and books when he wasn't painting or playing with Elliott. The two of them would disappear into the woods each day for a couple of hours, emerging cold and windblown, both happy to find refuge by the warm fire. Elliott usually curled up with Dixie close to the fireplace, while a freshly showered Zachary sipped coffee, wearing one of his long-sleeved loose shirts and warm pants, close to me on the sofa. I enjoyed the quiet rhythm of their life, pleased Dixie and I were able to slip into it without disturbing the pattern they had.

The first evening I was there, he showed me his huge selection of movies, telling me to pick one to watch. As I was going through the shelves, I discovered several unopened board games shoved onto the bottom shelf—dust-covered and ignored. When I questioned him, he admitted to having bought them when he first moved here, thinking when people were visiting, if the weather was bad, they'd be a good way to pass the time. "I loved board games as a kid," he told me pensively. My heart ached knowing the reason they were still unopened was there had been no visitors. I lifted both the Monopoly and Scrabble boxes up in my hands. "Your choice."

We spent hours laughing at each other while we played and tracked scores on tiny sheets of paper. He was, as I discovered, very competitive. I enjoyed watching him strategize as he moved his *boot* around the board, or tried to make as many triple-word scores as possible. He beat me in every game other than Scrabble. He chuckled and shrugged, saying it was only fair the writer should win that game. He admitted to also loving chess; occasionally when Chris was at the house, they would play a game or two—but only when Chris came alone. At my quizzical look, he shrugged and admitted he and Karen didn't get on very well. When I expressed my surprise, he also confessed to being rude to her the first day they met, when he ran into her in the forest.

"She surprised me," he explained. "I thought it was Chris. I never expected to see her. She was looking for some leaves or something. I may have startled her with my...brusqueness." He had the grace to look abashed while acknowledging he'd been aloof and stayed in the shadows. "The second time we met wasn't much better," he continued sheepishly. "I think we've avoided each other since. I don't think we'll ever be, ah, friends."

"You don't like surprises."

"Not like that."

"You're deliberately rude at times," I observed, trying to get him to open up.

"I'm aware." His tone told me that was all he had to say on the matter.

"Not everyone will reject you because of your scars, Zachary. Some people look beyond the surface of a person to what's inside."

The disbelieving look and dismissive shrug of his shoulders let me know the subject was closed.

I didn't push.

The way he was looking at me now, though, with a relaxed smile on his face, I hoped one day he would talk more freely and tell me so I wouldn't have to push.

The wind picked up, his dark hair falling over his brow and into his eyes. Impatiently, he pushed his hand through it only to have it immediately fall back down. I laughed at his irritated expression.

"You need a haircut."

"I know. Mr. Olson is still away. It always gets too long this time of year."

"Mr. Olson?"

"He owns the barber shop in town. I, ah, always go to him. He... he knows me."

"I could do it."

"I don't have any scissors that would work for cutting hair."

"Karen does."

"Yeah?"

I nodded. "She owns a salon. She has all the girly stuff here, including scissors." I wiggled my bright toes in my flip flops—no bare feet today. "That's where I got the polish."

"Nice."

"I'll grab a pair and get some more food for Dixie, then I can trim it for you, if you like?"

He hesitated, frowning. Slowly, he lifted his hand to the right side of his head, his fingers trembling as he touched the scars. I stepped closer, wanting to reassure him. "You can show me where not to touch, Zachary. I won't hurt you."

His eyes searched mine, and I waited patiently. His scars were his biggest weakness and I still didn't understand all the minefields that surrounded them. I had to let him lead me.

Finally he nodded. Pulling his hand down, I kissed his knuckles and smiled at him, almost euphoric at his trust.

"I'll go get the scissors. You wash your hair—it's easier to cut when it's wet."

His arms shot out, dragging me to him, his mouth crashing on mine. His kiss was deep and hard.

"I'll be waiting."

I felt the heat of his mouth on mine the entire time I was gone.

Zachary's damp head gleamed in the light. I stood between his legs, hesitating. "Off the top and sides?"

"Mostly the top. I, um, like it longer on the side. You can trim the back a little."

His request made sense, of course, because keeping the sides longer helped to cover the scars.

Taking a deep breath, I picked up the comb. "Does this hurt?" I wondered. "Combing your hair, I mean?"

His eyes were nervous as he looked at me. "It's sensitive in places."

"Show me."

He raised a shaky hand, clasping mine with it, and running my fingers over the uneven patches of skin. "There," he whispered.

Softly, I kissed the marred skin. "Okay," I whispered into his ear. "Hold on to me."

I ran my fingers over his scalp, letting him get used to my touch, ignoring his intake of air. His hands settled on my hips, their grasp tight. Carefully, I combed his hair through and started cutting. For a few minutes the only sound in the room was the snipping of scissors and Zachary's uneven breaths. As I worked away, I hummed, hoping it might soothe him. Gradually, his breathing calmed and he relaxed, his hold on my hips loosening.

"Have you done this before?"

I smirked a little. "Maybe you should have asked that earlier."

"Maybe."

"My friends and I cut each other's hair when we were in college," I chuckled. "It saved money and they never complained." I paused to look and make sure both sides were even. "Of course, they had way more hair than you so let's hope I get it right. Otherwise, you may not need another visit to Mr. Olsen until next year." I winked at him. "Karen cuts mine, and she showed me the basics. I think we'll be okay."

He buried his hand in my hair, tugging on the strands. "You have beautiful hair, Megan. I love how it feels in my hands."

My cheeks warmed at his sweet words.

He tugged again, bringing my face close to his, kissing me warmly. "I like doing that," he murmured, releasing my hair.

"Making me blush?"

"Yes."

"Why?" I asked, continuing to cut away, ignoring the increasing tempo of my heart.

"It's an honest response. It tells me I've either pleased or embarrassed you."

"I also blush when I'm angry," I challenged with a grin. "So how can you tell I'm not just angry all the time?"

"It's different."

I set down the scissors and ran my fingers through his hair. "Different?"

"When you're angry, you get...well, red. Instantly flushed. When you're embarrassed or pleased the color is like a flower on your cheeks...it spreads out—pink and soft."

I stared at him, my insides beginning to quiver, my breathing picking up. "You notice things like that?"

He nodded, tilting his head back. His eyes caught the light, swirls of blue and green staring at me. "You blush when aroused, too, Megan." His hands began sweeping the backs of my legs, sliding higher with every pass, the heat of his fingers burning through the thin material of my yoga pants. "I do?" I sputtered, clinging to his shoulders, feeling the coiled muscles contract.

His voice became low and husky. "Yeah, you do, but it's different. It starts on your chest and blooms up to your face, deepening the more turned on you get." He paused, the tip of his tongue peeking out and teasing his bottom lip. "Sort of like what is happening"—he tugged me closer— "right now."

I gasped as he lifted me into his lap, his mouth covering mine. His kiss was deep and carnal, his desire evident in the way his arousal pressed up against me. "God, I want you," he groaned into my neck. "I want you spread out on my bed all pink and soft for me—everywhere."

Yearning shot through me, hot and bright. I had no idea how he did this to me. One look, one sexy sentence uttered in his low, raspy voice, and I wanted him.

"Your hair," I protested feebly.

"Fuck my hair," he growled, thrusting into me. I moaned at his need, my own desire spiking. He could have anything he wanted.

"No," I shot back at him. "Fuck *me*, Zachary. Now."

He stood up, his arms holding me tight. "With pleasure."

———

Zachary was curled around me, head resting on my chest, fingers caressing my hair, tugging at the mess he'd made with his hands during our frenzied lovemaking. He certainly did love my hair. Once again, the floor was strewn with pillows and sheets, but the remaining lamp had been put in a different place for safety. In a gentle sweep, I slid my fingers over the back of his neck, feeling the slight shiver that went through his body at my touch.

"Zachary?"

"Hmm?"

I paused, trying to keep my voice light and even. "Can I ask you some questions?"

His body tensed, fingers stilling, at my words. He rolled over, an arm covering his eyes. Immediately, I missed his warmth. I moved closer, laying my hand on his chest, over his heart, and the small spattering of scars around it. "Does this hurt?"

"No."

I laid my head down on his chest, not speaking, unsure if he would elaborate.

The room was silent for a moment, save for his fingers drumming a restless beat on my arm. "My skin everywhere on the right side is incredibly sensitive, Megan. Some of the burns were worse than others. In some places, the skin around the scar is more reactive and the scar itself has no feeling in it at all. There're times I'm in pain and when I am, I take pills. I feel temperature changes easily. I wear loose clothing, my showers are barely warm, and I never, ever go outside unless I'm fully covered. I can't stand the feel of the sun. It's like being burned all over again."

"Oh."

His lips brushed my temple; a tender pass of affection. "In answer to your question, none of your touches hurt. You are far too gentle for that." He assured me, his voice quiet. "Your touch actually soothes me."

"But you tense up every time."

He exhaled deeply. "I've been alone a long time. No one has touched me for almost twelve years. In fact, no one has ever touched me the way you do—my entire life. It...takes some getting used to." His arm held me a little closer. "I'm trying, Megan."

My heart ached with his quiet admission.

His whole life?

"I know you're trying." I paused, glancing up at his face. "I don't want to hurt you, Zachary, or do something by accident to cause you pain. That's why I'm asking."

His chest expanded as he drew in a deep breath. "I don't like to talk about this."

"I need to understand." Pushing up, I met his nervous eyes. "I need to know the boundaries."

"Boundaries?" He frowned. "I don't understand."

"Things that make you uncomfortable—bother you. For instance, I've noticed you have no candles around. All your appliances are electric."

His mouth tightened, his fingers pulling on the blanket, twisting it up tight. "Yes. I don't like candles or things with open flames."

"But you have the fireplace? That doesn't seem to bother you as much."

"It used to. It took me a long time, but I slowly overcame the fear. I couldn't bring myself to brick up the fireplace, since it was one of the things I liked most about the house. It's more contained with the hearth and screen; I like how it smells and the sounds it makes, and Elliott likes the heat. I never sit close."

"And you're able to light it."

"I can control it. I'm very careful. I'm sure you saw the long fire-starter matches."

I nodded and thought for a moment. "So, ah, some fire frightens you?"

His eyes shut, his face warring with emotions. He pressed his head down into the pillow, bringing me back to his chest, his voice tinged with weariness. "I don't like it, but no, fire itself doesn't frighten me. What it can do frightens me."

"I don't understand."

"You think I should be afraid of fire because I was burned?"

"I guess I thought you would be."

"I'm sure some people are...afterward. It depends, I suppose—"

"On?"

Silence filled the room. I could feel his heart beating rapidly under my ear. Too rapidly. I was about to tell him I would stop pushing, when he spoke again.

"On how you were burned."

My stomach knotted at the sound of his voice—distant, removed.

"It's like guns, Megan. They don't kill people. The person pulling the trigger does." His voice dropped further, becoming more remote. "Fire itself didn't set out to burn me. The person holding the flame did."

Icy fingers of dread wrapped around my spine. I gasped for air, unable to catch my breath. Zachary's arm tightened as he lifted his head. "Megan?"

"I thought...I thought you'd been in an accident?" I choked out, horrified. "Someone...did this to you? Deliberately?"

"Yes."

"W...why?"

"To teach me a lesson."

My heart hammered in my chest as my breath came out in small bursts of air. I shook my head in disbelief. "No."

His eyes were flat, his voice cold.

"Yes. I deserved it."

13

MEGAN

"Yes. I deserved it."

I blinked at him in shock, not sure I'd heard him correctly. I struggled to draw in oxygen. It felt as if all the air had been sucked out of the room. The weight on my chest was hard and heavy, as I tried to process his words.

He deserved it.

How could he think that? I couldn't understand.

I couldn't even fathom it.

After he uttered those words, my stomach heaved. I continued to stare at him, shaking my head, my mind running his words on a loop, hot tears streaming down my face. Zachary sat up, confused at my reaction.

"Megan?" He placed his large hand on my arm, squeezing my bicep, his grip gentle. "Why are you so upset? Don't do this. Don't cry." He rested his forehead to mine, his warm breath washing over my skin. "I'm not worth it."

I pulled back, horrified.

Don't cry? Not worth it?

"You need to explain this to me," I gasped.

111

His eyes narrowed; the intimacy we had shared evaporated and his gaze became stern. "I don't have to explain anything to you. I told you my past wasn't pretty." He threw back the covers, his movements jerky as he grabbed his clothes, yanking them on, and headed to the door. "I don't want to talk about this anymore. Not now. I'm not ready."

My heart thundered in my chest. "Will you ever be ready?"

He paused, his hand gripping the doorframe, fingers wrapped tight on the wood. "I don't know," he admitted, walking out of the room.

Stumbling, I found my clothes and followed him downstairs, where he was shrugging on his overcoat, ignoring me. "Where are you going?"

"Elliott and I are going for a walk. It'll give you time to calm down."

"*Calm down?* You say *that* to me, refuse to talk anymore, explain, and you expect me to calm down? Do you really think it's that simple? Talk to me, Zachary!"

He turned; his eyes so dark and filled with anger, I flinched. "I told you I wasn't *ready* to talk about it. You keep *pushing!*"

"I wouldn't push if you would open up to me! That's all I'm asking!"

"That's all?" he sneered. "Why don't you ask for my soul on a plate?"

"The way you talk it sounds like you don't think you have one," I shot back, trying hard not to cry again.

"Not one worth this emotional outburst of yours."

"Maybe I think you're worth being emotional about."

He shook his head. "You barely know me."

"Because you won't let me in."

"Back to that again. You're beginning to sound like a broken record, Megan. Do you think I *owe* it to you to talk? To open up, as you say? Because we slept together?"

I let out a sharp gasp at his hurtful words. "I think after what we've shared the past few days you owe me that, yes."

"I owe you nothing. We're both adults. You knew what you were getting into when we slept together. I didn't promise you anything."

I stood, frozen, gaping at him, not knowing what to do. How did we get to this point so fast? I could see him, *us,* dissolving right in front of my eyes. His pain, his self-loathing was so evident and heart-breaking. I knew he was scared. Something in his past held him in overwhelming fear and such panic, he was lashing out. He was pushing me away because I wanted to help. Zachary didn't know how to accept help.

I held out my hand, not caring if he saw how hard it was shaking. "Please."

He stepped back from my touch. "Stop looking at me like that!" he roared. "Stop trying so fucking hard! Drop it, Megan!"

"What if I can't?"

His face transformed, his posture grew rigid; the warmth I had seen the past few days, gone. Standing in front of me, again, was the cold, dismissive man I met on the beach.

"Then you know where the door is."

The walls shook as he slammed out of the house with such force I even felt the shudder through the floorboards. My shaking legs gave out and I collapsed on the sofa. Dixie whined by my feet and I picked her up, holding her close, seeking the comfort of her warm body and the unconditional love she offered. I shivered, my body icy, as I struggled not to cry. Looking around the room, my eyes were drawn to *Tempest*. Its powerful imagery hit me again. I was at a loss to explain how a man who could stir and express such emotions on a canvas, could shut them off so totally in his life, and be so cold in the face of my own.

I buried my face in Dixie's fur.

I didn't know how to cope with that—to cope with him.

Or how I'd deal with any of it when he returned.

ZACHARY

I couldn't get away from Megan quick enough. I broke through the tree line, not stopping until the dense forest swallowed me up, hiding me in its dark grip.

My legs gave out and I fell to my knees, gasping for air.

Her eyes.

The pain and horror of her eyes, when I told her I had been burned by someone—a deliberate act of cruelty I had, for the longest time, felt I deserved—was shocking. Of course, she assumed I'd been in an accident of some sort. Nowhere in that gentle soul of hers would she ever be able to imagine inflicting that sort of pain on another human being or someone doing that to me.

Watching her fold into herself at my statement, then the fresh pain I caused as I flung cruel words at her, was devastating. The want, *need,* for her to back off, before I dissolved in front of her—an utter emotional wreck—had torn me apart inside. It felt like long, tearing claws ripped at my stomach as I saw what I was doing to her— how my words were affecting her—but I couldn't stop.

I had never wanted to speak those words out loud and allow myself to be comforted by her healing embrace, as much as I did in those moments. I wanted to feel her arms around me. I wanted her soft voice in my ear, telling me everything would be all right.

There was something holding me back, though. It was the knowledge that when she learned why I was burned—the type of man I had been years ago—her opinion of me would change.

It was her expressive eyes that haunted me at the moment.

No one ever looked at me the way she did. She hurt—for me. She felt pain because of what I had experienced, without even knowing why I had experienced it. From the moment we met, I was captivated by the emotions I saw in her eyes. Her gaze was soft, warm, calm. Always affectionate and accepting—never judging; even now, after I had yelled and cursed at her they remained judgment free despite the pain I caused.

How the hell was it possible someone like her even existed? I ran my hands through my hair, clutching and tugging the strands she had cut only hours prior, welcoming the pain as my scalp protested.

How the fuck had I let myself feel so much for her in such a short period of time? We barely knew each other, yet I felt closer to her than anyone who had ever been in my life—ever. Why my trust in her was so absolute I had no idea, but it was. She brought out feelings I didn't even know existed. Tenderness raged in me when she was close. The need to care for another person was so new to me, but she brought it out in me with ease. I wanted her laughter and smiles. I wanted her close. I wanted her comfort and healing touch.

I wanted her.

In order to have her, though, I had to tell her everything—risk everything—in order to move forward. But if she chose to walk away? My heart beat frantically under my ribs at the mere thought.

Elliott butted my chest, a low whimper in his throat. I stroked his great head, realizing I was still kneeling on the damp ground and he was waiting for me to lead him.

I looked behind me in the direction of the house, where I'd left her alone and upset.

Megan was waiting for me to lead her, as well, to open up to her and let her in.

That was if I hadn't broken our fragile bond.

I stood up, brushing the wet dirt from my pants, calling Elliott and walking farther into the forest. I needed to clear my head and give her time to calm down. Witnessing her emotions made me react in strange ways. I lashed out in fear, pushing her away when I should have been pulling her close, holding her as tight as I could as I told her everything. While I let out all the painful memories and allowed her tender strength to begin healing me.

I knew she was strong and could do it; she was stronger than she knew. She had suffered a huge loss because of her ex and she still pushed forward. She refused to allow me to ignore the feelings between us, winning me over with her sweet gestures and thoughtful gifts, which made me want to explore whatever this was with her.

She made me smile. She made me feel.

She gave me something I hadn't felt in years: hope.

She made me want to be better—for her.

Instead of telling Megan all that, I had treated her to a hearty helping of my temper, and pushed her aside.

Even after all these years, I was still a bastard.

I broke into a slow jog, needing the physical release.

An hour later, I emerged from the forest, winded but calmer. I stopped on the deck, my throat catching as I noticed a light in the house at the end of the beach. It hadn't been on earlier.

Walking into the house, I knew. It felt cold, empty. The silence surrounded me—intense like a painful scream.

I had pushed her too far. I was too late.

Megan had left.

I didn't even know if I could get her back.

My heart ached when I realized I wasn't sure I should even try.

14

MEGAN

I wrapped my hands around the coffee mug, trying to stop the shaking. I couldn't get warm. I couldn't stop the waves of nausea that kept rolling through my stomach as I thought about Zachary's detached, cold voice, how empty his eyes had been. He had dismissed my emotions without a thought and walked away. I couldn't stay there, in his house; the words he flung at me echoing in the empty room.

"You know where the door is."

He had made it clear, his need to have space and me sitting there waiting for him, still upset, would do neither of us any good. He knew where I was. If he wanted to talk, he could come to me.

I wiped away the tears that flowed down my cheeks. I wasn't sure he *would* come and find me. His anger had been so quick to flare, his defenses thrown up without a second thought. The gentler side to his personality disappeared in a heartbeat. The man who'd stared at me, cold and removed, wasn't the Zachary for whom I was falling.

He was right; we barely knew each other, yet my feelings for him were so strong, they shocked me. My body hummed with electricity every time he was near. I wanted to touch him all the time; the way

117

he stayed close, I thought he felt the same way. I knew he wasn't used to being touched, but the more time we spent together, the more comfortable he was becoming with reaching out to me. He'd hold my hand or play with my hair; small, simple gestures most people took for granted, but for Zachary, were huge steps. I loved watching him talk, and listening to his laughter, something that seemed to come easier to him the past few days. He told me I made him feel lighter, almost normal. To me he was normal. When I looked at him now, all I saw was Zachary: a man learning to live again, one capable of great tenderness and warmth when he allowed himself to open up. What I didn't see was the angry, pain-filled man with scars, who lashed out to push people away.

That was until he reemerged when we were arguing.

The sky darkened, night beginning to fall, and still he hadn't come to me. I thought when he knew I had returned to Karen's house and he'd calmed down, he would find me, but I waited in vain. Unable to take the silence, I turned on the radio and wandered the house, restless and edgy. The weather forecast came on predicting another storm headed our way. With a groan, I leaned my forehead on the cold glass while I stared out onto the beach below, wondering if that meant another migraine for me. There was such unusual weather—not only here—but all around the world. Zachary had mentioned it had been a colder, snowier winter than he'd experienced, and so far the spring had been one huge rainstorm after another.

Stepping on the deck, I glanced up at the house on the bluff. It had remained dark long after I came back, but now I could see the bright light on the top floor. Zachary was back home and in his studio, no doubt losing himself in his work. I wondered if he was still upset, or if our argument would be locked away in a corner of his mind, practically forgotten. If it was the latter, I wouldn't even enter his thoughts again until he emerged from his studio; if I entered them then. I had no idea what would happen. He was, I knew, capable of cutting off his feelings when he chose. Pain rippled in my chest as I thought about him choosing to cut me off for good.

Beside me, Dixie whined, wanting to go for a walk. She wasn't happy when I snapped on her lead before we descended to the beach. I couldn't risk her taking off in the direction of Zachary's house. I purposely led her in the opposite direction, ignoring her gentle pulls to head toward the light on the bluff. "Not tonight, girl," I whispered, patting her on the head. "We're on our own."

I swallowed the lump in my throat as I wondered if we would be on our own from now on. In my need to help Zachary, to reach out and show him how much I cared, I might have, in fact, pushed him away. Tears stung my eyes as I realized I wasn't sure if he would return to me.

I tossed and turned in my bed. Twice I got up and looked toward the house. Zachary's light burned all night. Sleep only came in small spurts; the next morning I was groggy and desperate for coffee. With a groan, I realized my cream was in Zachary's refrigerator and I would have to drink it black, as well as go into town and get some supplies. As predicted the skies were heavy, a dull gray blanket covering the world, so I decided to go in early and get my errands done before the rain came.

My phone rang with Karen's ringtone and I grabbed it off the counter, sitting on the sofa as I answered.

"Hi."

"Hey, stranger. How are you?"

"Good. You?"

"I'm fine. Everything okay there for you? You haven't called in a few days and your texts were rather short."

My eyes drifted to the window and the dark sky. "Um, yeah. Just been busy."

"Are you writing?"

"Trying."

Karen's voice sounded worried. "Megan, are you okay? You sound strange. Is Dixie okay?"

I cleared my throat, tugging on my ear in worry. How could I tell her what was happening? I had no idea how she'd react if I told her all that had happened since I arrived. I chose the easier route and fibbed a little. "Yeah, she's fine. I'm just fighting another headache. The weather's been quite bad. You know how it affects me."

"I know. Here as well—such strange weather for this time of year. Don't you have your meds?"

"No, I forgot them."

"Why don't you talk to the pharmacist in town and maybe they can contact your home pharmacy and do a refill for you?"

"That's a good idea. I'll go in today. I need cream anyway."

"Megan, are you sure you're okay?"

"I'm fine. Really."

"Do you need anything?"

I drew in a shaky breath. I needed Zachary. "No," I whispered. "Really, I'm okay. I'll call in a couple days once the weather breaks and I feel better."

"Promise?"

"Yes."

"If you don't, I'll come there and check on you. You know I will."

I smiled at her bossiness. She was a good friend and I knew she was worried. I cleared my throat. "I will. I'll get some pills, so I can sleep and feel better. I'll call you in a couple of days."

"Okay."

I hung up and walked over to the window again, leaning my forehead to the cool glass. My breath caught when I spied Zachary on the beach, standing with his back to me, as Elliott ran around. Moments passed while I stared, transfixed, at his distant figure, the long overcoat billowing out behind him. I reached for the glass door, yearning to go to him and beg him to talk to me. I wanted to wind my arms around him and feel his coat wrapping me close to his warmth. I longed to hear his steady heartbeat under my ear as he held me to him, nuzzling my hair with his lips. A tear ran down my cheek as I thought about what his low voice would sound like as he whispered he had missed me, that everything would be okay now, and he wasn't letting me go.

None of that happened, though. Without so much as a backward glance, he whistled for Elliott and together they disappeared from sight.

I slumped against the glass. The air I'd been holding in escaped, a deep sigh fogging up the window. Using my sleeve, I wiped away the dampness on both the glass and my cheeks. He didn't even look toward the house. He didn't come to check up on me to see if I was okay. He had closed himself off again.

He chose when I would leave and he pushed me away.

Grimacing, I wiped away the last of my tears. I was so tired, but I had to go and do some errands. Once more, I had to move forward.

Alone.

It was a huge effort to walk around the small town, picking up the few things I needed, and smile back at the friendly clerks as they wished me a good day. Karen was right and the pharmacist was very helpful; I now had some medication in case of another headache. The one I had I knew was from my overwrought emotions and lack of sleep. The drive back seemed endless and it took all my willpower not to continue up the road to Zachary's place.

After unpacking my things, I took Dixie on another walk, letting her run on the empty beach. Part of me hoped Zachary would hear us and Elliott would come out to run with her; and even more so, I hoped he would appear, but there was no sign of either of them. The studio was in darkness and there was nothing to indicate he was inside. I knew he sometimes went elsewhere to paint or sketch—maybe he wasn't home—or perhaps asleep. His studio light had burned all night; and he once told me sometimes he painted all night then slept all day.

I sighed, wondering if maybe he was looking out his window,

watching us, regretting the day I ever walked into his life, wishing I would leave, so he could return to his completely private life.

The thought of him being alone and isolated made my chest ache with sadness.

He was too full of life to cut himself off again. He didn't see it, but he had so much to offer, so much to give if he allowed himself the opportunity.

With one last glance, I turned and headed back to the house. I could feel the storm closing in, and Dixie and I needed to be safe when it hit. I scooped her up, holding her close as we made our way back to the house. "We'll make some popcorn and have a quiet evening, then go to bed early, okay girl? Maybe we'll watch a movie, just you and me, like old times."

I refused to think about how much cozier it had been when it was the four of us together and I was curled up beside Zachary watching a movie and eating popcorn.

Furious hammering on the door woke me from my restless drug-induced sleep on the sofa. I sat up in the darkness, blinking and confused, unsure of the time. My heart pounded in my chest as hope flared, wanting it to be Zachary who woke me, yet panicked it might not be him. Dixie whimpered from the end of the sofa where she'd been sleeping, and I put my hand out to soothe her. Rain was beating down on the roof and lightning streaked across the sky, silhouetting the shadow that stood outside the doors, as the beating resumed. Warily, I snapped on the light and pulled back the curtains to reveal Zachary's ravaged face pressed against the window. Sliding the door open, I backed up as he stepped inside. He was soaking wet, rain rolling off his broad shoulders, causing the water to puddle around his feet. His hair was plastered to his head, black and gleaming in the light. His eyes were dark and stormy like the waves that pounded on the sand outside.

Silently, we stared at each other. His chest heaved with his gasping breaths and I found my own breathing picking up as he gazed at me, a myriad of emotions flowing in his eyes, his mouth drawn tight. His body was rigid; rage and fear rolling off him, his hands fisted at his sides. I was powerless to move in the face of his pain. "I'm sorry," he pleaded. "I'm a fucking idiot and I'm so very sorry, Megan."

Relief punched through my chest, my hand flying to my mouth to stifle the sob that threatened to escape. He was here. He was apologizing.

"I only wanted to help."

"I know. I didn't mean it. Tell me you know that." He caught my hand and placed it on his chest. "Tell me you can forgive me."

Overwhelmed at his plea, I could only nod.

"I can't stay away from you. I've tried all day to resist it, but all I could think about was you. How you looked at me yesterday, Megan." His lips brushed over my shaking hand, his voice softening. "How do you say so much with those eyes of yours? How do you affect me so fucking deeply?"

Small bursts of electricity charged through me. My legs began shaking as our eyes held. "You do the same to me," I whispered. "You affect me, too."

"I can't sleep without you either," he hissed. "I tried, but I can't. How is that possible? God damn it!" He lunged, jerking me hard to his chest as his mouth covered mine possessively. I gasped as I met the coldness of his body. My shock fast became a hot, blistering need as he worked my mouth, tongues seeking, our breaths mingling, becoming one. Whimpering, I held him to me, needing to feel his roughness—to know he was real. My hands twisted in his wet hair, holding his face close to mine as I gave him what he wanted. I gave him everything I had and he took it; growling as he kissed and moaned, claimed and seized. He blindly reached behind him, shutting the door with a loud slam. He lifted me as if I weighed no more than a feather, walking down the hall to the bedroom, stumbling against furniture and walls, never loosening his hold.

Neither of us pulled away. Neither of us wanted to separate for even one, single second. My back hit the mattress, him on top of me; icy, wet rain running off and soaking into the fabric all around us. Neither of us cared.

His mouth pushed into mine, needy and hot, his chilly hands slipping under my shirt. Abruptly, he sat up, gripping and tearing; the material giving away under his strong hands like paper succumbing to scissors. His mouth closed around my aching nipple, sucking hard, and I gasped, arching closer to him. Back and forth he went, leaving no inch of skin untouched by his lips and tongue, laving and teasing, leaving trails of heat behind. He drew back long enough for me to pull his shirt over his head and then he was back on me, his cold skin welcome against the burning warmth of my mine.

We kissed and touched for what seemed like hours. Zachary's mouth and hands never ceased in their caresses and strokes. I reveled in his touch, thinking it had been lost to me forever. "Megan, I want you," he murmured, his breath hot in my ear, causing a shiver to run down my spine. "So beautiful." He moaned as he pinned me to the mattress with his body, heavy and possessive, the weight of him wanted and real. Grunting and pulling, the rest of our clothing was torn away, his erection hot and thick in my hand as I stroked him.

He hovered over me, panting, as he touched his forehead to mine. "Please."

Barely holding on to my sanity, his low, rough voice pushed me over the edge.

"Zachary," I implored, my need for him as desperate as his was for me.

His hands ran up my legs, his touch firm as he pulled my thighs apart and pushed inside me...hard. There was nothing gentle in his lovemaking tonight; it was all about possession. His hips thrust with power and speed as he took me, groaning and cursing, his head buried in my neck while he surged and claimed. Pleasure sparked and peaked as I held him tight, crying out his name as I came. I fell apart under him while he kept moving, crushing me to his chest so hard it was almost painful. He emptied himself inside me, moaning my name, his hot lips pressed to my skin. Shuddering, he collapsed, rolling so I was nestled into his side, but his hold not lessening.

Our ragged breaths filled the room as we calmed. I shivered as the sweat on my body cooled, realizing the bed below us was damp with rain and seawater. Zachary swore lowly and stood up, grabbing his pants, pulling them on. I watched in silence, dread filling my heart—he was leaving.

He turned on the light beside me and I blinked at the sudden brightness. "Do you have a robe or something?" he asked.

Embarrassment flooded my cheeks at his subtle rejection. I slid off the bed, fighting back tears, not wanting him to see how his words upset me. His hands wrapped around my biceps, stopping me. "Hey."

"It's behind the door."

"Why are you crying?" His voice sounded horrified. "Jesus. Did I...did I *hurt* you, Megan?"

"No," I whispered, grabbing my robe and slipping it on, needing to cover myself from his eyes. "Just go, Zachary."

"Go?" His voice was confused, his hand cupping the back of his neck as he stared at me. With a groan, he wrapped me in his arms. "Megan, I got up because you're shivering. I'm not leaving without you. I'm taking you home with me."

"What?"

His finger ran down my cheek. "I told you—I can't sleep without you now. I need you beside me."

I looked at the bed behind me. "But—"

He grimaced. "I was so fucking desperate, I came in here like a damn caveman, took you with barely a word, and your bedding is soaked. I can't let you stay in there."

"I can put it in the dryer."

"It's three in the morning. Let me take you back home with me and you can do that later today. I want you beside me in my bed. Please, sweetheart." He rested his forehead on mine. "Please."

The unexpected endearment brought the tears back to my eyes. He shook his head sadly. "A single word," he murmured. "One single kind word from me and you cry. You take all the harsh ones and roll with them, but one kind one does this." He gently wiped away the moisture. "I don't deserve your tears."

"I love you." I needed to say the words that had been burning in my head, out loud, needed him to know how I felt.

His hand stilled on my cheek. His face became lax with shock. The tension in his body increased, his eyes widening with astonishment.

"Nobody loves me. Nobody ever really has."

"I do."

"You don't even know me," he insisted.

I shifted closer, his arm wrapping around my back, holding me to him. "I do know you. I know you're alone because you choose to be. I know you're lonely. I know you have a beautiful soul that needs to be loved."

"You think my soul is beautiful?"

"Yes."

He shook his head. "It hasn't always been. My past...my past is ugly, Megan."

"It doesn't matter. I love you here. Now. Not for your past. Not for what happened to you."

"It might change your mind."

"It won't."

He searched my gaze. "How can you be so sure?"

"I simply am."

"But you want to know."

"I deserve that."

He held me closer, his lips grazing my forehead with a sigh. "Yes, you do."

"You'll tell me?"

He hesitated.

"I want, *I need*, to know all of you," I implored him. "Good and bad."

"Later today," he promised. "Come home with me and let me hold you. Let me make up for earlier. Then later I'll answer any question you ask." He paused. "I'll tell you everything."

"Okay." I wanted to stay beside him. I wanted to feel his arms around me.

I didn't fail to notice he didn't say I love you back.

15

MEGAN

I woke up slowly, my hand reaching for Zachary, only to find cold, empty sheets. Hearing muted barks, I padded over to the window, taking in the dull gray of the morning.

The overcast sky was dark, the ocean fast moving and angry, foamy waves of steel swirling with green as they pounded frantically along the shore. Trees and long grass bent in the wind, and farther in the distance, small boats bobbed furiously on the water. The storm was not done with us yet. Elliott and Dixie were running around the beach, barking and playing, wound up by the weather.

In the midst of all the chaos stood Zachary. A tall, solitary figure in his dark overcoat, standing in the shallow surf, staring out in to the unending distance. His hands were shoved in his pockets, hair blowing in the wind, feet deep in the frigid water. His stance screamed tension. The urge to go down and wrap myself around him, to offer him some comfort, was great. My fingers gripped the edge of the window tight in order to not give in to the desire. I knew our argument had upset him and his promise to tell me his story was weighing on his mind. The thought my declaration of love was also upsetting him caused a small ache in my chest.

My fingers plucked nervously at the edge of the long shirt I was wearing. After wrapping me in the damp comforter last night and scooping up Dixie, we had returned to his house. Zachary had carried both of us; his long gait across the wet, cold sand ate up the distance quickly. Once inside, a warm shower and gentle hands sliding a dry shirt over my head replaced the wet blanket and shivers. Slipping under the covers, Zachary's hard chest molded to my back, holding me close as his breath whispered across my neck. "Sleep, sweetheart."

It hadn't come easily—for either of us. His promise loomed too big, his tension so palpable that instead of the relief of quiet, blissful sleep, both of us were restless and trapped in our own dark thoughts. Physically close, the yawning gap between our emotions was vast.

Now looking at him, once again choosing to be alone, I wondered if possibly he was right. Maybe he was too damaged. Maybe I couldn't save him.

Maybe...he didn't want to be saved.

The fire was burning low when I went downstairs, and I added another log the way Zachary had shown me, resituating the fire screen. The coffee was cold, so I dumped it down the drain and made a fresh pot, then went back to the window to watch Zachary. He had moved farther down the beach, closer to Karen's house—his head now lowered, hands still deep in his pockets, shoulders hunched —as he slowly waded through the water. A shiver went through me watching him, trying to imagine how cold his feet must be, but he seemed immune to the icy water. He told me he liked how it felt against his skin.

When the coffee was ready, I poured a cup, unsure what to do next. Stay here and wait? Pour a cup for him and take it to him? The question was answered when I heard the door open and both dogs burst in the room, tails wagging, their coats damp and cold under my hands when I stroked them. After greeting me, they both ran into the other room where I knew they would be warming up by the fire. I hesitated, then poured another cup of coffee as Zachary walked into the room. He paused briefly in the doorway, his eyes meeting mine as he stepped forward, his hand wrapping around my neck and taking me to him. I gasped as his icy fingers grazed my skin, the coldness of the outside permeating his clothes as he held me to him, his mouth covering mine, soft and full. With him, he brought the scent of the ocean. The salty, sharp smell wrapped around me. The chill of his body seeped into mine, as he kissed me with so much adoration, it made my heart sing. My head was spinning when he drew back, dropping a couple more light kisses on my mouth. I opened my eyes to his weary gaze, the fatigue etched on his skin like a map of fine lines.

"Zachary," I uttered his name, concerned. "You look exhausted." Cautiously, I laid my hand on his cheek, a sense of relief rippling through me when he relaxed into my touch.

Slowly his head lowered until it rested on my shoulder, the weight heavy. Sliding my hand around his neck, my fingers slipped into his damp hair, caressing the strands.

"I'm tired, Megan. So very tired," he murmured, his voice rough and drained. I held him a little closer, knowing he didn't only mean physically. He seemed so vulnerable; my chest tightened with the sound of his pain. I rested my cheek to his head, pressing a kiss to his hair, wanting to offer him comfort.

"What can I do?"

He lifted his head, eyes pleading. "Would you come back to bed with me? Let me hold you while I sleep?" He paused. "I need to sleep. I can't...I can't talk right now."

"It's okay, Zachary. Yes. Yes, I'll come back to bed with you."

His head fell back to my shoulder. "Thank you."

He slept hard with his head buried in my neck, arms wrapped around me, warm and finally at peace. For the first time since I met him he sought my touch, groaning in satisfaction when I trailed my fingers along his arms and back. I slid my fingers into his hair, keeping my touch light as he relaxed. His body grew heavy as he gave into the weariness that plagued him.

Outside, the wind picked up as the rain started again, drumming heavily on the roof. His warm body, deep breathing, and the soothing beat of the rain overhead relaxed me, and shutting my eyes, I joined him in sleep.

Hours later, my eyes opened as Zachary stirred, his body moving, muscles shifting, his eyes finding mine. "Hi," he whispered.

I traced a constant circle on his back with my fingers, gently caressing his skin. "Hi."

"You're still here."

"I told you I would be."

"Sometimes I find that hard to believe."

"I've noticed."

He swallowed nervously. "I'm not used to people being truthful with me, Megan. The world I lived in, people said what they thought I wanted to hear, even when they didn't mean it."

"It doesn't sound like a very nice world."

"It wasn't a nice one, but it was the only one I knew...until now."

"Until now?" I questioned.

Leaning up, he placed a soft kiss to my lips. "You, Megan. You make it better."

"I want to," I admitted, smiling, liking that I could change his life for the better.

"You do."

He rested his head back on my chest with a quiet sigh; the tenderness flowed through me at his unconsciously needful gesture, making my eyes sting. His scarred cheek was pressed into my skin, the ridges feeling rough against me. I ran my hand through his hair, smiling as he relaxed deeper into my body, his weight feeling so right on me. He was rarely relaxed enough to let me feel him without restraint. I loved him most when he allowed himself to be vulnerable.

"It's late."

I glanced at the clock. "It's just two in the afternoon. You needed to sleep."

"You want me to talk."

"I do, but only if you can, Zachary. I want to know you; all of you."

He didn't say anything, but I felt his tension start to creep back. He began to pull away, but I wrapped myself around him. "Nothing you tell me is going to change how I feel."

"You can't say that for sure."

"I can. Your past is simply that—your past. I've already assumed, from the few things you've said, it isn't pretty or very nice. I know you're not proud of some things that happened, or some of the things you did, but it made you what and who you are today."

He looked up; his forehead furrowed. "What do you see me as today, Megan?"

I traced his skin with my finger, trying to smooth out the lines of anxiety. "A gifted artist. Haunted by his past. Alone. Scared to admit what he really needs."

"What do I really need?"

"To forgive yourself. " I drew in a deep breath. "To let yourself be loved."

"You still think you love me?"

"I don't think. I know."

"You shouldn't."

"I still do."

"You might not after I tell you."

"And I might very well love you more."

The startled look on his face told me he never expected to hear those words.

"Megan—"

"Tell me, Zachary. Tell me your story and let me judge my feelings. You want honesty?"

"Yes."

"Then give me yours and I'll give you mine."

His eyes searched my face. "I promise you I'll listen with an open heart," I pleaded in a soft, reassuring voice. "We can't move forward until we get through this. You know that."

He sat up. "All right, but not here, not in our bed. I need to have a shower and I'll meet you in the living room."

Grabbing some clothes, he disappeared into the bathroom.

Our bed.

I wondered if he realized those were the words he used.

He paced, walking around the room, adjusting pictures, shifting small items the slightest fraction to the left or right, only to push it back to its original place. He stood in front of *Tempest*, staring in silence—a frown on his face, shoulders rigid and unyielding. From my place on the sofa I watched, forcing myself not to get up and touch him, not to raise my voice and call to him. He had to come to me. He had to be the one to open the dialogue. He traced his initials in the corner with one long finger, over and again, eventually lowering his arm, resting his hand on the mantle. A deep shudder flowed through his body and he turned to look at me, defeat already in his stance. I couldn't take it anymore and held out my hand to him, pleased when he reached out and took it, coming to sit with me on the sofa. He stared down at our entwined hands, then lifted them and kissing my palm before pulling away. He leaned forward and took one of his peppermints from the bowl on the coffee table. The familiar sound of the candy wrapper being opened made me smile.

Without a word, he offered it to me, unwrapping a new one for himself when I took it out of his hand. The fresh flavor of sweet mint filled my mouth, reminding me of his taste when he kissed me. "You eat these, a lot."

He grunted in agreement. "When I woke up...after...my throat hurt and I had a funny taste in my mouth all the time. One of the nurses gave me this kind of peppermint and I liked it. It wasn't as strong as some kinds and I enjoy the sweetness." He bit down, his jaw flexing as he chewed on the mint. "I kind of became addicted to them, I think. Mrs. Cooper keeps that brand in especially for me."

"They are good," I agreed, hoping he would keep talking.

He fell silent again. The cushions shifted as he moved, his long legs stretching and bending. An irregular beat was tapped out by his restless fingers, but still he said nothing. He shifted forward, his arms resting on his thighs, staring into the fire. I could feel the tension starting to build in him, his lips thinning in a grimace, his face becoming determined, so I slid closer.

"Zachary—"

"I don't know how to do this, Megan."

"What can I do?"

"Maybe if you asked me some questions? Could you do that?"

"Are you sure you want to do this today?"

His eyes, tormented and worried, but determined, met mine. "Yes."

I slipped my hand into his.

"Okay then. Together."

He nodded.

"Together."

16

MEGAN

Zachary looked anxious as his hand clutched mine in a tight grip. So, I kissed his cheek gently, trying to let him know I was here and ready for whatever he had to say. I knew it wasn't going to be pleasant, but I was sure I could handle it. I prayed I could. I also tried to think of how to start the conversation in such a way he wouldn't immediately shut himself off.

Looking around the room, my gaze landed on his painting. "Have you always painted?"

"No."

I tried again.

"What did you do before you started painting?"

His inhale of air told me that maybe wasn't the best question to start with, but I forged ahead. "You must have done something?"

"I was an actor."

That surprised me. I racked my brains trying to remember his name, but came up with nothing.

"Sorry, I guess I'm not familiar with your work."

He shook his head. "Given our age difference that doesn't surprise me. Since you would have been about thirteen when I was at the height of my career, it's hardly a shock. You were probably far more into boy bands than older movie stars."

I had to smile at his remark; he was right. I loved music and books when I was younger—I wasn't much into movies. The same held true today.

"Besides, my professional name was Adam Dennis."

My eyebrows rose. Adam Dennis—that name rang a bell.

"You won an Oscar."

"I was nominated."

"I think I saw some of your films." My brow furrowed as I tried to remember. All I came up with was a vague image of a tall, slender young man playing a single father. "You look different now." I held up my hand. "I don't mean your scars."

He snorted. "I was young, Megan. Younger than you are now, for most of the films I made. Yeah, I've changed. I filled out, I've gotten bigger." He flexed his arms, causing the muscles to tighten and clench. "It happens when everything you eat isn't monitored."

"They watched what you ate?"

"I was a leading man. My appearance was carefully controlled; the length of my hair, my weight, the clothes I wore, all of it. I hated all that shit."

He stood up, pulling away. "I do remember your name, Zachary. You were huge."

"Emphasis on *were*."

"Why did you use a different name?"

"It's common. My agent thought Zachary was too long—and I hated being called Zach. I still hate it. It was my mother's idea to use my middle name and flip Adam to be my first. Dennis was her maiden name so she got that in there."

"Are you parents still alive?" He seemed alone in the world.

He shrugged, but I saw the pain that crossed his face while he struggled to remain composed. "I have no idea. I haven't spoken to them since I was eighteen."

"Why?"

"I grew up in England. I was born late in life for my parents. I wasn't exactly a welcome surprise, but as luck would have it, I was a good-looking kid. So, my mother started taking me to auditions and got me signed with an agent. I worked a lot as a child." He barked out a humorless laugh. "Earned my keep, so to speak."

He leaned against the wall; his gaze fixed on a spot over my head. "When I was in my teens, we moved to the States. I got a part in a popular sitcom."

"Did you like that?"

"I had no choice. I went where my parents told me to go. My father fired my agent and did that job; plus he acted as my manager and my mother was my handler. I just learned the lines and did what I was told. My happiness or what I liked never came into play."

In my head I pictured a young Zachary trapped in a world he despised. "So you weren't close?"

Bitterness tinged his tone. "Not even remotely. All I was to them was a paycheck. A way to live a particular lifestyle they enjoyed."

"Surely they loved you—they were your parents," I protested.

"My mother loved herself. She was a manipulative shrew, Megan," he spat. "My father did what she wanted because it was easier than arguing with her. She used anything she needed to in order to get what she wanted: anger, tears, threats. It didn't matter. The only thing my father loved was the money I brought in." He paused and squeezed his eyes shut, as if in pain. "What *my face* brought in, because that's all I was to them—a good-looking face that made money."

My stomach rolled at his cold voice. He could have been talking about complete strangers instead of his parents.

"When I was eighteen, I severed all ties. I left them the house, and I walked away. I fired my father and mother—from both my professional and private life." He pushed off the wall, pacing. "*Fuck,* what a scene that was. My mother sobbing because she knew the gravy train was gone and my father trying to convince me he hadn't stolen all the money I'd made over the years." He stopped his pacing, staring at me. I saw the hurt he denied, written all over his face. "All I was to them was money. They used me. Neither of them said a single word about losing me as their son, only that I couldn't walk away from them and leave them with nothing. My mother actually had the nerve to tell me how much she had sacrificed of herself over the years, always putting me first." Zachary threw his hands up in disgust. "I guess she forgot about what I had sacrificed: friends, school, a regular life. I never knew what it was like to have someone who liked me for me—Zachary. I never had what other kids had—a chance to be a kid, get a part-time job, make mistakes—I had to be perfect all the fucking time. Live up to the image they created—or suffer the consequences." He stopped pacing, his shoulders slumping. "Do you know what I missed most, Megan? What I wanted most of all?"

I shook my head, my hands balling into fists from the pain in his voice. "No," I whispered. "Tell me."

"Hugs. I'd watch other kids on the set get hugged by their parents or their agent. Sometimes they'd have a friend on the set. I never did. Not once. Between acting, being tutored, and all the bloody lessons they insisted I have, I never had time for friends. My mother hung around the sets for appearance sake but she didn't care about what I did as long as she got her designer bags and big house."

I swallowed a lump in my throat. "Your mom...didn't hug you?"

He sat down beside me. Cupping my face in one hand, he squeezed my cheeks lightly. "'Look at this face,'" he crooned snidely. "'My million dollar face.'" He withdrew his hand.

"That was the only time she touched me and that was what she would say—every single time. My face, Megan. She loved my face. Not me." His bottom lip trembled a little. "What a stupid kid I was, right? I knew they didn't love me, yet I still wanted their affection."

I wanted to weep. I wanted to wrap him in my arms, kiss his ravaged face, and tell him he wasn't stupid. I wanted to hold him until that kid felt how loved he was now and could start to heal, but he stood up and started pacing again. "Don't, Megan," he pleaded.

"Don't what?"

"Don't look at me like that. Don't feel bad for me. The entire time I grew up I was ignored by them. There was no guidance or care. I was a commodity. That was all I was to them; a mistake they used to their advantage. They lived a great life, thanks to me, and when I walked away that was what they mourned—not the loss of their son, but the loss of the money and the lifestyle they didn't want to give up." He grimaced and pulled in a deep breath. "They didn't care about me or anyone else, but I was the exact same way. My parents were shit, but I was a *great* student. I treated everyone like crap. I was the perfect image of a spoiled brat. I was catered to on set. Everything I wanted, I got. People did what I told them to do because of my name—because they knew if they didn't I would probably get them fired. And on occasion I did."

"So, you were a brat. It was all you knew. Children learn by example."

He laughed. "You're still defending me. You still think too highly of me." He shook his head, a sad expression on his face. "Except it didn't change, Megan. Even after I grew up, in fact, it got worse. After I got rid of my parents, I got a new agent and PR team. I became my own manager; I refused to let anyone dictate my life anymore. I surrounded myself with people who wanted from me what I wanted from them."

"Which was?"

"More—of everything. My father played it safe with my career. He kept me acting in the stupid sitcom because of the consistent money—even though I hated it and had for years. Every decision my father ever made was based on the dollar figure. Every stupid movie he put me in, every endorsement was because of the bottom line. I hated it. I hated him. So, I changed direction and branched into films. I wanted bigger roles and my agent, Ryan, was with me on that decision—more money, more power. I became a Hollywood bad boy. Drinking, drugs, women—all of it. Publicity was my friend because no matter what I did, I had something they wanted..." he sneered "... my fucking face. It was always about my face with everyone. Any movie they put me in was a sure fire winner at the box office and it made having to clean up my messes worth it. As long as I had my face, I had everything. I was worth something."

I was on my feet before I realized it. "You're worth something now, Zachary! Your face doesn't change that!"

Zachary stepped back, looking startled by my outburst. He held out his hands in supplication. "I'm only trying to tell you, Megan. Make you understand."

I sat down, my legs too shaky to hold me up. "I get it. Your entire life was based on your face. Don't even get me started on how fucking wrong that is."

He gave me a strange look. "That's how it was. It was all I knew."

"Still wrong," I seethed. "There's so much more to you than a face."

Suddenly, he crossed over and cupped my face again, but this time his touch was different; gentler. He dropped a soft kiss to my mouth. "Thank you," he breathed. Before I could react, he was gone again. My lips tingled from his kiss and the depth behind those two small words.

I shook my head to clear it. "Okay, so you were a bad boy now."

"I was an adult with the mindset of a spoiled child—a very bad combination. I went from an egotistical teen star, used to getting his way, to an arrogant self-obsessed adult. It was all about me. Just like my mother had taught me. Everything I wanted I got. I used people, Megan. Unless you were of use to me you weren't in my life, and once I was done with you: that was that. I had no one in my life that was loyal to me, and I was loyal to no one."

"Weren't you lonely?"

He shrugged, silent for a moment. "I never thought about it. I didn't know any different—I'd been doing that all my life. Who I was, the person I had been, never changed. I was conceited—selfish. I was considered a great actor, but an awful person. My reputation preceded me on every project I worked on." I shrugged. "And I didn't care. All my life I had been used and now I was using people. It was a vicious cycle.

"I enjoyed being an actor. I liked it, enjoyed the craft, and as I learned more, I got better roles, so I suppose I was happy with that part of my life. Outside of that, I filled my time with empty shit: parties, cars, stuff, women." He paused, looking uncomfortable. "Lots of women."

I swallowed nervously at his tone and body language; both were tense. "And none of them meant anything to you?"

"Never." He inhaled deeply. "I used them and they used me right back. I was a great way to get their name in the paper—a date with Adam Dennis. Being seen on my arm would guarantee publicity."

"And what would you get out of it?" I asked, sliding my hands under my legs so he couldn't see how hard they were shaking. I waited for his reply, already knowing and dreading the answer.

"Sex. Publicity as well, but often a blow job in the limo or a fast fuck before I went home." He stared at me. "I never stayed; ever. And...rarely, very rarely was there ever a second date. Unless it was something I wanted."

His matter-of-fact tone made my stomach roll, but I fought to keep my expression neutral. I knew if I got upset, he would stop talking and I needed to hear this; I needed to hear everything.

"You didn't form a...relationship with anyone? Ever?"

"No. I didn't want one. I saw how my parents used each other. How they used me. I thought that was what love did to a person. I watched people all around me use each other and walk away so easily from someone they claimed to love. I didn't want any part of it. I refused to let it happen to me."

"So bitter," I murmured.

He shook his head. "Realistic."

"Not always."

"In my world, yes."

"I don't think I like your world."

He barked out a bitter laugh. "My world didn't like me either."

His eyes narrowed. "I told you it wasn't pretty. Do you want me to stop?"

"No."

His voice softened, the cold edge melting a small amount. "It's my past, Megan. You asked me for honesty. I'm trying to give you that."

"I know. I'm fine." I inhaled deeply, willing myself to remain calm. "Was there anything good in your life, Zachary? Anything good at all?"

He turned to the mantle, his fingers drifting over his painting. "I went into rehab for substance abuse when I was twenty-two and part of the therapy was finding an outlet to express myself. I thought it was bullshit. I thought all of it was bullshit—until I picked up a paint brush." I watched, fascinated, as his hand moved fluidly over the swirls. I could see him recreating them in his mind, the paint being layered on the canvas as he created his work. "I could paint. I mean, I always liked to draw and sketch, but I had no idea I could paint." Abruptly, he turned. "So I guess that was good. I didn't share it with anyone, but it was something I could do, that was mine, you know?"

I nodded, my heart tugging in my chest. All he had was painting —and no one to share that with—no one he trusted. A small piece of himself he protected from the world.

"What happened, Zachary?"

He paced up and down in front of the fireplace—his steps measured and heavy as he walked. At one point he stopped and hunched down, running his hands over Elliott's head, his face awash in deep emotions, but he remained silent.

"I used people, Megan. Badly."

"So you said."

He looked up, the darkness in his expression causing my breath to hitch in my throat. "My last film, I was twenty-five. I was jaded and bitter. I didn't care about anything or anybody. I was rich, arrogant, and I took what I wanted." He sighed, standing up and dropping into the chair across from me. "I decided I wanted my co-star."

I started feeling ill at the mere thought of what was to come, but I still had to know. "And?"

"My agent warned me to stay away from her; Marni was married and the rumors were that her marriage was in trouble. He told me she was vulnerable. He even used the word 'unstable.'" His voice lowered, self-hatred coloring its tone. "I didn't care. It was perfect for me; a warm body to fuck while on location, then I could walk away when the film was complete. No strings."

"But that wasn't what happened?"

"No. The first few days I pursued her, charmed her; that was how I worked. The chase was fun; it always was for me...and we had an affair."

"Did she know about your thoughts on relationships?"

"I told her I wasn't interested in anything permanent. I thought she was okay with that."

"But she wasn't?"

"No."

The room was quiet, only the cracking of the fire and the sounds of the ocean in the distance could be heard. I wanted to ask him, to demand he tell me what happened, but he was so lost inside his head, I knew he wouldn't hear me.

"Ryan was right. It wasn't a good idea. She projected this bitchy, independent vibe, but she wasn't. When I look back, I think maybe she was as lost as me. I broke it off with her a few days before we wrapped. She was getting too clingy, and I was done with it all; it was time for me to move on. She was so angry and upset. We argued, and things got rather ugly. She, ah, told me she loved me."

He looked at me, his expression blank. "I told her I didn't care. She knew the rules at the start. It was her problem, not mine. I told her to go back to her husband."

"What happened?"

"We argued some more and I got tired of it, so I decided to leave. She was crying, which didn't bother me in the slightest and only made her angrier. I told her to use that anger when we filmed the final scene we had together a couple days later; that maybe, for the first time I'd see a decent performance from her."

"You were cruel."

He nodded. "She slapped me and told me I would regret my actions." He paused. "I laughed at her. I told her I already did, and nothing she did could make me regret it more."

A shiver ran down my spine.

Zachary's haunted gaze met mine.

"I was wrong."

1 7

MEGAN

My heart pounded in my chest as I waited for Zachary to talk. I felt the damp nervous sweat at the back of my neck, and I struggled to remain calm.

Zachary stared into the fire; silent, motionless. His long fingers were steepled together, his elbows resting on his thighs as he stared, lost to some deep memory in his head.

He stood up again, pacing, ignoring me. Back and forth he went, in constant motion. He was like a caged animal; tense and frantic. I couldn't speak. I was afraid if I tried, all the emotion I was holding in would burst forth and he would close in on himself again.

Finally, his pacing stopped. He braced himself against the mantle, his back to me, his voice filled with agony. The distance he fought to maintain was gone and his pain was tangible.

"I didn't see Marni until our final scene. She seemed fine. Distant, cold, but fine, which was okay with me. I wasn't feeling very responsive toward her, either. Ironically, the scene was me being a big man and letting the woman I loved go, so she could have a better life. Marni's character pleads with me, begs me to change my mind and in the final moment becomes angry. She was to throw the contents of her glass in my face, slap me and storm away." He paused. "The final shot would be of me watching her walk away, standing in the room where we'd made love, candles flickering, all very dreamlike. My face would be tormented, knowing I had done the right thing in letting her go. It was supposed to be very climatic and emotional."

He stopped talking abruptly and I could see his shoulders moving with his rapid breaths. I forced myself to remain where I was and not go to him. My own breaths were coming out fast, and part of me wanted to tell him to stop, that I didn't want to hear anymore, but I couldn't. I was the one who begged for him to talk and no matter how much I hated it, I had to listen.

I found my voice. "Tell me."

"We did a quick run through. We had already rehearsed it all thoroughly. Where we would stand, how much water was in the glass she threw, how she had to toss it, so it hit me properly. All of it. We were ready and I just wanted the scene done and over.

"Something was wrong—off. Marni was too calm and she looked...vacant. I was on edge and jittery. I expected attitude and anger, not a passive attitude. Then—"

"Then?" I prompted gently.

"We got ready to roll and she did something strange. She lifted the glass with the water in it and drank it. The set director started to come toward her and she laughed, waving him off and lifted the bottle she had with her saying sorry, she'd fill it herself. She made a joke that she was thirsty and forgot; everyone sort of laughed—she was known for being a little different, eccentric, that way." He turned to face me, not moving. I felt like the naked pain on his face was holding me in my seat. "But everything felt wrong, the hair on the back of my neck was standing up and I was jumpy. I felt as though I was on a precipice, waiting, but I didn't know what I was waiting for."

"Did you say anything?"

He shook his head. "Everyone was tense on set. They all knew what had happened between Marni and me, so no one was really comfortable that day. I told myself I was being paranoid. It was the final scene and I was anxious for it to be done. That was all."

"But it wasn't your imagination, was it?"

"No. We went through the scene up to the point of her throwing the water at me, and then we were ready to go." Zachary let out a deep sigh. "The cameras started rolling and we both slipped into our characters. It was perfect—both of us were on our mark. The last part of the scene, Marni picked up her glass and looked at me." Zachary's hand lifted to his face in an unconscious gesture of defense. "Her eyes were cold and determined and so fucking filled with insanity... that I knew. I knew right then something was going to happen."

His words were coming faster now, his accent more pronounced, his hands clenching and unclenching. "I couldn't stop it, I couldn't move. It was as if I was watching it from outside my body—looking in, and powerless to stop it." His breath started coming out in small gasps. "It was all choreographed. I was supposed to stand there and take it. Let her throw the water at me and not move; be stoic. We'd rehearsed it enough, I could watch the water come at me and not even blink. But it wasn't right. She wasn't right. As soon as she tossed the contents of the glass my arm came up." His hands balled into fists, his entire body trembling now.

"What was it?"

"Vodka. What everyone thought was water was alcohol; she replaced the water she drank with straight vodka. It hit my face, burning my eye and soaking into my shirt.

"Before I could react or anyone else realized what was happening, she picked up a lit candle"—he swallowed and lowered his voice —"and set me on fire."

My stomach lurched and I covered my mouth as I stared at him in horror. Not only had she done all that, but she'd planned it.

Zachary's eyes were wide, filled with the emotion of his terrible memories. He braced himself against the wall with one shaking arm.

"It happened so fast. Chaos broke out. I fell down, screaming in pain, Marni was ranting and shouting, trying to stop people from getting to me. The accelerant was everywhere so fire was burning on the set, as well as me. All I vaguely remember is the screaming and shouting as people rushed around." His voice became gritty with emotion. "I remember the smell of my flesh burning. The pain overtook me and I blacked out."

"And Marni?"

Zachary's head shook slightly, as if he was trying to clear his mind. His chest heaved with a large puff of air.

"She killed herself."

I shook with nerves. I'd never felt so cold in my life as I huddled into the blanket, my body physically reacting as Zachary's words kept repeating in my head—a constant unending circle. So many emotions raged within me. Grief and sorrow for Zachary's suffering. I felt a fierce, almost primal anger toward a woman I never met, for inflicting such horror and pain onto another person, then in a cowardly act, taking her own life. I drew the blanket closer; my hands gripping the soft material so tight my knuckles were white as I struggled not to be overwhelmed. I needed to be calm for Zachary when he returned.

After he told me Marni had killed herself, he had locked down. "I have to walk. I have to go. I need—"

I only nodded, unable to stop him. He paused at the door. "Will you be here when I get back?"

"Yes."

His shoulders lost a little of their tension and he called for both dogs, closing the door quietly behind him, leaving me alone with the deafening silence. I had no idea how long he'd be gone, but I knew this time he would be coming back. I had to wait for him and be here when he did. I had to be strong for him.

I was surprised when the door opened again not long after. I was silent as I watched him shed his coat and join me on the sofa.

Reaching out, he pulled me onto his lap, holding me tight as I gathered the blanket around us both. The tension in his body began to dissipate. "I'm sorry," he murmured.

"Why?"

"I shouldn't have said all that and walked away again. I know you have questions. I needed to clear my head, though."

"I understand."

A shaky sigh escaped him. "I needed to hold you. I needed to know you're for real."

"I'm not going anywhere."

His arms tightened and I snuggled deeper into his warmth. Minutes passed as we drew comfort from one another.

Slowly, my shaking stopped and I drew back. He looked so drawn and weary, his eyes dull and flat. "We don't have to talk anymore today."

"I want to."

"Are you sure?"

"Yes. I want to finish it." His hands cupped the back of my head, restlessly stroking my skin. "Help me finish it, Megan."

I nodded, understanding he needed my questions again.

"Can you tell me what happened...after?"

Gently, he lifted me off his lap and got up, once again on edge. As if sensing the growing tension in the room, the dogs crept away, heading for the kitchen. I wasn't sure if Zachary even noticed them leaving.

"I only know what I was told." He frowned. "I was out for a while. They weaned me off the drugs gradually, letting my periods of consciousness become longer, until I was lucid enough to understand what had happened. That Marni had done that for revenge. She had a total break from reality—Ryan told me she laughed as she watched me burn."

My stomach heaved as I listened. I wanted to get up and wrap him in my arms as he spoke, finally letting the memories that had festered and raged inside, out into the open. I knew, though, if I touched him right now he would shut down. I had to sit and let him talk, yell, scream...whatever it took.

"She died that day?"

"Yes. In the chaos she ran to her trailer and locked herself in. She, ah, shot herself. Besides the alcohol there were drugs in her system. She knew what she was going to do; she knew she was going to set me on fire, then kill herself." His eyes were filled with guilt. "I did that to her. Ryan told me she was unstable. He warned me she had a history of nervous breakdowns and she'd even attempted suicide once. She did a few strange things that should have set off alarm bells in my head, but as usual, I blocked them out. I remember waking up one night, finding her in my room, just staring at me—she had somehow got a copy of my key. Another time I found her going through my stuff, taking little things she thought I wouldn't miss. I chalked it up to her quirkiness instead of seeing the truth." He shook his head. "When I told Ryan he warned me again, but in my usual selfish way, I ignored him and did what I wanted. Took what I wanted. Only this time I paid a price. We both did."

"She made the decision to hurt you."

He shook his head. "She wasn't in her right mind. I pushed her over the edge with my cruelty."

Remembering his words from the other day, I cleared my throat. "You don't think you *deserved* what happened, do you?"

"No." He sighed. "Not most of the time, but at others, I think maybe I did."

I shook my head furiously. "No. Nobody deserves that to happen to them. Ever."

"What I did—"

"—was wrong. You were cruel. You were also only human; you made a huge error in judgment. She could have done a dozen things to show her displeasure. She was obviously sick, Zachary."

"I should have seen that more plainly, though."

"No. You weren't capable of seeing another person's suffering at the time."

"So you forgive me for what I did? So easily?"

I frowned at him. "It's not my place to forgive you. You need to forgive yourself. You need to forgive her."

He was motionless as he contemplated my words. "I forgave her a long time ago. I'm not sure I can ever forgive myself completely."

"Only you have that power," I reminded him gently.

"I know."

Nothing I could say would change how he felt. Nothing would change for him until he was ready, so I let it go for now.

"How did you end up here?"

The tension returned to his shoulders and he started moving around the room again, touching things, once again lost in thought. Absently, he picked up a small sculpture, his thumb tracing over the smooth glass.

"One day I was an actor—everyone wanted a piece of me. I thought I had everything: looks, money, a life most would envy—my whole future laid out before me. People to do anything I told them to do, women falling over me. I knew I was a complete and utter asshole, but I didn't care. They didn't care." He stopped pacing and looked out the window.

"Then I woke up. It was all gone. I had no future. It all changed in one instant. I changed. Everything I knew...everything my life was built around was my *face*. My looks. My entire life was because of how I looked." He sneered in disgust and looked down at his hands, as if he was surprised to see he was holding something. "My fucking face. God damn it, I *hated* my fucking face!"

With a roar, he threw the sculpture across the room, the glass hitting the wall and shattering into thousands of tiny shards. I covered my mouth to stop the startled gasp, my body trembling in the face of his sudden rage. He started shouting.

"I wasn't Adam Dennis the famous actor anymore! I was a scarred, ugly man who needed help! But I had no one who wanted to help me! I had surrounded myself with people just like me—cold and uncaring—and when I really needed someone there was nobody I could rely on." His voice broke and he stopped shouting, his chest heaving with exertion. He stumbled to the chair, almost falling into it. His head fell back, eyes shut. All I could do was stare, waiting for him to speak again. When he did, his voice was quieter and laced with sadness. "I was useless to anyone in my life; I held no value to anyone. I was in pain, and for the first time in my life I was scared. I had no one—not a single person to help me. My agent was distant; he knew my career was over, so I was of little use to him anymore. He played his role, but we both knew what was going on. The studio was in protection mode; too busy disclaiming any responsibility for the tragic accident on set that injured one person and killed another. All they wanted to do was throw money my way, and sweep it all under the rug and forget it. Forget me."

"That's what was said?"

"It was a closed set. They concealed it up as best they could; twisted the situation to serve their purpose. Her family didn't want what happened to be known. I didn't want the extent of my injuries out there. They paid money to the right people and covered it up. There were rumors and innuendos, but frankly, I was too ill to care much about that. I was in too much pain.

"Did you know, Megan," he murmured, his voice almost robotic, "if you're burned enough you get cold?"

My chest constricted as tears filled my eyes. "No."

He nodded, his eyes distant and unseeing. "It felt endless: pain, burning, cold. I shook all the time. My skin was on fire, but I shook all the time from the cold. Odd, isn't it?"

"Zachary—"

He kept talking, his voice an empty drone, as I cried without a sound, my tears running down my cheeks, unheeded.

"It was a cold that came from inside—nothing could warm me up. Every time I would start to wake up it was the first thing I felt. As though I was trapped in a burning iceberg. I didn't think it would ever end." He paused, a rough exhale of air leaving his lungs. "I thought I'd go mad before it was over. I wanted to die.

"Maybe it would have been better if I did."

My heart ached at those words. I couldn't even comprehend his pain.

He looked past me. "I struggled daily, just to make it through every day. Get past the physical pain and work through the mental part of it. They did what they could for me medically, although my head was in such a bad place I refused some of the treatments. My career was over—I knew that. I had a couple procedures to help with the scarring, but they were extremely painful and didn't make much difference in my opinion."

I wiped my face, my voice raspy when I spoke. "You didn't have anyone, Zachary? Anyone you trusted?"

"I was still stupid enough I thought I did, but the people I was unwise enough to think of as friends, couldn't be bothered with me. I was utterly alone...except for one person." His voice was deep with weariness. "One person stayed. A staff member I had never paid much attention to. She was there, and helped me over the next few months. I was so grateful." He snorted in disgust. "I acted like an idiot, I was so grateful; like a fucking stray dog someone takes home instead of kicking. That was what I had become—a stray dog nobody wanted. I trusted her, I believed everything she said. Until—" His voice trailed off.

"Until?" I prompted gently.

"Until she had enough pictures, enough of a story built up—she sold it to a magazine." He shook his head. "Once I was no longer of use to her, she left too, taking away the last bit of trust I had in humanity."

"Oh, Zachary."

"I caught her writing up her story on her computer. I was still pretty bandaged up, so the pictures didn't show how bad things were, but with her terrible, over-the-top story, it was enough to bring it all back into the public eye again. The whole tragic story of the leading man who lost everything."

He looked around the room. "I had bought this place a few years before this happened. It was always my sanctuary when that world became too much. I severed ties with my agent and came here. Disappeared from the world I had known. I made a different life—a new one. No cameras or fame. No one using me anymore for what I could do for them." He sighed, the sound forlorn. "I've forgiven myself as much as I ever will, Megan. I even had some counseling. I still live with what I did, though. I think there are some things a person can't ever really recover from. I thought maybe being alone was part of the penance I had to pay for the person I had been."

Tears poured down my face at his words. He was so broken and used, yet in the face of all the ugliness of the story he told, he was still beautiful to me. He had lost everything. Lost himself in a world where the only thing he was taught, that defined him, was taken away. He struggled to find the real Zachary and he did it all alone, assuming that was how he had to be, because it was all he knew.

A sob escaped my lips and Zachary looked up, his pain-filled gaze meeting mine. I was shocked to see the tears in his eyes. I had never seen him cry.

"Then I met you," he rasped. "You, with your sweet words and loving soul. You didn't care about my scars or my past. You saw me. You saw the pain I put on my canvases and all you wanted was to make it go away, to understand it."

His hands twisted and clawed at the fabric of his pant legs as he bared his soul. "I know you think you forced me, but I had to tell you the truth, even though I knew there was a chance you'd walk away, too. I was a bastard, Megan. I still am in many ways. I always will be.

"But I love you. God help me, I've tried to fight it, to fight you, but I can't. I love you so much it scares me."

I gasped at his words, my heart hammering in my chest.

He loved me?

He lifted his hand, shaking, reaching out to me. "What frightens me even more is how much I need you. I have never *needed* another person in my life. You're like the air I breathe. I can't be without you now, Megan." His voice was beseeching. "I can't."

I fell to my knees in front of him, my arms pulling him close as he buried his face in my neck, his emotions so strong he shook with the force of them.

I held on as tight as I could, his hands clutching at me in his desperation to be closer. "You don't have to be, Zachary—ever. I'm here. I'm staying right here."

18

MEGAN

We were huddled under the blankets, a mass of twisted limbs. Zachary trembled so violently it seemed to take forever to get him upstairs and into bed. His grip on me was tight, as though he was afraid if he loosened his hold, I would disappear.

Given what he told me earlier, I could hardly blame him for thinking that. Everyone in his life, up until now, walked away. Proved to him what he already felt about himself: he wasn't worth sticking with unless he had something to offer.

He still couldn't see the greatest thing he had to offer anyone was himself.

I had no intention of repeating that pattern he had seen over and again. I wasn't sure, though, if I could ever convince him of his own self-worth.

He pressed into me, warmth beginning to return to his body as I held him, stroking my fingers through his hair, up and down his back while my foot ran over his calf, letting him feel me tight against him everywhere. I needed to feel him as much as he needed to feel me.

The shock of hearing his story had been great. His reaction to letting it out, even greater. Watching him cry, elicited a deep need to

156

protect and care for him, causing me to brush my own tears aside. I was sure I witnessed a side of Zachary no one had ever seen: him at his most vulnerable.

He had expressed so many emotions: grief, torment, pain. And then, in the last few seconds of his tortured confession: a declaration of love.

Zachary loved me. He said the words—his need so fierce, desire so great, there was no room left for doubt. His emotional outpouring left me speechless and unable to do anything as he raged in my arms, his tears so thick they soaked my shirt. It was then the tremors took over, and I knew I had to get him upstairs into bed. The day had been one emotional upheaval after another, and he was losing his strength. I struggled under his weight as he leaned into me, grateful when we finally reached the bedroom.

There was no rest, though, not yet. He was still overwrought and needed reassurance; he also wanted to give me as much information as he could. It was as if, now he had opened up the floodgates, he wanted the words out in the open.

"Will you stay with me?"

"Yes," I soothed, running my fingers though his hair.

"Even though you know now what a bastard I am?"

"I don't think you're the same person anymore, Zachary. Do you?"

He lifted his head. "I don't want to be. I try not to be, although I know I fail at times."

"We all fail at times. I don't expect you to be perfect." I paused. "And you shouldn't expect it of yourself."

"I want to be for you."

I shook my head. "I'm not perfect, either. Don't set yourself up to fail. Just be Zachary." I kissed him, my lips soft on his skin. "That's all I need. Just Zachary."

"*Just* Zachary has never been enough for anyone before now."

"It is for me."

"That will take some getting used to."

"I know. I'm not going anywhere."

"Ask me some more questions, Megan. Please. Help me."

I wanted him to rest, but I knew he wouldn't—not until he had purged as many memories as he could. Unsure where to begin, I traced down one of the scars on his face, so much deeper and harder than the others. "I, ah, was wearing a heavy chain as part of my character's wardrobe," he explained to my unasked question. "When they were trying to get to me, I was knocked down and the hot metal got pressed into my skin. It caused the most damage." He hesitated. "Does it feel strange when I kiss you? The way my mouth feels, I mean?"

I thought about it, remembering the first time I had felt the hardness of the scar against my lips, but after that, I stopped thinking about it. "No. It feels like Zachary is kissing me." I moved my mouth with his. "I like when you kiss me."

He looked almost shy when he returned my smile. "I like kissing you."

I drew his head back to my chest, feeling him sinking into me.

"Do you ever go back to England?"

"I haven't for a long time. Not since...I was burned."

"Do you miss your old life?"

"No."

"Nothing? The glamour, the parties?"

"No. It was empty. The life I live here is quiet and secluded, but it has more...meaning, if that makes sense."

"Maybe because you have people here who care about you —friends."

His head lifted. "Friends," he repeated slowly, as if the word was totally foreign to him.

"Don't you consider Jonathon and Ashley friends? Mr. and Mrs. Cooper? I think, if you asked, they would consider you one. Especially Ashley. She's very fond of you."

"I'm not used to being a friend, or having them."

"They care about you, Zachary. Help you. They're all very protective. To me, that means being a friend."

His brow furrowed as he thought about it. I swallowed the painful lump in my throat as he looked at me from under his lashes. There was disbelief in his gaze. "I never thought about it that way," he admitted.

"I know you only see him on rare occasions, but Chris, as well. You do have people who care now." I cupped his face, stroking the skin. "Your life has changed. You need to allow yourself to feel and accept."

He chuckled dryly. "You sound like Doc Webber."

"Who?"

He rolled on his back and nestled me to his side. "After I got here, I hid for a while. Mrs. Cooper was kind enough to deliver groceries to me. She knew who I was since I'd met her several times after I bought the place. They had a sideline business and cared for houses in the area when owners weren't around and I hired them."

"Yes, Karen told me that. That's how I got her key."

"So, she knew of the accident and she was very, ah, respectful. She treated me the same way she did before, which to her credit, was no different than the way she treated anyone. I wasn't a big Hollywood star here. I was simply Zachary."

"You didn't go by Adam?"

"No. This was a place I was just me. No one, not even Ryan, knew about this place."

"I see. Your hideaway."

I felt his lips brush my head. "Exactly."

"So, I was here," he continued, "running low on pain meds, and I knew I should be looked at. I called the town doctor and told him I needed a house call, and it needed to be that day. He told me to go to hell."

"What?"

"I was my, ah, usual, demanding, egotistical self when I called."

159

Well, that would explain a lot. I'd heard his demanding tone on more than one occasion.

"He asked if my legs were broken and when I told him no, he wasn't polite," Zachary chuckled. "He told me when I could address him civilly to call back, or better yet, get my lazy ass down to his office."

I tried not to laugh at the image I had of Zachary's face after being told off by someone. "Oh. What did you do?"

"I hung up and cursed him out. I threw stuff and yelled a lot."

"Did you feel better?"

"Not really. Plus, I had a mess to clean up."

"I see." A small chuckle escaped and Zachary's lips grazed my hair again.

"A couple days later, when I was getting desperate, I called back and asked, *politely*, if I could come see him, after hours. He agreed and I went to see him.

"I was a fucking nervous wreck leaving the house. His practice was out back of his house and I sat in my car for a good ten minutes before I went in." Zachary snorted. "What a cantankerous, grumpy old man he was." His voice became softer. "One of the best things that's ever happened to me."

I captured his hand that was restlessly waving as he spoke and laid it on his chest. "Tell me."

"He was fine. Didn't react to my face or comment on it. He checked me out, agreed I needed more medication and sent me on my way. Or at least let me get to the door, before he asked me if I played chess. I told him yes, and he nodded. That was it. I was almost to my car when he came out and informed me he lived alone and spent his evenings sipping whiskey, wishing he still had a chess partner. He pointed to the side door. It's always open, he'd said. Then he went inside without another word."

"You went back?"

"Eventually."

"He counseled you?"

"Doc didn't believe in fancy shit like counseling. He believed in talking. So we did—sometimes. Sometimes I talked, sometimes he did. Some nights we said nothing and he beat my ass in chess, like he always did. I spent a lot of nights at his kitchen table."

I ached at the sadness in his voice. The way he spoke, I knew Doc wasn't around any longer. "Did he pass away?"

"No. He missed his wife, who had passed away a few years before I got here. His daughter lives in Boston and he missed her, too. She wanted him to retire and come live with her, so he did. He left a couple years ago."

His pain was so evident. I hated the thought he'd been alone for so long. "You miss him."

Zachary's voice was quiet. "As gruff as the old guy was, he helped me. He never told me how I should feel or what I should do. He kind of let me talk until I figured it out myself."

"He was your friend, Zachary."

He thought about it before nodding. "Yes. Yes, he was."

"Did he know? What happened, I mean?"

"It took me almost a year to tell him."

"What did he say?"

"He told me I was right. I was a bastard."

I gaped up at him, but he didn't look upset. "He also told me I needed to let it go and move on. I couldn't change the past, but I could learn from it. He told me I could choose to be different and not be a bastard anymore because I knew better now."

He was quiet for a moment. "I remember one night, he got angry at me. Told me I needed to stop blaming my parents for everything wrong in my life. He agreed they were terrible parents and lousy human beings, but he pointed out the fact that although they started me on the road, I had been the one driving for a while. I made the decisions. And I could have chosen different." He exhaled a deep rush of air. "As usual, he was right and I started accepting the blame for my own actions. God, Megan, the man could make me talk about shit I didn't even realize I was holding in."

"Do you ever think of contacting them? Your parents, I mean?"

He pulled back, his eyes dark. "No. That part of my past is dead. Doc was right in many ways, but I never want to see them again. Ever. The subject is closed."

"All right," I soothed. "I only asked."

His face softened. "That's behind me. That whole part of my life is done. Once you're part of my past, I don't go back. That will never change for me."

"No second chances?"

"No. I don't give second chances."

A chill went through me at his tone: firm, unyielding, cold.

"Don't look so upset, Megan. Even Doc agreed with me on that subject—they'd had more than their share of chances to be decent. Like he said, having a baby doesn't make you a parent. They should never have had children."

"Don't say that. You wouldn't be here. I don't—" My voice caught on the last word. "Don't say that."

He kissed my head. "Sorry."

"Do you ever talk to, um, Doc?"

His voice was gruff. "No. He moved on."

He was denying his feelings—I could tell how much he missed the man. "You should call him. I bet he also misses you."

"No. I'm sure he's busy with his grandkids. I don't want to bother him."

I rolled my eyes at his stubbornness. "He needed to be with his family, Zachary. That doesn't mean he doesn't still care. Sometimes we have to leave the ones we love behind, but it doesn't mean we've forgotten them."

He eyed me warily. "You think he'd, ah, like it if I called?"

"Yes."

He glanced away, but I saw the shimmer of more moisture in his eyes. "Maybe I'll try next week," he mumbled.

I pulled him back to my chest, cradling his head. "I bet he'd like that."

"He said something I didn't really understand until now."

"What?

"He said once I let myself feel something good, it would change me. It would change how I felt about the world." Zachary tugged me closer. "He was right. How I feel about you makes me want to change. You make me feel something I haven't felt—ever."

"Can you tell me?" I whispered.

He lifted his head. "You give me hope, Megan. Hope I can be better. Hope I can be the man you need me to be. Hope I can leave my past behind me and find a happy future—with you.

"I don't know how to love someone. I've never experienced that emotion." He traced my face with his fingers. "Before you I didn't experience many good emotions, but I want to try."

I turned my face, touching my lips into his palm. "I know."

"I'm going to fuck up."

My lips curled into a smile. "I know that, too. We both will."

"Promise me you'll stick with me."

"I will."

He burrowed into my neck, a heavy, weary sigh blowing across my skin.

"Then that's all that matters."

Z achary slept...hard. Wrapped around me, his head burrowed in my shoulder, his weary body and soul slumbered deep into the evening. I couldn't move; when I shifted, he would grimace, moving with me, as if afraid to let me go, even in sleep.

Sleep didn't come for me, though.

His words, his pain, and his final sweet declaration kept running through my mind.

I had grown up knowing I was loved. Safe in the care of my parents, I had what I always felt was a boring, normal life. There were the usual ups and downs of being a child, but there was always love. Hugs when I needed them for comfort or joy, kisses for scraped knees and good report cards. Conversations over dinner and bedtimes with stories—all of those things I took for granted.

Zachary had never experienced any of them. There was nothing normal about his childhood. He grew up thinking his only use, his only purpose in life, was provided by his face. There was no love given by his parents. They denied him the one thing he wanted more than anything, even if he couldn't admit it then or now: love.

With slow, gentle motions, I ran my hand through his hair, lifting it away from his face. His face was pale with the emotion of the day, his rough skin and the jagged ridges of his marks standing out in vivid detail. I couldn't imagine the pain he had endured, or the sense of loss he had felt when he woke after the incident, knowing his entire world had changed.

The guilt, the pain, and the sadness he had carried all these years had made him bitter. He was right; he would never be what would be considered normal. He had experienced too much loss and rejection in his life. He was always poised for flight, ready to walk away and shut off his feelings rather than risk being hurt again. I ached for the loneliness and isolation he had felt his entire life. What most people would consider a gift—his striking good looks—had been nothing but a curse to him. They were, he felt, what defined him. Then when they were taken away he was proven right. His entire world disappeared.

Panic fluttered, building as I studied his face. I wanted to help him. I wanted to prove to him the world wasn't all bad. If he could accept there were people who actually cared for him, not for what he could do for them, I knew he would find his way, but he had to learn to trust. Somehow I had to teach him to trust.

Could I be enough for him? Could he accept me as a person who made mistakes and not the perfect image he seemed to have of me?

Was there something I could do that he could not forgive? That part of his world was so black and white; could I ever get him to see gray?

I loved him so much already. The image of him walking away caused a low, throbbing pain to lance in my chest. Closing my eyes, I concentrated on my breathing—deep, slow lungfuls of air until my pulse calmed and the pain lessened.

Then I remembered his words. He needed me. He reached out for the first time in his life to another person: to me.

I needed patience. We would take it one step at a time. Together.

Zachary shifted, muttering in his sleep, holding me closer. "Megan...love you—" He relaxed, deep into sleep again, his face peaceful, all the stress and tension he carried erased.

For a brief second, I wondered what he would be like if his childhood had been different. If his parents had shown him love. If he hadn't been used and become bitter. His handsome face not marred and his smiles easily offered. I wanted to be able to go back in time and find the child he had been; keep him safe from all he had faced and protect him from the pain.

But that was something I couldn't do; all I could do was show him life was worth living and that he was, now, loved.

I could also protect him—and I would.

19

MEGAN

"Stop that."

I glanced up, distracted with my thoughts. "What?"

Zachary smiled at me, pulling my hand down. "Tugging at your ear."

"Oh." I hadn't even realized I'd been doing it again.

He reclined back in his chair, sipping his coffee, regarding me with a smile. "You do that when you're thinking—usually when you're thinking too hard about something. Want to fill me in on what's going on in that pretty head of yours this morning? You've been rather quiet since we got up." He paused, frowning. "Was yesterday too much, Megan? Have I given you second thoughts about me?" His voice caught. "About us?"

I shook my head furiously. "No."

"What is it then? Tell me."

I looked past him to the window. The storm was gone; the sky blue and the sun glimmering on the water that lapped along the shore in long, lazy waves. The dogs had already been out scampering around the sand, happy the oppressive air had dissipated. Zachary had slept most of the night, exhausted from his emotional outpouring.

I had held him, only dozing, ever vigilant to his movements and quiet mutterings when he would stir and tighten his grip, as if needing to know I was still there.

I smiled at him, clasping his hand that was stretched toward me on the table. "I'm a little tired. That's all."

"Megan."

"I'm fine, Zachary."

I couldn't tell him why I had been unable to sleep. Images kept flashing though my mind of what happened to him. The thoughts of his skin burning, of the pain he endured, tore at my heart all night. Thinking about how alone he had been his entire life caused tears to soak into the pillow as I cried in silence for his loneliness. The fear I wasn't what he needed, I couldn't be strong enough to help him, or that the love I felt for him wouldn't be enough, made my chest ache in suppressed worry.

"You're exhausted. Did you sleep at all?"

"Not much," I admitted.

"Why don't you go back to bed, while I go into town? Ashley let me know some things I ordered arrived, so I'm going to pick them up."

"I'm fine. I need to do a few things myself."

"Like?"

"Check emails, laundry, tidy Karen's place." I gave him a knowing look. "The guest room is rather...messy."

I was surprised to see the tips of his ears turn red as he nodded. "I imagine there are also a few dried up puddles..."

I couldn't stop the giggle that broke from my lips, as I remembered the path of chaos we left behind. "I imagine so."

"I feel like I should help you, since I was the cause of all the mess."

I waved him off. "No. I can do it in between laundry and emails. Bring something for dinner and we'll call it even."

He winked. "I'll even cook it."

"Done."

"Okay, so I'll go into town, you do what you have to and we'll meet back here later? Anything else you need?"

I shook my head. "Only you."

His mouth and voice were warm as his lips lingered on mine. "You have me."

I smiled as I watched him rinse out his mug and disappear to get ready. The last part of our conversation felt so normal. Planning our day, discussing dinner—knowing we'd be back together in a few hours.

I wanted to be normal for him. I wanted him to know what that felt like.

When he reappeared a few minutes later, he looked apprehensive. "What about the dogs?"

"I'll take them with me."

"Okay." He hesitated, his voice a little more anxious, his keys jingling as he played with them. "You'll be here when I get back?"

"If not, I'm only down the beach. You can come find me." I met his gaze. "I'll be waiting."

His chest heaved as he let out a long rush of air. "Okay."

"Okay."

I groaned in frustration at the number of emails from Jared. I was sure they were full of staged, empty pleas and more veiled threats about me withdrawing my claim that his work was in any way connected to me. I had changed my cell number a few days prior to leaving Boston, so his emails had become more frequent, and more bothersome. My head sunk to my chest, too heavy to hold up anymore. I had to do something and end this situation...for good. I couldn't fight him without a huge cost I couldn't afford, though. Especially, given the fact that through my own inane behavior, I had basically handed him the book on a platter and left myself with nothing to prove it was mine. The only choice, then, was to walk away.

I paced the room, my mind racing. Two years I had spent writing that story. Was I ready to give it up and let him have it? Knowing it would be published under another name and allow that scumbag to take credit for my work? The thought made my hands clench and my stomach churn.

Karen and Chris had offered me the money to fight this battle, but I couldn't take it knowing the chances of me winning were slim to none. My parents were still off on their trip of a lifetime and had no idea what had happened. They had saved and scrimped all their life for this vacation and there was no way I was asking them to help. I knew, without a doubt, they would head home and help me in any way possible, but I refused to ask them. As much as I missed them, I wanted them to enjoy their well-deserved trip.

Which brought me to Zachary. I could ask him, even for a loan. I had no doubt he would give me the money. Standing at the window, I looked over the water that shone in the sunlight. I thought of what fighting Jared would entail: lawyers, court, investigations. I would have to go back to Boston for an undetermined amount of time and leave Zachary behind. Our relationship might come to light. His privacy would be invaded. The one thing he protected—above all else —the one thing that brought him some comfort in this world.

I couldn't do that to him.

I could write another book, but I couldn't replace Zachary. I wouldn't risk losing him.

I caught a glimpse of my reflection in the window and smiled as I lowered my hand. I was tugging on my ear again. I knew if he was here, he'd shake his head at me.

I sat back down at my computer, my decision made, and sent off an email to Bill. I added all of Jared's emails into the file I had and quickly went through the others that were waiting. I read my mother's long and newsy one, telling me all about their adventures in Europe. I answered it, filling the page with silly bits about Dixie and being at the beach, knowing she wouldn't see it until they were back at some hotel on a break. They thought I was staying here to help

Karen and do some more writing. They had no idea the real reason I was hiding out in Cliff's Edge. Luckily, they were far away enough the story wouldn't reach them. When they were home, a few months from now, I would tell them, but right now I remained quiet.

Using the house phone, I called Karen, but got her voice mail. I assured her I was fine and we would speak soon. I told her the ever-present storms seemed to have moved from the area, my head was clear and all was well. I hung up, hoping that would set her mind at ease.

I worked around the house, tidying. I mopped up the puddle marks, remade the bed, and pitched out the food that had gone bad since I'd been staying with Zachary. I was changing the laundry over when I heard the excited barks of the dogs and the door opening. I listened to Zachary greeting the dogs, the deep timbre of his voice filling the house. There was so much affection in his tone as he spoke, a gentleness he probably had no idea was even there, that permeated his voice when he spoke to them. It was also present when he spoke to me.

Stepping into the living area, I smiled at the three of them. Zachary was on his knees, both Dixie and Elliott soaking up the attention as he stroked and talked to them. He glanced up, the warm look in his eyes causing my throat to tighten as we stared. He stood, placing a large bag on the sofa, then slipped his hand around my neck, bringing my face close to his. His breath, sweet and minty washed over my face as he lowered his mouth to mine. "Hello."

"Hi," I whispered.

His lips were gentle as they brushed over mine. His fingers tangled in my hair, holding me close as we kissed. It was soft and light; a greeting that said *I missed you—I'm happy you're here.* Drawing back, his lips grazed my forehead. "Almost done?"

"I still have the last load of laundry to finish. Did you get all your errands accomplished?"

He nodded, his grin actually reaching his eyes, lighting them a bright blue. "Yep. Dinner and everything." He paused, the grin fading. "I was going to get you some soup—from that café you like." He swallowed, as his fingers moved faster on my neck. "I tried, Megan. I parked in front of the café and I looked in the window. I even shut off the engine." His eyes glanced everywhere except at me. "But I couldn't go in."

The sadness in his voice pierced my heart. He tried—for me.

"Hey," I called softly. I waited until his eyes, now serious, met mine. "You tried, Zachary. That's amazing. Maybe next time we can try again, together, yes? Or maybe start smaller—like a walk in the park." I cupped his cheek, stroking his scars as tenderly as I could, letting him relax into my touch. "Thank you for doing that."

"But I failed."

"You tried. That's all that matters. You tried for me. You didn't fail. I love you for doing that."

He clasped me into his arms, holding me close. "I love you," he murmured.

I held him tight, pure happiness radiating through me at his words. "I love you, too."

"Why don't you take the dogs and head back. I'll be there in a while."

"I'd rather wait for you."

"Okay. It's so beautiful out—how about we let them run on the beach while this last load is going?"

He nodded and we headed toward the door. I picked up my jacket, lifting the bag Zachary had left on the sofa, surprised at how heavy it was. "What's this?"

He stopped, staring at the bag. He took it from my hands without a word. Twice he opened his mouth, but nothing came out. I noticed the tips of his ears turn a deep red again—a sure sign of embarrassment for him. What was in the bag that would cause such a reaction?

"Some new books, Zachary?" I asked, trying to get him to explain.

"Sort of," he mumbled, his ears darkening further.

Now I was really intrigued. If he didn't want me to see them, why did he bring them in? I poked him in the side, my tone teasing. "Were you just putting on a front with the whole 'suspense-thriller sort of guy thing'? Did you order some of my romance books online?"

His eyes snapped up as he shook his head furiously side to side. He shoved the bag at my chest. "It's for you."

"What?"

"I bought them for you."

My smile faded. "You bought me a gift?"

His lips thinned, and he started talking so fast, the words were running together. "I saw them. Ashley had them. She just got them in. They were pretty. I mean nice. Well, she said pretty. I thought maybe you could use them. Maybe if the words found you again, you'd want a place to put them. So I bought them. For you. Yeah. A gift." He paused. "I've never bought anyone a gift—ever." He looked at the bag again, pulling it back a little. "Should I have wrapped them? Ashley offered, but I said no. It wasn't your birthday so I didn't think I should. Was that wrong? *Fuck*. Maybe it is your birthday? I don't even fucking know that." His eyes widened in panic. "Is it your birthday, Megan?"

I gaped at him a little over his unusual rambling as I began to understand. He bought me a gift—something he'd never done, and now he was nervous about giving it to me—beyond nervous. It was the sweetest, most touching thing I'd ever seen. I blinked at the moisture in my eyes as I pried the bag from his hands. "No it's not my birthday, Zachary. It's in June."

"Okay, then." He pushed the bag at me. "I hope you like them."

"I will."

"You haven't looked yet."

"You bought them for me so I'll love them, whatever they are." I leaned closer, kissing his cheek. "Thank you."

His smile was shy and his ears got redder. Reaching up, I ran my finger over the inflamed skin. "I'm not the only one with ear issues," I teased. "I never saw this until I cut your hair."

He swatted my hand away, but he was still smiling. "Open your gift," he commanded.

I sat down and lifted the heavy items out of the bag, gasping in delight.

Journals.

Thick, embossed leather-bound journals, all encased in a heavy black box. Five in total, all different colors: forest green, rich, deep red, a warm, golden yellow, the richest blue and a vivid purple completed the set. The paper was heavy and rich under my fingers, lightly lined, with an intricate border on each page. A lovely, matching satin ribbon bookmark edged in pewter was attached to each of them. I stared, speechless, at the thoughtful, decadent gift. Zachary was trying to give me back the gift of writing. A place to put my words if they came back. He knew the computer wasn't what I needed. These lovely journals were.

I lifted my eyes to his anxious gaze. My damaged, beautiful, scarred, worried man. A man, who felt he had nothing to offer another person, yet with one caring gesture, proved he had everything to give and more.

Reaching in his shirt pocket, he pulled out a package, his hand shaking with nerves. "Ashley said these pens were very good, and you'd like the way they wrote on that paper." He nodded to the journals and cleared his throat. "If, ah, you don't like them you can exchange them for something else."

I shook my head, letting the tears fall. "They're perfect."

"Yeah?"

"They're the most perfect gift I've ever received."

Zachary shook his head, his fingers wiping away the tears. "Don't cry, Megan." He sighed. "I hate it when you cry. It makes me feel...strange."

"Strange?"

"Your feelings make me feel odd. I'm not used to feeling anything for another person. For caring how they feel about something."

I wrapped my hand around his. "It's called love, Zachary. When you love someone you feel their pain and joy. You become part of it—of them."

"I only want you happy."

"I am."

"But you're crying."

I sat the heavy books on the table and cupped his face. "Your gift touched me. I love it. I love you."

He yanked me flush to him, his mouth hard on mine. Winding my hands into his hair I dragged him closer, my passion matching his. He pressed me back, my body falling onto the sofa with him on top, a mass of entwined limbs and pressing lips. I was on fire for him, arching into his warmth, wanting closer. Zachary's hands slipped under my shirt, caressing my back, moving and stroking, making me moan with want for him. Everything faded away except his nearness. I needed to feel more of him, be closer, taste him more.

Until a voice startled us both.

"Whose truck is that in the driveway, Megan?" The voice turned horrified. "What the hell is going on?"

The dogs were running around barking, as Zachary flung himself away from me. I stared up in shock at Karen.

"What are you doing here?"

Glaring at me, she tossed her hair, crossing her arms over her chest in a gesture I knew meant she was pissed. "*You* were supposed to call and let me know you were okay. That was two days ago, Megan. *Two days!* I was so worried, I drove up here to check on you! I expected to find you sick, not locking lips"—she flicked her hand toward Zachary—"with him!"

I stood up, my stance echoing hers. "Be polite."

"Oh, sorry." Her voice dripped with sarcasm. "Hello, Zachary. How *nice* to see you again."

He grunted out a curse and I shot him a look of annoyance. He wasn't helping the situation. I smoothed down my shirt, grateful the house was tidy, given Karen's sudden appearance. "My cell died and I forgot to charge it. I'm sorry you were worried. I did leave you a voice mail a while ago, but I guess you were already on the way."

"Not soon enough, it would seem."

Zachary stepped forward, his hands fisted at his sides. "What does that mean?"

I laid a hand on his chest, stopping him. "I need to talk to Karen for a while. I think you were going to take the dogs home?" I suggested with a raise of my eyebrows.

For a moment, he stared at me as my eyes beseeched him to cooperate.

"Yeah," he huffed. He glanced at Karen. "And make us dinner."

Her eyebrows shot up even higher.

"I'll walk you to your SUV." I looked at Karen and pointed to the floor mouthing, "Stay here," at her. Her face said it all—we'd be talking as soon as I was back in the house.

Zachary loaded up the dogs, shutting the door with far more force than necessary. "Come with me."

I wrapped my arms around his waist, pressing into his chest. "She drove for miles to see me and make sure I was all right. I have to stay and talk to her."

"She'll try and convince you not to come to me."

"I won't listen."

"She doesn't like me," he mumbled, sounding like a petulant child. "She thinks I'm rude."

I started to giggle. Tilting my head back, I grinned up at him. "You are—at least with her."

"She is with me, too," he pointed out, with a small smile tugging on his mouth.

"Well, the two of you need to get over it."

"Get over it?"

"I love you both. You have to learn to coexist."

I heard the back door open and I resisted the urge to roll my eyes, as Zachary's gaze shot daggers her way. I could only imagine the looks she was shooting back.

His face softened as he looked back at me. "Only for you."

I pulled his head down and kissed him. "I'll be over soon."

His gaze flickered to her again. His voice was worried. "Promise?"

My hands tightened on his face. "Yes."

He tucked his cell phone into my hand. "I'll find yours and charge it. Call me if you need me and when you're coming over. We'll meet you on the beach."

"Okay. "

He climbed into his SUV, still looking worried, and I tapped on the window, leaning in. "Thank you again for the journals. I love them."

His face relaxed a little and he tugged me to his mouth, kissing me, hard and fast, with so much passion I was breathless.

"I love you," he murmured against my lips.

With one last glare thrown at Karen, he drove away.

We shared a look before she turned and went inside.

I squared my shoulders, and followed her, preparing for another heavy conversation.

20

MEGAN

When I entered the house, Karen was busy making coffee, our usual beverage when we talked. I grabbed the mugs and cream, then sat down at the table and waited for her. She was quiet as she brought over the coffee; the only sound in the kitchen was the clinking of metal hitting the side of the mugs as we stirred in our cream and sugar.

Taking in a deep breath, I met her eyes over the rim of my mug, preparing myself for her ire. Instead, a deep sadness met my gaze as she spoke. "Were you even going to tell me, Megan?"

I set my mug down and reached for her hand. "Of course I was!"

"How?" she asked quietly. "How on earth did you meet Zachary and become—?" She paused. "I don't even know what you are. Lovers?"

I sighed. "We're together, Karen. I love him."

"You love him?" She gaped at me. "I don't understand. You've only been here a short time. How did you even meet him? Get close to him? I've been coming here for three years, and I've only seen him a few times." She shook her head. "And the few unfortunate times we've been in each other's company, hasn't been pleasant."

"He mentioned that to me."

"You talked about that?"

"We talk about a lot of things."

She took a drink of her coffee, her nails tapping the porcelain impatiently. "Chris likes him. He says he's a smart man. Lonely. They play chess sometimes."

"I know."

Her eyes narrowed. "What else do you know, Megan?"

I rolled my eyes. "We're still pretty new, Karen. So just like any other couple, we're still discovering each other. I know about his past, he knows about mine."

"He knows about Jared?"

I nodded, grimacing. I hated hearing his name. "I told him."

"How did you meet?"

I filled our cups and stood up, restless. Walking around the room, my gaze automatically went to the beach. "Out there," I pointed. "He was out with Elliott, who had made friends with Dixie the day before. I introduced myself."

"I bet he was his usual charming self," she stated dryly.

I shrugged. "It's a defense mechanism."

"It works."

I turned and faced her, my hand tightening on the handle of my mug. "He uses it to keep people away. You're as rude to him as he is to you. Stop judging him, Karen, or I'll stop talking."

My tone seemed to surprise her. She stared at me and held out her hand. "I'm sorry. He rubs me the wrong way for some reason, and frankly, today has been a bit of a shock to say the least."

I sat back down, squeezing her hand. "All of this has been a shock to me."

"Can you tell me?"

For the next hour, I talked. She listened, frowned on occasion, or muttered a profane name about Zachary under her breath, but she didn't interrupt. I was honest and told her everything, until I got to his past. That was his story and I wasn't comfortable sharing his history with her. I trusted her, but it still wasn't my story to tell.

"Chris has a couple of Zachary's paintings in his office. He says they remind him of this place and help him relax on bad days."

"They would. He captures the feelings so vividly on canvas."

"He isn't very good at expressing feelings to people."

"Not yet," I agreed, feeling the sad tug at my heart. "He's getting better at being verbal. I love his paintings—he's very talented."

She nodded. "I'll give him that, he is. Not my style, but they are good."

I chuckled. "Don't knock yourself out with the praise."

"Sorry." She looked away, then bent closer. "Did he tell you what happened? How he got those scars?"

"Yes."

"Was it an accident?"

I paused, shaking my head. "No."

"But you won't tell me."

"I can't."

She nodded. "Maybe one day?"

"Maybe."

"It's a shame. He'd be a handsome man without them."

"He's a handsome man with them!" I slammed my hand on the table. "His scars don't define him! His face isn't the reason I fell in love with him, damn it!"

Her eyes widened. "I was only saying—"

"You were only saying what everyone else thinks, I know! Poor Zachary; too bad about his face. He isn't poor Zachary! He's just Zachary!" Then I burst into tears. Long, deep sobs that ripped from my chest. Tears I didn't even know I was holding in, as words poured from my mouth.

"You don't know," I sobbed. "You don't know what he's been through. How much hurt and pain...all his life...so much..."

Karen's arms wrapped around me, her voice soothing as she

stroked my back. "I'm sorry Megan," she crooned. "Let it out. Let it all out."

I sobbed on her shoulder, incoherent words and thoughts escaping between the gasps and cries. I told her how much I loved him, how alone he was, that I knew how much he needed me and I, him. I cried for his pain and what he'd gone through. I cried because I was so afraid of what the future held for us.

When the tears finally stopped, I sat back, dropping my head into my hands. "I love him so much," I muttered, my voice thick. "So much it scares me."

Karen's hands covered mine, removing them from my face. "I've never seen you like this, my dear friend."

"I've never felt like this—ever." I drew in a shaky breath. "I need you, Karen. I need you to be my friend and support me. I feel so lost."

She stood up, bringing me with her. "I'm right here, Megan. Now go wash your face, and we'll talk some more."

I emerged from the bathroom, my face refreshed and feeling calmer. Karen was sitting on the sofa, a bottle of wine open and waiting. "Done with the coffee?" I teased.

"I thought we needed something stronger." She smirked, handing me a glass.

I took a sip, enjoying the deep flavor of the Merlot.

"What's next?" Karen asked quietly. "What are your plans?"

"I've been thinking about that, actually."

"Jared came to the salon," she blurted out.

I sat up so fast, my wine splashed over the edge of the glass. My hands started to shake. "What?"

"He wanted to know where you were. He went by your apartment and your landlord told him you hadn't been there for a while. He told me you weren't answering his emails and you changed your cell number."

"You didn't—?"

"Of course not! I told him to fuck off. Well, first I told him what a weasel he was, then I might've accidentally tripped, spilling the hair color I was applying all over his expensive pants." She shrugged. "But, you know, that's the danger of coming into a salon wearing clothes like that."

I started to laugh, imagining the look of horror etched on his arrogant face. How I ever thought he was attractive, I didn't know. "I'm sorry he bothered you."

"He's getting desperate."

"I know."

"Stop tugging your ear. It's not your fault."

I dropped my hand. "I emailed Bill to set up a meeting."

"To what end?"

"I can't fight him, but I'm *not* taking his payoff."

"His publishers won't go ahead with this hanging over the book."

"I'm aware."

"He'll be so angry."

"I know," I admitted. "I was hoping, maybe, you'd let me stay on here for a while?"

"Of course," she agreed immediately. "You may have to share the place with Chris soon, but you're welcome to stay here for as long as you want." She gave me a mischievous smile. "Unless, of course, you move up to the big house."

I blushed a little under her gaze. I was thinking Zachary might ask me to stay with him eventually.

"Are you coming back, then—for the meeting?"

"I was hoping to let Bill handle it."

"You should be there, Megan. Face Jared, tell him what you think of him." Leaning over, she clasped my hand. "Chris and I will give you the money to fight this mess. You know we will. Bill will help you to find the right lawyer."

"I have nothing to fight *with*. He has everything. Even my file of changes I thought I wanted to make." I shook my head. "It's my word

181

against his. There are parts I wrote so long ago, I don't know if I'd remember them. He'd be able to quote it all if needed. He has it all, Karen. I handed it all to him like a blind fool."

"You trusted him."

"Big mistake."

"A mistake you've paid for dearly." Her shrewd eyes regarded me. "Is the money the only thing holding you back?"

"No. The thought of a trial and what he would say and do bothers me. What might come out about, ah, what's happening in my life now. I can't risk it."

"You're worried about Zachary?"

"His privacy is important. I can't risk exposing him."

"Have you told him he's part of the reason you're not going to fight?"

"No. Don't try and change my mind, Karen. I'd pretty much decided this before Zachary came into the picture. Now I'm sure." I hesitated. "But maybe you're right. I should come back and face him, end it once and for all. Leave him to deal with his publishers. I won't fight him, but I'm not going to make it easy on him either.

"I want to put this behind me and start fresh. I have a different life to lead now, I think." I smiled as I looked at the journals on the table. I had already shown them to Karen. "Maybe I'll try writing again."

Karen smiled. "It *is* a thoughtful gift."

I nodded, encouraging her small allowance toward Zachary. "It is. He is thoughtful—and sweet. He only has to warm up to you."

She laughed. "I'm not sure we'll ever warm up to each other."

Zachary's phone buzzed in my pocket and I read the screen, chuckling at the fact he was using my cellphone.

Is she leaving soon?

Smiling, I replied.

I don't think so.

I could almost hear the resignation in his answer.

Would you like to ask your friend if she wants to join us for dinner?

I grinned as I typed.

Can you handle that?

His response was swift.

At least that way I get to see you again. I'll be polite.

I looked up at Karen. "Now's your chance to find out. Zachary wants to know if you'd like to join us for dinner. He promises to be polite." I left out the other comments.

"Well, this I have to see for myself," she snorted.

She's looking forward to it. I typed, trying not to laugh. I knew he would read that and roll his eyes. Somehow I knew I would spend the evening refereeing the two of them.

"I'm leaving early tomorrow. Do you want to come back with me?"

I shook my head. "No. I'll come in the next day or so. I have to do a few things here, then I'll drive myself in."

"Okay. Maybe you should stay at our place so Jared can't get to you. Our building has great security."

"Good idea. I'll go to my place and get some things. Tidy it up, since I left in such a hurry."

Karen stood up. "Okay. I'm going to shower and get ready for this big dinner."

I rolled my eyes. "You have to be polite, too."

183

"I will."

"You better." Picking up our empty glasses, I headed for the kitchen. "I'm going to walk over and help him with dinner. Come over when you're ready?" I called out as I texted Zachary to tell him I was on my way.

I heard her laughing down the hall. "Help with dinner. Yeah. That's a good one. I'll knock before I come in this time."

I was chuckling as I walked onto the deck. My breath caught as I saw Zachary hurrying down his steps to the beach. The dogs were in front of him when they hit the sand. His steps never lagged as he began jogging toward me, and I descended to the beach, my own feet moving faster than normal.

Soon, I was in his arms, held tight to his chest. Warm lips nuzzled the top of my head and I gripped his neck, happy to feel him close to me. I looked up at him, the emotion in his eyes catching me by surprise.

"Hey."

His minty breath washed over me as he touched his mouth to mine in a series of small, light kisses. "Hi," he whispered, relief evident in his voice. "I'm glad to see you."

"Did you think you wouldn't?"

His silence said it all.

I brushed my mouth to his. "I missed you."

"How long 'til we have company?"

"About an hour, knowing Karen."

A surprised gasp left my lips as he swooped me up in his arms and began walking back to his house.

"Good. We have some unfinished thank yous from earlier."

I giggled. "She said she'd knock this time."

"She'll have to—I'm locking the door."

I sighed as I looked down at my plate again. I was beginning to believe Karen was right: they would never warm to each other. I looked between them in frustration. It didn't help that Zachary was about as communicative with her as he had been with me the first day, answering most of her questions with grunts or brief yeses and nos. The fact Karen kept pushing him on things he obviously didn't want to discuss was making him terse.

I threw my napkin down, shoving my plate so hard, my wineglass tipped over. Luckily, it was empty, but the noise drew both their gazes toward me. "Could the two of you try, please? For me?"

Karen's eyebrow rose as I addressed her. "Why don't you ask him about his paintings, or his photography?" I waved my hand around the room. "He took most of these photos." I pointed to the mantle. "That painting? That's the one I saw the day in the gallery before we met." My voice softened as I smiled at Zachary. "I fell in love with him because of that painting."

He ducked his head with a shy grin on his face, his eyes crinkling in the corners. His smile fell when I shook my head at him. "And you. Karen is my best friend. She asks a lot of questions, all the time—it's not only you. You have a voice—a lovely one, in fact. Use it. Answer her—maybe even ask her a few questions. The two of you might be surprised how much you have in common." I stood up, taking my plate. "You both love me, maybe that's a good place to start." Spinning on my heels, I walked into the kitchen, slamming my plate down and grabbing the coffee pot.

"Well, I guess we were told," Zachary's voice drawled from the dining room.

"You are rude," Karen retorted.

"Right back at you, lady. You're exactly like the women I dealt with all my life. Bitchy."

I groaned, my head falling into my hands. They were both impossible.

To my surprise, Karen chuckled. "That's my cover. Owning my

own business, I have to be a bitch at times. And I kind of like being a bad-ass."

There was a pause before Zachary spoke again. "Is it a hard thing, owning your own place?"

I straightened up. That was the first real question Zachary had asked all night.

"At times. Suppliers, landlords, staff, maintenance. There're times I wish I was simply a hair dresser again, and not running the place."

"Megan is a customer of yours?"

"Yes, that's how we met. We got to talking and became friends." She paused. "I love her like a sister."

Zachary was quiet, his voice warmer when he spoke. "I love her, too."

"You better not hurt her."

"I don't want to."

"Then don't. It's that simple. I can't let her be hurt again. That asshole did a number on her."

"I'd be glad to take him to task for that."

"I'd join you."

I heard their wineglasses clink and like an idiot, I clasped my hands together in a silent sign of glee, waiting to see how they proceeded.

"If your customers look half as good as she does when they leave your place, you must be very good at your job."

"I am good."

"Modest as well, I see."

"I call it how I see it."

I rolled my eyes.

At least they were talking.

Karen stretched and stood up from the table. "I'm off very early, so I'm heading home." She glanced at me. "Should I say goodbye now?"

Unsure how to answer, I hesitated. In truth, I knew I should go and stay the night with her since she had driven up here, but I really didn't want to leave Zachary alone.

I was surprised when Zachary spoke up before I could answer. "I'll walk her over later. I'll make sure she gets there safe."

Karen pursed her lips, her voice almost teasing. "What about me, Zachary? Don't you want to make sure I get there safe? Or is Megan the only one you think some sea monster is going to attack?"

Zachary leaned back, a small grin playing on his lips. "I think you could probably handle a sea monster your own bad-ass self, Karen, but if you like, I'm happy to walk you home." Then he smirked at her.

Smirked.

I thought my jaw was going to hit the floor. They sounded almost...friendly.

Karen's eyebrow arched—a look I knew all too well. "You don't think Megan could handle a sea monster?"

Zachary's voice sent shivers through my spine. "She could—but she doesn't have to. That's my job now."

Karen blinked, looked at me, then blinked again.

"Well, then, I guess there's nothing else to say."

She stopped at the door. "Are you sure you won't come back with me tomorrow, Megan? You really have to stay?"

Beside me, Zachary froze. I closed my eyes, inwardly cursing. I hadn't yet talked to him about me going back to Boston. We'd barely managed to get dressed before Karen arrived for dinner.

Slowly, he unfurled himself from the sofa, his voice quiet when he spoke. "Are you certain, Megan? I'm sure whatever is keeping you here can't be that important if you're ready to return to Boston."

I stood up, my heart sinking at his words. He thought I was leaving him. Looking past him, I smiled at Karen, struggling to remain calm. "I'm sure. I'll only be in Boston a few days when I come, and I don't have that meeting set up."

She shrugged, totally oblivious to the turmoil she had caused. "Okay then, thought I'd try. The drive is always nicer with two people." She drew on her sweater. "Thank you for dinner, Zachary."

He moved past me, avoiding my touch. "I'll let the dogs out and watch you to make sure you arrive home safely."

The door closed, shutting off her laughter.

I walked to the kitchen, automatically straightening up, needing to stay busy, my mind racing. His first instinct—his first thought—had been I was leaving. He still couldn't accept he was loved or he came first to someone. He actually thought I would walk away from him.

My head snapped up at the sound of the door opening. When Zachary appeared in the kitchen, I shut the door to the dishwasher and turned to face him. I expected anger and confusion on his face. I expected him to start yelling or to close in on himself, but all I saw was sorrow. His eyes were resigned, his shoulders slumped as we stared at each other.

He was composed—too composed. "You're leaving."

I stepped forward. "Karen shouldn't have said anything."

"She probably thought you told me." There was no doubt I was hearing some hurt in his voice.

"I only decided this afternoon when I spoke with her. I was going to tell you." I smiled, trying to get him to understand. "You, ah, had me pretty busy before she arrived."

A glimmer of a smile appeared on his mouth, but then he shook his head and frowned. "Why, Megan? Why are you going back there?"

I stepped closer until we were almost touching. "I'm not leaving you, Zachary."

He started to speak, but I cut him off.

"I'm not leaving you," I stated clearly. I needed him to understand.

"What are you doing, then?"

"I have to go back and meet with Jared. Then I'll be back. "

His composure disappeared. "What? Why the fuck would you want to do that?"

"I have to put this behind me."

"Fine. I'll give you the money for a lawyer and they can fight it for you. Hire experts to prove he is lying."

"I'm not fighting it. I'm walking away."

"You can't do that. You have other options."

My eyes narrowed. "No, I don't have other options. I can and I am. It's my decision."

"He stole your work."

"Yes, he did, and without me accepting his payout or recanting my story, he might not get it published." I shrugged. "We both lose."

"Fight it! I'll give you the money! I have plenty!"

"I don't want your money!" Weeks of pent up anger exploded, and suddenly I was yelling. "It's a lost cause, Zachary! He has the book—my notes—even my fucking ideas about the cover! He has it all! I worked for him! Slept with him! Do you know how this all looks to people?" I paused, dragging in a deep breath. "His story is airtight! *He* told *me* about the book. *He* showed *me* the chapters. He even managed to show a date line! He's an established, successful author. I'm the ex-girlfriend who's doing this because she's bitter about the breakup and wants to make a name for herself, since she's trying to become a writer." I sat down on the chair in front of him, tired. "There's nothing to fight. It's done." I looked up at him. "I'm only going to finish it. Please understand."

He kneeled in front of me, cupping my face. "I hate the bastard."

"I'm not so fond of him myself. I can't take your money, Zachary."

He nodded in understanding. "I don't want you to go."

I wrapped my hand around his, stroking the hardened flesh tenderly. "I have to. I'll only be gone a few days."

"You'll come back?"

I nodded. "I'll bring a few more things with me."

"Megan"—he hesitated—"does your decision not to fight this have anything to do with me?"

I closed my eyes and nodded. "I'd already made up my mind for the most part, but it factored into my final decision. I won't risk your privacy."

His fast intake of air and the way his hands tightened on my skin made me open my eyes. "I hate you're giving up because of me."

"I'm not giving up. I'm moving on. Don't ask me to change my mind, and don't be angry with me, please."

"Anger isn't what I'm feeling right now."

I searched his face. "What is?"

His mouth hovered over mine. "Love. Only love, Megan."

21

MEGAN

I inhaled the clean ocean air. I would miss the smell, even if it was only for a few days. My small bag was packed and I was ready to go, even though I really didn't want to. I wanted to let Bill handle it, tell Jared I refused his "generous" offer, and stay here with Zachary.

I had to confront him myself, though. I wanted to see the look on his face when he realized he wasn't getting his way, and I wouldn't be bullied. I didn't care what happened with the book now—if it got published or not was irrelevant at this point. I was going to move ahead, in Cliff's Edge with Zachary. Together, we'd find our own path and when I was ready, I would try writing again. More than once, Zachary had hinted at me staying close to him. He had reminded me Ashley hired staff in the busy summer months at the gallery and the hours were flexible, which would leave lots of writing time. Karen told me I could stay here at her beach house as long as I needed. My lease was up on my apartment in the fall, and the thought of living here was a far more pleasant one than staying on in Boston. It would be a fresh start. Dixie loved it here, too.

Her excited little bark made me turn my head to see Zachary and Elliott coming toward us. Dixie turned in frantic little circles of excitement as they came closer. I giggled as I realized, if I could, I would do the same thing when I saw Zachary. He was almost larger than life, striding toward me, his overcoat billowing out behind him, stretched taut across his broad shoulders. My stomach did strange little flip flops every time I saw him. The longing to feel his arms around me grew with every step he took closer, and a small sigh of pent up emotion escaped my lips when I was wrapped up in his embrace.

"Ready to go?" he asked, his voice rough.

I tightened my arms around his waist. "It's only a few days. I'll come back as quick as I can."

"I know." His lips nuzzled my hair. "You're sure about Dixie?"

I tilted my head back. "Yes. I'm staying at Karen's and I'll be busy. If she's here with you, she'll be happier and I won't worry."

"And you'll come back."

I tamped down my frustration at his words. He still couldn't accept I'd come back anyway. I reminded myself he needed time. The longer I was with him, the more comfortable he would become, and he would accept this was real. We were real. I kept my voice patient. "I *am* coming back, Zachary. Even if I took Dixie with me, I'd come back. I'm coming back for you. For us."

His mouth covered mine, his kiss hard and desperate. He surrounded me, molding my body to his as he wrapped us both in his coat, seeking the reassurance my touch would give him. Slowly, the kiss morphed into a tender, gentle one of farewell, and he released me with a quiet exhale of air.

"I'll walk you to your car."

I swallowed back the unexpected sting of tears. I didn't want to leave either.

"Hey."

I looked up at him, his expression one of surprise. "Don't cry, Megan." He wiped away a small tear under my eye. "I'll be right here, waiting. Hurry back to me."

I wanted to ask him to come with me, but I knew that wasn't possible. So, I nodded and forced a smile. "I know."

We were quiet as I slid into the car. Zachary kneeled beside the open door. "Drive safe. Call me when you get there."

"I will."

He dropped a kiss to my forehead, his lips lingering, his expression forlorn. "I'll miss you."

He shut my door, and without a backward glance, walked away. I knew he was fighting his emotions, and all his doubts were messing with his head. He still didn't believe he mattered enough. I wasn't sure he even understood what that meant. So accustomed to rejection and being used, his insecurities crippled him. The cold, indifferent face he showed to the world was a far cry from the unsure, caring soul he kept hidden.

I knew I had to be patient. I hoped with time he would realize it. Once enough time passed and his trust grew, he would know how much he meant to me. His first instinct wouldn't be one of distrust and worry, but rather the assurance that came with the acceptance of love. My love for him. One day we'd get there—together.

His tormented, worried eyes haunted me the whole drive back to the city.

I wished for Zachary's presence beside me as I faced Jared in the boardroom at his lawyer's office. Both Bill and I would have preferred the meeting elsewhere, but in the end, we had agreed to meet here. I hardly slept last night and hadn't been able to even look at breakfast, my stomach was so tied in knots. We were kept waiting, which only increased my anxiety, and more than once, I realized I was tugging on my ears, trying to remain calm. I caught my reflection in the mirrored tile on one wall and grimaced at how bright pink the right lobe had become.

Jared's arrogant stance and nasty attitude were even more

obvious than the last time I had seen him as he strode into the room, a smug look on his face. He was sure I was coming to sign his offer and disappear, so he could move ahead with his plans. When Bill informed him I would not be accepting the deal and refused to withdraw my claims the book was mine, he became angrier, addressing me directly, even as his lawyer tried to override him.

"Take the damn money and sign, Megan," Jared hissed through clenched teeth.

"No." I shook my head, refusing to back down or show him fear. "I'm not taking your payout. I can't fight you, but I'm not going to let you take my work."

"It's mine. We both know that!"

"It doesn't matter how often you say it. It will never be the truth. I'm not signing."

He slammed his hand down on the table, the water jug and glasses shaking with the force of his action. An ugly sneer marred his face—the face I now knew to be his real one. What I ever saw in him, I couldn't remember now. "Your inane declarations are tiresome. My publishers don't like any of this bullshit. They may not publish the book with this hanging over it."

"Good. It's not your book to publish."

His eyes narrowed. "It is."

I glared back at him. "Well, we're never going to agree on that fact."

"I want my book published."

"Then finish writing your *other* book, Jared. You can't have mine. I don't want your money."

He glared at me. "What do you want, then?"

"For you to give me my book back."

He shook his head, contemplating me with a knowing jeer. "I can quote ninety percent of this book to you right now, Megan. Can you do that? Since, as you say, it's yours."

"Of course not," I snapped. "I wrote most of it two years ago and you made changes. You can quote it because you memorized the damn thing as you copied it. It proves nothing."

He shook his head again, an evil smirk twisting his lips. "It proves it's mine."

Bill spoke up. "I think we're done here. Ms. Greene isn't signing."

I shook my head as Jared let out a string of muffled curses.

Leaning forward, I scowled at him. "Stop harassing my friends. Leave me alone. I'm moving on with my life."

"Oh?" He snarled. "Anything you want to share?"

I stood up. "No. I made the mistake of sharing with you once. I won't do it again."

Pivoting on my heel, I walked to the door, gasping when Jared's hand closed around my bicep. "You'll regret this, Megan," he warned in my ear. "You're fucking me up and I'm gonna return the favor."

I shook his hand off. "You already did, Jared. Good luck with publishing *my* book."

I walked out of the room quickly, so he couldn't see how hard I was shaking. Bill could finish whatever needed to be done, but I had to get out of there before I lost it totally on Jared. I pushed the elevator button, praying it would come fast. Once I was safely down in the lobby, I sunk into one of the chairs scattered around and waited for Bill.

I didn't feel better having faced Jared. If anything, I felt worse. He was so smug and arrogant. I cursed myself for ever seeing only his handsome face and not seeing the darkness that lurked behind his easy smile.

I longed for Zachary. Even in his anger he was honest. I wanted to hear his voice. I had only spoken to him briefly when I arrived, then again this morning. He didn't like to talk on the phone, and kept our conversations short. He did, however, assure me earlier he missed me and was looking forward to me coming home. I had stared at the phone for a while after he had hung up.

Home.

It was amazing how fast home had become the place where Zachary was. His very presence made me feel safe, and the way he seemed to need me made me feel complete. Here, without him, I felt very empty.

Bill sat down beside me, shaking his head. "It's not over, Megan."

"What now?"

"He may come after you. He's threatening slander or defamation of character, something. He's desperate to discredit you."

Weariness settled over my shoulders. "You think I should sign? Give him my book and let the world think I lied?"

"It's not my field of expertise, but I'll fight this for you," he said, holding up his hand when I started to shake my head. "We've been friends a long time, Megan. I'm not asking for payment. I'd do this as your friend, but it could get ugly, and there's a very good chance we'll lose. It would certainly stop the book from coming out, though."

"I can't let you do that. Your firm—"

"Takes some pro bono cases. I could do this—for you."

"And if I lose, he gets the book anyway."

"It's a risk. We have to see what his next move is." He hesitated. "Can I ask you something?"

I nodded.

"Can you write another book, Megan?"

"Yes."

"As hard as it would be to do, wouldn't the money help you figure out the next step? Give you a break for a while to do that?" His voice became guarded. "Can you recover from this if he chooses to come after you?"

I shut my eyes as I thought about it. I could write another book. I could find a job and move ahead with my life. I could take the money, walk away, and not have to worry how it would affect Zachary. A dull throbbing started behind my eyes and I rubbed my temples, trying to ease the headache that was coming on. "I don't know," I admitted quietly.

"Think about it. We can talk in a couple days. The next move is his, if he decides to come after you."

"I will."

"Are you staying here?"

"No. I'm going back to my place to get a few things, then head to Cliff's Edge tomorrow." The mere thought of getting back there eased some of the tension I was feeling. "I'm anxious to get back to Zachary," I added without thinking.

"Who is Zachary, Megan? Your next mark?" Jared's voice was snide as he spoke from behind me.

Slowly, I stood up, trying hard not to show my panic. How much had he heard? I didn't want him to know anything about Zachary or where I was staying. Internally, I cursed myself for slipping up. I turned to Jared, who was eyeing me closely, a calculating expression on his face. I shrugged nonchalantly, hoping he bought my act. "Not that it's any of your business, but I got a new dog."

His expression didn't change. Desperate to throw him off track, I pulled out my phone. "Want to see a picture?" I asked, knowing full well he had no interest at all in seeing one.

My ruse seemed to work. He sneered at me as he shook his head. "No, thanks." With a nasty grin he turned to leave. "Think about what your lawyer said, and what I said, Megan. I meant it...you know I did."

A long, cold shudder ran through my spine as I watched him walk away.

Karen was perched on the countertop, watching me clean out the refrigerator in my apartment. "I hate to say it, Megan, but maybe Bill is right. If you won't accept the money to fight it, maybe you should walk away."

I threw another container of bad yogurt into the bin. "So he wins."

Her voice was filled with sympathy. "I think he already did."

The expired pasta sauce hit the edge of the garbage bin with more force than I intended. For a second I thought I had overthrown it and I would have to clean up another mess, but then it tipped into the can and I sighed in relief. "I guess he has."

"At least you get some money. Maybe the book will suck and there won't be any sales." At the rather insulted look I threw her, she chuckled. "I meant with the changes he made. Maybe it won't be as good."

"I don't want to take his money. It feels all sorts of wrong."

"Don't think about it. Think about what it means. You don't have to deal with him anymore. You can move forward with your life, and like Bill said, write another book."

I snorted as I tied the top of the bag shut. "Like any publisher would ever touch me with all of this attached to my name."

"Then you self-publish under another name and build up your reputation that way. You can do this, Megan. I know you can."

I adjusted the temperature and shut the door. "Maybe I should just walk away. Withdraw my statement and be done with it."

"I think if you're going to do that, you should take the money." She tilted her head. "At least get some compensation out of it. I bet if Bill went to them and said you'd take the money, they'd word the statement in a positive way."

"Like what?" I shook my head. "That I was mistaken?"

"I'm sure they could figure something out. If Jared got what he wanted, I'm sure he'd be happy to word it, ah, in a kind fashion."

"Yeah." I nodded, sarcasm edging my voice. "He's such a kind person."

"Give him what he wants, he might be. Think about it," she urged.

"I will."

She jumped off the counter. "Okay enough of this shit. No more about Jared or the book. We're going to the salon and you're getting the works: mani, pedi, facial, and I'll trim your hair. Then we'll order in pizza and drink our weight in wine. What time are you going back tomorrow?"

"I have some errands to do, plus an appointment at the bank, then I'll head back. I plan on being there in the early evening."

"Okay. Got your stuff packed?"

"Yep."

"Good." She grinned at me. "I call girls' night officially started."

I couldn't help but return her grin. She was right. I needed a break from everything else.

"Girls' night it is."

I woke up early the next day, my head surprisingly clear, considering how much wine we'd consumed the previous night. Karen and I had sat up late talking, drinking—the way we often had since we met.

A hot shower swept away the last of the cobwebs, and feeling ambitious, I went to the kitchen to make coffee. I moved around quietly, knowing I was the only one up. Chris was away and Karen wasn't going into the salon until late morning. My laptop was taking up counter space and I pushed it aside to fill the coffee pot, frowning when memories of last night's wine-induced idea came back to me.

In a moment of weakness, while I was lamenting missing Zachary, I had typed his professional name into a search engine. I was shocked at the amount of hits that came up, considering he had been such a big star before the age of internet had fully hit. There was a vast amount of information regarding both his personal and professional life. Karen and I had looked at some pictures, agreeing he was incredibly handsome. I was embarrassed to realize I had downloaded some of them. As I studied a couple, I also recognized something else: all the pictures showed his rugged good looks, but if you looked in his eyes, you saw the truth. They stared at the camera, void of any emotion, even ones where he was smiling. Lifeless and cold, his eyes made me shiver and think that perhaps I wouldn't have liked that person very much.

The Zachary I had come to know, who was beginning to open up, to show his feelings, was indeed a different person. What had happened—his past—had changed not only his physical appearance, but also the person inside. I thought about how different he was since we had come together: warmer, gentler. Maybe, I thought with a smile, I had changed him. Maybe the love I had shown him, helped make him that way.

I groaned when I looked at my history and saw not only a large number of pictures, but I had even purchased and downloaded an unauthorized biography on his life. I remembered thinking it was a good idea at the time, and that knowing more about him might help me to understand him better.

Now, with a clear head, I knew if there was something I wanted to know, I should just ask him directly. I wondered how he would respond if I showed him some of the pictures and asked him more questions. Hearing Karen moving around, I opened a new folder and transferred all the pictures and the book into it, labeling it Zachary. I would go through it all later, and delete most of it, once I made the decision about talking to him.

At the exact moment, I needed coffee.

———

Small excited tremors ran through my stomach as I drove into Cliff's Edge mid-afternoon. Thanks to my early start, I had accomplished not only my errands, but also managed to move the bank appointment up, so I was on the road prior to noon. Zachary wasn't expecting me yet, so I was hoping to surprise him. I stopped, grabbed a few things at the store, and even dropped by to say hello to Ashley, telling her how much Karen loved the scarf I had given her. She showed me a couple new pieces Zachary had brought in, and we chatted for a few minutes. Her smile, when she told me she had never seen him look so at ease or happy, made me blush a little. The fact he admitted to her he missed me, made me long to get home even quicker. Before I left, she handed me some tubes of paint he had ordered. Outside, as I was putting them in the trunk, the breeze caught the small order form, lifting it high and swirling away across the parking lot, coming to rest part way across the pavement. I hurried over to grab it, almost reaching it, when it lifted back up, drifting higher and landing on the road. I watched it with pursed lips as it drifted far out of my reach, then decided not to chase after it. If he needed another copy, Ashley would make him one. Right now, my only goal was to get to him.

I pulled up behind Karen's house, and after a few minutes of hesitation, carried my bags inside. I had most of my things here, although it seemed more of my possessions were up at Zachary's daily. Still, I wasn't sure how he'd feel about me arriving at his place with suitcases. Moving quickly, I put away the few groceries, even though I hoped most of them would end up at Zachary's later.

Opening the glass door, I inhaled the fresh air and reveled in the sound of the waves crashing along the shore. My eyes immediately went to the house on the bluff. As usual, I admired the way it nestled on the edge of the forest and overlooked the vast expanse of water in front of it. It appeared deserted, but I knew chances were he'd be in his studio, given the bright light of the day. All the windows were treated with a special film that blocked out the harmful rays, while still allowing light in so he could work and be comfortable. I could picture him in there, surrounded by his canvases, holding his paint palette, lost to the vision in front of him. I loved watching him create, deep in concentration.

I ran down the steps, hurrying across the beach. It felt as if there was an invisible string pulling me to his house—to him. About halfway across, both dogs suddenly appeared at the top of the stairs, barking and running toward me. Falling on my knees, I hugged them both, picking up Dixie to snuggle, her little body quivering with happiness.

I sensed his presence, and looking up, I was met with the vision of Zachary standing at the top of the stairs, watching me. Wearing loose pants and one of his long-sleeved, white linen shirts, his dark hair blowing in the breeze, he looked so good to me. My heart rate picked up as he began moving, taking the stairs two at a time and heading my way, his feet pounding against the hard sand. I stood up, rushing to meet him, images of a romantic lovers' reunion filling my head. He would swoop me in his arms and swing me around, laughing joyfully at my return—of this I was certain.

Until, that was, I tripped, falling head first into his chest and sending us both crashing to the beach, a mass of entwined arms and limbs. "Oops," I muttered, feeling my cheeks darken.

"I thought only steps were your problem."

"No, flat, stable surfaces also present difficulties at times," I mumbled into his chest.

He chuckled, the sound deep in his throat. His long fingers found my chin, lifting my head. Our eyes met and what I saw in them, made me forget my embarrassment. Deep, intense emotion that was lit with blue and green gazed at me, filling me with warmth. Love filled his eyes as he smiled, one long finger running over my cheek. "You're home."

Never had a word felt so beautiful.

I nodded, unable to tear my eyes away from his.

"Early."

"I missed you," I rasped out, my throat thick with unspoken words and feelings.

He dragged me up his chest, his arms encircling me like a vice. Lifting his head, he peppered my face with small, light kisses over my warm skin. "Megan," he murmured, his voice sounding incredulous that I was back with him.

Threading his hand into my hair, he brought my mouth to his, parting my lips and kissing me deeply. I moaned as his taste exploded, filling my senses. Mint, coffee, and Zachary—nothing could be better. His chest rumbled beneath me as he held me close. His lips were soft and pliant, and his hand slipped under my shirt to stroke the skin of my back, causing shudders to run through me. The dull ache that had been present in my chest the past couple days disappeared now that I was in his arms. My entire body came alive against his as he welcomed me back, his mouth commanding mine. He teased and caressed, leaving me panting and breathless when he drew back, tucking me under his chin. A long sigh of pleasure blew across my head as he nuzzled my hair.

"Thank you."

I knew he was thanking me for more than a kiss on the beach. He was thanking me for keeping my word by coming back to him.

"Always," I whispered against his throat.

"I love you."

Now, I was home.

22

MEGAN

"Are you planning on eating that monstrosity, or only drowning it?" Zachary's amused voice interrupted my thoughts.

With a grin, I lifted the bottle of corn syrup, snapping the lid shut and putting it on the table. I'd put on quite a lot. "I'll share," I offered.

He shook his head. "Syrup is for pancakes, Megan. Not ice cream."

"No, maple syrup is for pancakes. Corn syrup is perfect for ice cream. It makes the yumminess-factor even better."

"Yumminess-factor?" he repeated, curiously. "Did they teach you that phrase in writing school?"

I nodded, answering around a mouthful of the sweet treat. "It's a good phrase."

He chuckled and shook his head as I held the spoon out to tempt him. "No, I think I'll pass."

"Please?"

Rolling his eyes, he leaned forward, opening his mouth. I slipped the heaping spoonful inside, his full lips closing around the spoon slowly. I sat back and waited for his approval. He turned the sweet concoction around in his mouth and swallowed. "God, that is wretch-ed." He shuddered. "It's like eating pure sugar."

I grinned, eating another large mouthful. "Nope. Delicious."

He sipped his black coffee. "Whatever. When you go into diabetic shock, don't say I didn't warn you."

"Okay, peppermint boy."

"That's different."

"It's still sugar."

"Sharp sugar."

I arched an eyebrow at him. "Sharp sugar?"

"It's a good phrase. I made it up all by myself."

I started to laugh, Zachary's mouth quirking as he gave in and laughed with me. He placed his hand on my knee and squeezed it affectionately, then picked up his book again, still chuckling.

I loved it when he laughed. It was still something rare, but when it happened, he laughed with his whole body, the sound rich and low. His shoulders shook, his eyes crinkled, and his mouth stretched into the widest smile. His entire appearance changed—the constant lines on his forehead dissolving, the serious expression he always wore morphing into one of playfulness. It made my heart soar knowing, for even the briefest moment, I did that for him.

God, I loved him.

Since coming back from Boston, we'd barely been separated. Even when he was in his studio I was with him. He had piled up some pillows and blankets, making me a little nest in the corner, where I happily curled up and read or napped while he worked. On occasion, I'd hear the click of the camera shutter and open one eye to see him snapping away. He'd grin, ignore my glare and continue shooting until he was happy. Daily walks with the dogs, quiet nights by the fireplace, waking up wrapped around him every morning—the past week had been all about us, and I enjoyed every moment of it with him.

I finished my ice cream and set down the bowl. Although I didn't want to admit it, it was rather sweet, given how much syrup I had poured on. Grinning, I leaned over and took the mug from Zachary's hand and sipped his coffee, shuddering a little at the bitter taste. He liked it strong and black and drank far too much of it. It did help clear away the sweet taste, though, and I giggled a little at the look he gave me for stealing his mug.

He placed his book on the table. "I forgot to look and see if that paint was still back ordered." He looked around. "Where did I put my laptop?"

"I think it's upstairs." My smaller laptop was on the table, so I grabbed it and passed it over to him. "Use mine." I'd been using it earlier when I contacted Bill and told him my decision to accept Jared's offer. As much as I hated to do it, I'd take the money and move on with my life. What I had in Cliff's Edge with Zachary was more important than fighting a battle I knew I was destined to lose. It had been a hard decision to make, but now I had made it, I was at peace with it. I hadn't told Zachary yet; I was waiting for the right moment to bring up the subject.

He smirked at me as he took my laptop. "Are you going to give me back my coffee?"

"No."

He opened my laptop, shaking his head, muttering about thieving women. His long fingers flew over the keys, pausing as he studied the screen with a frown. "Still back ordered."

"Can you get it anywhere else?"

"No, it's a rather exclusive shade. I need to ask Ashley to research it again and see if she can find another source."

Another few clicks of the keyboard and he started to shut the lid. He paused, his face freezing, a frowning glance at me as he started clicking the mouse again. He was silent, his body becoming tense as his shoulders squared and his frown deepened. I stared at him, wondering why he looked so angry. He was glaring at the screen. I sat up, realization of what he was looking at flooding my head. A small tremor shot through my spine, working its way from the pit of my stomach to my throat, tightening the muscles as it worked upward.

"Zachary—"

He spun the laptop my way. "Why do you have a file of me, Megan? Pictures?" He clicked again. "A fucking book on my past?"

I swallowed, the words dying in my throat at the fury on his face.

"Why?" he demanded again. "Why do you have this shit on here?" His eyes narrowed, his face becoming the cold mask I'd seen the first time I met him. "Are you researching me for something?"

"No!" I gasped out. "It's not like that at all, I promise!"

"Then tell me what it *is* like."

"I was drunk with Karen and missing you," I offered, knowing how lame those words sounded.

"And?"

"I googled you, okay?"

He pushed the laptop off his knee, standing up. He towered over me, his anger evident in the set of his shoulders. "Why?"

"I was...curious."

"Why wouldn't you ask me? Why look on the internet or hide the fact you were curious?" His eyes narrowed, filled with suspicion. "What else are you hiding?"

I became angry, as well. How could he think I was lying to him? I wasn't anything like the people from his past. "I'm not hiding anything, Zachary." I waved my hand dismissively at the computer. "If I was, would I leave it in a file with your name on it for you to find, if I was hiding something?"

"You never expected me to look on your computer."

"I gave you my computer! I forgot it was there!" I stood up in my fury. "I was drunk, thinking of you and my curiosity got the better of me! Yes, I looked at some pictures of you when you were younger, before you were scarred. Yes, I downloaded a stupid book about you. I never read it!" I flung out my arms in supplication. "Haven't you ever done something in a moment of weakness?"

His face softened—only by a small degree—but it was enough. I stepped closer to him, lowering my voice. "I was missing you. I meant to delete the files, but I forgot."

He stared at me, his gaze still filled with distrust. I tamped down the hurt I felt over how easily he could doubt me, remembering how fragile his trust still was in people: in me—in us.

"I was being silly. I'll erase it."

His voice was tight. "If you want to know something, ask me."

"I will. I never did it to hurt you."

"I don't like to look at those pictures or remember the person I was back then." He drew in a sharp breath. "I didn't like that person. I might have been good-looking, but inside I was rotting."

"I know."

I edged closer, glad when he didn't back away. "Your eyes were dead in those pictures. You looked so removed in them." I lifted my hand up, the motion slow so he knew what I was doing, and laid it on his cheek. "Your eyes are alive now. They speak to me."

"You brought them to life. You brought me to life, Megan. I can't"—he swallowed—"I can't stand the thought of you being anything but what I think you are: sweet, honest, and real." He shut his eyes as a shudder racked his entire frame. Pain and worry clouded his vision when he opened his lids again. "It would end me if you were lying. Forever."

"I'm not." I stroked his damaged skin gently. "I'm not, Zachary. I love you."

Our gaze locked, and I refused to break the connection. I wanted him to see the honesty. See the love I had for him, and him alone.

His shoulders loosened, his expression softening.

"I'll erase it." I held out my hand. "Give me my laptop."

He shook his head. "I'm being an ass. I hate reminders of my past, and I overreacted." Turning his head, he kissed my palm. "Forgive me."

"At some point, you have to trust me."

"I do."

"Your trust isn't absolute."

"I'm trying."

My chest felt heavy and weariness sunk into my bones. I didn't want him to try anymore. I wanted him to believe. In himself, in me, in us.

I picked up my bowl.

"Megan—"

I didn't turn around. "Try harder."

The fire danced in the grate, the flames twisting and burning, glowing orange, yellow, and red, its heat welcome. I glanced at the door, wondering how long Zachary would be gone. He had told me he was taking Elliott for a walk, and even asked if I wanted to join him, but I said no, and for him to go without me. He hadn't been for a tramp in the woods for a couple days, and I knew he needed a little space to think about what happened. I supposed in some ways, his reaction was to be expected—he'd always assume the worst. I was grateful this time he let me explain, and he didn't walk away, but I hated the fact he was still so mistrustful.

With a small sigh, I picked up my laptop and clicked on the file that upset him. I scanned the pictures and clicked delete. I glanced through the pages of the book, skimming. It was rather inane, bland fodder and I shook my head at the badly written passages. It looked more like a pile of cut and pasted articles from gossip magazines than a biography. The only line that made me pause was in the last chapter where the author claimed that Adam Dennis's disappearance would be a hot topic for years to come. The book stated the desire for the real story of why he left Hollywood and what really happened to his co-star was a mystery that would never die. I frowned, wondering if that still held true. I knew how much Zachary valued his privacy and distanced himself from his past. He'd hate the thought of being thrust into the limelight again—the entire new world he built for himself destroyed. He lived in constant fear of exposure and ridicule over his scars. The thought of the real story coming out filled him with dread. Groaning, I deleted the book, reminding myself the next time I decided to drink, not to have my laptop close.

The search engine Zachary had been using was still open. I clicked on history and found the name of the paint for which he was searching. Starting a new request, I typed away and twenty minutes later I was successful. The paint was located and I could have it shipped to the gallery in two days. I rubbed my hands together in glee and placed the order, emailing a copy to Ashley so she'd know to play along when Zachary talked to her about it. Somehow, I'd find an excuse to take him into town, and pick it up as a surprise. Instead of discussing it with Ashley, she could hand him the package. He'd be thrilled.

At least that time, I'd done something good with my laptop.

His cheeks were red and cold when he came back. His eyes were calm and remorseful as he leaned in, touching his mouth to mine. He ran his finger over the blank journal in my hand. "Writing something?"

"No, I was looking at them. They're so beautiful."

"Not feeling inspired?"

"Not right now."

"Some people use them to write out their feelings." He looked down at the floor and hesitated before continuing. "Like if someone pisses them off or does something stupid, they write it out."

"I'm not pissed with you."

"You should be."

"I'm...sad."

"I made you sad?"

I was completely honest with him. "Yes, you did."

"I'm sorry, Megan."

"I know you are, but you need to stop and think sometimes."

His shoulders bowed. "I know. I react to memories rather than what's happening now." He reached for my hand, his touch tentative. I wrapped both my hands around his, squeezing. "I'll push you away one day, won't I?"

"No. I won't let you."

He exhaled deeply, lifting our hands and kissing my fingers. "Promise?"

"Yes."

———

It was warm in my little nest. The sun high in the sky, and the studio filled with light. Zachary had opened the windows and the breeze felt soothing on my skin as it drifted by. He was buried behind a canvas while the strains of sultry jazz played in the background. Every so often, his hand would wrap around the edge of the canvas as he stood close, etching some detail into his work. Other times, his arm would flash as he struck a jagged stroke on to his creation. I had often seen other artists working at street festivals or along the boardwalk when on vacation, standing in front of their canvas, silent and inert, but not Zachary. He was in constant motion as he worked, the odd muttered word escaping his mouth, and at times he'd hum or sing along with the music.

His singing voice was terrible.

I felt lazy today—I had since I woke up from my fractured sleep. In fact, for the past couple days, I had felt weary. I wasn't sure if it was emotion, or if I was coming down with something, but when Zachary had come up here to work, I was happy to join him, knowing I'd nap for a few hours. Neither of us had slept very well last night, and for the first time since I returned from Boston, we didn't make love after going to bed. He held me, but he had been restless most of the time, causing my own sleepless night. His quiet apology this morning was tinged with worry when he informed me I looked tired and questioned the reason, thinking I was still upset. I assured him I wasn't, and he seemed relieved when I followed him up stairs and settled into my corner.

Movement caught my eye and I grinned as he lifted one foot and used his toes to scratch the top of his other foot. It was rare he stood still while painting, his bare feet hitting the planked floor in an uneven rhythm as he moved and shifted, stopping only for the briefest periods as he contemplated his work. I sunk deeper into the pillows, my eyes feeling heavy. I let my book fall to my chest and shut my eyes allowing the soft music, the sound of the brush hitting the canvas and Zachary's awful tenor to lull me to sleep.

Warm lips ran over my throat, a soft tongue swirling on my skin. Groggy, I opened my eyes meeting the darkened gaze of Zachary as he loomed over me. Sliding my hand around his neck, I buried my fingers in his thick hair that curled around his shirt collar. "You have paint on your cheek," I mumbled, my voice still thick from sleep.

"Azure blue," he whispered, dropping gentle kisses to the side of my mouth. Grinning, he rubbed his cheek along mine. "Looks better on you."

"You got paint on me."

He sat back, dragging his shirt over his head. "Allow me." With light touches, he wiped the paint off my cheek, following the linen with his mouth. "I'll kiss it all better."

"You missed a spot."

His voice was husky. "Show me."

I tugged his face closer, so close I could feel his breath wash over my face. "Here," I whispered, flicking my tongue out and touching his bottom lip, trailing along the full flesh.

Groaning, he covered my mouth, slipping his tongue inside and kissing me. It was a kiss filled with tenderness and want. One that said *"I'm sorry,"* and *"I'm here—I want you."* His taste filled my mouth, and the scent of him—musky, warm, citrusy—wrapped around me, enveloping my senses as he pressed us deep into the blankets and pillows. Heat surged through me at his touch, shooting down my arms and legs, warming my body. I needed him. I needed to feel him hard and moving inside me—claiming me, and making me his. I whimpered into his mouth as he touched me, delving under my clothes to feel how much I wanted him. Piece by piece, clothing disappeared, our mouths only separating for the briefest of moments before coming back together again. He caressed and teased with his hands and mouth while I arched under him wanting more—wanting closer. He crooned, whispering how much he wanted me, how beautiful I was, how good I felt to him as he slipped inside, rocking into me. I felt his love seeping into my skin as he thrust forward, my name falling from his lips, his rhythm slow and deep. He captured my restless hands, pinning them beside my head, staring down at me, his emotions naked and glaring. Everything I needed to know, every insecurity he tried to hide, blazed from his wide stare as he opened himself to me. I cried out as my orgasm hit me, exploding like glass shattering against stone. Thousands of shards tore through my bloodstream as Zachary gathered me to his chest, burying his head into my neck and groaning his release.

Wrapped in the safety of his embrace, I felt the emotion well in me. It was during our lovemaking he opened himself up most. Trusted me most and gave the most of himself to me. I wanted that trust all the time.

Gently, he laid me down, curling his body around mine. "Shh," he whispered. "I have you, Megan. I'm right here."

I nodded, unable to speak or explain my sudden tears. He didn't utter a word either, but ran his hands up and down my back in long comforting strokes.

"I'll do better," he whispered into my ear. "I promise."

I held him closer, praying he could.

23

MEGAN

Two days later, my phone beeped with an incoming text from Ashley. The special paint had arrived, and so had both sets of brushes I'd ordered the day I came back from Boston. I wanted to give him a gift, and after asking her advice, she kindly offered to get two different sets in for me, and allow Zachary to choose which he preferred. He'd want to hold them in his hand, feel their weight and balance before deciding, she explained. Now that the paint and brushes had arrived, I couldn't wait to surprise him, but I hadn't thought to ask the price at the time. I frowned as I looked at the screen—they cost a lot of money, but I'd manage it. I really wanted to give him something special and I knew he'd love the brushes. We could go into town today and pick them up.

Zachary still seemed a little withdrawn; the effects of the other night still lingering between us. I thought maybe a change of scenery would be a good thing for both of us.

"What's that frown for?"

I deleted the message, not wanting to spoil the surprise. "Nothing."

He glanced down at the phone as I set it on the table. "Problem?"

I resisted rolling my eyes at him. "No."

His gaze lingered on the phone, then he returned his attention to the paper. He didn't look convinced or happy. I stifled a sigh, resisting the urge to remind him of our trust discussion.

"It's nothing, Zachary."

He shrugged a little, but didn't say anything. I was a lousy liar and I didn't want to give the surprise away, so I changed the subject. "I'm going into town today. You want to come?"

He glanced out the window at the dull sunshine. "Not really. Can it wait until tomorrow?"

I chewed on the inside of my cheek. I really wanted to go and get his gifts. He had been muttering again yesterday about this color he wanted and talked about checking online to try and find it. I wanted to give it to him before he had the chance. I was looking forward to seeing his reaction to the brushes and watching him choose the set he wanted. I could already picture him holding the brushes, his long fingers wrapped around the carved wood as he tested them in imaginary strokes on a blank canvas. His eyes would light up when he felt the connection and glow with warmth as he smiled my way, banishing the lingering unease of the past couple days.

"No, I, ah, need a few things. I have to go in today."

He took a sip of his coffee. "Like what?"

I searched my brain trying to think of something. "Um, cream... and some ah, personal stuff."

"Personal stuff?"

"Girl stuff, Zachary."

"Ah."

"We're almost out of popcorn and corn syrup."

He snickered, his mood shifting a little. "Well, if you didn't drown ice cream in it and eat popcorn every evening, maybe we wouldn't have to run in to town so much. Do we have any ice cream left?"

"Only a little."

"I'll add it to the list. I'll let Mrs. Cooper know."

"Okay. You'll come with me?"

"You go without me."

"Oh."

He studied me, his eyes curious and wary. "Is it so important I go with you?"

"I had thought—" My voice trailed off. It wasn't worth pushing him. Ashley would let me bring the brushes home and return whichever ones he didn't want, and my other plan could wait. "Never mind. I'll go alone."

"You thought what?"

"I wanted to go in today, and I wanted you to come with me. It's quiet in town. I thought maybe we could have lunch at the café."

"Pick it up, you mean?"

I shook my head, swallowing hard. I'd been thinking about this a lot. "No, I thought we could eat *in* the café."

His entire body stiffened. I wrapped my hand around his. "It's still slow—only the locals. You said you'd try."

"What if...what if it's busy?" His voice dropped. "What if they stare?"

"If it's busy we'll try another day. If they stare, then they're rude. It's their problem, not yours." I shifted closer. "You've already done this, Zachary. More than you realize, you've accomplished so many firsts. You go to the store, the doctor, the gallery, and even the park. At one point, you told me you didn't think you'd ever leave this house, but you did it all, and you've done it by yourself. I'll be there with you today." I squeezed his hand. "It's only lunch."

His eyes were filled with fear and his head already shaking no.

"For me?" I pleaded, shifting closer. "How about we go into town and do our errands, then decide? Don't say no right away. We can decide when we're there."

I felt the shudder run through him. I started to tell him to forget it, I'd go in myself and we'd do it another day. I could pick up his gift, bring it home with me and surprise him there. He'd still love the gesture. Then, to my amazement, he straightened his shoulders.

"Okay. I'll come with you. We'll decide when we're there, but if I say no, it's no. We'll come home."

The breath I was holding, huffed out in relief. Maybe today would be a good day.

"Okay."

"Your friend was in again, not long ago, Megan. He asked if you'd be in today."

I frowned at Mrs. Cooper in confusion. "I'm sorry—my friend?"

She nodded as she packed the last few groceries into the box. "He was here the other day, as well. Ah, what was his name again? Nice looking young man. Tall, blond hair. Jamie? Gary?"

An icy shiver, long and hard, ran down my spine. "Jared?"

"Yes! That's it. He said he was visiting you and Zachary last week and didn't want to go to the house to surprise you if you were coming into town. He thought he'd surprise you here, instead. I told him you had called to say you were coming in."

My hands started to shake. Jared was in Cliff's Edge.

How did he find me?

He had overheard more than I realized. If he was here, it was for only one reason.

He was here to destroy.

I swallowed, my throat dry and tight.

Zachary.

He was across the street, talking to Jonathon. I was supposed to meet him there when I was done, so I could surprise him with the gifts Ashley was holding for me. Then we were going to decide on lunch.

That wasn't going to happen.

I somehow knew. Jared was going to approach him—say something to him.

But what? What was he going to do?

217

Panic built in my chest, expanding and pushing the air out of my lungs.

"I'll be back," I almost whimpered, running from the store, leaving everything behind me. I hurried across the road, cutting across the parking lot at the back of the gallery. Somewhere in my brain it registered there were more cars around than usual. I noticed the small crowd of people at the edge of the lot, but ignored them. My solitary focus was getting to Zachary.

I almost made it across the pavement when the back door of the gallery burst open. Zachary stormed out, his face dark, everything about him screaming rage. He froze when he saw me, the expression on his face akin to revulsion. His skin was ashen and pale, his eyes horrified, and tension screamed from his stance. I stumbled in the heat of his hate-filled glare as fear shot through me, twisting like a snake around my spine. Then, I saw someone else.

Jared.

He smirked at me as he stepped beside Zachary. "The lady of the hour," he mocked. "Come to watch the show, Megan?"

I opened my mouth to speak, to plead, to do something, but no sound came out. Zachary kept staring; his hands clenched into fists so tight, his knuckles were white. A large wad of paper was crumbled in one rigid fist, and I watched as he threw it to the side, and if possible, his stare became darker. The crowd I had noticed earlier moved, and before I even understood what was happening, Zachary was surrounded. Flash bulbs went off, people were shouting, microphones were being shoved in his face. Horrified, I watched him go into protective mode, his head lowering, using one hand to shield his face as he used the other to push people away, and struggling to break free of the turmoil surrounding him. Without another thought, I lunged forward, pushing and shoving, screaming at them to leave him alone, trying to get to Zachary. A hand wrapped around my bicep, gripping me hard, tugging me back from the crowd and I spun, expecting to see Zachary. Instead Jared's cruel, smug face towered over me. "What have you done?" I gasped, struggling to get away.

He yanked me to his chest, his voice close to my ear, his fingers digging into my skin, pinning me in place. "What you deserved," he gloated, then raised his voice. "Gentlemen, our own little investigative reporter! The woman who located and brought you the infamous Adam Dennis!"

I was blinded by the flashes. Loud shouts and calls filled my ears. Jared kept my arms pinned at my sides and I watched gasping and helpless as Zachary broke free, sprinting to his SUV. He paused only for a brief second as he tore his door open, his eyes meeting mine.

I knew what he saw. Jared holding me, surrounded by a crowd he thought I'd sent to find him. I shook my head, tears filling my eyes as I struggled to get free from Jared's constricting grasp.

There was only indifference in his gaze: blank, unforgiving, cold. He looked at me as if I was a stranger.

No second chances, his voice murmured in my head.

My head fell to my chest as I sobbed.

The squeal of his tires would echo in my head for days.

***

Hands tore Jared's painful grip away from my arms. An arm wrapped around me, pulling me into the safety of the gallery. Stumbling blindly, I sank onto the floor, shaking and crying. Voices talked around me fast and panicked. I caught only snippets of words.

He said...

She did this...

She wouldn't...

And one word that kept repeating.

Zachary.

I wept until there were no tears left to cry. When I opened my eyes, I realized I was in Jonathon's office. The only other person in the room was Ashley, who was regarding me with anguish. "Tell me you didn't do what he says you did. What he told Zachary you did."

"I love Zachary," I rasped, holding out my hands in supplication.

"I didn't do anything." A wave of nausea ran through me and I clapped my hand over my mouth, my shoulders heaving. In sympathy, she pointed to a door and I rushed into the washroom, retching until there was nothing left. Washing my face and hands, I avoided looking in the mirror, knowing what I'd see—what Ashley saw when she looked at me.

Guilt.

Because of me, Jared came after Zachary. I might not have done anything, literally, but I caused it to happen.

She was waiting for me when I came out. "Sit down."

"I have to go. I have to find—"

She shook her head. "Jonathon is dealing with the police and chaos out there. You can't go anywhere right now. The gallery is closed." She shuddered. "I hope Zachary is safe. He isn't answering his phone."

My stomach lurched again and I wrapped my arms around my torso to try and stop the shivers that kept running through me.

She drew in a deep breath. "I want the truth, Megan. Who was that man?"

My voice shook as I told her. I told her everything. About my book and what Jared did. How I met Zachary. I told her all of it. When I was finished, she was quiet, her fingers tapping out a fast rhythm on the arm of her wheelchair. "What did he say?" I asked, knowing the answer, but wanting to hear it.

She shook her head, disgust written all over her face. "I didn't hear or see the start of it, but what I did witness was awful. There were people in the gallery keeping both of us busy and he cornered Zachary in the office. He told him you had set him up. You became curious about Karen's reclusive neighbor, did some checking and thought you'd found a great story. You were using him to write a book on his life—a real exposé. He went on and on about how you contrived meeting him, your innocent act. He said the whole story about him stealing your book was only a cover to get you sympathy." She met my eyes. "He took great pleasure in telling Zachary the two of you were lovers, but you had gotten greedy about not sharing the book with him, so he decided to speed things up." Her voice dropped. "He also said you were getting tired of keeping up the act of being in love and letting Zachary touch you like he was"—she hesitated —"normal."

I whimpered. Without even knowing it, he hit all of Zachary's weak spots. "What happened?"

"Zachary hit him. Only once, but it was hard. He went down and Zachary bolted." She shook her head. "That's when he ran out the door and into the mess back there. Jonathon called the police and went out back and grabbed you."

I shut my eyes as fresh tears gathered. So easily broken. The fragile bond I knew would take time to strengthen had been so easy to break. Small cracks had been forming, and today, the final blow had been delivered.

"I didn't do this, Ashley. I'm not writing a book about him. I didn't expose him." The tremor in my voice grew stronger. "But, it is my fault."

"What?"

"Jared heard me say his name and where I was staying. I thought I covered it up, but obviously I didn't. He was looking for a way to discredit me so no one would ever believe me about my book, or anything else." Bill had been right. A sob erupted from my chest. "It worked." I met her eyes. "Zachary will never listen to me. He'll never give me a chance to explain."

She rolled forward, clasping my hand. "I believe you."

"You do?"

"No one could fake the way you looked at Zachary, or how he looked at you. He was different with you." She squeezed my hand. "You have to make him listen, Megan."

"He left without me."

"He was scared and in shock. The person he thought he could trust betrayed him."

I opened my mouth to protest, but she waved my words away.

"The truth or not, that's what it looked like to him. Think about it, Megan. He's been here for ten years and until now, felt safe. Out of the limelight and away from his past. Then you enter his life—" Her voice trailed off.

"The one thing he needed, the one thing he counted on—his privacy—was suddenly taken away from him and he was told you were responsible. He knows this'll be all over the news. He'll hide for a while until he figures out how far this will reach in the media and how adversely it'll affect his life." She shuddered. "I hope they don't know where his house is located."

I stood up, gasping. "I have to get to him."

She tugged me down. "Jonathon will drive you once he thinks it's safe. You can't be followed, either."

"What if he won't listen to me?" I whispered.

"You have to give him some time. Let him think it through. Once he calms down, I'm sure he'll realize who is actually the one lying.'"

"You didn't see how he looked at me."

"I saw how he looked at you before this happened. You need to hang on to that image."

I shut my eyes, my entire body exhausted.

I was pretty sure that wasn't the image I would remember.

Time passed as I sat in Jonathon's office. Slowly the crowd dispersed, the town once again quiet. When they realized there were no more pictures to be taken, and no one in the town would even talk to them, the reporters left, although I was sure they'd be back.

I stood in the shadows outside, waiting for Jonathon while he went to pick up my purse at the store. He was not as convinced as Ashley was about my innocence, but he was at least being polite. I tried calling Zachary, but the calls went straight to voice mail. Every time I heard his terse message, I began to cry again, so I didn't leave him any messages. I doubted he'd listen to them anyway. I needed to see him face to face.

A ball of paper caught my eye and remembering it had been in Zachary's hand, I bent down, picking it up and unfurling it. My eyes widened at the pictures. Zachary and me on the beach the day before —close up and zoomed in on his scarred face. Another one of us walking in town. Then others, of me with Jared, his arm around me, taken when we were dating. All the pictures were date stamped, but the ones of me with Jared were falsified. They were dated so it looked like they were taken last week when I was in Boston; made to look like we were still dating. To make Zachary believe I was the horrid person Jared said I was.

A figure moved and I tensed when Jared appeared.

"I've been waiting."

"How?" I whimpered.

He laughed, the sound cruel. "Did you forget what I did before I started writing, Megan? I was a researcher for the publishing house. I checked facts, dug up information." He sneered. "You made this little project so very interesting for me." He sniggered. "I passed you on the highway last week, and waited for you here. I heard you talking to your lawyer and say where you were staying, so I rented a different car and followed you. Once I was sure where you were heading, I drove in front of you and waited." His eyes narrowed. "So worth my time, too."

"Why, Jared?" I asked, my voice shaking with barely concealed hatred. "Why did you do this?" I threw up my hands, shaking the fake pictures. "It's a book, it's only a book!"

"A book you wouldn't give me."

I shook my head. "I emailed Bill the other night and told him I would accept your offer. You didn't have to do this. You didn't have to destroy someone else's life!"

He laughed again, the sound low and evil. "Don't you get it, Megan?"

"I guess not."

He stepped forward, close enough I could see the bruise forming on his face from Zachary's fist. "I get what I want. I warned you not to fuck with me. Thanks to your stupid, inane mouth, I get it all. Luckily for me, I know you well enough to know what a lousy liar you are and there was no new dog. Good thing no one else has figured that out yet, and now they never will." An evil smile curled his thin lips. "Even if this little story dies a fast death, which it probably will, no one will ever believe a word you say again. I get your book and discredit you,"—he smirked—"and, I get it all for free. I don't have to pay you a dime."

Revulsion tore through me. "You're the most despicable person I've met. I regret the day I ever heard your name."

He leered at me as he shrugged his shoulders. "Regret away, Megan. I still win." His eyes glinted, dark and nasty as he shoved some more papers into my cold hand. "You made it all so easy, as well." Then he turned and walked away, leaving me looking at the order receipt from Zachary's paint, which had flown away, and some more pictures of the two of us together. He'd been here and seen me —he'd been watching us—following us. He found the information he needed because of my careless mouth and a piece of paper I let blow away. I hadn't noticed him, never saw him passing me on the highway or watching us.

I swallowed the bile rising in my throat again. I had led him right to Zachary.

Jonathon came around the corner, frowning when he saw Jared's departing figure. His eyes softened when he saw my tears, and he slipped his hand under my elbow to steady me. "Are you all right?"

I shook my head, unable to speak.

"Let me take you home, Megan."

Home.

Zachary.

"Yes," I mumbled. I had to get to him.

I stumbled into the house, refusing Jonathon's offer of help. I needed to be alone and think before I went to see Zachary. The roads had been deserted, so I knew no one followed us from town, but I still hoped Zachary was safe in his house. I stopped at the sight of Dixie on the sofa, my hand clutching the doorframe for support. She'd been at Zachary's when we left.

Why was she here?

I gasped as my eyes swept the room. Sitting on top of the mantle was a canvas I would know anywhere. *Tempest* was leaning on the wall; one long rending tear slashed diagonally across the painting, the image ruined. With slow steps and fresh tears falling down my face, I crossed the room, my fingers tracing the edge of the tear gently, the meaning behind the gesture plain.

He was destroying what I loved, because he thought I destroyed him.

A small piece of paper was tacked to the corner.

Finally. You got something you really wanted.

Sinking to the floor, I buried my head in my hands as I sobbed. I didn't have to go to his house to know he was gone. His house would be vacant, the rooms echoing with silence.

He had left. I didn't know how to find him and tell him the truth.

He left thinking once again he'd been used and discarded. He believed that I used him, because he was unworthy of really being loved.

A small bundle of fur crawled into my lap, and I pulled Dixie close to me as I wept. He brought her back to me and left me with the thing he believed I wanted most.

Except it wasn't the painting I wanted. It was him.

Now, both were destroyed.

24

MEGAN

Someone was tugging at my arms. "Megan. You have to move."

Blinking, I looked up into Karen's concerned eyes, then took in my surroundings. The room was dim, and I realized I must have cried myself to sleep sitting on the floor.

When did she arrive?

She shook me slightly. "Stand up," she commanded, her voice firm but patient. With her help, I struggled to my feet and moved to the sofa. She handed me a glass of water. "Drink."

I sipped at the liquid, the coolness feeling good on my parched throat.

"How—"

"Ashley called. She said you needed me. Right away."

"Oh."

All the memories came back, my eyes widening and filling with more tears. Karen took my glass and clasped my hands. "Tell me."

Between sobs and hiccups, I told her everything. She listened, cursing at times, rubbing my back on occasion, while I cried and got out all the words.

"Bastards," she hissed. "Both of them."

I frowned at her, shaking my head. "This isn't Zachary's fault. You can't blame him."

"He believed Jared! How could he do that?"

"Jared did a thorough job." Sniffing, I pulled the crumbled paper out of my pocket, showing it to her. "He covered all the bases—again." Another sob wrenched from my chest. "For the second time, I handed it to him. Only this time, I'm not the only one hurt."

"Stop blaming yourself. You had no idea Jared would do something like this, Megan."

"I should have, though." I stood up, pacing. "I should've taken the damn offer, like you and Bill said. Put it behind me. He stole my book, then had no problem calling me a liar and defaming me everywhere. I should've known he wouldn't stop." I held out my hands in a pleading gesture. "I dropped a receipt with Zachary's name on it. I didn't know Jared had followed me." I choked back a fresh sob. "I didn't know he was watching."

Karen grabbed my hands and tugged me back down beside her. "I know," she soothed.

"You should have seen his face," I sobbed. "He believed him. He thinks I used him the way he's been used all his life. He looked at me as if he hated me, Karen!"

"He's upset. He'll come around."

"No! He's gone!" I indicated the painting. "He did *that* then he left! His cellphone is off, and he and Elliott are gone!"

She got up and examined the painting, shaking her head. "Coward," she muttered.

"Don't," I pleaded. "Don't call him names."

"How can you defend him?"

"Because he's hurt! He's out there alone, thinking everything between us was a lie!" My voice rose, panicked. "I don't know where to find him!"

"I don't know why you want to after the way he behaved today."

I stood up, shouting now. "Because I love him! And now, once again, he thinks he isn't worthy of being loved. Jared's stunt only proved to him he'd been right along! Can't you see that, Karen?"

She stared at me, gaping. I didn't think she'd ever heard me raise my voice in anger.

My legs gave out and I fell back to the sofa. I stared at her beseechingly. "Don't you understand? He's alone, in pain, and I can't reach him. I can't hold him and let him feel how much I love him." I wiped the tears off my face. "I don't think I'll ever have the chance to do that again."

"Maybe he'll calm down and reach out to you. Maybe he'll think it over and come back in a few days."

I shook my head. "He doesn't give second chances—ever. He told me that on more than one occasion." I drew in a shallow gulp of air. My chest felt so heavy I couldn't get in enough oxygen. "Jared did such a good job; Zachary will never believe anything else now. He won't come back here for a long time—if ever. He'll never give me another chance"—my voice dropped to a whisper—"or maybe even another thought."

I walked to the window, looking at the bluff. Squinting, I could make out the shape of the house, its lines barely discernable in the dark. There were no lights blazing in the studio, no one moving around the rooms, or quiet music playing. The house looked dead—it was as empty as my heart.

"And yet you forgive him."

I turned to look at her. "He has a whole life of pain and rejection to draw from. Of course his first instinct would be to believe he'd been deceived again. Used again. We'd only just started, Karen. He still questioned *why* I would love him. He never got the chance to know how deep that love went. We never got the chance to stand the test of time. I have the luxury of *knowing* he loved me, that what we had was real—he thinks my love was a lie."

My chest tightened; the simple act of breathing causing me pain. "We argued the other day over those stupid pictures I downloaded. It planted a seed of doubt—or maybe added to the doubt he already felt.

Then I practically insisted we go into town today. I was so excited about giving him a gift, I begged him to come with me, even though he didn't want to. I can only imagine how all the pieces fell together in his head once Jared started spewing his lies and the reporters descended." My head fell back against the glass as I met her concerned eyes. "How easy it was for him to believe I betrayed him."

Karen rubbed my arm in what she meant to be a soothing gesture. Except, there was no soothing me. My body felt like a live wire, burning and snapping in waves of shock. "What are you going to do now?"

Turning back to the window, I stared into the night.

"The one thing I can do," I whispered. "Keep breathing."

The sun rose, lighting the sand and water around me as I walked up and down the beach in constant motion. I hadn't slept all night—every time I closed my eyes, I'd see Zachary's face and the dead look in his eyes as he glared at me. Feel the waves of anger when he turned and left. Nausea would run through me and I'd have to sit up, waiting for it to pass. Finally, I had given up, and Dixie and I had gone down to the beach. More than once, I ended up at the bottom of his beach stairs, staring up at his house. I prayed for some miracle, wanting him to appear at the top of the steps and tell me he had panicked, but came back.

Of course it never happened, so I'd call Dixie from her exploration of the deck and we'd walk away. Her soft whines told me she was as sad over not finding Elliott there as I was over missing Zachary. I scratched behind her ears. "Sorry, girl. We're on our own again."

I stood back from the lazy waves that rolled up onto the beach, staring out over the long expanse of water. Out of the corner of my eye, I saw Karen coming toward me. She slipped her arm around my waist, standing in silence beside me.

Finally she spoke. "Did you sleep?"

"No."

"Have you been thinking or wallowing?"

I chuckled a little at her directness. "Some of both."

"I wish you were angry."

"I can't be. I'm too numb." I shrugged. "I'm not sure I can ever be angry with him. The urge to believe the worst is so deeply engrained in his psyche, I'm not sure it'll ever change. I think maybe it was going to happen one way or another." I glanced at her, the sadness sinking back in. "Time was against us."

"I checked the net—there are a few stories and some pictures, but it isn't huge. It's been twelve years and they didn't get very much information. Chris says there were only a few small articles in the paper."

"Good. I hope it dies down quick for Zachary's sake." I sighed. "Not that it will help me, or my image in any way. Jared won that round."

"What are you going to do about him?"

"Nothing. What can I do? Spar with him through the media? It's done; he won—he won it all."

"Megan—"

"Don't," I pleaded. "I need a little time, Karen. Give me that, please. Let me work it through in my head and my heart." My voice shook a little. "I'm overwhelmed right now."

She wrapped her other arm around me. "I'm staying here. I'm not leaving you alone."

I rested my head on her shoulder, grateful for her and her friendship. "Thank you."

The next day we were out on the beach for another walk. I walked a lot, trying to sort things out in my head. Karen was often beside me, allowing me to talk when I wanted and remain silent at other times. Dixie let out a little bark, running toward Zachary's steps. My body started to shake with anticipation, even as my head snapped to the side, my eyes glued to the stairs and the figure that appeared. A rush of disappointed air escaped when I realized it was Mrs. Cooper gingerly making her way down the steps. Karen squeezed my arm in comfort and we walked toward her together. She smiled—her eyes sad and somewhat nervous—as she greeted us. Frowning, she cupped my face with her hand. "Child, you look so tired."

I smiled and shrugged. "I'm fine, Mrs. Cooper, really, I am."

She nodded, although she didn't look convinced.

"Has the town returned to normal?" Karen inquired.

"I think the last of them left yesterday. They sniffed around, asking questions and taking their stupid photographs," Mrs. Cooper huffed. "Nobody would talk to them, though." She smiled grimly at us. "It isn't like many people even knew him well enough to comment on his life now, never mind what happened years ago."

"Did you know?" Karen asked, her curiosity getting the better of her. "Did you know who he was before he came to live here?"

"I knew who he was when he first came here. He would come to the store at the strangest times—early in the morning or late at night so he wouldn't be seen. He was always polite, but distant, and we gave him his privacy. He seemed to need it. After his, ah, accident, he came back and it broke my heart to see the change in him—not only physically. He was broken—bitter. He didn't leave his house much."

She paused, lost in memories. "We had become a little closer. Mr. C and I looked after his house when he wasn't around. Then when he came to live here on a permanent basis, I brought him groceries for the first little while. He hid himself at first, but when I offered to let him send me his lists and come through the back to pick up his groceries, he agreed." She sighed as she looked over my shoulder at the water. "I thought maybe, with some encouragement, he would start rejoining the world, but he never really did." She focused her gaze on me. "Until you came into his life, Megan. I thought he had finally turned a corner."

My chest tightened further. I thought so, too.

"I didn't do this to him," I pleaded, my voice full of honesty. "I would never hurt him this way."

"I know," she assured me. "I don't know what all happened with that other man, but I know he was the one responsible."

"He was!"

"The lesson of not judging a book by its cover most certainly applies here, doesn't it? He's such a nice looking man, only to be such a terrible person. I'm sorry I even let him in my store. He seemed to know both of you so well, the way he spoke."

"That's what he does, Mrs. Cooper. He fooled me, as well."

She nodded in understanding, patting my shoulder. "I wish I could help."

My fingers pulled at the sleeve of my sweater. "Why are you here?"

She hesitated, heaving out a large gust of air. "Megan, I had a message from Zachary last night."

Hearing his name, my heart started to pound in my chest. "Is he all right?"

She looked surprised at my question. "I believe so. He instructed my husband and me to come close up his house."

Pain lanced, constricting my chest. I pressed my hand to my heart, trying to stop the ache that was forming. "Did he say for how long?"

"Indefinitely."

Tremors ran through my spine. He wasn't coming back.

Mrs. Cooper shifted, looking uncomfortable. "He asked me to check and see if you had taken your things. If not, to remove what belonged to you and return it before I locked the place up and engaged the security system. He wants you to give me the key."

I hadn't been back. I couldn't face going into his house and the echoing silence that would greet me. I shoved my hand into my pocket, fingering the silver key resting inside. He'd only given it to me a few days prior, now he wanted it back; he wanted my things removed.

There would be no chance to explain—no conversations—no second chances.

I looked at Karen, fighting the tears. "I can't—" I swallowed the lump forming in my throat. "I can't go in there."

She shook her head. "I'll go with Mrs. Cooper. Can you tell me what's there?"

"Some clothes and toiletries," I rasped out. "My laptop." I racked my brain. "I don't know...I don't know what else is there." I couldn't think; I could barely form the words over the roaring in my head.

He wasn't coming back.

Karen took the key from my shaking hand. "I'll assume I need to take anything feminine or that I recognize is yours. Go back to the house, Megan. I'll take care of this for you." She grabbed my arm, frowning. "Can you make it back to the house? You're scaring me a little."

"I need a moment," I pleaded. "Just give me a second."

Karen and Mrs. Cooper exchanged a look. I shut my eyes and inhaled deep gulps of air, willing myself to calm.

I had spent the last two days in denial. I kept telling myself it was over, even as a small hope inside me stayed lit. Hope said he would realize how wrong he had been and that I couldn't possibly be the awful person he was led to believe. Hope told me he would come back and we'd talk and face this together.

But hope just died.

"Anything else?" Karen asked.

"My journals he gave me," I whispered, making a decision. "They're on the table." He had brought them over, hoping I would open one and start writing, but they were still empty.

He gave them to me and I wanted them. A tangible reminder, that at one point, I had meant something to him. The first gift he ever gave another person. I had meant enough to him that he made such an immense gesture.

I needed my journals.

"Okay, I'll get them. You go back to the house and sit down before you fall down. Please."

I nodded, watching them as they climbed the stairs, Dixie following them. I didn't try and stop her. I turned, and with slow, measured steps, walked to Karen's house, alone.

Reminding myself, the whole way, to keep breathing.

When night fell, it felt endless. Darkness descended in slow motion, like ink dripping from a bottle, one drop at a time, until the sky was filled with blackness. The only light I could see were the stars that shone like small diamonds, set into the ebony velvet of the heavens. I inhaled, the scent of the ocean all around me in the night. I huddled farther into the blanket I was wrapped in, as I sat on the deck staring into the sky. I had given up trying to sleep. I knew it wasn't going to happen. The past weeks played and replayed in my head on an endless loop. Every word, every touch, the tiniest of details of my time with Zachary screamed at me. I couldn't shut them off.

I knew Karen was worried. Every morning she shook her head as she watched the circles under my eyes grow darker. Her sighs of frustration grew louder with every meal I picked at, and each word I uttered in Zachary's defense. She refused to leave, saying she was too worried about me, and I refused to go back to Boston with her. I wasn't ready to leave yet. We were at an impasse.

Another long shiver ran through me and I knew I had to go back inside the house. The days were warming up, but the nights were still cold and I had been outside for a while, gazing at the darkened horizon, wondering if by chance, Zachary was doing the same thing wherever he was. With one last look, and a shaky sigh, I got up slowly and stepped back inside.

I curled into the corner of the sofa, Dixie beside me, her warm body heavy with sleep. I stroked her fur, wishing I could sleep, as well, but that peacefulness wouldn't come to me. Instead, when I shut my eyes, images bombarded me, and rest proved to be elusive. I didn't know how to move forward—to get past all these feelings and memories.

My gaze fell on my journals. I had picked them up numerous times over the past couple days, after Karen had carried them in and set them down. My fingers had traced the supple leather over and again, remembering the expression on Zachary's face as he gave them to me. He said he wanted me to fill the blank pages with my words; how when they came back to me, the books would be there, waiting.

Before I realized what was happening, I had removed one journal from the box and opened up the thick pages.

I had the words.

Our words. They needed to come out of my head and live on these pages.

The pages of us.

I picked up one of the special pens he had chosen and began to write.

Time slipped away, and it was the clearing of Karen's throat that broke my concentration. Startled, I looked at her, realizing the room was filled with the morning sun. I looked down at the journal in front of me surprised to see I had filled about a third of the book.

"You're writing," Karen's voice was surprised but pleased.

"I am."

"A new story?"

I shut the book, putting the cap back on the pen, tracing my finger over the spine. "My story."

She sat beside me. "Your story?"

"I can't stop thinking, Karen. The words play continuously in my head. I have to get them out."

"So you're writing about you and Zachary?"

"Yes. I thought—"

"Tell me," she encouraged, sounding concerned.

"I thought if I wrote them out—let all my feelings and thoughts flow into these books—these journals he gave me—maybe I could find some peace. Figure out a way of moving forward."

"Makes sense."

I looked over her shoulder. "Can we go into town later?"

Her eyebrows flew up. "Sure. Why?"

"I want to take *Tempest* to Ashley and Jonathon. I want to see if they know someone who can fix it."

"Why?"

"It means something to me. It has from the second I saw it. I need to have it repaired."

"Megan—"

I held up my hand. "Don't say it. I want it repaired for me."

"Okay, then, we'll go into town later. Coffee and toast first, though."

Leaning forward, I squeezed her hands. "Sounds good."

Ashley was horrified went she saw the damage to the painting, but knew a professional restorer who could repair it. It would never be whole again—the same way Zachary would never be whole. It could be repaired and to the unknowing eye, look fine, but it would never be the same—undamaged. The symmetry was almost ironic, and not lost on any of us. She told me she had a quick email from Zachary stating he would be out of touch for the foreseeable future and not to expect any new work. She shook her head as she told me he must've also canceled his email account since her reply bounced back. "He isn't answering his cell phone, either," she informed me. "His voice mail says messages would be checked infrequently. Mrs. Cooper might have other information since she looks after his house."

The news saddened me further, but I wasn't surprised. I hated that he was closing the door on the few people who truly cared for him, and wasn't listening to anyone who was trying to reach out. I also knew if Mrs. Cooper had more information, she would respect Zachary's privacy and not give it to me.

I was surprised to see how empty the back gallery was, and she explained they had removed Zachary's paintings with all the reporters around. "Zachary would hate the thought of people buying them to resell, or use as part of the stories that will come out. We'll hang them back up when it all dies down." She squeezed my hand. "It will die down, Megan. Especially with him gone."

I nodded, masking my anger. He shouldn't have had to go anywhere. Cliff's Edge, this small, laid-back town was his home, but because of me, because of Jared, he had left.

A small voice in my head whispered he shouldn't have run. He should have given me a chance and believed in me, in us, more. Ignoring the pain those thoughts caused, I thanked Ashley and hurried across the street where Karen was picking up a few things. I kept my head down, hoping no reporters had returned and recognized me. I didn't want to experience that again.

Karen was ready, so we headed back to her place, with plans to watch a movie and an early night. "I am tired," I admitted, when she commented on my appearance, gazing at me from her chair.

"Will you sleep tonight?"

My eyes drifted to my journal. "Yeah, I think I might."

She tilted her head. "You sound clearer this afternoon—better. You still look like shit, but you sound more like you."

"I think I found my path."

"Writing your story?"

"Yes. I made a decision I want to talk to you about."

"Sure."

"You mentioned with the big job Chris is now on, and how busy the salon is, you were afraid this place would sit empty most of the next few months."

She nodded.

"Would you consider letting me stay on here for a while? I'll pay rent, of course."

"What about your place in Boston?"

"I'll sublet it."

"Are you...waiting for him?"

"No." I closed my eyes as I admitted the truth. "He isn't coming back."

I shifted in my chair as I tried to explain. "Aside from you, there isn't anything in Boston for me now, and I like it here. I don't have a job to go back to; I spoke with Ashley earlier and she's willing to hire me for some hours during the next while. I can write, work, and find my feet." I shook my head. "The way I planned to do when I got here, before...Zachary."

"Are you writing that story for you or to publish?"

"No, it's for me. Only me. Maybe, though, once it's out of my head, I can find more words and write again."

"Any plot bunnies up there?"

"Maybe." I smiled at her.

"I have to go back to Boston."

"I know."

She pursed her lips, studying me. "Will you be okay here alone, Megan? Will you fall apart when I leave?"

"No, I'm done falling apart. I need to move on."

"Can you?"

I shrugged. "I have no choice, do I? No one can do it for me, so I have to."

"You'll have to share the place on occasion when we can make it down."

"I know. I'm good with that."

"You know, one of the girls at the salon was looking for a place. She broke up with her boyfriend and literally left everything behind. She'd probably take most of your stuff, if you wanted. The rest you can bring here or store at our place. I can ask her, if you want me to?"

"That would be great."

She stood up. "Okay. I'm going to call Chris and tell him I'm coming home tomorrow." She hesitated. "If you need me you'll call, right? Or if you can't stand being here alone, you'll come stay with us?"

Warmth flooded my chest at her words. "You're such a good friend."

"Takes one to know one."

She left the room and I smiled sadly. I would miss her, but it was time. She needed to get back to her life and I needed to find mine. I wasn't sure if this move was permanent for me, but for now, it was where I wanted to be. I was under no illusion that Zachary would reappear at any time, seeking me out, yet I was loath to leave this place.

Maybe once I finished our story. Maybe once I exorcized the pain and made peace with what happened I'd be able to move forward and find my direction.

It must have happened for a reason. I refused to believe what Zachary and I went through, what we shared, how he started to open up and accept he was worthy of being loved, was for nothing.

I only had to figure out how to find the reason, accept it, and move on with my life.

25

MEGAN

I stopped tracking the passage of time. The minutes became hours, morphing into days, and three weeks later, I had filled four of my journals. The world around me ceased to exist when I picked up my pen and relived the past months, starting with the events that led up to me coming to Cliff's Edge and my too brief time with Zachary. Moments I'd forgotten, small flashes of his smile, tender words from his full lips, even fiery explosions of his eyes came back to me as I wrote. Sweet, quiet seconds and dark, angry moments, were all carefully recorded in brutal honesty. My tears often fell onto the pages as I wrote feverishly, gripped in some memory, wanting, *needing* to get the words out of my head and onto the paper. Every day, I prayed *today* would be the day the pain would lessen. One more sentence, one more memory aired, would ease the ache that was never-ending. It was a constant reminder of a part of my life that was so intense, fraught with land mines and pain, yet, in so many ways, the happiest I'd ever been.

Karen checked on me often, making sure I wasn't losing myself in my writing or wallowing in tears. Dixie and I walked the beach every day, some days even succeeding in pretending the house on the bluff was only that: another empty house on the beach. After a few days, she stopped running toward the stairs looking for Elliott. I never made it as close as the stairs before I had to turn back, my chest tightening, my legs starting to shake. I convinced myself I had stopped waiting for Zachary to appear; if my eyes drifted toward the house, it was only by accident. Chris would be pleased to know I was keeping an eye on Zachary's house. I even looked at the Smith's house on occasion. I saw Mrs. Cooper in town when I drove in for supplies and a few times I waved at Mr. Cooper when I saw him checking out both vacant properties.

I ate the food Karen insisted on bringing with her on visits, even though I had no appetite. Everything tasted like ash in my mouth, but I chewed and swallowed, thankful for her concern. I smiled and nodded when she asked if I was all right, hoping she wouldn't delve too hard, or stay too long. Her salon was busy, so she rarely spent the night, usually only coming down for a day. I listened to her stories and laughed when I was expected to, so she would believe I was doing better. I walked every day and went into town when I needed to. I chatted to Ashley, smiled at Jonathon. I was pleasant and friendly to the people at the pharmacy and café. I slept, although it never relieved my exhaustion, and functioned, being sure to keep the pain hidden unless I was alone and my pen was in hand. Then it leaked out of me, drop by drop as the ink and tears flowed, filling the pages.

Most of the time I felt like a walking corpse: weary, only existing, barely able to make it from one day to the next, but still, I pushed on. Some days, I even managed to convince myself I was fine. Other days I admitted I wasn't, but I knew one day I would be. There were moments of sudden anger when I allowed myself to rage at Jared, the situation, and even Zachary. I cursed his lack of faith; how easy it seemed to be to cast my love and me aside. To walk away from me—from us—without question, not looking back, locking my memory from his heart. I wondered if he ever, in the deepest, darkest moment of the night, questioned his decision to leave, or if I ever crossed his mind. If he missed me at all the way I missed him. I wanted to know if his chest ever ached with agony, so strong he wanted it to burst open, hoping the poison would leach out and cease destroying him little by little. Then, guilt would seep back in, and my anger would dissolve. He ran away from his life because of me. I brought him pain and regret. It was my fault his simple existence was shattered.

It was far easier to remain angry at Jared.

Karen was upset over the fact I'd still done nothing in regards to the situation I was in. In truth, I had no idea what to do. I knew I was hiding from my problems, yet I couldn't figure out the next step; most of the time I couldn't find it in me to care. Jared had my book; he had destroyed any chance of my claims being credible by throwing Zachary to the proverbial wolves and pointing the finger of blame toward me. He had withdrawn his offer of money, and now I had no clue what to do next; even Bill was flummoxed. His last email stated we needed to sit tight for a while and see what happened next.

I sighed, scrubbing my face in the early morning light. The last journal was open; its pages spread, the lines empty, waiting for my words. For the first time, my mind was as blank as the paper I was looking at. The other journals all contained our story—the unexpected beginning and the tumultuous middle. This one would contain our end. My mind went over and over all the things I had missed those final days—things that were so obvious now. Zachary's constant disbelief, which I should have paid more attention to at the time, instead of assuming it would ease off the longer we were together. I never really accepted the fact our time could be limited. I should have made sure he knew, without a doubt, how much I cared for him. I thought of his overreaction to the pictures on my laptop, which caused the seeds of doubt to be planted in his head. Seeds Jared liberally watered and fed, so they bloomed strong and fierce when he encountered Zachary that day in the gallery. Maybe if we'd been even more strident in our own honesty, we could have withstood Jared's poison.

I thought of the dark sedan with the tinted windows that flew past me on the highway when I was returning after the last terrible meeting with Jared. I remembered muttering about impatient drivers and assholes behind the wheel as it sped by. I saw a similar car parked on the street, but never once gave it a second thought or even assumed it might be the same one. I never even considered the fact Jared had overheard enough of my conversation to know where I was staying or that he would follow me. I thought I had fooled him, when in fact, he had fooled me. Again.

The receipt I let carelessly blow away. He'd been right there, watching. For all I knew, he'd been in the gallery listening to me while I was talking to Ashley. He picked up the piece of paper and instantly knew the **Z D A** on the paintings in the gallery and the Zachary on the paper were the same person I mentioned to Bill. For someone like him, smart at research, desperate to silence me, it was all he needed. I had no idea if he stayed in town or went back to Boston and returned, but he had pictures from the day we'd been in town which he used to convince Zachary he was telling the truth. I knew he'd been to the beach at least once, but hadn't approached the house, or if he had, dismissed it quickly, knowing it was too open and he'd be seen. In town he could blend in, though, and he did it well; even making sure Mrs. Cooper thought he was a friend.

A long shiver ran through me as I picked up my pen, not sure I'd be able to handle writing all this out, but knowing I had to. As painful as it was, the story deserved the same honesty at the end as the beginning. This part wouldn't fill the journal—there would be pages empty at the end.

Pages I wondered if I would ever fill or if they would remain as empty as the hollow in my chest.

I filled my lungs with oxygen, exhaling fast. My breath flew over the pages, teasing the edges of the thick stock. The deep red of the satin bookmark fluttered with the air, and I tucked it farther into the book.

I pressed the pen to the paper and began.

Hours later, the opening of the back door startled me and my head snapped up. Night had fallen outside; standing in the shadow of the doorway were Chris and Karen. I was so deep into writing, I hadn't even heard the car arrive. They both looked serious and a rush of dread filled me, my heartbeat speeding up as fear shot through me.

Karen sat down on the coffee table and I reached out, my hand shaking. "What?" I begged her. "Did something...my parents?" My voice trailed off in a whimper when she shook her head. "Zachary?"

Her hand wrapped around mine. "No, honey. No, I'm sorry. We didn't mean to frighten you like that."

Chris sat beside her. "It's Jared."

I shut my eyes, fighting panic. What had he done now? What more did I have to lose?

"Tell me."

"Megan," Chris began, "look at me, please."

I opened my eyes, surprised at the calm gaze that met mine. I relaxed a little.

"You need to come to Boston with us."

"Why?"

"There was a fire at Jared's house. It was basically destroyed."

I frowned at him, unsure what this had to do with me. "Was he, um, hurt?"

"No."

"I don't understand." Why did he want me to go to Boston?

"In the chaos of the fire and the aftermath, his desk was over-turned." Chris paused, glancing at Karen. She squeezed my hand to get my attention.

"Do you remember his desk, Megan?"

I nodded. "Yes. It was an old oak one with lots of drawers. Jared said it was so big it had been in the house since it was built. You couldn't get it out of the room. He didn't let anyone touch it."

244

Chris smirked. "Well, they did more than touch it. When they flipped it to get to the wall, searching for hotspots, they triggered some mechanism and a secret compartment opened up."

"Secret compartment?"

Karen leaned forward. "It had manuscripts in it, Megan."

"I'm sorry—manuscripts? What manuscripts?"

"Stolen manuscripts. Your book was in there—the original manuscript you penned."

"My book?" I echoed in disbelief.

"Yes. It's over, Megan. Jared's been lying all this time."

Those were the words I'd wanted to hear all along. "He admitted it?" I whispered, unable to believe what I was hearing.

"He couldn't deny it. The concrete evidence was right there."

A memory stirred as I looked at Karen. Zachary stating he thought Jared was "either very clever or he'd done this before and knew all the loopholes." He'd been right all along.

"There were other books?"

"His entire series. He stole all of it."

"What?" I gasped. "The whole series?"

"Bill will explain everything to you. We need you to come back to Boston with us and see him. Jared's lawyer and publishers, or ex-publishers, want to meet with you."

"Why didn't you call? I could have driven myself in."

"We didn't know how you'd react," Karen admitted. "Bill did email you yesterday, but you didn't respond."

"Oh." I looked over to the counter where my laptop sat. "I forgot to plug it in. You were worried. I'm sorry."

"It's okay. We decided to come out and get you."

I smiled at my friends. I was lucky to have them in my life and I knew I needed their support right now, perhaps more than ever. "Thank you."

Bill smiled as he handed me a glass of water. I turned back to the window, taking in the view from his office high over the city, staring as the city bustled and teamed below me. It was so different from the vast expanse of water I was now used to. Surrounded by massive buildings and noise; cars and people moved fast, hustling to their destinations. When outside, I found the noise too much to handle. I stifled a sigh as the longing for the open space of Cliff's Edge swept through me. I inhaled a deep gulp of air, frowning as the scent of Bill's coffee hit me, and I had to swallow my sudden nausea. My nerves were certainly getting to me today. I sipped the cool liquid gratefully and rubbed my weary eyes.

"Are you all right, Megan?" Bill asked in a concerned voice. "You look very pale."

"I'm fine. It's a lot to take in."

"I know. Are you sure you don't want to put this meeting off? I can postpone it."

"No. I want it done." I walked over to the chair across from Bill and farthest away from his coffee. "I know the firefighters discovered the hidden manuscripts and they're now in the hands of his publishers, but how did Jared get them in the first place? Besides mine, I mean."

Bill leaned back in his chair. "He discovered them by accident. Something was stuck in a drawer; he was trying to get it out and triggered the mechanism. The back opened up and there they were—dusty and forgotten. His proverbial ship had come in."

I shook my head in disgust. As always, he would grab onto the opportunity—the easiest road for Jared. Whatever required the least effort and the most reward—that was how he worked.

"He did some checking and found out the manuscripts had been written by a previous owner of the house. His only living relative was a grandson who barely knew his grandfather, who became a recluse in later years. No one knew about the books. Apparently, like you, he didn't like to talk about his writing. His grandson has vague recollections of his grandfather telling him made-up stories when he was young, but had no idea he had turned those simple stories into novels. Three complete novels and the outline of the fourth, all waiting for him to lay claim."

"Why did he take mine? I don't understand if he had such a good thing going. It makes no sense."

Bill drained his coffee and set his mug on the desk, folding his hands on the dark wood. "Ah, there's where he made his biggest mistake, Megan. He'd worked at the publishing house as a researcher and he's a smart man. He had a passing knowledge of the business and what they were looking for in manuscripts—he was able to rework some details and modernize the books so they were current. He made friends with a couple editors and got the first one looked at."

Of course he "made friends." That was what Jared did; it served his purpose.

"It was huge; it made him a great deal of money."

Bill smirked. "Made, as in past tense. The books have been removed from circulation and the legal ramifications are huge for not only Jared, but the publishers, as well."

I tried not to feel a sense of satisfaction from those words, but I failed.

"The second and third books," Bill continued, "were even bigger. Now Jared had a choice. He could have ended it at the third book and rested on his laurels. He certainly made enough money to do so. There was talk of a movie deal and merchandising—the whole ball of wax—but his ego came into play. He believed his own press and decided he could use the outline to write the fourth book."

I remembered reading the draft. How unlike the first three books it was—badly written and choppy.

"He couldn't write it."

"He couldn't write his way out of a wet paper bag." Bill laughed. "All his life he did the least amount of work possible, getting by on his looks. His talent was research, finding loopholes. He did it as a profession and used the same pattern to run his own life. The outline wasn't complete and he was drowning. " He tilted his head, regarding me. "Then you came in and—"

"Handed him my book," I interrupted him. "I know what an idiot I was, Bill."

He shrugged. "You trusted him. He's good at getting people to trust him. He fooled an entire country, Megan.

"But he screwed himself. Instead of destroying the evidence, he kept it. The manuscripts were like trophies to him. He caused his own downfall. You were in the right place at the wrong time and he needed your book to buy him some time." He snorted with disgust. "He thought, and I'm quoting here, 'all he needed was a little more time to write the last book.' He had no conscience when it came to stealing your work. Or the work of a dead man. Jared has no morals."

My stomach rolled as I thought about Jared. How could I have not seen what a terrible person he was behind his handsome face? I stared into my lap, my hands curled into tight balls of anger and embarrassment.

"Don't beat yourself up, Megan." Bill's voice was kind. "You had no idea."

"Why is he cooperating?"

"He has no choice. His career is over. His bank accounts frozen. The public is up in arms over this. His publishers are furious and out for blood. He had no time to prepare for what happened; with his huge ego he never thought ahead, assuming he wouldn't get caught. He's facing penalties, legal fees, and criminal charges—many of them. Probably jail time." Bill sat back with a satisfied smile. "Basically, he's fucked."

"Will he, ah, be there today?"

"No. His lawyer will be, as well as a rep from the publishing house and their lawyer. Probably his agent, too."

Relief flooded my chest, easing the knot of fear in my stomach. I never wanted to lay eyes on him again. "Good."

"We're going to get your property back today, Megan. That's why

I asked you for a list of what was in the satchel, as best as you could remember. I'm sure they also want to know if you plan on pressing any charges against Jared."

"No. I want my work back. I want to forget he even existed." The thought of facing him in court made me shiver. "By the time all this is through what would I get anyway?"

"Probably not much but satisfaction."

"I only want my book back."

He glanced at his watch. "Then let's go to the boardroom and do just that, all right?"

I sat across the table with Bill, staring at my leather satchel. I'd know it anywhere. The handle was bent and thin from years of use. The leather was dull, the edges frayed. I knew when the flap was lifted my grandfather's faded initials would be inside, the ink barely visible after all these years. I knew exactly where to find them. To anyone looking at it they would only see an old beaten-up bag. For me it was a sentimental link to a man who read to me, who taught me how to spell my name with his large hand wrapped around my smaller one, as together, we traced the letters over and again. My fingers itched to reach out and touch the leather, but I wasn't allowed to—not yet.

Voices had been droning on, with me partially listening. I heard the words fraud, charges, and a lot of legal terms I didn't understand. Mr. Chalmers, the lawyer for the publishing house, explained they were now working with the grandson of the real author, trying to work out legalities and settlements. As Bill had told me, book sales were suspended and the PR side of the business was trying to handle the maelstrom of negative press Jared's deception had caused. Jared himself had lost his career, his house, his entire lifestyle, and with every indication, his freedom. There was a very large part of me that felt a grim satisfaction knowing he would finally be punished for his actions.

Beside me, Bill spoke up, bringing my attention back to the people at the table. "Ms. Greene would like her property returned to her...immediately." He slid my list across the table. "There's a full description of the satchel and where you can locate the initials inside. There's also a list of the notes and drawings the satchel contained, proving that she's the rightful owner."

I watched anxiously, my chest tight and fighting queasiness again. My stomach had been in knots since I came back to Boston. I had hardly kept a thing down and Karen was beside herself in worry. I needed this done and over.

After more discussion, tears filled my eyes as my satchel was handed to Bill, who placed it in my hands. I ran my fingers over the worn leather, remembering all the times I had watched my grandfather do the same thing. The faint scent of smoke came off the leather from the fire. The thought the satchel and all it contained could have been consumed in flames stilled my fingers for a moment. If that happened, I would never again have held this small piece of my past in my hands. Somehow, it was even more important than the documents it held. I sent a small prayer of thanks out to the firefighter who had noticed the books and thought to remove them from harm, as well as to the neighbor who had contacted Jared's agent to hold them in safekeeping until Jared returned. It was because of his agent's honest, horrified reaction to the discovery of what the books actually represented, we were now fully aware of the depth of Jared's deceit.

My hands shook as I slipped the knot open and took out my book. My eyes widened as I took in its condition. Long slashing strokes of a felt pen, scribbled notes and comments covered the pages with Jared's attempts to make is *his own*. Luckily, I could still read my own words, at least most of them. The fact he had touched them, desecrated the pages with his words, made me even more nauseous. I vowed to rewrite the book in its entirety, and burn this copy. I wanted no reminder of him.

"Ms. Greene," Mr. Dunn, one of the owners of the publishing house, addressed me directly. I looked up, feeling dazed and confused. "My partners and I would be interested in discussing your book with you at another time, when this has all been resolved—if you'd be open to the idea?" He cleared his throat. "We read through the original draft and felt it was even better than the one Jared had submitted. We'd like to work with you in the future, if you're willing."

I glanced at Bill, unsure what to say or even think. He nodded. "I'll discuss it with my client and we'll get back to you."

I flipped through the rest of the documents grateful Jared hadn't touched my drawings and obviously ignored all my notes. I could recreate this—make it mine again. A small flutter of excitement bloomed in my chest—a purpose, something I could work on and could be part of my future. I had options. I spoke up. "We'll get back to you soon."

Heads nodded, smiles were offered my way, and I lowered my head, concentrating on the papers in front of me.

Unbidden, thoughts of Zachary entered my mind. Would he ever know all this happened? Would he realize how wrong he had been? How would he feel if he found out everything Jared did was a lie, and I had loved him? That what we had was real? Would he contact me? Where was he? I closed my eyes at the burst of pain that erupted in my chest.

No second chances.

I had to remember that.

Bill came back to Karen's place with me, and I let him fill them in on the meeting. He explained more of the legal ramifications Jared would be facing and answered some other questions we all had about the whole situation. He quietly informed me he would be happy to help me proceed with the book once it was ready. He assured me I'd have good council from the firm where he worked, since this wasn't really his specialty.

"I still can't pay anything," I reminded him.

He laughed. "With all the press this is getting, my firm would be thrilled to help you, Megan. In fact, my boss insists on it." He winked at me. "This might fast track my way into partnership."

We all chuckled with him, knowing he was trying to lighten up the moment.

"You may want to think about submitting this to other publishers as well, Megan. There's so much media attention around Jared and the stolen manuscripts, plus what he tried to do to yours, I'm sure your book would be given serious consideration now. You don't have to use the publishers that once rallied against you."

I nodded, mulling it over. They had only done what they thought was right and backed up their own author. They had no reason to believe Jared had been telling anything less than the truth—but maybe another publisher would be a good idea. Finally I spoke up. "I'll think about it, Bill. I'm not rushing into anything right now."

"Good idea." He stood up. "I have to go. I'll be in touch." He laid his hand on my shoulder. "The worst is over, Megan. You can move on, now."

Chris also stood up, announcing he had to get to the office. I curled into the corner of the sofa, dragging a blanket over my lap. I was constantly cold. Thoughts of the day swirled in my head as I stared at the satchel on the table. *Move on*, Bill said. Was I ready to move on now?

Karen's voice broke through my musings as she handed me a cup of herbal tea. "Are you okay, Megan? You look so tired and worn-out."

"It's been a lot to take in," I answered, sipping the warm beverage. "I haven't slept well the past couple nights."

She frowned. "It's more than a couple missed nights. You look positively exhausted. You're hardly eating, and I hear you throwing up all the time."

I shrugged, struggling not to cry at her words. "Nerves. It'll get better now."

"No, it's more," she insisted. "You're killing yourself."

"I'm doing the best I can," I whispered as the tears broke through.

She wrapped her hands around my cold ones. "I know, sweetie, but I think you need to see a doctor. It's more than a broken heart." She squeezed my hands, frowning. "You can barely keep water down. I'm worried. Please let me make an appointment with your doctor."

"If it'll make you feel better, okay." I drew in a deep breath. "Then I'm going back to Cliff's Edge." I smiled at her, wiping the tears away. "I have a book to fix."

"Will you finish your story?"

"Yes. It's time to close that one and start fresh."

"Can you?"

I shut my eyes, Zachary's scarred, hurt face filling my mind. He was gone and he wasn't coming back. Bill was right—it was time to move on. "Yes."

"Okay, then. Deal."

2 6

ZACHARY

The house smelled musty. I'd arranged for it to be cleaned before I arrived back, but it still carried the lingering odor of neglect. Elliott ran ahead of me, sniffing and pawing around. Walking from room to room, I opened the windows, letting the rush of the cleansing, salty air flow through the house. I hesitated at the door to my bedroom. It was clean and tidy—the bed made fresh, but I swore if I drew in a deep breath, I'd still be able to catch a trace of Megan in the air; the scent that had haunted my mind all this time. Cursing at my own stupid thoughts, I flung open the window. If there was any remaining scent lingering, it would be gone soon enough. Neither she nor her scent had a place in my life anymore.

It was more difficult to enter the studio, since the room hadn't been touched, even by the cleaning staff. The last painting I'd been working on was still on the easel, unfinished and sparse. What made my chest ache, though, were the pictures of Megan. She was smiling in the sunlight, laughing, angry, glaring at me, and the last one: her sleeping on the blankets that were still piled on the floor in the corner.

I'd developed the photos and created a collage, dry mounting them on a large board. She was beautiful and life-like as I stared at the images, lost briefly in memories of times I thought were the happiest of my life. Fuming once again that she was invading my thoughts, I shoved the board behind a pile of blank canvases, turning the pictures to the wall for good measure. I would get rid of it in the next while, since I never planned on transferring the images to canvas now. I opened the window and turned around, staring at the almost empty space. My eyes fell on the blankets in the corner of the room. Megan's nest, as she liked to call it. Without another thought, I crossed the room, bending down and running my fingers over the thick material, once again remembering her.

Remembering *us*.

The vision of her curled on the pile of blankets and pillows filled my head. She had been sitting, reading as I worked away that afternoon, and fallen asleep. When I'd looked up, I'd had to capture the moment, grabbing my camera, trading it for my paint-brush. Her bright hair spilled over the blue blanket, eyelashes dark laying on her pale skin, and the way her hand curled up under her chin, as she slumbered, called to me. I snapped away, embedding more of her images onto film, thinking one day I would attempt to recreate them on canvas. I recalled rousing her with my touch, slowly bringing her awake with warm kisses and trailing fingers. We made love on those blankets, my body telling her all the things my mouth couldn't yet say. My apology and conflicted feelings had been silent but powerful as I surged into her warm, welcoming body.

It had been the last time she was in my studio. Our world had ended only a couple days later. I looked down to see my hand fisting the material, grasping it so hard, it was tearing. I stood up abruptly, shaking my head. Why was I thinking about that afternoon?

I wondered if it was a mistake coming back to Cliff's Edge. Maybe it was too soon. Perhaps I should have never returned, but something kept nagging at me it was time to come back, and finally I gave in.

Walking out of the studio, I closed the door behind me, shutting out the memories.

The next few days, I spent settling back in. Other than closing the window, I kept away from the studio. Mrs. Cooper had been kind enough to send Mr. Cooper out with groceries so I didn't have to venture into town. Elliott and I walked the beach and in the woods, not surprised that, as usual, our private area was deserted, except for me.

It had been three months since the day I left, throwing a quickly packed case and Elliott into the SUV, then driving straight to Canada. There, a small cabin, and an even smaller town offered me refuge, while I figured out my next step. For days I paced and cursed, the pain in my chest threatening to overwhelm me. I couldn't eat or sleep. Dormant feelings of rejection and worthlessness simmered under my marred skin, making it feel as if it was stretched too tight over my bones. I shied away from the news or radio, not wanting to know the stories and rumors that had occurred. In desperation, I immersed myself in books, photography, and painted like a man possessed. Canvas after canvas came to life under my hands as I lost myself in a world where I didn't have to think—only create. The views there were different from my house in Maine. The scope was vaster, the scenery angrier, my perception darker. Some of the pieces were magnificent. Most of them I left sitting in the cabin, knowing I would never share them with the world. They were too personal. The paint on those canvases was thicker and edged with rage in many places. Rage was an emotion I could hold on to. Rage over my own foolishness. Rage over what had occurred and how I opened myself up to a world of hurt because of a pair of wide, brown eyes that gazed up at me in seeming adoration.

I wanted it to be hate. Hate for those eyes and the woman behind them. Hate for what she had done.

Yet, I was never able to feel that hate. Not for her.

No matter how hard I tried, it was impossible.

Somewhere, deep in my heart and my brain, was the smallest

seed of disbelief. Doubt that the woman I had finally lost my heart to could have ever betrayed me that way. I wanted it to be real; I wanted to believe her sweet words and gentle ways had been real—meant only for me.

I wanted to believe she had seen the man behind the scars and loved him, despite them—despite his past.

A tiny part of me refused to believe she hadn't loved me. In the darkness of the night, when I lay awake and the memories washed over me, that quiet voice told me I'd been wrong.

I was missing something and Megan loved me.

Which only fueled the rage even more.

Any reporters that had been hanging around Cliff's Edge had long since left. The story became old and not interesting enough to stick around for in case I reappeared, but, as a precaution, I was determined to keep a low profile. Early fall was now upon us, and the town slowly began to empty of tourists, yet I still stayed close to the house and beach. I only ventured into town once, late at night, to pick up supplies. I hadn't even let Ashley and Jonathon know I was back, and I knew Mrs. Cooper would never violate my trust. She was the only person I had contacted when I returned.

Jonathon had been in touch on the rare occasion I would check emails in the small café that had internet access. My cabin was far too remote to offer such amenities. He begged for my return or at least for new pieces to sell. Every painting the gallery possessed was sold, and he wanted more. I never answered back, but I had a few upstairs he could have if he wanted them, as well as the ones I had brought back with me. Perhaps being back would help inspire me. I shook my head as I took a sip of wine, unsure I would once more feel inspired. I returned to close this part of my life, to decide whether or not to sell the house. I wasn't sure I would ever feel the same about the place now, or ever feel as safe as I had before everything happened. The memories were too many and far too fresh.

As hard as I tried to deny it, Megan was everywhere. I could hear her laughter in the house; see her walking on the beach. Certain times when I would walk into a room, I swore I could smell her fragrance lingering in the air, even though I told myself it was impossible. This morning, when I awoke, a bright color caught my eye. Tucked behind the lamp was one of her many hair ties. She was forever losing them and I would find them scattered all over the house. For a brief moment, I stared at it before lifting it to my nose. It smelled of her—floral and light. A burst of anger tore through me and I grabbed the trash can, tossing in the hair tie. In the bathroom, I found her lotion in the cupboard and flung it in the can. I yanked the top dresser drawer open, almost snarling at the sight of some of her socks. She always had cold feet and was in constant need of warmth. My fingers closed around the fuzzy material, an image of her feet resting in my lap, as we watched a movie, caused my eyes to burn with unshed tears. I emptied the entire drawer, not caring what all was inside.

Downstairs, I grabbed a trash bag and dumped the overflowing tin into it. Megan, or whoever had removed her things, had done a lousy job, and I was determined to finish it. Elliott followed me, low whimpers escaping his throat. I tore open cupboard after cupboard, ignoring his discomfort. A half empty bottle of corn syrup ricocheted off the floor as I flung it blindly, remembering her sweet smile I thought was only for me. The pictures Jared showed me proved I was wrong. An unopened jar of raspberry jam hit the bottom of the bag so hard it shattered, as I thought about licking the sticky mess off her fingers one morning, then making love to her on the kitchen floor. Her face that morning had been glowing and alive. Not like the last time I saw her, pale and ashamed, a face in the crowd, *his* arm holding her. With a roar, item after item went in the bag. I wanted no reminders of the woman who deceived me. Nothing that would sneak up on me and cause the ache in my chest to burst into life and throb with an intensity I thought would kill me.

Tucked under the edge of the sofa, I saw a pair of her flip flops. I shoved them in the bag and walked all around the house dragging the bag behind me. I paused at the bottom of the stairs, panting. All that was left was the studio—the pictures.

The memories.

Leaving the cumbersome bag, I walked up the stairs, my feet feeling heavier with each tread. Outside the door, I paused, glancing toward Elliott, who was lying with his face buried in his paws, low whimpers in the back of his throat. I knew he could sense my anger, and it was upsetting him. I wasn't entirely sure myself where all my anger had come from after so many months. With determination, I stepped inside and yanked the collage board out, planning on carrying it downstairs and disposing of it. Instead, I leaned it on the wall and stared. Her sweet face, *Megan's* sweet face, with those wondrous eyes, stared back at me. Ice-cold fury morphed into pain. Twisting, ripping pain that made my throat tighten and hands shake. Weariness draped over me, as I realized: she was still there, in my heart. As firmly entrenched as my hatred of my parents, was my love for her. No matter what had transpired, no matter how much I wanted to hate her, I never would. I couldn't forgive or forget, but she would always reside there. She would always be with me.

I fell back heavily against the wall, my legs too shaky to hold me up. I had to leave this place. Go away and start over. It didn't matter if I emptied the entire house; she would still exist within these walls.

I slipped the board back to the front of the pile. It didn't matter if I tried to hide it. I could see it, and her, every time I closed my eyes.

Quietly, I shut the door and went back downstairs, calling Elliott to come with me.

I left the bag where it lay.

Later that night, I was startled by three sharp raps at my door. Elliott stood up—a low whimper in his throat, meaning whoever was at the door wasn't a stranger. Warily, I approached it, the evening light casting a shadow through the covered glass, showing me it was a woman. My heart skipped a beat and my hand tightened on the knob. The person on the other side was small; surely it wasn't Megan. She couldn't know I was here. The house down the beach was empty. I hadn't seen anyone since I arrived back.

I opened the door, surprised to find Karen standing on the other side. Her expression was less than friendly, a scowl on her face as she gazed at me.

"So, it's true. You're back," she snapped as she breezed past me, stopping in the hall.

"Do come in," I murmured, sarcasm dripping from the words. "Make yourself at home." I walked past her into the living room. "Can I get you a glass of wine? Or would you prefer my balls on a plate?"

"Since I don't think you have any, I'll take the wine."

I arched my eyebrow at her but fetched a glass and poured her some wine, unclear as to why I wasn't simply ordering her out of the house.

"How did you know I was here?"

She tossed her hair in defiance at my annoyed tone. "Chris was here last week. He said he heard Mrs. Cooper on the phone with you arranging the house to be cleaned and groceries brought in."

"Ah. I should have emailed, I suppose—less ears. Shame the place I was staying at had very little internet access." I sat down in the chair across the table from her, feeling weary. "What do you want, Karen?"

She slammed a large manila envelope on the table in front of me. "I brought you this, Zachary."

I eyed the thick package with suspicion. "What is it?"

"The truth."

"According to you, you mean?"

"Listen you egotistical, insufferable man. Take your head out of your ass and read what's inside."

"I don't think I'm interested in more stories, but thanks anyway."

Her eyes narrowed in anger. "Are you always this pig-headed and stupid?"

"So I've been told." I pushed the envelope back toward her. "Thanks for dropping by."

"Have you really been that out of touch?" she asked, her voice incredulous. "Have you not been keeping up with the news?"

"Aside from the local paper, which is a weekly publication where I was staying, and is about six pages in total, no. I didn't need to read more bullshit and gossip, but I can fill you in on the current price of local fish, if you're interested." I sighed, growing impatient with the conversation. "Whatever"—I swallowed, having trouble even saying her name—"*Megan* sent you here to tell me, I'm not interested."

"She has no idea I'm here."

"Which is why, again?"

"Maybe because I can't stand to watch her suffer anymore."

I shrugged, trying to ignore the small pang of pain at the thought of her suffering. "Guilt can do that to a person."

"She blames herself, but not for the reason you think."

I was getting aggravated and I wanted her to leave. "You're not making any sense."

"Megan blames herself for what Jared did, but not because she was in on it. He used her as much as he used you. That's what he does—uses people."

"What?"

"She didn't lead him to you. He followed her here, Zachary. He watched you together. He decided to use *you* to crush *her*. He found out who you were, then he caused this disaster. Not her—she had no idea."

"So she says," I argued, but my eyes looked at the envelope sitting on the table.

Karen stood up, slamming her hand down on the table. "It's the truth. She blames herself because you were hurt in all of this mess. She wasn't even surprised how easily you believed his lies. She told me you were so used to being hurt and taken advantage of it would be your first and only reaction." She paused, her voice becoming softer. "She forgives you, you know."

I bit back my angry retort. "I will ask again, Karen. Why are you here?"

She pushed the envelope back so my hand was touching it. "Read this."

"Maybe later; after dinner with my coffee. I like a good story while I digest."

"You'll find it very enlightening."

"Enlightening? Does it give me insight into how to find love? Heal the broken heart you think I have?"

"I'm not sure at this point, you have a heart."

I laughed, the sound dry and forced, echoing off the rafters above our heads. "Now you're getting the picture. If there isn't anything else, I have things to do."

She stood up, anger emitting from her body like the waves pounding out on the beach.

"Read it." Her hands were clenched at her side. "If you won't do it for me, then do it for my husband, who I know you respect. If he hadn't been so busy right now, it would've been him handing this to you, not me. I know you wouldn't refuse him."

I frowned at her words. Why would Chris want me to read this so much he would send his wife to deliver it? I had no idea, but I didn't like how I was feeling right now: trapped, cornered, on edge.

"Is there a pop quiz later?" I snapped.

"I don't know why I bothered," she hissed, turning and hurrying out the door, the slam of it behind her shaking the window glass. I watched as she stomped down the steps and crossed the beach. Once she turned around, flinging her arms up as she yelled words carried away by the wind and waves. I highly doubted they were pleasant.

I shook my head as I regarded the innocuous looking envelope, wondering what it could contain.

Why I was bothering to find out, I didn't know. Chris had been a quiet, but good friend over the years—I knew him far better than I knew Karen. He never asked about my past or scars, accepting me as merely his neighbor. He had my email address and was kind enough to let me know, a couple times, that he was watching the house after I fled last time. He never mentioned Megan, for which I was grateful. But now this envelope—it had to be important to him.

Sitting down, I opened the flap and dumped the contents on the table. News articles, press releases and documents piled up; and as I went through them, I saw they were all clipped together in some sort of fashion, and date order.

With a sigh, I topped up my wine and started to read.

Two hours later, I was banging on Karen's door. I paced the deck waiting for her to answer, my heart pounding in my chest, my mind racing with the information I had read. Thoughts and words echoed in my head, the envelope clutched in my tight fist.

The door slid open and I pivoted around when she stepped out, her arms crossed over her chest. We stared at each other, my eyes searching hers for answers.

"Do you have something to say, or did you want to borrow a cup of sugar?"

I stepped closer, my fingers jabbing at the envelope. "It's true? All of it is true?"

She huffed as she straightened up. "Yes. All of it is true. Not only did Jared steal Megan's manuscript, they've proven he stole all the books he published. She didn't lie to you, Zachary. About her book or anything else."

"She didn't use me."

Karen's arms flung out, gesturing wildly. "Hallelujah! The man finally gets it!"

I grabbed her arm. "Why, Karen? Why are you here? You hate me—why did you come to give me this information?"

Her brow furrowed. "I don't hate you, Zachary. I don't understand you, but I don't hate you."

"Why?"

She stepped back. "You'd better come inside."

I followed her in, my knees almost crumbling as I inhaled.

Megan.

She was everywhere.

Her scent soaked the air. Her favorite sweater was draped over the back of the chair. Her sneakers were lying on the floor by the door, looking as if they had been kicked off moments ago. The journals I'd given her were sitting on the table. I looked around in panic, expecting Dixie to come running, barking out a greeting, or to see Megan's sad face looking at me.

My gaze flew to Karen, who shook her head. "She isn't here."

"But she was."

"Yes."

Reaching behind me, she shut the door. I stepped forward, only to let out a muffled curse. In three strides, I was across the room, standing in front of *Tempest.* My fingers flew over the canvas, confused. I had left it behind. In one angry stroke of a knife, I had destroyed the image. Severing the completeness of it, the way Megan's betrayal had severed my heart. I left it to her as a symbol, torn and jagged, yet it was here, mended and complete.

"How?"

Karen stood beside me. "It broke her heart—almost as much as you leaving. She asked Ashley for help to have it restored." A small humorless laugh left her mouth. "She wouldn't take money to fight Jared, or accept help for anything, but she asked me to loan her the money to fix your painting." She moved away and sat down. "It arrived back this week. She was going to give it back to Ashley for you, but she couldn't bear to part with it yet."

I sat down across from her, my legs feeling too weak to hold me up anymore. "Where is she?"

"You don't have the right to know the answer to that question."

"Please."

A weary sigh shook her frame. "She's been staying here."

I swallowed the thick feeling in my throat. "But she's gone now?"

"She went back to Boston. She was meeting with some people about her book."

"She's being published?"

Karen shrugged. "She hasn't decided yet. Things are...complicated right now."

"Is she all right?"

"Do you really care?"

I had no idea how to answer that loaded question. For months I'd been fighting feeling anything besides anger and betrayal. I'd been trying, so hard, not to feel anything except contempt for her. It was a battle I knew earlier today I had lost before I'd even begun to fight it. I missed Megan so much, it made me even angrier, which made my denial stronger, and the whole time I'd been wrong.

So fucking wrong.

"Yes, I care."

"You have a strange way of showing it."

"I thought she lied to me. I thought she was using me."

"Because you chose to believe the lies of someone other than her. You never even gave her the chance to explain!"

I could hear the anger in her voice. "It made more sense," I offered, knowing it was a feeble excuse.

"It made more sense than her loving you?"

"Yes."

"You're more fucked up than I even thought, aren't you?"

"I don't understand love."

"You made that obvious."

I frowned at her, not understanding. "Did Megan not tell you my past?"

Karen leaned forward, almost sneering at me. "Listen, Zachary, and listen well. Until a very short time ago, I knew nothing about your past—about who you were. Megan kept it all private." She sat back, her eyes drifting to the table. "Until this moment, I didn't realize how well she wrote it."

"Wrote what?"

She stood up and picked up Megan's journals. She held them in her hands, as if making a decision. She withdrew the red colored one and placed it on the table, then handed me the rest of the books. "She wrote your story."

I was shaking as I took the books. "Why?"

She sat down again. "Partly to get the memories out, I think. Mostly though, to heal. She wanted to remember all of it. She didn't plan on doing anything with them, except to write them out of her head. It was better than her sitting here, staring into space, which is what she did for a few days. I got up one morning and found her writing, as if her life depended on it. I knew she'd be okay—it would take some time, but she would recover. If she could write it out, she'd get through this." Her eyes narrowed. "And she has."

"She's moved on." My voice sounded clogged, almost choking as I spoke.

"How long are you staying here?" she asked abruptly, ignoring my statement.

"I don't know."

"You need to read those books."

"Why are you keeping one?"

"It's the last book. The ending, if you like. Once you read those, we'll talk. I'll decide if you get the last one."

"Why are you giving them to me at all?"

The room was silent as she mulled over my question. "I don't really like you, Zachary. I don't understand what Megan sees in you that inspired the love and loyalty she feels toward you. I don't know why my husband thinks so highly of you—even now." Her fingers traced over a pattern on the arm of the chair, back and forth, almost hypnotically. "But I love both of them, and he asked me to give you the information on Jared. Megan still feels something for you, although I don't understand why. Their opinions have to be counted, so I'm giving you the benefit of the doubt—for their sakes." She stood up, signaling she was done with me. "Read the journals. Then we'll talk."

I walked to the door. "Does Megan know I'm back?"

"No."

"Will you tell her?"

"We'll talk after you read the journals."

I knew that was all I would get from her for now.

Without another word, I opened the door and headed across the beach, the journals feeling heavy in my hands.

27

ZACHARY

Four days. I waited four days—hoping, praying Megan would return. I wanted to see her again on the beach and go to her; hear her voice, and see her sweet face. I yearned for her more every day.

The days passed, though, with was no sign of her anywhere. Maybe she had decided not to return once she found out I was back in Cliff's Edge. I had no doubt Karen told her I'd come back, since she promised me she would. For the first two days, I read Megan's journals. I relived moments I hadn't allowed myself to remember, smiled at the way she saw me through her eyes, frowned at how often I'd caused her tears. The tenderness, only she could trigger, raged again, as she described reading my moods when my eyes changed color—something I wasn't even aware happened. I blinked away the moisture when she compared my smile to a morning sunrise—slow and warming the air around me. I rarely smiled before she entered my life, feeling the scars made that gesture look twisted and wrong. She saw only good and beauty.

Twice, I had begged Karen to tell me where Megan was, but she refused, saying the decision was up to Megan, not me. Despite my assurances of how much I loved her, Karen's opinion of me still remained skeptical; her protectiveness was fierce. I had to respect her for that above all else. The morning she left, I found the last journal on my doorstep, but I had yet to finish reading it. The pain it contained was so raw and overwhelming I hadn't read past the day I fled from Megan and Cliff's Edge.

The morning of the fifth day, I was attacking the canvas in front of me, all the rage and bitterness toward myself splashing on the stretched material in angry, bold swipes of black, indigo, and gray. The storm on the painting was bleak, dark and massive; overtaking everything in its path—much like the burning pressure in my chest.

The pain hadn't lessened; in fact, it had gotten worse since I returned. I hadn't slept and barely eaten—Karen's words and Megan's writing playing repeatedly in my head. I had read and reread everything Karen gave me. The proof staring me in the face, the truth I knew all along, and refused to admit, ashamed at my actions. The things I'd done, the assumptions I'd made, the pain I'd inflicted. All done because once again, I believed in what I saw, not what I felt. I failed to trust the one person in the world I should have listened to.

I stepped back, feeling the great weariness from lack of sleep cover me like a thick blanket. I dropped my brush into the jar beside me and wiped my hands on the rag as I stared at the chaos on the canvas. The picture I looked at was void of anything but pain—much like my heart.

Elliott's head snapped up, a low whimper happening in the back of his throat as he stood, his tail moving side to side in agitation while his huge eyes looked behind me toward the beach. Slowly, I approached the window, reaching out a hand to steady myself on the frame.

Megan.

Standing motionless on the packed sand, just out of reach of the shallow surf.

She was wearing a long, thick coat clutched loosely around her body. Her shoulders were hunched against the wind that blew strong and cold, while her glorious hair streamed out behind her, the sun catching the color, and turning it bright copper. She seemed so small amid the vastness that stretched out before her, yet it was only her that my eyes could see.

Dixie ran around on the sand, sniffing and exploring, her excited barks barely rising over the swell of the waves and the wind. Behind me, Elliott paced, knowing Dixie was there. He was as anxious to be reunited with her, as I was to see Megan.

Unlike the reunion they would share, though, I had no expectations of a joyous reception from Megan. Her journals were vast and rich—our story laid out in all its sweetness and horror. I saw us falling in love, and felt my walls crumble in those pages as I opened myself to her. I felt her elation and read her pain, the pages bearing the evidence of her emotion as she wrote about the last awful day, a few new ones added of my own as I read her words. All of the journals showed the tears that had fallen as she wrote, the watermarks appearing more often as the story grew to a close. I had no idea what the end part of the last journal contained. I still hadn't read it; every time I picked it up, a wave of nausea would rush through me, knowing I could very well read Megan's final farewell to me in it. I knew I would read and live her pain of the past few months she'd been alone. Her words would convey the same loneliness and longing I'd felt all this time, as well as the hurt I caused both of us by leaving. As much as I admired her strength before, now I dreaded reading how she used it to move past me.

Slowly I walked down the stairs, Elliott ahead of me. Shrugging into my coat, on impulse, I slipped the last journal into the pocket. I hesitated, my hand gripping the door handle, knowing once I opened the door there was no turning back. Elliott would be out like a shot and within seconds, Megan would know I was coming. There was a chance she would turn and walk away.

Nonetheless, it was a chance I had to take.

E lliott was out of the door and on the beach before I even got to the top of the stairs. I stood watching as Dixie and he raced toward each other, the barks of welcome ringing out, echoing loudly. A smile tugged on my lips, watching the two furry friends reunite. Megan turned, watching as well, her head lifting, looking my way as I stood on the steps. Deliberately, she turned back to the water, her shoulders now straight. There was no doubt what emotion she was feeling at the moment.

Wrapping my coat tighter, I crossed the beach, stopping before I was too close. The urge to wrap myself around her was almost over-whelming. All I wanted was to reach out and touch her, but I knew that wouldn't be welcomed.

She spun around, the movement so abrupt and unexpected, it startled me and I stepped back. Emotions I'd kept buried, memories I refused to allow to surface, broke free, tearing though me like a tornado.

Her eyes—swirling, deep pools of brown so rich and vibrant stared at me, filled with a thousand emotions. Her sweet face was pale, the freckles standing out on her skin like flecks of wet sand on a bleached seashell. She was thin and tired looking—yet so very beautiful.

How could I have forgotten how beautiful she was? How much she made me feel simply by being close to her?

I stepped forward, but her hand flew up, halting my movement.

She was also very angry.

I held up my hands in supplication. "Megan," I breathed.

Her eyes dropped, but she didn't move, instead pulling the coat she was wearing closer around her like armor. "Why are you here?"

"I had to come back."

"Why?"

How did I explain it to her? There weren't enough words for what I wanted to tell her. "Please, look at me."

Slowly her eyes lifted, my heart aching with the pain and hurt I saw in them. Pain and hurt I caused. Her hands tightened on the coat, the material twisting in her fists. "You believed him. You believed his disgusting, terrible lies," she spat.

"I'm sorry." Two words that weren't anywhere near adequate, yet the only ones I could think to say.

"You're sorry?"

"I have so much to say, Megan. I don't know how to start."

"Why don't you start with where you've been for the past few months, Zachary? After you left me here! Alone—facing that sea of reporters who were screaming and yelling questions, calling me names, while he stood there, fucking smirking as you walked away— no—ran away like a coward! You arrogant, selfish, asshole! You just left me there!"

Her voice had steadily risen until she was screaming at me and I flinched at her words, but didn't stop her diatribe. Everything she said was true.

"And then I come back here to find you gone! You disappeared without a word, the whole time believing his lies!"

"I did believe them. It made so much more sense than you really loving me."

Her shoulders sagged, her voice now weary. "I never did anything but love you."

"I know that now."

"How did it feel when you realized I wasn't lying? That every-thing I said was the truth? That we were real? He used *me*. He used *you* to get to *me*. Not the other way around. How did that feel?"

"It made me ill."

"How do you think I felt?"

"I have no idea, Megan. I can only imagine you were devastated."

She nodded. "I was. And, I was alone again and had to start over."

I closed my eyes at the sound of her pain. "I'm so, so sorry."

"So you keep saying."

"I don't know what else to say. I want to take you inside and talk to you. Sit down and hash this all out. Listen to whatever you want to tell me. Maybe get you to listen to me." I inhaled sharply. "I know it might not mean anything now, Megan, but I love you."

She drew in on herself, taking a step back as her eyes widened. "You love me...*why*, Zachary? Why exactly do you love me?"

Watching her reaction to me was torture. The need to draw her close clawed at me and I pushed my hands into my pockets to stop myself from touching her. My entire world was hanging by a thread in front of me, and I knew it could snap at any second. She could turn and walk away—out of my life for good.

My fingers closed around the journal in the bottom of my pocket, nervously clutching the smooth leather, remembering her words of love. I needed to make her feel them again. "Why? Because of how I felt when I was with you. How you made me feel about the world around me. That maybe, it wasn't such a terrible place. That perhaps I had a place in it, as long as you were beside me."

"You were so quick to throw it away."

"I know. I was scared and caught off guard when my past hit me in the face. I reacted and I hurt you. I'll never forgive myself for that."

"Why did you come back? You came back before you knew the truth. You said yourself you don't give second chances—ever."

My brow furrowed. "You aren't the one who needs the second chance. I am, Megan. I need *you* to give *me* a second chance. I've fought against it for months. I kept telling myself the only thing I felt for you was contempt, but I was lying to myself. I missed you so fucking much, I ached with it." My hands clenched at my side, desperate to reach out, *needing* to touch her. "You want to know why I came back? Because somewhere, some part of me knew I had to try and find you. There was a small voice telling me it was real. You did love me and I'd fucked up the one good thing I ever found in my life."

I paced up and down the sand, needing to move as the tension grew inside me. "I told myself I was coming back here to clear out the house and sell it, move on and forget this place and that you ever existed." A humorless laugh escaped my lips as I stopped pacing and stood in front of her. "As if I could ever forget you—or get over you. The day I walked back into the house you were there—you were fucking everywhere. All I could see, all I could feel, were all the good things about you, about us. All I could think of was you. Your voice, your scent, the way you looked at me and cared for me. All I could feel in that house was your love.

"Then Karen came to see me. She gave me all the articles about that fucking bastard and what he'd done. It was then I realized how deeply I'd wronged you. Wronged us."

"You believed him so easily. You walked away without even questioning it."

"I did. It proved I was right all along. I wasn't worthy of being loved. Only used."

"I didn't use you."

"I know. *Fuck*, I know that now. I knew it months ago, but I was too afraid to admit it. Too afraid I had been wrong." My fingers dug into the skin at the back of my neck. "Karen gave me your journals to read and I saw how you'd written our story." I stepped forward, my voice wavering. "I read your words—I read your love for me, Megan. I saw your tears on those pages. I saw the truth. I knew how wrong I'd been, how much damage I'd done, and I knew I was probably too late."

"Is that why you're here now, Zachary? Because of the story, because of what you found out at the end?"

Found at the end?

I frowned at her. "I haven't finished reading the last book yet, Megan."

"I don't believe you."

"I haven't. I was too...afraid to read it."

"Why?"

"I didn't want to know you didn't love me anymore. I didn't want to read your goodbye." I pulled the book out of my pocket, offering it to her. "I wanted to see if I could beg you to rewrite the end. If you thought you could forgive me, and let me try and show you how much I still love you."

She looked between the book and my face. Up and down her gaze moved. "You need to read it the way it is right now."

My arm dropped, the book now weighing too much to hold it. "Is there no chance?"

Megan moved closer. Close enough, I could see the gold in her eyes; smell the gentle floral scent of her hair. "You want to know if I can forgive you."

I wanted to yank her into my arms and feel her warmth. I wanted to bury my face into her hair and breathe her in, but I couldn't—not without her permission. Like I was in a trance, I lifted my hand and tucked one long strand of hair behind her ear. "Yes."

"I forgave you the day you left me. You'd only known love for a few weeks, Zachary. You weren't even sure of everything you were feeling yet. What you knew best was being hurt." I froze as she rose up, the soft brush of her lips on my cheek surprising. "But you have to read the rest of our story, then decide if you want to move forward. We have so much to recover from, and it won't be easy or happen overnight." She stepped back, the glimmer of tears in her eyes. "I started again without you, and I'll keep going because I have to. If you read that book and decide you have to leave, just do it. Don't come see me. Don't give me hope again. I'll pack my things, go back to Boston, and carry on where I have some support. " A tear rolled down her cheek. "I can't take it and I won't let you hurt us again. I won't recover from that."

Then she turned and walked away.

The journal mocked me from the table where it had been sitting since I walked in the house. I had stood and watched Megan move across the beach, away from me. Her figure grew smaller as the distance between us lengthened. I watched her until she disappeared, struggling not to run after her and beg her to tell me what was in the book. That it didn't matter, because I loved her. I wanted her to let me hold her until I felt the horrible pain ease away, and I was strong enough to be what she needed. I would prove to her I wasn't ever going to leave her again.

I didn't want to hurt her anymore.

I pulled the book closer, almost with fear. I opened the cover; flipping to the page where the satin red ribbon marked the spot I stopped. That last, awful day when I allowed my insecurities to blind me to the truth—truth I was too weak to believe. Megan's unique, almost old-fashioned script filled the pages. I flipped to the last page, noticing, for the first time, the book was only about two-thirds full.

I sat on the sofa closer to the fire, an unusual chill running through my body. The contents of this journal were going to change my life, of that I had no doubt.

I looked out the window, watching the waves as they surged and ebbed. I felt my tension easing as I matched my breathing to the long swells.

Finally, I lowered my gaze to the book, wondering if I was strong enough to read it and accept what it said.

Two hours later, the book fell from my hands as hot tears poured down my face, her words swirling around in my head. So many emotions flooded my heart. Her raw pain at my leaving and how she struggled tore at my soul. I left her alone at a time I should've been beside her; giving her what she offered me so freely: unconditional love and support. I had failed her in so many ways, yet her words brought with them the flash of another emotion: hope. Hope for the future, hope for us. With that hope, came joy for the news our story contained.

Bending down, I picked up the book. She hadn't finished our story. The pages were still blank as if she was waiting, unsure how to finish.

I had to get to her. Plead with her to allow me to be part of those blank pages.

To allow us to finish the story together.

MEGAN

I shivered under the blanket at the cold that seemed to be a permanent resident inside my body. I thought I was prepared to see Zachary. When Karen told me he was back and what she had done, I was shocked—and furious. Her decision, she told me, was based on the fact he seemed as lost and struggling as I appeared to still be, even though I tried hard to cover that fact. When she told me he was waiting for me, I almost didn't believe it.

Seeing him this morning, it took all I had not to throw myself into his arms. The way he looked at me almost broke my resolve. His insistence he hadn't read the last journal to the end, that he was still in love with me, made it all that much harder to believe he was even standing in front of me. He didn't give second chances. He told me that multiple times—why would he change his mind for me?

The sudden fury I'd felt when he was standing in front of me was shocking. The anger I denied, the names I refused to allow anyone to call him, fell from my lips...and he took it. He took it all and let me rage until the moment passed, his gaze never wavering. He stood tall and firm, admitting it was his own doubts that he listened to, his own fears he allowed Jared's words to penetrate. He apologized continually, asking for only one thing.

For me to give *him* a second chance. To believe in him and us enough to allow him back in my life. My aching heart and weary soul wanted to give him what he desired. I still loved him, but it was no longer only about me. He had to know the whole story. One of the hardest things I ever did was to turn from him and walk away. The next step was his and his alone to make.

I burrowed deeper, once again feeling exhausted. It hit me at the oddest times and nothing could stop my eyes from closing. My body demanded rest, and with a sigh, I gave in.

Sun streamed in the window, warming my face as I slowly woke up. When my eyes opened, they found Zachary, sitting, a silent sentinel, watching over me. In his hand was the last journal. His face was inscrutable, but his posture was rigid, his fingers clenching the journal so tight his knuckles were white. I shook my head, clearing my throat. "I guess I forgot to lock the sliding door."

I sat up, swinging my legs off the sofa. When he spoke, his voice was surprisingly tender. "Do you need anything?"

I blinked, my brow furrowed in confusion. "I'm sorry, what?"

"A drink, something to eat. Can I do anything for you?"

"No."

He laid the book down between us on the small coffee table. "Your work is brilliant. Honest to a fault."

"It's *our* story. It deserved honesty."

"Why, Megan? Why did you write it?"

I cleared my throat. "I thought if I wrote it out, the pain would lessen. Maybe if I got it out of my head, I wouldn't ache so much."

"Did it work?"

"No."

He nodded in silent understanding. "I thought if I ran away and didn't see you, I could hate you the way I wanted. I thought I could stop the rage I felt."

"Did it work?"

"No." He paused. "I had one huge flaw in my logic, though."

"Oh?"

He leaned forward, his hands splayed across his thighs. "My rage was directed at myself because I knew, somewhere inside, I knew, I could never hate you. No matter what I thought you did, I would only ever love you."

His honest words caused an ache in my chest. My hands tightened around the edge of the blanket as I fought the tears that were never far beneath the surface.

He picked up the journal. "I hurt you so much. I also left you alone to face so much more than some reporters."

"Yes," I whispered.

"Tell me."

"You didn't read it?"

"I read your words. I want to hear you tell me." He paused, swallowing as his voice shook. "Tell me about the day you found out, Megan."

"Karen made me go to the doctor—she wouldn't let me leave until I did."

He nodded.

"They took blood and checked me out, ran some tests. Karen stayed with me because I was so nervous, even though I was sure he would tell me it was stress."

"It was more. So much more." He came closer, edging forward, his gaze never faltering.

A tear rolled down my cheek as I recalled the moment. "He told me I was pregnant."

The smallest smile ghosted over his face, his eyes bright. "How did you feel?"

I thought back to that day and the myriad of emotions I went through.

"Surprised—scared—upset—angry."

"With me?"

"No." I leaned toward him, wanting to explain. "I forgot my shot, Zachary. I missed it. I was angry at myself." I drew in a deep breath. "But then, I wasn't. All I felt was joy. So much joy, I thought my heart would burst."

"Even though I left you alone?"

I closed my eyes as I nodded. "It was as if I had a new sense of purpose. I was determined to move forward and give this child all my love—create a life for the two of us. I had a small piece of you left I could love."

His voice became thicker. "You loved our child even though I deserted you?"

I met his gaze, shocked to see tears in his eyes. "Or course I did. We created this life together." I lowered my voice. "You didn't know. Neither of us did at that point."

"And I never would have, if I hadn't come back. You would have been alone with our child." His voice grew angrier. "Raising our child on your own, because I'm a coward."

Hot tears splashed on my shaking fists. "You're here now," I offered, almost afraid to say it. I had no idea if he would stay.

"By the grace of God, yes." He got up and began pacing. "How can you forgive all this? How can you forgive me? If it's not bad enough I didn't have the same faith in us you did to stay and find out the truth, now I find out I left you alone and pregnant?" He stopped, dropping to his knees in front of me. "Why would you even keep the child? How can you forgive me all that, Megan?" His eyes searched mine, looking for answers. "I don't understand."

The depth of emotion in his gaze was overwhelming. Pain, regret, and torment churned in his wide stare. The edges of his eyes were so red-rimmed I knew he'd been crying before this conversation happened. He gasped as I reached up and cupped his face, his hands moving to cover mine right away, pressing them into his skin. "When you truly love, you forgive," I whispered.

Hope colored his words. "And do you?"

I knew we had so much to work out—so much to talk about and deal with. His leaving, the pain he caused, the fears I'd been dealing with alone. The months I spent trying to rebuild my life. I didn't even know where he'd been, or what he'd been doing all this time. There were fears I would have to face about him staying as well, but I also knew I still loved him.

"Yes."

"The baby?"

"—is a part of us; it was all I had to hold on to of you."

His hand lifted, shaking, and began to lower again, but then he drew back, his face uncertain. I lifted the blanket aside and clasped his wrist, guiding it to my stomach. The warmth of his skin felt good against the cold of my own. Slowly his fingers opened, moving and caressing the small swell beneath his touch. "I never planned to have a child," he whispered. "I didn't know if I'd be a good father." He looked up, a worried frown on his face. "You know I didn't have a very good example growing up."

I studied his face, seeing the wonder in his expression.

"How did you feel when you read about the baby?"

"How did I feel?"

"Yes. You wanted my words, Zachary. Now I want yours. I need them. What made you cry?"

He stared, his brow furrowed. "I was ashamed that I'd deserted you. Worried I was too late and you may not forgive me." He paused, his gaze dropping to my stomach. "Then the happiness of knowing you're carrying my child. That you were here, safe, and maybe I had a chance—I've never felt happiness like that before, Megan. I've never wanted something so much, either."

He swallowed and looked back up at me. "You didn't finish the story. Why didn't you finish?"

"I didn't know how it was going to end."

"Let it end with me—with us. Give me the chance, Megan. Please."

"Do you want this child?"

Both his hands were on my stomach now. Skimming, touching, spreading out in a protective gesture covering the entire surface. "Yes. *God*, yes. "

"Do you think you can love our child?"

"I already do."

I lifted his chin. "Then you'll be fine."

"What about"—he hesitated—"us?"

"We need to work on us. I need time."

281

"You'll stay on here?"

"Yes."

"Will you let me be a part of this, of our child's life?"

I sighed. "Yes, of course."

"Do you—"

"Do I what?"

He leaned closer. "Do you think you can love me again, Megan?"

"I do love you, Zachary. I need to be able to trust you again—to know you won't run the next time something happens that upsets you. I can't do that to our child. I won't allow that to happen."

"You won't have to. I'm never leaving again. I can't," he declared as his voice trembled. "I've been so lost without you."

My voice caught. "I've missed you so much."

He moved even closer, his breath washing over my face. "Forgive me. Please forgive me."

"I have."

His eyes dropped to my mouth in a silent question. My head dipped with permission as his lips, so soft and familiar, molded to mine, the pressure gentle. His hand wove into my hair as his fingers stroked the back of my head in light caresses. His scent surrounded me, the taste of him in my mouth easing the dull ache I carried for months. A long shiver ran through his body as he whispered my name, the sound so pleading, I whimpered as he brushed his lips over mine once more. Zachary's kiss was languid and indulgent; long sweeping passes of his tongue, sweet pecks of his lips, gentle nips of his teeth as he pulled my bottom lip into his mouth. He wrapped his arm around me, holding me close, while his other hand stroked my stomach in never ending circles.

There was nothing rushed or hurried. No long, deep moans of raging passion. It was a kiss of welcome, one of sweet reunion, of letting go of the hurt and starting again.

It was a kiss that promised a future.

Our future.

He drew back, his breathing deep. Touching his forehead to

mine, his voice shook. "Never, Megan—I'm not leaving again. I will fight and struggle to stay with you—for you, for our child." His fingers curved over my rounded stomach. "If you let me?" He paused, and I felt a shudder run through his long frame. "Please let me."

"This is your only chance," I whispered. "I have to protect our child."

He shook his head. "You'll never have to protect our child from me, or guard your heart again. I promise you with everything I am."

"I love you."

He gathered me to him, lifting me onto his lap and wrapping himself around me. His warmth soaked into my skin, as his fingers stroked through my hair in long, gentle passes.

"That's all I need." He pressed a kiss to my hair. "That's all I'll ever need."

I rested my face onto his chest, doubt still lingering.

"I hope so," I whispered.

"With all that I am, Megan, I swear."

For now, it was enough.

28

MEGAN

Warm lips lingered on my temple. "Morning."

I snuggled deeper into the comfort of the blankets with a little groan. "Too early."

"Your doctor appointment is in an hour, Megan. I let you sleep as long as I could." Zachary's voice was tender as he spoke, his fingers stroking through my hair in long passes.

Opening my eyes, I smiled up at him, the feeling of wonder still fresh. Even after three weeks, I found it hard to believe he was back and home with me. We had been taking things slow. I was still staying at Karen's in the guest room. Zachary slept on the sofa, refusing to leave me alone at night, but knowing I wasn't ready for anything else quite yet. We'd spent endless hours talking, sharing, crying, and at times, even yelling. But the past week there had been less of those dark conversations and more of the lighter moments. We were both letting go of the past sadness and moving on. Zachary's smiles were easier these days; quick to appear, often followed by the low laughter I liked so much.

Today, I had an ultrasound scheduled and he was coming with

me. He'd been hesitant when he asked permission; I'd been overjoyed he wanted to be there. He spent a lot of time reading pregnancy books, asking me questions, and when I was lying down, talking to my tummy. Last week, I'd woken up to find him beside me murmuring in a gentle tone, his lips close to my skin.

"You'll love it here, little one. There's sand and water and all sort of things to discover." He chuckled suddenly. "You don't know what Daddy is talking about do you? You don't know what sand and water is!" His lips moved on my tummy, as his hand ran gentle circles over it. "I'll teach you everything. Daddy loves you so much and I can hardly wait to meet you. Mommy, too. She's taking such good care of you." He glanced up, meeting my tear-filled eyes.

"Ah, the book says to talk to them so they get used to my voice," he mumbled, the tips of his ears turning red. I nodded, unable to speak as I took in the look in his eyes. They were soft, peaceful, and filled with love. There was none of the wariness, no distrust in the depth of his gaze. His lips lingered against the swell of my tummy again as his large hand wrapped around mine. "Thank you," he breathed.

Today he would get to hear the heartbeat of our child, and if possible, we would find out the sex. Zachary was beyond excited for both things to occur. It was also special for me, since, for the first time, I wouldn't be alone in the waiting room. Zachary would be beside me.

"Megan?"

"Hmm?"

His hand rubbed the back of his neck as he hesitated. "I'm nervous."

I ran my fingers through his hair—it always seemed to relax him. "About the ultrasound, or going to the hospital?"

"Both."

"The ultrasound is easy. All you have to do is hold my hand."

"I can do that."

I wrapped both of my hands around his, which was resting beside me. "As for the hospital, how about I hold *your* hand? Would that help?"

His lips curled into a shy smile, his entire face relaxing as he nodded. "Yes, that would help a lot."

He helped me to stand, then wrapped his arms around me, holding me close. I could feel his love surround me. Every day I accepted it a little more, believed him a little more.

Believed in us a little more.

The drive was quiet, Zachary's tension evident. I reached over and rubbed the back of his neck as I sang along with the radio, ad-libbing the words I didn't know, making him chuckle. I was pleased when his shoulders loosened a little, giggling when he winked and turned up the radio, putting an end to my impromptu concert.

When we arrived at the hospital, his nerves returned. He kept his head lowered and his hand wrapped around mine so tight I needed to ask him to loosen his grip. "Sorry," he muttered.

In the elevator, I turned to him, ducking low so he was forced to meet my eyes. "No one is going to judge here, Zachary. This is about our child. Not you." I drew in a deep breath. "Stop expecting rejection—give people a chance before you assume the worst."

His eyes widened and his expression changed from wary to open. "You're right." He nodded and nestled me to his chest, nuzzling my temple. "Our child."

The elevator doors opened and we stepped out. I offered him my hand again and with a tight smile he took it. "You can do this," I encouraged.

His grip tightened. "With you, I think I can do anything."

We were both smiling when we entered the doctor's office.

Dr. Booker didn't even blink when I introduced Zachary to him. He smiled warmly and clapped him on the shoulder, telling him he was pleased to meet him, then ushered us both to the ultrasound room. Zachary relaxed more in the dimly lit room and gazed around, his nerves still showing with the drumming of his fingers on his thigh. Dr. Booker explained the procedure to us both and answered a few questions Zachary had for him as he watched the doctor set things up. He was patient and made sure we both understood everything before starting the ultrasound. I gasped a little as the cool gel hit my tummy, grinning when Zachary mouthed "amateur" at me. Compared to the temperature of the water he stuck his feet into every day, the gel was nothing. His smile was wide when I stuck my tongue out at him, thrilled that he'd relaxed enough to tease me. Bringing him closer to the examination table, I watched his face, transfixed at his expression as the rapid sounds of our child's heartbeat filled the room—the wonder and awe of the moment erasing everything else. His hand tightened on my arm, his gaze fixated on the screen in front of him. He leaned closer, peering at the image, his eyes wide and filling with tears. He turned his head, his voice filled with emotion. "Our baby."

Dr. Booker chuckled. "Your baby is cooperating today. You want to know the sex?"

"Yes." Both Zachary and I spoke at the same time.

"It's a boy."

My own eyes filled with tears. A son. We were having a son.

Zachary pressed his lips to my temple, his damp cheek rubbing on mine.

"I love you," he whispered.

It was a different man who escorted me out of the hospital. Zachary's shoulders were straighter, his head held high. He ignored the few, more open, curious glances; his entire focus on me. I nestled into his side, amazed at the change, proud of his courage. Even his hold felt different; more possessive and sure. Once at the car, he insisted on fastening my seat belt, then laying his hands over my tummy and stroking the swell.

His eyes were shining when he looked up. "My boy."

I stroked his cheek. "Your son."

He held up the sonogram picture, his voice filled with wonder. "Our son." Leaning forward, his lips grazed mine; soft, gentle touches of adoration. "My sweetheart."

My heart thumped at his use of his endearment. I always felt so loved when he murmured it to me. His eyes were soft as he shut my door, never leaving mine as he walked around the vehicle and slid inside.

A yawn escaped me as he settled beside me, inserting the key. "I have to pick up the stuff from Mrs. Cooper, then I'll take you home."

I nodded, still amazed at how something so small, like a trip to the doctor, could tire me so much.

I beamed when Zachary went inside the store, the picture still gripped in his hand, smiling proudly when he came out. There was no doubt he'd been showing it off to Mr. and Mrs. Cooper. I knew if he wasn't so worried about taking me home to rest, he'd have gone to the gallery to show it to Ashley, as well. I knew a trip to see her would happen in the next couple days. I loved seeing how proud he was as he tucked the picture into his sun visor, glancing up at it often during the remainder of the drive.

I frowned nervously when the SUV rolled to a stop by his back door.

"What are you doing?"

He stared straight ahead, his hands wrapped around the steering wheel. "Will you come inside with me, Megan?"

I hesitated. I hadn't been back to his house yet. There were so many memories there and Karen's place was neutral ground for us. Zachary spent time in his home studio, while I worked on my book at Karen's, happy when he would appear at some point. There were always warm kisses and gentle words of hello, and although I knew he hated to leave again, even for a few hours, he understood I needed time.

However, maybe it was time to expand our world again.

"Please," he whispered, turning to me, his face and voice vulnerable. "I have something to show you."

I turned around in a circle in the upstairs bedroom, speechless. Zachary had renovated the room closest to his into a nursery. The once mocha-colored walls were now painted the softest blues and yellows. The heavy glass and metal desk and filing cabinet were gone, replaced by a simple maple crib, which was set up in the corner with a matching dresser and change table placed in close proximity. Right by the window, a large, cushioned rocking chair and table were nestled, waiting. I loved every piece in the room. "You can finish it with all the other stuff we need." He spoke from the doorway, his hand rubbing the back of his neck. "If you don't like anything, we can return it." He crossed the room and picked up a huge teddy bear from the rocking chair, holding it out to me. "I thought maybe the baby would like this."

"How—" I choked, my throat thick with emotion, as I reached for the bear, hugging it to my chest.

"I wanted to surprise you. I chose these colors thinking they'd be good for a boy or a girl. I thought they were...soothing."

"I thought you were painting in your studio."

"This was more important." He stepped forward, his voice wary. "I wanted to get this room done so if you decided—"

"If I decided?"

"To come back to me." He drew in a deep breath. "If you decided to come back to me, I'd be ready; for both of you." His warm hand cupped my cheek, brushing away the tears with his thumb. "Please come back to me. Give us a chance."

"Zachary—"

He shook his head interrupting me. "Please, sweetheart, listen to me. You told me Karen and Chris were coming down this weekend."

I nodded.

"Come stay here with me. Please. At least try."

He indicated the room around us. "I want this to be our son's room. Our...home." He stepped closer. "I want you here with me, so it feels like home again, Megan.

"I know we have a lot to work out, but I can't stop thinking about you here. Being able to touch you anytime I want. Knowing you're downstairs while I'm painting. Falling asleep with you." His head fell to my shoulder. "I slept so well with you beside me."

I curled my fingers into the hair that fell over his collar. I felt a deep rumbling sigh in his chest. He lifted his gaze to mine, his eyes bright with emotion. "I want a life with you, Megan. In this house, or somewhere else, if that's what you want. Wherever you want to be, I'll follow—anywhere."

I knew what he was saying. If I went back to Boston, he'd give up his private life here, to be with me—to be with us. I blinked away fresh tears.

"I want to stay here."

"With me?"

The two small words were spoken with so much want. He showed his vulnerability in both his actions and words. He created this room for his child. He wanted me to stay with him.

He was handing me his heart, unsure how I would receive it, and willing to take the chance of being rejected.

Despite what happened, and the pain we'd both gone through, I still loved him.

I would always love him.

"With you."

Zachary's eyes filled with tears. "I'll take good care of you and our son. I won't ever leave you again." He stroked my cheek. "Nothing will ever take me away from you. I love you, Megan."

The feeling I'd been missing so much welled up inside me. It seeped into every molecule and settled deep into my skin, blooming and taking hold. The feeling of being complete.

With Zachary I was complete.

"I love you."

His smile was brilliant, and I gasped as he swooped me up into his arms.

"Let's go get your stuff."

29

MEGAN

A light breeze pushed through the curtains, the gauzy fabric billowing in the air as I stepped out of the shower. I heard the sounds of laughter and barking, the noise drawing me to the window. Below, on the beach, was my favorite sight in the world. Zachary, tall and strong, standing ankle deep in the water, holding a small figure in his arms. Our son's tiny fist clutched the material of Zachary's shirt while his other hand gestured toward something in the water he wanted. I knew Matthew would be talking a mile a minute in his daddy's ear, directing him to pick up whatever stone, seashell or piece of wood that had caught his eye.

Sure enough, Zachary lowered Matthew down to the watery sand and bent low to capture whatever treasure from the sea our son had demanded. He crouched down, the two dark heads touching as Matthew crowed in delight at his find. Both heads were so similar you couldn't tell where one began and the other ended. When he stood up, I chuckled. Even standing, they were alike. Both clad in jeans and long sleeved, white shirts, their pant legs rolled up, feet bare and submerged in the cool water. Like his father, Matthew loved how the water felt against his skin; I'd given up trying to keep shoes on his little feet and losing them to the surf as they got carried out to sea.

Behind them, Dixie, Elliott, and Rex, our newly adopted dog, chased each other around on the sand, tails wagging, excited barks filling the air. After a minute, Matthew pushed his new find into Zachary's hand for safe keeping and joined them in their game of tag. Soon his happy giggles were added as his favorite playmates welcomed him with enthusiasm. Not to be left out, Zachary joined the group and more laughter and shouts rang out from the beach.

I rested my head to the glass and gazed on in wonderment. It never ceased to amaze me how Zachary had changed. Not even a shadow remained of the angry, bitter man I met on the beach over three years ago. The last of his former self had fallen away the day our son was born. His newfound joy was reflected in every aspect of his life. His paintings were filled with light, exploding with color and brilliance. His eyes only reflected trust and love when they met mine. His hair-trigger temper rarely ever showed and on the odd occasion it did, it burned itself out as fast as it ignited. There was a peace about him now, one that permeated every aspect of our life.

Watching him with our son was wonderful. His patience and capacity for play was boundless, his desire to teach and encourage, endless. His favorite times were spent with his son beside him in the studio, tiny fingers clutching a brush that dabbed and jerked on the paper as Zachary praised and cheered him on. Many of Matthew's "masterpieces" hung on the walls all around the house. My parents and Auntie K were also gifted with many for their homes. The post office in Cliff's Edge was well used to sending out tubular packages containing rolled up works of art, and greeted Zachary and Matthew with enthusiasm when they walked in.

His all-encompassing love surrounded both of us. Coming from a man who insisted he never understood what love was, it was a rare gift.

I ran my hand over my stomach in secret delight, knowing the news I could share with him today would be greeted with nothing but elation.

The need to feel him close filled me, and I hurried to get ready and make my way downstairs to my boys. The aroma of coffee filled the kitchen, and wrinkling my nose, I hurried past it. The same as when I was pregnant with Matthew, coffee was my nemesis. My first clue I was pregnant again was when the scent had made me nauseous the other day. Zachary hadn't yet noticed my aversion to coffee—but I didn't drink anywhere near as much of it as he did.

I stepped outside, inhaling the crisp air. Dixie spotted me right away, barking and racing toward the steps to greet me. In a synchronized move, two dark heads snapped my way, Matthew's little hands waving frantically as if afraid I could miss spotting him. Zachary stood up, ruffling his hair, leaning down and speaking to him as he handed Matthew something from his pocket. Little legs pumped fast and I dropped to my knees to scoop up his warm little body. I peppered tiny kisses all over his sweet face and he giggled and squirmed trying to escape. "Look, Mommy!"

Grinning, I held out my hand for the small rounded stone, admiring it before giving it back for his collection. "Is this a keeper?"

He nodded with enthusiasm. "It has stwipes!"

"Ah." Stripes or multi-colored ones ranked high.

He pushed off me, heading for the water. "Me get mo'e!"

I laughed as he passed his father, exchanging a rather glancing high-five. The air caught in my throat as Zachary came closer, dropping beside me on the sand and covering my mouth with his.

"Hi, sweetheart," he breathed against my lips. "You look pretty this morning. Well-rested."

"You let me sleep."

"Hmmm. You were so tired last night, you didn't even move when I came to bed."

"You should have woken me up."

"I tried," he growled as his warm lips ghosted over my cheek, dropping soft kisses on my skin. "Am I losing my touch, woman?"

I chuckled. "Your touch is as effective as ever." I grinned up at him, placing his hand on my stomach. "Highly effective, I'd say."

For a second he frowned in confusion, then his eyes widened, his excited gaze flying to mine. Both hands spread across my stomach, his long fingers fisting the fabric. "Really?" he murmured. "Another baby?"

"Well, I hope it's a baby. Not an alien or anything. 'Cause that would be hard to explain."

In an instant, I was in his arms, held tight to his chest. He buried his face into my neck and held me for a long moment, not saying anything. I felt his tears on my skin, warm and fast, as his emotions welled. I held him close, running my fingers along the back of his neck, giving him the time he needed to calm himself. I watched our son play with the dogs, smiling as I thought about this new little life joining him in a couple years.

Zachary drew back, eyes damp, but filled with light. "I won't miss any of it this time."

"No."

"Another child."

"Yes."

"Are you feeling okay?"

"Aside from the fact coffee makes my stomach turn and feeling tired, yep."

"You went to the doctor?"

"Yesterday."

He chuckled. "That was your errand?"

"I wanted to make sure."

He ran his hands over my tummy, his voice anxious. "Everything is all right?"

"Everything is perfect. You can come for the first ultrasound next time."

He kissed me again. "I like ultrasounds."

"I know."

"I guess we'd better pull back on the writing."

I chuckled as he settled behind me, drawing me into his arms. "I'm still capable of writing, Zachary. We're almost done."

When Matthew was about a year old, Zachary told me he wanted to write his story. I was surprised, but pleased when he asked me if I'd help him. A few days later, I left a pile of heavy, black, leather-covered journals on the shelf in his studio and didn't say another word. He would let me know when he was ready.

Slowly, Zachary wrote his story. I never tried to push him, letting him set the pace. Sometimes weeks would pass until he picked up a pen. Other times, he wrote daily. His dark, bold script covered the pages of the journals. Some days he wrote on his own, bent over the kitchen table, his pen embedding the words so deeply onto the page you could feel the indents from the nib. Other days, his memories were lighter and the pages turned faster as the words poured out. The worst days were the ones he would sit, pulling me onto his lap as he spoke in low measured tones, while I recorded the pain and turmoil he allowed to escape. When it became too much, I would lay the book aside and wrap him in my arms, healing him the only way I knew how: with my love. That happened more as of late. He still found talking about what happened with Jared and our separation difficult. I knew, without a doubt, once he got past that part, he would be able to finish it himself. He wrote joy well.

He settled behind me, drawing me into his arms, and tucking me under his chin. "We'll take it as it comes."

I knew that was as far as we'd discuss it today, so I hummed in agreement. "Okay."

"Is it too soon to tell people?"

"Maybe my parents, and Karen and Chris next time they're down. Other people can wait a bit."

Karen and Zachary were still, to this day, restrained. They both accepted their place in my life and made great efforts to be cordial, but I knew they would never be close. They couldn't see how similar they were, and still liked to argue over the most inane things, trading insults with each other until Chris or I stepped in. There were times I swore they did it on purpose, secretly enjoying riling each other up.

Zachary and Chris were closer and spent many evenings bent over the chessboard; often with a curious Matthew disrupting their game. Some very unique forms of chess were played by the three of them.

My parents supported me, having come to accept Zachary. They knew the whole story and it took them a while to warm to him, but they adored Matthew and visited when they could.

Our world was still fairly isolated. Zachary was far more comfortable now, but still wary of strangers. We both knew once Matthew was older we would need to move closer to another town for him with school, but we both agreed our life was best in smaller, more remote places. The fallout from Jared's stunt had been minimal, affecting our lives in the smallest sense. To be safe, Zachary installed a gate at the end of the road, protecting our privacy even further. He was relieved to discover he'd been gone from the spotlight long enough that the odd reporter who did surface, quickly moved on to newer, bigger stories when a lead to Adam Dennis didn't pan out to much of anything. Slowly, the fears of his past ebbed from our life and we were able to move forward—together.

My book had finally been published and was successful. My second book was now in the hands of editors and the outline of a third was taking shape in my head. Much like Zachary, I disliked the publicity side of my work and kept a very low profile. My publishers were pleased with the success of the books, and I still enjoyed the process. Although I had learned what made me happiest was the world I had here with Zachary and Matthew. My life with them fulfilled me like nothing else.

I no longer wrote the stories out by hand—Zachary's gift of an ultra-light laptop had ended that habit. It was far more productive to type out the words as they came to me, saving the document when a certain little boy would interrupt the process. It also gave me the protection for my work, which, after all that happened with Jared, was a professional gift I treasured.

Zachary had converted a small room on the third floor into an office for me. I would sit, tapping away at the computer, finding the same inspiration in the beautiful vista spread out before me as did Zachary. He had tucked my desk underneath a large window and built shelves around it, which held some of the treasures found by Matthew. They also contained countless journals—a never-ending gift from him. I never knew when a fresh one would appear on the shelf, waiting to be filled. Now they contained happy memories I wrote out of our life together. He loved reading through them and reliving those special times we shared as a family.

Wrapped in Zachary's arms, we watched our son playing in the low waves, picking up bits and pieces off the beach that the tide had deposited overnight; adding them to the small pile he'd started. We did this most days. Picking, sifting, sorting through his treasures, keeping only what he loved best, and putting it with the larger pile on the deck of the house.

Zachary's hands covered mine, resting on my stomach. His fingers continually traced the back of my hands, finally tapping out a steady rhythm on my ring finger. I glanced up at him, caught in the intensity of his stare.

He lifted my hand, kissing my finger. "It's time, Megan."

"Time?"

"I want the mother of my children to share my name." He tapped my finger again. "I want to put a ring on here and marry you."

"Oh," I breathed. We'd never discussed marriage. Neither of us felt the need of a piece of paper to know we were a couple. Until it seemed, this moment.

"Please. Live your life with me." He paused and smiled softly. "Let me tell the world you're mine."

His.

I liked the idea of belonging to Zachary, and him to me.

I drew his head down, pressing my lips to his. "Yes."

His arms tightened, his lips warm on mine. I could feel his wide smile against my mouth.

A small shout broke us apart, as Matthew pointed to some new curiosity he saw just out of his short reach. "You're being paged, Daddy."

Another warm kiss was dropped on my lips and Zachary stood up. "Hold that thought, Mommy."

I leaned back on the sand, watching my family and smiling, already anticipating the day there would be another little set of legs standing beside Zachary in the low surf. I thought of the years ahead of me, watching my family grow, Zachary and me together.

My smile grew wider.

ACKNOWLEDGMENTS

To Trina, Caroline and Tracy, words can't express how much your help and encouragement has meant to me.

Flavia and Meire, your belief makes me smile.

Meredith—so many thanks are needed and I can't possibly express them enough.

Deb, your red pen and hard work made it so much better, but your friendship is what I treasure the most.

Suzanne—there aren't enough mangos in the world.

Your help and guidance made this journey so much better.

My readers (online and otherwise) who support me so strongly – thank you.

You make my life so much richer.

Vested Interest Series

BAM - The Beginning (Prequel)

Bentley (Vested Interest #1)

Aiden (Vested Interest #2)

Maddox (Vested Interest #3)

Reid (Vested Interest #4)

Van (Vested Interest #5)

Halton (Vested Interest #6)

Sandy (Vested Interest #7)

Insta-Spark Collection

It Started with a Kiss

Christmas Sugar

An Instant Connection

An Unexpected Gift

The Contract Series

The Contract (The Contract #1)

The Baby Clause (The Contract #2)

The Amendment (The Contract #3)

Mission Cove

The Summer of Us

Standalones

Into the Storm

Beneath the Scars

Over the Fence

My Image of You (Random House/Loveswept)

ABOUT THE AUTHOR

NYT/WSJ/USAT international bestselling author Melanie Moreland, lives a happy and content life in a quiet area of Ontario with her beloved husband of twenty-eight-plus years and their rescue cat, Amber. Nothing means more to her than her friends and family, and she cherishes every moment spent with them.

While seriously addicted to coffee, and highly challenged with all things computer-related and technical, she relishes baking, cooking, and trying new recipes for people to sample. She loves to throw dinner parties, and enjoys traveling, here and abroad, but finds coming home is always the best part of any trip.

Melanie loves stories, especially paired with a good wine, and enjoys skydiving (free falling over a fleck of dust) extreme snowboarding (falling down stairs) and piloting her own helicopter (tripping over her own feet.) She's learned happily ever afters, even bumpy ones, are all in how you tell the story.

Melanie is represented by Flavia Viotti at Bookcase Literary Agency. For any questions regarding subsidiary or translation rights please contact her at flavia@bookcaseagency.com

Connect with Melanie

Like reader groups? Lots of fun and giveaways! Check it out Melanie Moreland's Minions

Join my newsletter for up-to-date news, sales, book announcements and excerpts (no spam): Melanie Moreland's newsletter

Visit my website www.melaniemoreland.com

facebook.com/authormoreland

twitter.com/morelandmelanie

instagram.com/morelandmelanie

Made in the USA
Monee, IL
18 March 2023

30153526R00174